THE EDGE OF
FEDERAL SPACE BOOK 3
NOWHERE

ZACHARY JONES

ACKNOWLEDGEMENTS

So, now there are three of them! For those readers who do take the time to read the acknowledgments, thank you. I will only delay you for a moment.

I would first like to thank my wife, Sarah, for being my first beta reader and number one fan. It's always good to know at least one person likes my writing.

I would next like to thank Cathrine at Ebook Launch for helping clean up my manuscript for publication.

And finally, I would like to thank the folks at Damonza for slapping cover on this thing and formatting it for publication.

And to you, the reader, please leave a review to let me know what you think. Now off to the adventure!

CHAPTER 1

THE BATTLE OF Triumph had been a victory, but it had cost too much to feel like one. That didn't stop Admiral Moebius from reinforcing Osiris Squadron with volunteers from other squadrons and sending them right back into action.

Squadron Leader Mason Grey sat in the cockpit of his Lightning as he waited for *Independence* to make the last jump to Pluto, the first step in Operation Allegiant Dragon. All fine and good, except Mason couldn't guess why Admiral Moebius had decided on Pluto as her first toehold in Outer Sol.

Pluto had only one major settlement, the mostly buried city of New Lowell on the Sputnik Planitia, which existed to support and house the scientists and staff of the hundreds of observatories that surrounded the city. As a scientific outpost with minimal military value, New Lowell had fallen quickly during the initial invasion of Outer Sol by the Ascended—or "Cendies" as they were more often called—when they had taken control of everything outside the asteroid belt.

But while Mason didn't think Pluto was important, the Cendies did, if intelligence was anything to go by. They had built a large military base on the surface right atop New Lowell, with Turtleback landing ships that housed thousands of Cendy soldiers landed on the surface.

The Cendies had installed several missile and kinetic weapon batteries on the surface, making it very dangerous for any starship that entered the skies above Tombaugh Regio. However, though powerful, the weapons were designed for trading blows with starships in orbit. Against low-flying strikecraft, they were helpless.

The alarm sounded, the battlecarrier vibrated as the drive keel discharged, and *Independence* appeared over Pluto. She was not alone.

Independence led a taskforce comprising four cruisers and twice as many destroyers. The carriers *Goshawk*, *Hyena*, and *Cassowary* each led their own taskforce with identical escorts. A fifth taskforce, this one centered on the assault ship *Ashigaru*, carried a full regiment of Federal troopers and an armored company of Pele superheavy tanks.

The armored doors covering Mason's hangar bay opened, and the light reflecting off Charon and Pluto spilled in. Even so far out, the Sun's light provided ample visibility for the unaided eye. Not that Mason could see it with his eyes given his Lightning's opaque canopy. Everything he saw was filtered through his fighter's multitude of AI-managed sensors.

The catapult kicked his Lightning away from the battlecarrier, and after a moment of jarring acceleration, Mason and his fighter floated weightless for several seconds until he cleared enough distance to activate his longburn drives. A gentle acceleration pulled him into his seat, settling his body into the layer of acceleration gel inside his hardsuit. The carriers and the assault ship blossomed with strikecraft launches as they threw their entire complements into space within a minute.

Mason couldn't help but feel a little awed at the massive dance involving dozens of starships, hundreds of small craft, and thousands of spacers, all working in practiced coordination. Twenty-four assault shuttles and fourteen carryalls launched from *Ashigaru*. Each assault shuttle carried two platoons of troopers, and each carryall lugged a single Pele superheavy tank.

It was the single largest concentration of Earth Federation ground-fighting power Mason had ever seen deployed. And it looked extremely vulnerable as the assault shuttles and carryalls gathered into a dispersed formation.

"All squadrons, *Independence* Command," echoed Admiral Moebius's voice through the general channel. "Operation Allegiant Dragon is a go."

That was all that needed to be said. Mason fired his longburn drive and aimed for a predetermined vector that cut close to the surface of Charon on the way down to Pluto's surface. Hundreds of small longburn drives lit up the space over Pluto and Charon as fighters, assault shuttles, and carryalls accelerated for the surface. The starships fell away behind them as the strikecraft accelerated at 1.5 g, the maximum the carryalls could handle while they were laden with Pele superheavies.

The formation dispersed as it opened the distance from the starships until hundreds of kilometers separated the squadrons, with dozens of kilometers between the individual craft within each squadron. Fighters ventured ahead, while vulnerable assault shuttles and carryalls lagged behind.

Mason kept his attention on the space far beyond his squadron, toward Charon and Pluto, where the danger would come from. There was nothing to suggest the Cendies had set up defenses on the surface of Charon, but that didn't mean the deep scans and reconnaissance ships had not missed dangers hidden atop or within the ice.

The braking burn started ten thousand kilometers above Charon and continued as they made their closest approach. A rush of adrenaline coursed through Mason's veins as he flew backward over Charon's surface at orbital velocity. Nothing leaped from the surface of Charon as the formation passed close over its surface, but not long after, the first signs of opposition appeared from behind Pluto.

"Contacts! Cendy fighters incoming," called Squadron Leader Harrison Blain, commanding the 121st "Daggers" Fighter Squadron, the vanguard of the formation's fighters.

Mason's sensor AI counted a hundred Outriders rising from Pluto to intercept the Federal attack—a number confirmed dozens of times over by the interlinked sensor AIs of every friendly craft in the formation.

Most of the Lightnings aborted their braking burn and turned to start accelerating toward the enemy fighters, but not Mason's squadron. The sixteen fighters of the Osiris Squadron had a more specialized task.

Minutes later, Lightnings and Outriders clashed in a brief, violent battle as both sides launched mass volleys of interceptors at each other. The Lightnings came out ahead thanks to their superior numbers and the protection afforded by their Stiletto pods. Each pod was filled with miniaturized interceptors meant to counter other missiles. Cendy Outriders were wiped from the tactical display while the escorting Lightnings suffered light losses.

Mason's squadron was the first to reach the end of the braking burn just a few kilometers above the surface of Pluto, transitioning to horizontal flight over the dark reddish ice of the Cthulhu Macula and proceeding east toward New Lowell.

Mason opened the squadron channel. "Flight leaders, everyone still awake?"

"Up and alert, Hauler," responded Flight Lieutenant Dominic, his second-in-command and leader of Osiris Squadron's Second Flight.

"We're ready to rock," confirmed Flight Lieutenant Sabal from her lead position in Third Flight.

"My flight's on the deck and alert, Hauler," said Flight Lieutenant "Skids" Gottlieb, one of the most senior of the newcomers to Osiris Squadron.

"Excellent. Stay on alert as we approach the target. Proceed to mission objectives as soon as we engage the Turtlebacks."

Once his flight leads had acknowledged the order, Mason switched to his flight's channel and asked for a status check.

"All weapons, including the big gun, are ready, Hauler," Flight Lieutenant Sienna "Marbles" Armitage, his wingmate, said.

"Raiden cannon and Atlatl pods report ready status," Flight Lieutenant Seymore "Seesaw" Sawyer said.

"All systems online. Raiden ready for action," Flying Officer Octavia "Slap" Dash said. She was the most junior member of Mason's flight.

"Good. Arm Raiden cannons and prepare final system checks," Mason said. "I want to be ready to fire as soon as we get line of sight on the Turtlebacks."

Mason began the arming sequence of his own Raiden cannon. The belly doors of his Lightning's weapons bay parted, and the massive cannon descended from inside, the telescoping barrel extending until the muzzle almost reached the nose of his fighter.

The Raiden cannon had five shots, dictated not by power requirements or the size of the ammo but by the revolver-like cylinder that contained the counter-recoil charges. Without them, recoil from firing the Raiden would tear it off its mountings.

Five shots meant careful aiming. The small penetrators didn't usually cause much damage. But when skillfully deployed, they could penetrate deeply into the hull of a starship, far enough to take out critical systems, including main reactors and control systems. Thanks to the experience gained from the fight over Triumph, Mason knew precisely where he needed to place his rounds for maximum effect.

"Launching recon drones," Mason said.

Whereas all the other Lightnings in Osiris Squadron had two Stiletto pods and two Atlatl missile pods mounted on their dorsal hardpoints, Mason had two Augur drones, replacing the Atlatl pods, to give his squadron a last-minute intelligence update before coming within line of sight. He launched the drones one at a time, ejectors kicking them off his fighter before they fired their shortburn drives and rocketed up and away. The drones fanned out as they accelerated ahead and climbed to a higher altitude, feeding data directly to Mason's sensor AI.

As soon as they got a line of sight on New Lowell, fresh data flooded into Mason's tactical display.

Four Turtlebacks were exactly where they were expected to be, but the Augurs provided extra details. The Turtlebacks had landed at four corners directly atop the buried city of New Lowell, a deliberate choice to deter the use of nukes or other heavy ordnance, thus necessitating the use of precision ordnance and a ground assault to neutralize the Cendy threat.

Though landed, the Turtlebacks were hardly vulnerable when on the ground. Indeed, they were as much fortresses as they were landing ships. Not only did they carry thousands of Cendy soldiers but they had facilities inside to produce both new soldiers and weapons for them to carry.

The Augurs didn't last long after they started streaming data. The Turtlebacks launched interceptors as soon as they came into view, and one by one, Mason lost telemetry on each of his drones.

"Okay, that's it for the drones," Mason said. "Break formation and proceed to your firing positions." The four ships of Mason's flight separated to flow on their individual courses.

Letting each of his fighters fly off on their own ran against everything Mason believed in, but it was a necessity for dealing with the Turtlebacks. And it wasn't like they were alone. Not with the rest of the Osiris Squadron holding back to come to their aid when needed.

With five shots apiece, Mason had had his pilots practice ahead of time where to place their penetrators—two to the main reactors deep inside the Turtlebacks and one to the command center where the Cendy navigatrix—essentially the ship's captain—resided. The remaining two shots were aimed at their banks of interceptors in the hope the penetrators would set off the solid fuel propellant of their shortburn drives.

The key was timing. Turning to kill each Turtleback one at a time would just give the Cendies more time to kill his pilots. So all the Turtlebacks had to be engaged at the same time.

Mason picked the Turtleback that was furthest to the west and the riskiest one to engage. He would have to move the fastest of all his fighters.

Flying fast and low over the white ice of the Tombaugh Regio, skirting the southern edge of the Sputnik Planitia, Mason had to fight his fighter's attempts to gain altitude as he flew above orbital velocity.

His pilots fell off his tactical display as he lost line of sight. The Turtlebacks would shoot down any relay satellite they tried to put up to maintain their data link.

All Mason could do was make sure he did his part and have faith in his pilots that they would do theirs.

At the first waypoint, Mason made a hard left turn, using a burst of power from his longburn drives to wrench his vector to the west. Anyone with halfway decent thermals would have seen his engines flare from a light-second away, but the mission didn't rely on stealth; it relied on speed.

He made a second hard left turn, flying up the western edge of the Sputnik Planitia, and then another. The last turn put him on an easterly course, aiming directly at his target. If everything went to plan, his four-ship flight would approach New Lowell from each cardinal direction. All that was left was to wait for his target to rise over the horizon as the surface of Pluto streaked beneath him.

Mason's path took him directly over the largest radio telescope array on Pluto. Hundreds of antenna dishes all pointed toward a single point in the sky above. The briefings before the mission had made it very clear that damage to any of the observatories around New Lowell was to be avoided at all costs.

Mason worried about Cendies with handheld missile launchers

hiding under one of the dishes and taking a shot at his fighter, but none appeared as he flew past the telescope array. Ahead, his target started to come into view.

The Turtleback's flat, rounded hull rested on the ice, with sensors and weapon systems fully deployed. Its radar lit Mason up the moment he came into view, and trails of interceptors launching from the back of the Turtleback were accompanied by the whine of Mason's missile launch alarm. He ignored both as he lined up his targeting reticle with the center of the Turtleback, right where the reactor would be.

As he pulled the trigger, his Lightning shuddered from the blast of the counter-recoil charge as the first round went flying toward the Turtleback.

The Turtleback's hull flashed from the first impact just before Mason fired his second penetrator into the reactor. Adjusting his aim while the second penetrator was still in flight, he fired his third at the command section.

His fourth and fifth went into the missile batteries along the side of the Turtleback facing him.

As soon as the last penetrator had left the barrel, Mason turned away from New Lowell and fired his longburn drive at full power. As he flew low over the ice, the exhaust instantly vaporized the nitrogen on the surface, sending up a long trail of gas behind him as he violently changed course.

The interceptors fired by the Turtleback plunged toward him, their engines still burning as they rapidly gained speed.

The sensor AI was already at work trying to throw off the lock of the interceptors. But against the cold surface of Pluto, Mason's Lightning burned like a star in their thermal sensors. His ventral dazzler laser turret burned out the seeker heads of a few interceptors, causing them to go stupid and plunge to the ground, but others kept their locks.

Mason launched decoys in a continuous stream, leaving a fiery trail. The combat AI automatically started launching Stilettos from the two pods on his dorsal wing hardpoints, ripping them off in rapid succession. The sky above him flashed with interceptors vaporizing each other, while an instant later, more drove themselves into the ice, chasing decoys into the ground.

Alarms stopped screaming, and Mason found himself still alive, rocketing over Pluto's surface at an unsafe speed. Forcing himself to relax, he lowered his throttle and allowed his fighter to gain altitude. In an instant, he regained his connection with the rest of his squadron and was relieved to see all sixteen still active.

All four Turtlebacks were leaking gas from where Raiden penetrators had breached their hulls, their active sensors and weapons systems now silent.

"All Turtlebacks are neutralized. Silverback, Hardball, Seesaw—sanitize the landing zone."

"Roger that—going in," Dominic responded.

"First Flight, form up with the assault shuttle," Mason said as he retraced his path around New Lowell, flying higher and faster than before with the Turtleback neutralized.

The landing zone was just two kilometers west of New Lowell in an area of clear ice between the city itself and another array of radio telescopes. The assault shuttles and carryalls flew slowly over the ice, giving Osiris Squadron time to make their runs against the landing zone.

While the four fighters of Mason's flight had Raidan cannons in their weapons bays, the other twelve Lightnings of Osiris Squadron carried eight cluster missiles. In a single volley, each Lightning fired one cluster missile, which leaped into Pluto's black sky before plunging to the ground.

Several kilometers up, the missiles released their submunitions—clouds of conical bomblets. At fifty meters above the surface, the submunitions detonated, shredding the ice below with shrapnel and briefly saturating the landing zone with a shower of deadly metal.

After that, the assault shuttles flew in low and fast until they reached the landing zone and fired their braking thrusters to slow themselves down rapidly. At the same time, they opened their tail ramps and dropped lines of troopers behind them, carried to the ice by the thrusters of their hardsuits. The troopers came under fire even before they reached the ground, calls for air support from embedded combat controllers flooding Mason's tactical display.

An icon appeared on Mason's tactical screen marking the location of a Cendy firing position. In the magnified optics, Mason saw the glowing, warm bodies of a squad of Cendies hunkered down in an entrenched position, their muzzle flashes lighting up the ice before them.

Mason armed a Hammer missile and launched it from one of his wing-mounted Atlatl pods. The missile streaked directly for the squad before executing a pop-up maneuver, climbing rapidly before diving on the Cendies and exploding, obliterating them with a cone of shrapnel.

Troopers were on the ground by then. Most lay prone, trading fire with the Cendies, while others busily erected ballistic barriers under fire. Free of their passengers, the assault shuttles provided close air support of their own, savaging Cendy positions with rocket and cannon fire.

The fourteen carryalls were the last to arrive, flying in a line-abreast formation as they approached the fighting troopers from behind. The carryalls didn't land under fire. With Pluto's weak gravity, all they did was slow to a safe speed and then release the superheavies, allowing the tanks to land themselves on the ice as the carryalls retreated to a safe distance.

The Pele superheavies were large targets as they floated toward the ground, attracting heavy Cendy fire. Small-arms fire bounced off their armor as missiles streaked toward them. Point-defense guns atop each Pele's turret opened fire, spraying the incoming missiles with dense streams of projectiles that blotted out the anti-tank missiles before they had a chance to hit. Each superheavy tank made it to the ground unharmed and started rumbling forward, their tracks throwing up clouds of ice as they moved.

More missiles arched over the ice from Cendy fighting positions and were struck down by the point defenses of the Peles. Troopers formed up behind the superheavies, using their armored bulk for cover.

The main guns of the Peles flashed, and Cendy positions down range erupted with geysers of gas and ice.

"Iron Leader to Osiris Leader, request fire missions against Cendy positions along the western edge of New Lowell," said the commander of the lead Pele.

"Understood, Iron Leader," Mason said. "Seesaw, your flight's up. Engage targets as they present themselves."

"Acknowledged, Hauler," Sawyer said. "Rolling in."

The four Lightnings of Sawyer's flight approached New Lowell from the north and unleashed a torrent of Hammer missiles against the Cendy positions. They detonated inside dug-in positions or over exposed infantry, annihilating them.

The Cendies didn't let up, even under the heavy fire of the Peles on the ground and the Lightnings and assault shuttles overhead. It was one thing that Mason had come to respect about the Cendies. Their soldiers never panicked, never routed, and almost never surrendered. Any that weren't killed simply picked themselves up, stepped over the bodies of their comrades, and continued fighting.

An assault shuttle took a hit from an infantry SAM, trailing gas from multiple points where shrapnel had breached the fuselage.

"Badger 5 hit!" called out the assault shuttle pilot as the craft tried to gain altitude. Mason could see one of the longburn drives on its tail was dark and trailing gas.

Two more missiles streaked up and detonated around the assault shuttle, shredding it with shrapnel and knocking out its remaining longburn drive.

"Badger 5 is going down!" the pilot cried in panic.

In the airless environment of Pluto, Badger 5's pilot had to use what was left of the assault shuttle's maneuvering thrusters to slow its descent. It was clear it didn't have enough control to turn toward friendly lines and was coming down behind Cendy positions.

"This is Osiris Leader. We'll cover your landing, Badger 5," Mason said.

"Understood, Osiris Leader, though calling it a landing might be optimistic," the pilot responded.

Mason targeted the Cendy positions nearest the projected crash site and launched a volley of hammer missiles as Badger 5 approached the ground. It came under small-arms fire as it closed with the ground, its hull flashing where the bullets struck. The Cendies defending New Lowell knew they were doomed yet still fought to kill as many Federals as possible.

The assault shuttle came down hard and slid across the ice for several hundred meters, taking fire the whole time. The fighters of Mason's flight kept up their fire support, hitting Cendy positions wherever they saw muzzle flashes and quickly expending their Hammers.

As Badger 5 came to a stop, there was no immediate sign of life inside. Not that that stopped the Cendies from trying to kill the crew. A group of Cendies popped out of a hole in the ice near the assault shuttle and started charging toward it.

A hatch in the side of the assault shuttle opened and one of the crew opened fire on the Cendies with a battle rifle. The Cendies were too close to the shuttle for Mason to use heavy ordnance without endangering the crew inside.

"Osiris Leader rolling in with guns. Keep me covered," Mason said, arming his cannon. He approached the crash site at a steep angle and fired, cutting a line of impacts across the ice and over the Cendy soldiers.

He pulled his nose up and fired his longburn drives to accelerate away as the Cendies launched infantry SAMs at him, but the small missiles lacked the reach to catch a climbing Lightning.

"Good shooting, Osiris Leader!"

"Good to hear you're alive, Badger 5. What's your status?" Mason asked.

"My copilot and I are both injured, and one of our crew chiefs is dead. I don't think we'll be able to leave on our own."

"Just keep your heads down, Badger 5. We'll keep you covered until help arrives," Mason said. Turning to the Badger Leader, he asked, "Badger Leader, can you spare an assault shuttle for pickup?"

"Negative, Osiris Leader. That area's too hot. I'd just lose another assault shuttle."

"I might be able to help," Iron Leader said. "I'm sending a platoon toward your position. Iron 13 and 14 are moving in to secure the crash site."

Two Peles had broken off from their advancing brethren and were rolling toward Badger 5 at full speed, firing away with their weapons even as their point defenses warded off the Cendies' anti-tank missiles.

"Roger that, Iron Leader. We'll keep the Cendies off Badger 5 until you get here," Mason said.

"Hauler, we've got more Cendies coming out of the ground east of Badger 5!" Armitage warned.

"I see them. Cendies must have holes all over the area," Mason said. "Marbles, you plug the holes as you see them. Skids and I will deal with the Cendies out in the open."

"Got it, Hauler," Armitage said, launching a Hammer into the entrance of one of the Cendy tunnels.

Mason flew in low for another strafing run, taking out a Cendy squad a few dozen meters short of the assault shuttle, turning bodies into white mist as they skipped over the ice. On the western side of Badger 5, Iron 13 and 14 continued to advance, pouring fire into the Cendy fighting positions between them and the fallen assault shuttle.

Mason had to evade more missiles—this time fired from directly in front of him; the Cendy soldiers were starting to anticipate his strafing runs.

"Skids, keep their heads down while I make my runs," Mason said.

"I'll plow the road for you, Hauler," Gottlieb said.

Mason didn't quite catch the analogy, but he understood her meaning. As he came in for another strafing run, Gottlieb fired a wave of Hammers that impacted the ground ahead of him, killing or suppressing Cendy firing positions before they could launch more missiles.

Firing his cannon, Mason cut another line of impacts across the ice, cutting down Cendy squads attempting to close with Badger 5. Before he could make his next run, the Peles rolled in. Iron 13 came to a stop on the eastern side of Badger 5's crash site, turning around to face its rear toward the downed assault shuttle and backing up until it almost touched.

Iron 14 rolled around to Badger 5's western side, guns blazing away as it rolled to a stop and similarly put its back to the assault shuttle.

Though determined, even the Cendy soldiers weren't willing to face tanks over open ground. They started withdrawing into their tunnels, throwing the occasional missile at the Peles, which were promptly shot down by the superheavies' point defenses.

"This is Iron 13. We've secured the crash site. Maintaining position until Badger 3 arrives."

"Understood, Iron 13. Badger 5, what's your status?" Mason asked.

"Still alive, though there are quite a few extra holes in my assault shuttle," the pilot said. "Thanks for the cover."

"Our pleasure, Badger 5. We'll maintain overwatch until you're picked up," Mason promised.

Beyond Mason's small area, the ground battle for New Lowell

continued. Peles rolled forward, spraying down a continuous barrage of machine-gun fire while other members of the Osiris Squadron provided air support.

From behind the tanks, troopers advanced, checking for the entrance of any Cendy tunnels in the ice. Each one they came across was sealed shut with a demolition charge that threw up spouts of shattered ice. The constant fire created a haze of ice and gas over the battlefield, giving the impression of an atmosphere that wasn't there.

Badger 3 set down near Badger 5, right next to Iron 13's Pele. Troopers from Badger 3 skipped across the ice to the downed Badger 5 and came out minutes later with members of the assault shuttle's crew.

In a matter of minutes, Badger 3 took off again, headed spaceward to deliver Badger 5's dead and injured to *Ashigaru*. With Badger 5 abandoned, Iron 13 and 14 departed from their guard positions to rejoin the main fight.

Soon the surface of New Lowell was secured by the superheavy tanks with air support. All that was left was for the troopers to clear the surface buildings, a job that Mason could do little to help with from above.

"Osiris Leader, your job's finished. Return to *Independence* for debriefing."

"Roger that, *Independence* Control," Mason said, burning for orbit with the rest of his squadron in tow.

Behind him, the Battle of New Lowell entered its final phase, the tense voice of troopers engaging in close-quarter combat echoing through the data link.

CHAPTER 2

The capture of the Cendy mothership was the intelligence haul of the century, but Jessica wondered whether she would need several centuries to explore its bulk. Even after scrounging every drone that she could find and recruiting every spacer and trooper not otherwise occupied, it had taken weeks to do a cursory exploration of the mothership's interior.

The starship was as large as a mid-sized habitat station and far more complex internally. It had three distinct segments. The rear segment was taken up by massive engines fed by appropriately large fuel tanks. The middle was dedicated to housing, feeding, and growing new Ascended. And the front of the vessel was a factory that could build small arms, starships, and everything else the Ascendancy might need. The entire cylindrical ship was wrapped around the largest drive keel ever recorded, dwarfing those of even the interstellar superfreighters.

The mothership was an engineering marvel, a triumph of starship construction that would humble the greatest of human starship architects.

But for Jessica, it was a gigantic haystack filled with precious few needles.

There was no use interrogating the crew. They were all linked to a shared simulation, and ever since Earth Fed had started abiding by the liberty accords, there was no forcing them to talk. The only hope of learning anything from them was Miriam Xia, who had been linked to the Ascendancy simulation since shortly after their surrender.

They did find the ship's navigatrix, the Ascendency's rough equivalent to a captain. The navigatrix was the disembodied brain of an Ascended inside an armored shell linked to all the mothership's systems. Unfortunately, the navigatrix was quite dead when Jessica's search parties discovered it; the life support system that had kept it alive had shut down weeks before. Jessica wasn't sure if that had been done by the crew or by the navigatrix itself, but the fact was, anything the navigatrix knew was forever out of reach.

The computer systems weren't much help either. They had all been wiped clean, and Jessica doubted all the computing power in 61 Virginis could recover any useful information from the vast amounts of junk data left in the mothership's hardware.

Jessica sighed and took a swig of tea from her drinking packet. "I'll be as old as Miriam before I'm done with this place," she said to the walls of her inflatable hab.

Colonel Delores Shimura had set up a base camp in the bottom of the mothership, near the massive shaft that the Cendies had used to bring in metals harvested from the asteroid of 30 Skeksis to feed the production line building Turtleback landing ships for the invasion of Triumph. Dozens of Turtlebacks in varying stages of construction still filled the dormant factory, a still-life image of the Cendy war machine.

Jessica set her packet down, placing it on a magnetic strip to keep it from floating away. The gravity of 30 Skeksis functioned as little more than a gentle reminder of which direction down was.

She kicked herself away from the control console and turned to the wall, where a net held dozens of small artifacts she had sampled during her search of the mothership—weapons, tools, and replacement parts. Most of the items looked similar to those of human manufacture. After all, there were only so many ways to design a rifle or a screwdriver. But unlike any human equipment, the Cendy equipment was completely devoid of markings. No branding, proof marks, instructions, or serial numbers. There weren't even numbers on any of the tools to denote the size of the fastener they were meant for. Instead, every piece of Cendy equipment, from assault rifles and portable infantry missile launchers to hammers and wrenches, had near-field communications chips embedded in them. Cendies talked to their tools in the same way they talked to each other: over short-range, line-of-sight radio.

And that lack of markings extended to their ships too. While the interiors of Federal starships were covered in all manner of symbology and signage, Cendy interiors were bare and sterile. There wasn't even art to be found. It gave Jessica the impression that the Cendies were stereotypically robotic. But she was certain that that impression was wrong, that there was something she wasn't seeing, and it had to do with the virtual world the mothership's crew had all retreated to.

Hopefully Miriam would have something to say when she woke up. If she woke up. All Jessica could tell from reading the outputs from Miriam's mobility rig was that she was experiencing events in the mothership's virtual world in real time.

Jessica heard the hatch crack open and turned to see the tall figure of Colonel Shimura stooping under the lip and then reaching up to open a latch on her collar and pull her helmet off. Her short hair fluttered in the low gravity.

Jessica saluted her.

"At ease, Lieutenant," Colonel Shimura said. "Learn anything?"

"Just the scale of this project, Colonel," Jessica answered. "I think trying to eat this elephant in pieces is going to take a long time."

"Just need to get more mouths to help with that," Colonel Shimura said.

"Are you feeling hungry, Colonel?"

"Always, but that's not what I mean. The League has cleaned up the situation on Triumph enough that they're sending a group over to examine the mothership. I want you to work with them."

"It's going to feel weird working with the people I've spent most of my career spying on, Colonel," Jessica said.

"I know, Lieutenant. It's an adjustment for me as well. But 30 Skeksis is League territory, and they are technically our allies now."

"Can we trust them, Colonel? Technically speaking?"

"We have to. Just make sure they're here to learn the Ascendancy's secrets. Not ours."

"I shall be circumspect."

"I'm sure you will be," Colonel Shimura said. "I have some news from Sol, by the way. Admiral Moebius has liberated Pluto."

"And Mas— ahem. And Squadron Leader Grey?" Jessica asked.

"He's fine. Played an important role in Pluto's liberation," Colonel Shimura told her.

"So, likely a dangerous one."

"Such is the nature of his job," Colonel Shimura said. "I know that's not comforting."

Jessica shrugged. "He does have a knack for surviving dangerous situations. That's how he got on our radar in the first place. Though I do wish he wouldn't make a habit of it."

"You're one to talk, Lieutenant."

"Touché, Colonel," Jessica said. "So, what do you know about our League guests?"

"Technically they're our hosts. What with us being in their territory and all."

"A point I suppose they won't let us forget," Jessica said. "What should I share with them?"

"Everything we've learned about the Ascendancy in general and the mothership in particular. All without revealing too much about us."

"I suppose the League has quite the dossier on you, Colonel," Jessica said.

"And you, Lieutenant. I give it even chances that the League knows the extent of your cybernetic enhancements, and they would be very interested in getting a peek at all the highly classified intelligence-gathering technology embedded inside you."

"So why do you want me working with League Intelligence if you're worried about what they might learn about me?" Jessica asked.

"Because of what you can learn from them," Colonel Shimura said. "The League is going to use this opportunity to gather intel on the Special Purpose Branch—to assume otherwise is naïve."

"So, be generous with what we know about the Cendies without revealing too much about us?" Jessica summed up. "All the while trying to sneak a peek behind the League's curtains."

"That's the size of it, Lieutenant."

"When do they arrive?"

"Within the hour. Their shuttle is currently on braking burn to 30 Skeksis."

"Huh, well, in that case, I'll make myself presentable to meet them."

※

Jessica followed Colonel Shimura to the improvised landing zone set up beneath the giant hole blown into the mined-out chamber below the mothership. In the low gravity of 30 Skeksis, they didn't walk or use a rover; they flew.

Using thruster rigs, they flew from the belly of the mothership into the mining chamber and over the smooth, blackened rock until they reached the perimeter of the landing zone, marked out by a circle of blinking LED lights.

Assault shuttles from *Amazon* rested in neat rows on one side of the landing zone, their boarding rams open to the vacuum. Light spilled out of the hole in the chamber, casting a bright circle that moved on the floor in time with 30 Skeksis's rotation. Jessica couldn't see any stars through the hole. The ambient light of 61 Virginis drowned out any starlight.

It didn't obscure the League assault shuttle as it drifted down through the opening. The shuttle was a wedge-shaped flying wing with sharply raked winglets at the tips. It was sharper and leaner than the Federal assault shuttles resting on the chamber.

The League pilot guided the craft to one of the empty landing spots and extended the landing gear just before touching down. Immediately Federal ground crews flew up to the League shuttle with their suit thrusters, trailing cables to attach to the shuttle and secure it to the ground. Their unfamiliarity with League equipment was evident as they fumbled around, looking for the points to attach their hooks to. It made Jessica wonder how much time they had to study the manuals for the hardpoints on League assault shuttles.

Colonel Shimura kicked off the ground and flew toward the assault shuttle under the power of her suit thrusters. Jessica followed, landing on the colonel's right.

Once the ground crews had finished securing the shuttle, the hatch jutting out of the tail between the engines opened, exposing figures wearing pressure suits.

The figures hopped down the ramp, pushing themselves to the ground with their suit thrusters. Jessica counted sixteen Leaguers disembarking from the shuttle, all wearing pressure suits in the gold and gray colors of the League Interstellar Intelligence Division. Four officers took up the front, while the remaining dozen filed behind them. A full colonel, a major, and a pair of first lieutenants made up the officers of the League contingent.

The League IID was its own discreet branch of the League military, unlike the Special Purpose Branch, which was an organic part of the Federal Space Forces. Secretive even to their own people, the IID had a well-earned reputation among friend and foe alike for being dangerous.

And for members of the Special Purpose Branch, mortal enemies.

Jessica knew that even during times of official peace between the Earth Federation and the League, their mutual intelligence services had duked it out in the shadows: proxy wars in the independent systems, infiltration, more than the odd assassination.

As Jessica stood with Colonel Shimura before the IID team, she could not help noticing that they all carried sidearms holstered on their hips.

"Welcome to 30 Skeksis, Colonel Miller," Colonel Shimura said.

"Colonel Shimura, it's a pleasure to finally meet you in person," Colonel Hieronymus Miller responded. "I must say, I never expected to meet you in such circumstances."

"The Cendies have made many seemingly impossible things happen," Colonel Shimura responded.

"Yes. Your second visit to Triumph must have been radically different from your first."

Colonel Shimura didn't answer.

Jessica wasn't aware that Colonel Shimura had been to Triumph before, but Colonel Miller's statement, if true, did not surprise her. She knew there was a lot she didn't know about her on-again-off-again commanding officer.

"If you will follow me, we've got an inflatable hab inside the mothership where we can get out of these pressure suits and make proper introductions."

"Please lead the way, Colonel."

They traversed a kilometer of empty mining chambers to the access tunnel and then flew up under the power of their suit thrusters. From there, it was an easy transition through one of the many airlocks of the inflatable habs.

After stowing their pressure suits, Jessica, Colonel Shimura, and their guests from the IID all gathered in the hab's common area. Coffee, tea, and low-gravity-appropriate snacks were already laid out, and a few of the Leaguers eagerly helped themselves.

Colonel Miller was tall and lean, with black skin several shades darker than Jessica's own. His head was shaved, and he wore a goatee so precisely trimmed, it looked like it had been cut with a laser. He gestured to his second-in-command, a woman whose hair was cropped on the sides of her head but grown long on top and gathered into a tight ponytail that whipped in the low gravity with every move of her head.

"This is Major Isobel Hesme, my XO," Colonel Miller said.

"A pleasure to meet you," Major Hesme said, giving Colonel Shimura a salute before glancing at Jessica with a curious look.

"Major," Colonel Shimura said, "this is Lieutenant Jessica Sinclair. She is leading the search of the Cendy mothership and is as close to an expert on the Ascendancy as we have. She'll be more than happy to brief you on what we've learned so far."

"Well, let me finish our introductions and I'll be sure to bend Lieutenant Sinclair's ear," Colonel Miller said. He proceeded to introduce his two junior officers, both first lieutenants. The taller of the pair was a square-faced, dark-skinned, dark-eyed woman with the build of an Olympic weightlifter who went by the name of Lieutenant Sy. The shorter was a squat, pale man named Lieutenant Tyrell.

Jessica nodded to each in turn, but she could tell by looking at them that they were less interested in small talk than in getting to the part where she dished out the details on the Cendies.

"Well, I suppose you've all read the reports," she began. "Where should I start?"

"How about with what you found out about their origins?" Colonel Miller suggested.

"Yes, that," Jessica said. "Well, they go back to the early founding of the Earth Federation, before the First— err, before the War of Independence. A group of scientists, engineers, and futurists built a massive colony ship, the largest of its time, and departed Sol for an unknown destination. The destination they filed on record was falsified."

"And you know this because you spoke with Miriam Xia?" Colonel Miller interjected.

"Yes. Well, sort of," Jessica answered. "Her digitized consciousness was preserved, and I was able to convince her to share what she knew. In fact, she was instrumental in convincing the crew of the mothership to surrender."

"And she's currently with them in their virtual environment?" Colonel Miller asked.

"Yes," Jessica confirmed.

"When do you think she'll be back? I would very much like to speak with her."

"That will depend on her, Colonel," Jessica said. "Thus far, she has not disconnected from their virtual world."

"Almost like she's plotting something," Major Hesme said.

Surprised, Jessica said, "Plotting? To what end?"

"There's an army of tens of thousands of Cendies she helped create," Major Hesme elaborated. "Who's to say she's not plotting something with them?"

"Not now, Major," Colonel Miller interrupted. "Please continue, Lieutenant."

Jessica cleared her throat. "I think, Major, that you misunderstand Miriam's relationship with the Cendies. Yes, she helped finance the Ascension Foundation and the construction of their colony ship. But she had no direct involvement in the creation of the Cendies themselves. That didn't happen until after *Ascension* departed Sol."

"How do you know that?" Colonel Miller asked.

"Because the Cendies are not what Miriam Xia expected to result from the Ascension Foundation's efforts," Jessica explained. "She was told by the Ascension Foundation's leader, Doctor Julian Marr, that he would create a race of explorers. When she learned that the Cendies instead had come back to try to conquer the Earth Federation and the League, she was genuinely shocked."

"Humph, interesting," Colonel Miller said. "Seems you have learned quite a lot about the Ascendancy in the past year."

"Mostly just narrowing down what we don't know about them, sir," Jessica said.

"Well, that's still progress," he said. "What can you guess as to their intentions?"

"Other than what the Cendies themselves have claimed their goals are?"

"I would like to know why they're trying to pacify us," Colonel Miller said.

Jessica shrugged. "If I were to speculate, I would say that they're protecting something. Maybe they decided their mission of exploration is threatened by the presence of a violent civilization."

Colonel Miller's eyebrows shot up. "Us?"

"Yes," Jessica said flatly.

"What do you think they're protecting?"

"Your guess is as good as mine, sir," Jessica said. "I know the Cendies value knowledge, both of science and the arts. But what they would find valuable that we might threaten? Until we know more, the possibilities are endless."

"And you're sure it wasn't the Ascension Foundation's original intent?" Colonel Miller probed.

"That's what they told Miriam Xia, and she's not inclined to believe they lied to her," Jessica said.

"And you think they were telling her the truth?"

"I don't know," Jessica admitted. "They might have lied to her from the start, though I doubt it."

"Why is that?"

"From my research into the Ascension Foundation's members, including Doctor Marr, creating a race of conquerors seems ... out of character for them," Jessica said. "It's possible that they changed their minds after they departed Sol. My guess is the Cendies deviated from their original intentions."

"You don't think the Foundation is controlling the Cendies?"

"Controlling? All the members would be long dead, even with life extension," Jessica said.

"Not if they were digitized like Miriam Xia."

"Is it the opinion of the IID that the Ascendancy is acting under the direction of the digitized ghosts of the Ascension Foundation's founders?" Colonel Shimura interjected.

"No. I'm merely making a supposition," Colonel Miller said.

"If that were the case, Colonel," Jessica said, "it would still be out of character for the founders of the Ascension Foundation to prosecute a war against Earth Fed and the League."

"I thought they didn't like the rest of humanity?" Major Hesme said.

"They didn't," Jessica said. "But they assumed the human race would eventually die out on its own. To them, we were a problem that would solve itself while their creations were busy exploring the Universe. And besides, the behavior of the Cendies is inconsistent with a war of extermination."

"A fair point," Colonel Miller granted. "The Cendies weren't exactly gentle in their invasion of Triumph, but there weren't any of the gratuitous acts of cruelty that usually happen in war."

"You would be an expert on both," Colonel Shimura said.

"I'm in good company," Colonel Miller retorted.

"So … before I … we continue, I must ask, do you two have a history together?" Jessica asked.

"No," Shimura and Miller said simultaneously.

After a pause, Shimura spoke first. "We know each other by reputation. Colonel Hieronymus Miller has quite the dossier."

"As does Colonel Dolores Shimura," Miller said.

"Yes, we spent a lot of time fighting from the shadows for our respective governments. But that is history now. The Ascendancy has upset the old paradigm," Miller said. "It will be curious how that paradigm changes when this war is over."

"We need to win the war first," Shimura pointed out.

"True. I suppose we should find out how to do that," Miller said.

CHAPTER 3

WHILE THE TROOPERS cleaned up on Pluto, Mason and his squadron recuperated in their quarters. The mission of Operation Allegiant Dragon had been one of the shorter missions the Osiris Squadron had been assigned since its inception—hours instead of days. Or, in the case of the Battle of Triumph, months.

Mason spent his downtime in the officers' lounge adjacent to Osiris Squadron's berthing. A vessel as large as *Independence* had a habitat ring divided into segments, like a train looped around itself, all housed inside the starship's hull between the main gun turrets and the hangar bays.

Mason reclined in his seat, enjoying the light but authoritative pull of .3 g holding him down while a packet of warm coffee rested on the table in front of him, along with a crumb-free donut wrapped in a napkin.

Dominic walked up, his uniform clean and freshly pressed, and stood with the air of someone trying to wash off the last few hours of space flight.

"Can't sleep?" Mason asked sympathetically.

"Nah. I prefer to let the stims wear out on their own rather than take a downer," Dominic said. "At my age, you try not to take more drugs than you have to."

In the first half-century of Flight Lieutenant Tanner Dominic's life, he had been a successful software engineer, doing well enough not to have to work again, even when modern life-extension technology was factored in. Instead, he had decided to join the Federal Space Forces as part of an adventure retirement. New old-timers like Dominic were hardly unheard of. Military service was traditionally the domain of the young, but that was not due to necessity, as in days past. Though gray and wrinkled, Dominic was just as fit as any spacer a third his age.

"Take a seat, Silverback," Mason invited. "Might as well enjoy the reprieve from duty."

"Thanks, Hauler," Dominic said, setting down his own packet on the table. "So, what do you think of the mission on Pluto?"

"Glad it went off as well as it did," Mason confided. "It's nice to come back with as many pilots as I left with."

"Couldn't agree more with that, but that wasn't my question," Dominic said.

"You're wondering why, of all the places in Outer Sol, Admiral Moebius picked Pluto as her first step?"

"Yeah. It's something that's been bothering me," Dominic admitted. "I get that New Lowell is the only major settlement this far out in Sol, but it's a scientific community—mostly astronomers and their families here to operate all the telescopes they built out on the Tombaugh Regio. Doesn't really lend itself as a staging point for the liberation of the rest of Outer Sol."

"We're not here to liberate Outer Sol just yet, Silverback," Mason reminded him. "We're just clearing the way for the tankers."

"Fair enough. But my point still stands—we could use any little dwarf planet in Sol as a staging ground. As far as I can tell, all Pluto gets us is a few hundred thousand civvies we have to look out for."

"Your mistake is assuming Admiral Moebius wanted Pluto for a staging ground," Mason said.

"Why else?"

"For the exact reason there are a few hundred thousand civvies on Pluto," Mason said. "Pluto's observatories."

"Those observatories are for looking at things billions of light-years away," Dominic said. "As in, any information they gather is already ancient—not very useful in a war dictated by the pace of faster-than-light travel."

"That would be true if we were fighting the League," Mason said.

"Okay, Hauler, how is this different?"

"The difference is that the League never had cloaking materials they could hide their ships behind at the edge of a star system. All the observatories on Pluto can detect very faint objects from extreme distances while covering almost the entire sky," Mason explained. "I think Admiral Moebius intends to use Pluto's observatories to search out any cloaked Cendy warships in Outer Sol and deal with them before the convoy arrives. Mark my words, once we get those observatories up and running, we'll be sent out to kill Cendy ships hiding in the Kuiper Belt."

"And where did you learn this? Did Admiral Moebius tell you?" Dominic asked.

"Nope. Just conjecture," Mason said. "I was there when they got the first sample of a Cendy cloak from a captured Fusilier. Stuff has one side that absorbs all radiation while the other reflects all radiation. You put a ship on the reflective side and it's all but invisible to anything on the black side."

"But not to Pluto's observatories."

"That would be my guess."

"Your guess?"

"I'm not an astronomer, Silverback," Mason said. "I'm not sure how those observatories are going to spot any Cendies in Outer Sol, or if they even can, but I bet Admiral Moebius believes so, hence why she set up a whole operation to take the planet. Why do you think our orders specified not damaging any of the telescopes?"

"I figured it was due to their scientific and cultural value," Dominic said. "We'd piss off every astronomer in settled space if we damaged Pluto's observatories."

Mason shook his head. "Like you said, Silverback, there are plenty of dwarf planets in the Kuiper Belt we could use without endangering civilian lives or priceless scientific equipment. Admiral Moebius didn't want us damaging Pluto's observatories because she intends to use them."

"And what makes you think the Cendies haven't thought of that?"

"They probably have."

"So why did they leave them intact?"

"Best guess? Knowledge is sacred to them, at least according to Jessica."

"How is she doing, by the way?" Dominic asked, diverted at the mention of Jessica.

"Drowning in intel they're gathering from the mothership we helped capture," Mason said. "And that's all she's had to say on the matter."

"You two still together?" Dominic asked.

"As far as I know, though 'together' is a funny concept when the parties involved are light-years apart," Mason said with a rueful smile.

"Hard to maintain a relationship over distance even when there's not a war going on. But good on you both for trying."

"I'm not sure how my relationships are your business, Silverback," Mason said with a smile.

"I'm your XO, Hauler. Your well-being is my business, and Lieutenant Sinclair is the best thing to happen to you since this war started," Dominic said firmly.

"I'm glad you think so," Mason said. "You sound more optimistic than I feel."

"You don't think you can maintain the relationship?"

"Have to be alive to do that," Mason said. "And I don't think the Cendies are going to make that easy for us."

"True. But just because death might be around the corner doesn't mean you shouldn't try and live."

"I suppose you would know."

"Hey, that's ageist," Dominic said and laughed. "Death is hardly knocking on my door, biologically speaking."

"I get your point," Mason said. "I'll make sure to draft something to Jessica before I turn in."

"Good on you. I'm sure she'll appreciate the distraction from her work with the Cendy mothership."

A notification appeared on Mason's HUD.

"What is it?" Dominic asked.

"That obvious?"

"The way your head tilts to the side is a strong tell you got a message on your brainset," Dominic said. "You'd make a terrible poker player."

"I know," Mason said. "Marshal Singh wants to see me in the war room. My guess is Admiral Moebius has another perilous mission for us."

Dominic saluted Mason with his coffee packet. "I look forward to hearing about it."

Finishing his coffee, Mason dropped the empty packet down a recycling chute and walked anti-spinward toward the war room, which was part of the flag module in the habitat ring, a segment set aside specifically for flag officers and their staff to run a war from.

A pair of troopers guarded the hatch, and they stopped Mason to check his brainset, as if a Cendy in disguise could have infiltrated *Independence*. Once the troopers had verified that he was, in fact, Squadron Leader Mason Grey, they ushered him through to the main level of the flag module, a long, squared-off hall with workstations lining each side and a large holotank dominating the center. The holotank backlit Marshal Singh's towering figure, the tip of his turban barely clearing the overhead.

Mason walked up and snapped a salute to Marshal Singh, who crisply returned it.

"Thank you for being prompt, Squadron Leader."

"I take it you have another job for us?" Mason asked.

"I just got out of a meeting with Admiral Moebius and the admirals commanding the other taskforces. With Pluto almost secure, we're moving on to the next phase in our operation."

"I'm all ears, sir," Mason said.

Marshal Singh waved Mason over to the holotank, which displayed the Solar System out to the orbit of Neptune. The marshal reached into the holotank and manipulated the display, zooming in to Neptune and revealing both the orbits of its moons and the locations of Cendy ships in orbit.

"The Cendies have established gas mining operations on Uranus and Neptune and are transporting the fuel out to an unknown location," Singh explained. "Our assumption is that the fuel is being taken to Cendy motherships to fuel their new starship construction. We're going to disrupt that supply chain by destroying the gas mining operations in Uranus and Neptune." Singh paused a moment before continuing, "In sixty hours, taskforces Alpha and Bravo will jump out for Uranus while taskforces Charlie and Delta will head for Neptune."

The Edge of Nowhere

Marshal Singh tapped a control, and two groups of Federal starships appeared in the holotank at the edge of Neptune's jump limit. Taskforce Charlie centered on FSFV *Cassowary*, and Taskforce Delta centered on *Independence* herself.

"Upon arrival over Neptune, *Independence* and *Cassowary* will launch a full strikecraft attack. Most of our squadrons will be tasked with dealing with the space-based infrastructure, except for Osiris Squadron. Your job will be to fly down into the atmosphere of Neptune to hunt down and destroy their gas skimmers. Those are the hardest-to-replace parts of the Cendy supply chain and will result in lasting disruption. Any questions, Squadron Leader?"

"Yes, sir," Mason said. "If all our carriers are engaging the enemy, who will be defending Pluto?"

"The troopers on the surface are already fortifying the city. By the time we jump out, there should be a few hundred surface-launch torpedoes and interceptors ready to oppose any Cendy counterattack against Pluto," Marshal Singh said. "Though given that the majority of the Cendy force in Sol is currently occupied with menacing the 1st Fleet in Inner Sol, it's unlikely they'll have the force to mount an effective attack."

Mason wasn't sure he agreed with that assessment. The Cendies always seemed to have some nasty surprise for unwary Federals. "How will we track down the skimmers in the atmosphere, sir?"

"*Independence* sensors should be able to track them through Neptune's atmosphere. Your pilots won't need to hunt them down. Just descend directly to their position and engage them."

"And what opposition can we expect to face, sir?"

"Over Neptune, there's a taskforce of Fusilier battlecruisers and Assassin arsenal ships," Marshal Singh said. "In Neptune's atmosphere? Unknown. It's possible, even likely, the Cendies will have fighters escorting the gas skimmers to oppose just the sort of attack we're planning. And that's not taking into account the kind of armament the skimmers might have."

"You think they have armed gas skimmers, sir?"

"We don't know, but it wouldn't be hard to mount some defensive missiles or even point-defense guns on a skimmer. They are more than large enough for that," Marshal Singh said. "I'll leave it to your discretion how your fighters should be outfitted."

"Triumph did give us a lot of practice with air-to-air combat," Mason said.

"Just remember that Neptune has no surface. Fly too deep into the atmosphere and it will crush your fighter like an insect."

"The same will happen with those skimmers if we damage them," Mason said. "So we don't need to take heavy ordnance. A few Atlatl pods full of Skylances should do the job."

Marshal Singh nodded. "As well as you should. Nuclear warheads aren't unlimited."

"There's reason to worry that we'll run out of nukes, sir?" Mason asked.

"Unless we can establish our line of communications with Earth and Luna, yes, Squadron Leader," Marshal Singh said. "The Battle of 61 Virginis has largely depleted our stockpiles of nuclear weapons. Our manufacturing capabilities outside of Sol simply cannot keep up with demand."

"Just how bad is it, sir?"

"Until we establish a stable supply chain with Luna, the nukes we have are all we're likely to get for a while," Singh said. "We departed 61 Virginis with much of Earth Fed's remaining stockpile."

"So there's not much room for error, then."

"Hasn't been since the war started, Squadron Leader. The fact is, even with our recent successes, Earth Fed's back is still against the wall."

"Then I'll see about trying to give us some breathing room, sir," Mason said. "I'll need to confer with my crew chief to see about getting my fighters prepped for flying in Neptune's atmosphere."

Marshal Singh nodded. "I'll leave you to it, Squadron Leader. But make sure to get some rest before we jump out."

Mason saluted. "Will do, sir."

༄

"Shit, flying through Neptune's not going to be easy on my birds, sir," Chief Rabin complained after Mason had briefed him on the mission.

"Can your crew get our Lightnings ready by then?" Mason asked.

"They're more or less ready now, sir, though I'm going to have my people inspect their airworthiness just the same," Chief Rabin said. "But Neptune's atmosphere's going to have a mix of abrasive ice crystals and corrosive hydrogen sulfide in the cloud deck. That's going to eat into the outer skin of the fighters, not to mention take a hell of a bite out of the service life of the intake turbines for the engines."

"Any of that going to be a problem in-flight?"

"No, but it will become a problem later on if I'm not given enough time to properly fix up my birds before the next mission," Chief Rabin warned.

"I'll make sure to let Marshal Singh know when we get back, then," Mason said.

"There's another problem, sir," Rabin said.

"What is it?"

"I don't have any balloons to outfit the cockpits of your fighters, sir."

"I guess someone forgot to tell the logistics people we'd be flying through gas giants," Mason said. "So if one of my pilots has to punch out, they're in for a long fall to their death."

Chief Rabin nodded. "That's right, sir."

Mason shrugged. "It's not like the Cendies take prisoners. I don't think it would do my pilots any good if they were left floating helplessly in Neptune's atmosphere until their life support ran out, do you?"

Rabin sighed. "You're right, sir. I still don't like letting your pilots fly without proper safety equipment."

"Neither do I, Chief, but we can't use what we don't have. We'll just have to make sure our fighters don't get shot down inside Neptune's atmosphere."

"I doubt the Cendies will be all that accommodating, sir."

"True. So let's make sure the Cendies have as little chance of killing my pilots as possible before we jump out."

※

"During our burn toward Neptune, *Independence* will provide continuous updates on the position of Cendy skimmers in the atmosphere," Mason briefed his pilots. "Obviously, *Independence* will only be able to track skimmers that are on the side of the planet facing toward her, so our operations will be confined to that hemisphere of the planet.

"Long-range surveillance of Neptune suggests the Cendies have at least fifty skimmers operating in and around Neptune. About half are in orbit transferring fuel at any given time. Those in the atmosphere will mostly be operating along the equator, on the same plane as the orbiting refineries and tankers.

"Best guess is that we'll have a dozen skimmers in sight of *Independence*'s sensors at any given time. I'll want us divided into two hunter-killer teams, each tasked with knocking down at least one skimmer, with the discretion to engage more if they become available.

"Now, here's the part where I stress caution. We don't know what kind of defensive armament the Cendies have on their skimmers, but I'm willing to bet they're going to carry nasty surprises, so I want us to leverage our main advantage over the skimmers—altitude and speed.

"In other words, engage the skimmers high and fast, giving our Skylances as much extra range as possible. That way if the skimmers fire missiles of their own, you all will have time to react and defend yourselves.

"I'll leave it to each pilot's discretion how many missiles they want to use against the skimmers. If the first volley is not sufficient to bring the skimmer down, continue to engage from maximum range and altitude. If I see in the after-action report that someone made a gun run on a skimmer, I will make every effort to make you regret surviving the experience. Any questions?"

Sabal raised her hand. "What kind of fighter opposition are we likely to run into in Neptune, Hauler?"

"Don't know, Hardball," Mason admitted. "I would say there's a non-zero chance that some Outriders will fly down to engage us, but that will depend on how they prioritize defense against the space-based attacks. Suffice it to say you should keep an eye out for getting bounced."

Gottlieb raised her hand. "Will we be in contact with the other hunter-killer teams while in Neptune's atmosphere?"

"Good question, Skids," Mason said. "Though the squadron will be divided into two hunter-killer teams, we won't be out of contact with each other. We'll have *Independence* overhead acting as a heavily armed relay satellite. If we run into trouble that any two Lightnings can't handle, help will be available."

"Speaking of help, Hauler, what about fire support from on high?" Armitage asked.

"*Independence* and the other starships will be engaged with Cendy space-based forces, so don't expect the big guns if we run into heavy opposition, Marbles," Mason said. "Anything down in Neptune's atmosphere will be up to us to kill."

When no more questions came Mason's way, he concluded the briefing. "Get a good rest. I want everyone up and checking your fighters four hours before *Independence* jumps out. Dismissed."

CHAPTER 4

It didn't take long for Colonel Miller's team to settle in. Colonel Shimura had assigned the Leaguers an entire inflatable hab so they didn't have to share bunk space or low-gravity toilets with their former enemies.

However, Colonel Shimura and Colonel Miller did agree that the Leaguers needed to be integrated with the Federal personnel studying the mothership. His junior officers and personnel were embedded with teams of Federal troopers and engineers exploring the mothership's vast interior, while Colonel Miller and Colonel Shimura worked directly with each other.

Major Hesme was assigned to work with Jessica, and it appeared she viewed it as her job to pick Jessica's brain bare.

"So, you figured this out because of a book?" Isobel asked after Jessica had summarized the trail of breadcrumbs that had led her to Miriam Xia.

"Yes."

"Never thought the first step in figuring out the Cendies would be learning their reading habits," Isobel remarked.

Jessica shrugged. "Had to start somewhere. That was the first clue that let me narrow down the possible origins of the Ascendancy."

"I suppose you had the advantage of knowing that the Ascendancy came from Sol. We had no such luck trying to figure out where they came from, though we assumed their origins would lead back to Earth. All roads lead there if you go back far enough in history."

"Including the League's," Jessica couldn't help but say.

"Yes—a point that was used when you tried to conquer us," Isobel said. "At least the Ascendancy doesn't use history as an excuse."

"No, they use the future as their excuse," Jessica said. "And I would be remiss if I didn't point out that the League attacked first in the second war between our nations, using an excuse not too dissimilar to the Ascendancy's."

"That's not how it's framed in our history classes," Isobel said.

"I bet it isn't," Jessica said. "But that's not germane to our current situation. So, what would you like to do?"

"I'm curious about the virtual world the Ascendancy has on this ship," Isobel said. "The one Miriam Xia's construct has been inside."

Jessica shrugged again. "In lieu of having crew quarters or lounge areas, the crew instead spend their non-working time in a virtual world."

"So, like a virtual game world?"

"Perhaps," Jessica said. "I haven't been in there myself, and Miriam's yet to unplug and tell us about her experience."

"It's been weeks since she entered," Isobel commented.

"Yes. I'm guessing Miriam and the Ascended are catching up with the last two hundred years. Or two years from Miriam's point of view, given she ran underclocked during that time."

"The way you speak of Miriam Xia sounds like you are friends," Isobel probed.

"That's because we are," Jessica said. "She's a very personable woman. Quite brilliant too."

"But she isn't real," Isobel pointed out.

"That's a philosophical question," Jessica said. "Do you not approve of uploaded minds?"

"I've always found the practice of some wealthy Federals of digitizing their consciousness before death distasteful."

"Not a fan of sentient AIs, I take it?"

"I have nothing against sentient AIs," Isobel said. "I think they're entitled to the same rights as you or me. I just don't like the idea of an elderly human imposing their identity on an AI construct in a vain attempt to extend their life."

"Miriam doesn't seem to feel too imposed upon by her identity," Jessica said dryly.

"Of course not. She was programmed that way. She was never given a chance to develop her own identity."

"That's a curious outlook you have there," Jessica said. "At first I thought you might have a religious objection."

"My husband is an AI programmer," Isobel said. "He's got strong opinions about the ethics of creating sentient AIs, and I admit many of his values have rubbed off on me."

"Does your husband work for IID?" Jessica enquired.

"If he did, I couldn't tell you about it," Isobel retorted. "Are you married?"

"No," Jessica said.

"I highly recommend it."

"Yes, well." Jessica decided to steer the conversation back on course. "I can't get us into the mothership's virtual world just yet. But if you're willing to suit up, I can take you to the compartment where Miriam and the mothership's crew are housed."

"That could be interesting, Lieutenant Sinclair."

"Jessica, please."

"Isobel, if you will."

"Thank you, Isobel. Now, shall we?"

⁂

"My stars!" Isobel exclaimed involuntarily after she followed Jessica into the Great Chamber.

Thousands of Cendies occupied thousands of reclined seats, still as statues.

"This feels like a massive tomb," Isobel said.

"Everyone in here is very much alive," Jessica assured her.

Interspersed among the Cendies were armed and armored troopers acting as guards for the prisoners. "Are those troopers enough if the Cendies all wake up at once and revolt?" Isobel asked a little nervously.

"The troopers are there to make sure the Cendies aren't disturbed,"

Jessica explained. "The promise that any resistance would be met with the destruction of their mothership is what's keeping the Cendies honest."

"Still hard to believe they surrendered," Isobel said.

"Something about this ship makes it too important to destroy," Jessica said. "I believe what's contained within the virtual world is the reason."

"What might that be?"

"Knowledge of some kind," Jessica said. "Perhaps the accumulated experiences of the crew or some interesting scientific discovery. I'm speculating based on the Cendies' apparent obsession with knowledge."

"It would be interesting to find out what that is."

"That's something I hope Miriam will tell us when she wakes up," Jessica said. "Speaking of whom, she's over here."

Resting in a retrofitted seat taken from an assault shuttle, Miriam Xia's beautifully made mobility rig lay supine. "Spared no expense, I see," Isobel said.

"I doubt Miriam would've tolerated being stuck inside an ugly mobility rig."

"Doesn't look like her, though."

"There wasn't time to get a custom model."

"You were there?" Isobel asked, surprised.

"You didn't know I was the one who recruited her?"

"I just didn't realize it was done in person," Isobel admitted. "How did you manage to get to Earth through the blockade?"

"With difficulty," Jessica said.

Isobel bounced over to Miriam's seat and looked at the reading coming off the display. "She's streaming a lot of data with the Cendies."

"About what you'd expect with a full-brain simulation, Isobel."

"Is there any way to listen in, Jessica?"

"We've been trying, but their encryption is top-notch, and that's not the biggest problem."

"What is?"

"There are hundreds of thousands of individual Cendies streaming data between each other, and we have no way of knowing which, if any, is actually useful."

"So our only way to know what's going on is to get inside," Isobel summed up. "And Miriam Xia is thus far the only outsider allowed in."

"Yes, that's the size of it, Isobel."

Isobel crossed her arms. "So we're just supposed to wait until Miriam Xia decides to wake up?"

Jessica shrugged. "Yes."

"And we can't just unplug her and ask what she's been up to?"

"We could, but that could anger her," Jessica said. "Right now, I think the best thing to do is to be patient."

"Hrmm, I can't say patience is my greatest virtue."

"Well, there's nothing else here to do other than wait," Jessica said. "And I generally prefer to do that in shirtsleeves with a packet of coffee and easy access to snacks."

Hrmm." Isobel turned away from Miriam and pushed herself over to the nearest Ascended, a worker with hand-like feet lying supine in the seat.

She kneeled and examined the tubes and wires running out the bottom of the seat and tapped on the thick tubes. "This is where the blood gets circulated?"

"Yes," Jessica said, following her over. "I take it you've read the report?"

"These are blood works where Cendy blood is circulated to have waste removed and nutrients and oxygen added."

"Yes," Jessica said. "Workers like this don't even have lungs. They're totally dependent on the ship's blood works to survive. Which is why we can't take them off the mothership. There's nowhere else we could support them."

"And the soldiers and emissaries?"

"They only make up a small percentage of the ship's crew. There weren't a lot of emissaries to start with, and few of the soldiers survived long enough to surrender."

"Seems like a rather limited existence to be so tied to one's ship. To never be able to exist anywhere else, be anything else but a worker drone on a massive starship."

"The Ascended don't think like we do," Jessica said. "And I suspect they get their enrichment from their virtual world. They only come out into the real world to get work done."

"I imagine that makes for a short commute at least," Isobel said, standing up slowly. "I think I've seen everything I need here. Is there anything else I should see?"

Jessica shrugged. "What interests you? Because the mothership has about it all. There's a shipyard, small-arms manufacturing, refining, propulsion, galleries of birthing tubes—you name it."

"Areas that my colleagues are no doubt exploring with yours," Isobel said. "Let's head back to the hab. I think I want to return to some relative comfort."

They left the sleeping chamber and its thousands upon thousands of residents and proceeded down one of the corridors that ran along the side of the ship, more floating in the weak gravity than walking.

The long tunnel was lit the whole length, but it was thousands of meters long—too long for Jessica to see either end. It just stretched forever, with endless handholds running up the sides for Cendy workers to scurry up and down. Though long, it was not difficult to make the kilometer-long trip back to base camp. Low gravity made for low exertion. They emerged at the bottom of the construction chamber near the vast hole leading into 30 Skeksis.

"What's going on over there?" Isobel asked.

A few hundred meters beyond the base camp, near one of the ruined Turtlebacks, Jessica saw the flashes that had drawn Isobel's attention. "Looks like someone's shooting," Jessica said. She brought up her HUD and pinged the IFF system to identify whether the figures in the distance were friend or foe. The HUD marked the Federals in blue and the Leaguers in yellow. One of the figures in the distance was Colonel Shimura, standing toward the rear of the group.

"Looks like your colleagues and mine have set up a shooting range," Jessica said. "Want to check it out?"

"Sure," Isobel said.

They skip-floated past the inflatable hab and toward the silent flashes of gunfire. As Jessica got closer, she saw paper targets had been set up, with the wreck of a Turtleback being used as a backstop.

It became evident that it wasn't a simple shooting practice. The weapons borne by the shooters were neither Federal nor League issue but

Ascendancy weapons. That piqued Jessica's curiosity, because she thought only Cendy soldiers could fire their weapons.

"When did we figure out how to fire the Ascendancy's guns, Colonel?" Jessica asked over the radio.

"Armorers were able to retrofit conventional triggers onto the Cendy weapons," Colonel Shimura said. "It was a task to keep them occupied. We've got half a dozen battle rifles ready for use. Interested in giving them a try?"

"I am very interested. Major Hesme is with me," Jessica said.

"She's welcome too. Her colleagues seem to be enjoying themselves."

As they walked up to the improvised firing range, two Leaguers stepped off the firing line. One was Colonel Miller, the other Lieutenant Sy.

"I was wondering where you two went off to," Colonel Miller said, holding out a Cendy rifle for Isobel.

"Lieutenant Sinclair was showing me the Cendy sleeping chamber," Isobel said as she accepted the rifle from Colonel Miller.

Lieutenant Sy wordlessly held out a rifle for Jessica. She accepted it and examined the work of the armorers to make the weapons usable for non-Cendies.

It was ... not attractive. It appeared the armorers had grafted the grip and trigger from a Federal battle rifle. How they had interfaced it with the Cendy battle rifle's fire-control system was beyond Jessica. She was happy to note that the fire selector was set to "Safe."

"How do these shoot?" Isobel asked.

"Walk up to the firing line and find out," Colonel Miller told her. "Fire controls work like you would expect them to on a Federal battle rifle."

Jessica wasn't surprised that League Intelligence officers were familiar with Federal weapons.

"Shall we, Lieutenant?" Isobel asked.

"Let's," Jessica agreed.

As they walked up, little drones turned down the firing line to replace spent targets with fresh ones.

"Well, let's see ..." Jessica shouldered the weapon. With no visible sights, she just looked down the length of the barrel and lined it up with the target, then flipped the selector to single fire and pulled the trigger.

Nothing happened, not even an anticlimactic click.

"It's not loaded, Lieutenant," Colonel Shimura told her.

"Ah, right." She looked around and noticed a stack of box-shaped magazines. "Is that the ammunition?"

"Yes. It loads from the sides, long end parallel to the barrel."

"Strange," Jessica murmured as she picked up the magazine. She examined it, noting the fresh round popping out of the box at one corner. Looking at the sides of her rifle, she saw there was an empty magazine inserted in a matching hole in the rifle.

"Load the fresh magazine through the left side and push the spent one out the other side," Colonel Shimura instructed.

Jessica did so, making sure the magazine was lined up correctly before pushing it through. It slid in easily, pushing the empty one out and locking into place with a tactile click.

Trying again, Jessica set the weapon to single fire and pulled the trigger. The weapon kicked back harder than she expected, and a hole was punched through the right side of the target.

"Well, I'm not going to give full auto a try, at least not without a hardsuit to eat the recoil," Jessica said.

"Good plan. Not that you have the option. I told the armorers to disable full auto just in case. They fire heavier projectiles than our battle rifles," Colonel Shimura said. "Sixty rounds to a mag versus a hundred for ours."

"Heavier rounds explain the recoil," Jessica said. "Curious they would penalize their ammo capacity for bigger rounds."

"My guess is to take advantage of their warform's large size," Colonel Shimura said.

Jessica glanced over at Isobel, who was happily firing away with her Cendy rifle, leaning forward against the recoil of each shot.

Jessica mimicked her posture and brought her rifle up to bear, firing again. The weapon kicked just as hard as before, but she found the barrel snapping back on target almost an instant later. The weapon was clearly not designed with humans in mind. It was too big and kicked too hard.

But the large size and heavy build of Cendy soldiers more than offset that problem. Federal battle rifles had to be smaller and lighter, recoiling so they could be used without the benefit of a strength-augmenting hardsuit.

By the time she had finished her magazine, Jessica's shoulder was starting to hurt, despite the padding provided by her pressure suit, and her target was thoroughly shredded with a scattered grouping. Though the range was only twenty meters, the lack of sights made hitting the target difficult.

Jessica stepped back from the firing line and set her rifle down to the side. "I'm guessing the Cendy soldiers use an internal aiming system so their weapons don't need built-in sights."

Colonel Shimura nodded. "Autopsies of Cendy soldiers show they have hardware in their heads that corresponds to an internal aiming system. We believe they interface with their weapons wirelessly—hence why they don't have triggers or any other external controls."

"I imagine making their weapons impossible for their enemies to use is also a factor," Jessica said.

"The Cendies left hundreds of thousands of such useless weapons on Triumph," Colonel Miller said. "We've ended up just piling them up until we can figure out a way to dispose of them."

Isobel stepped off the firing line, presumably after emptying the weapon's magazine. Clearly she was more tolerant of the weapon's recoil than Jessica was.

"Can't say I'm in love with the ergonomics," she said as she propped the weapon against the side of the crate next to Jessica's former rifle. "Feels like holding a fish."

Jessica looked down at the weapons and the curved contours of their stocks. "I admit, the resemblance is undeniable."

"The design makes sense for their soldiers, though," Colonel Shimura said. "They don't vary in size or build like humans do, nor do they have to worry about what armor they might be wearing. It's easy to make a one-size-fits-all weapon when your soldiers only come in one size."

"What about the other types of Cendies?" Isobel asked. "Do they have the same hardware for interfacing with weapons?"

"They don't appear to have the extra targeting equipment that the soldiers do, so I suspect even if they could fire the weapons, they wouldn't be able to aim them," Colonel Shimura said.

"Which fits with how they seem to specialize themselves," Colonel Miller said. "Their soldiers probably can't use the tools the workers can, or the emissaries for that matter."

"And their navigatrices and pilots are hard-wired with their vehicles," Jessica said.

"Yes. It's a shame that this mothership's navigatrix killed itself," Colonel Shimura said.

"Does imply that what they knew was worth dying for to keep out of their enemy's hands," Colonel Miller said.

"All the more reason we need to figure out what's in the Cendy virtual environment." Colonel Shimura turned to Jessica. "Anything new with Miss Xia?"

Jessica shook her head. "She still hasn't had anything to say."

"Have you tried getting her attention?"

"I figured it was best to wait while we explored the ship, Colonel," Jessica said.

"Well, I think we've been waiting long enough. After twenty-four hours, I want you to try to bring her back to the real world."

"She won't be happy about that," Jessica warned.

"Tough," Colonel Shimura said. "You'll have to remind her that this isn't a vacation."

CHAPTER 5

While standard Federal fighter squadrons had twelve fighters deployed to a carrier, special operations squadrons like Osiris had sixteen. To make room for the extra fighters, *Independence* had had to repurpose hangar bays 49 and 50, the bays usually reserved for the battlecarriers' assault shuttle and utility craft.

Hangar bays 49 and 50 were larger than the other hangar bays in order for each to fit a single assault shuttle and four smaller utility craft. As a result, there was barely enough room for two Lightnings to squeeze in if everything else was sacrificed.

Mason had picked hangar bay 50 as the home for both his fighter and Gottlieb's. The two Lightnings were stowed, wings folded, in a staggered position. Mason's Lightning was the closest to the closed hangar doors, and there was just enough room to maneuver the fighter onto the catapult for launch.

That did mean that when they were ready for launch, Gottlieb would be directly in the path of Mason's longburn drives. And despite the multitude of safeties meant to prevent a longburn drive from activating inside *Independence*, having a pair of cavernous drive exhaust engines facing you was not unlike having a gun pointed at your face.

It made Mason glad that the privilege of rank meant he got to be in front.

The hangar crew in their orange jumpsuits floated around the fighters, inspecting the ordnance bolted onto the wings. The four dorsal hardpoints each had a Stiletto pod for anti-missile defense while in space, while the four ventral hardpoints each had an Atlatl pod loaded with six Skylance air-to-air missiles apiece.

The interior weapons bay of each Lightning carried sixteen more Skylances mounted in pairs inside the eight-shot rotary launcher. That gave each of his pilots twenty-eight missiles for taking down the skimmers as well as engaging any Outriders that might attempt to engage them while in the atmosphere. He didn't include any Javelin interceptors. There would be plenty of those carried by the other Lightning squadrons.

Gottlieb floated next to her fighter, grabbing onto a handhold near the cockpit while the rest of her armored body floated in the air. Her helmet was off and clipped to the side of her hip.

"Something wrong, Skids?" Mason asked.

She looked down at Mason and shook her head. "Just working through some jitters, sir. First combat mission in a gas giant."

"It'll be different—no doubt about that," Mason said.

"Yeah. That's why I accepted the assignment when I was offered a spot with Osiris Squadron," Gottlieb said. "I guess I didn't realize how different it would be."

"I'm still surprised myself," Mason admitted.

A buzzer sounded, and Chief Rabin shouted to his crew to start leaving the hangar. "Hangar will depressurize in a couple of minutes," Mason said. "Better get buttoned up."

"Will do, Hauler. See you outside," Gottlieb said.

Mason nodded and kicked himself toward his fighter. Adjusting his approach with puffs from his hardsuit's thrusters, he grabbed the rim of the open cockpit with one hand and swung his legs in with practiced ease.

He made sure his helmet was sealed, then held down the toggle switch to close the canopy. It sealed shut with a hiss, leaving Mason closed off from the rest of the Universe in the windowless cockpit of his fighter. He locked the backplate of his hardsuit to his seat and started the process of bringing his fighter to life.

The Lightning had already been warmed up by the hangar crew, so it came to life in an instant. Being connected to his brainset, it treated

Mason to the disorienting sensation of the entire fighter becoming transparent as the sensor AI fed him external data.

Red lights started flashing inside the hangar bay as pressure dropped. Open valves in his cockpit opened to let air evacuate with that of the rest of the hangar and then closed once the hangar was depressurized. Then inert gas filled the cockpit until his hardsuit read the atmospheric pressure.

With that, his Lightning was fully powered up and ready for flight, held back only by safeties that prevented her longburn drives from activating while inside *Independence*.

A drone tug, held down to the deck by internal magnets, rolled into the hangar and toward Mason's Lightning, attaching itself to the front landing gear with a pincer arm, and slowly started to tow his fighter to the catapult.

With careful positioning, the drone turned his fighter toward the closed hangar door and locked the nose gear to the catapult. It then detached itself and rolled toward Gottlieb's fighter.

It was still five minutes until *Independence*'s jump to Neptune—five minutes that Mason spent running redundant checks, not so much to catch problems but to distract himself from his own nervousness.

"Osiris Leader, jump in sixty seconds and counting. Go, no-go for launch?"

"I'm go, *Independence* Control," Mason said.

"Roger that, Osiris Leader. Prepare for the jump."

Mason let out a long calming breath while his fingers danced on his dormant Lightning's control stick. A buzz that he felt more than heard traveled up through his seat, marking *Independence*'s jump to Neptune, and then the hangar doors parted.

"Oh, man," Mason breathed as vivid blue light poured through the opening slit in the doors. He hadn't expected his side of the battlecarrier to be facing Neptune after the jump, but as the hangar opened, he was looking right at the gas giant.

"Osiris Leader, brace for launch."

"Here goes …" The catapult kicked Mason out of the hangar and into open space.

The battlecarrier fell away from him as he gained control of his fighter. He unfolded the wings, waiting for them to lock before he lit his longburn drive.

Accelerating with a gentle one-third of a g, he pointed the nose toward Neptune and waited for the other fighters to catch up. On the tactical display, fighters and bombers continued to launch from *Independence*, while the same happened with *Cassowary* over a thousand kilometers away.

In a matter of minutes, a hundred Federal strikecraft burned for Neptune.

Osiris Squadron fell into formation around him in an echelon off his right wing.

Several kilometers away, *Independence*'s other squadrons formed up. Wildcard and Dagger squadrons were in full anti-strikecraft kit with Javelin interceptors and Stiletto pods, while the Conqueror bombers of the Nova Squadron carried a heavy anti-starship ordnance.

At a preplanned point away from *Independence*, Mason pushed his throttles forward, and the gs started adding up. All around him, every fighter and bomber added throttle and increased acceleration.

Over the course of a minute, Mason went from one-third g to ten gs. Increasing his weight thirty-fold in the space of a minute was not pleasant but well within the limits of what was expected of a combat pilot in the Federal Space Forces. Multiple expensive augmentation surgeries had reinforced his body against heavy gs, particularly his cardiovascular system, allowing him to keep conscious while minimizing the chance of a stroke. His hardsuit added support for his body, the inner gel layer distributing his weight and a steady stream of drugs keeping his mind sharp and alert.

It didn't take long for the Cendies to respond. Six Fusiliers and two Katyushas escorted the refinery ships. All at once, they lit their longburn drives and started to push themselves on an intercept course with the strikecraft. Outriders detached themselves from the Fusiliers and entered close defense formation.

Not counting Osiris Squadron, the Outriders matched the number of Lightnings. Stilettos gave the Lightnings the advantage in a fight, even if the Outriders got support from warships.

After passing the flip-over point of their burn, Osiris Squadron broke off with the rest of the Federal formation to begin their approach to Neptune. None of the Cendy forces in space attempted to intercept, evidently content to let Mason's squadron approach Neptune if it meant sixteen fewer Lightnings they would have to deal with in space.

As talking was impossible at ten gs, Mason was forced to use subvocal communication: *<Independence Control, it looks like we have a clear shot down to Jupiter. Requesting guidance to suspected skimmer locations.>*

"Roger that, Osiris Leader. We're uploading contacts now."

Data flooded in from *Independence*, and icons appeared on Neptune marking the suspected position of Cendy skimmers. There were at least fifteen contacts visible from *Independence*'s vantage in high orbit.

Mason briefed his pilots: *<All fighters, we've got our targets. Each pair gets one skimmer to shoot down. Exercise extreme caution. If things look too hairy, bug out to orbit. Remember, you get shot down over Neptune, there's nothing to keep you from falling to crush depth.>*

With targets assigned, Osiris Squadron separated as each pair of fighters vectored on targets scattered across the planet. The target Mason picked for himself was over a dark spot in Neptune's northern hemisphere. Flying over the storm would likely cause some interesting turbulence.

Gottlieb: *<You sure you want to fly toward that thing, Hauler?>*

Mason: *<Nervous, Skids?>*

Gottlieb: *<Flying over a storm larger than some planets does cause me some anxiety, sir.>*

Mason: *<Our Lightnings can handle it. Just don't fly too low and the monster storm won't be a problem.>*

Gottlieb: *<Roger that, Hauler.>*

Space over Neptune lit up as the other squadrons engaged Cendy space forces. Outriders and Lightnings traded volleys of interceptors, with the Cendy volley being blunted by the Stilettos the Lightnings carried. A few Lightnings winked off the display from hits, but the Cendy Outriders suffered worse despite remaining under the cover of the starships. And because the Cendies kept their fighters close to their ships, the Conquerors made their bombing runs unmolested.

The twenty-four bombers attacked from four different directions, with each bomber launching ten torpedoes, each concentrated on one of the Fusiliers. The Cendy battlecruisers' spinal-mounted guns were a deadly threat to the ships of taskforces Delta and Charlie. A solid direct hit would punch through the frontal armor of even *Independence*.

The arsenal ships launched waves of interceptors at the Federal torpedoes while the bombers burned hard to escape.

Interceptors met torpedoes in tiny flashes. Point-defense guns opened fire in the last sections before impact, and then all at once, the surviving torpedoes detonated.

Rather than making a direct impact, each torpedo detonated at a standoff range while pointing its shaped charge warheads at its target, blasting it with a concentrated cone of nuclear fire.

The icons of all four Fusiliers blinked to indicate they were hit, with one turning gray, indicating a kill. The remaining three were still active but damaged, indicated by the gas and debris Mason's sensors picked up.

The Conqueror bombers continued to burn away with the Lightnings in tow, the surviving Outriders remaining close to the remaining Fusiliers. The strikecraft were vectoring to return to the carriers, while the cruisers and destroyers of Taskforce Delta increased their acceleration to finish off the Cendy warships.

Mason had to admit that he wanted to watch the big ships duke it out, but Neptune loomed behind him as he neared the completion of his braking burn.

The braking burn concluded in the upper reaches of Neptune's atmosphere. As soon as the drives cut, Mason flipped his fighter over to place it in a nose-up attitude as he descended into Neptune.

It wasn't long until he felt the first bites of Neptune's atmosphere, with jitters and shakes that never happened in open space. The dark-blue expanse of the storm stretched across the horizon, while above him, the blackness of space gradually turned bluer and bluer as he flew deeper and deeper into the atmosphere.

Far below, Mason's sensor AI tracked the skimmer as it flew in a wide circle over the storm, picking up the valuable gases it brought up from below. It didn't seem to react to the presence of two Federal fighters approaching from above. Hopefully it was just a dumb drone going about a pre-programmed route without a care for the dangers that might be lurking above.

"Skids, you make it into the atmosphere okay?" Mason asked.

"Everything's intact and I have a good fix on the skimmer," Gottlieb said.

"Let's configure for atmospheric flight and head down and kill it, then."

"Right behind you, Hauler."

Mason opened the air intakes covering the turbines. These directed Neptune's air to heat exchangers to superheat it and expel it out the back for thrust. It was an even more efficient method of propulsion than long-burn drives, as no propellant had to be expended. A Lightning could fly in the atmosphere almost indefinitely. Mason hoped to be finished in less than an hour. He didn't like flying over a giant hole big enough to swallow Ganymede with room for seconds.

Gottlieb closed a kilometer off his right wing, entering a closer echelon formation preferred for atmospheric flying.

"We'll attack the skimmer together. Maintain supersonic speeds on approach. We're going to launch at long range, and I want the Skylances to have as much kinetic energy as possible when they launch."

"Roger that, Hauler."

The skimmer continued its lazy turn in the distance as Mason approached at supersonic speed. He selected four Skylances, one from each underwing Atlatl pod.

"We'll give the skimmer four missiles each," Mason said.

"Four missiles each—roger."

Mason continued his approach, waiting for the range to close for his Skylances. The skimmer took no evasive action.

Just before Mason entered firing range, multiple objects dropped from the skimmer and started flying toward Mason and Gottlieb. "Incoming missiles!" Gottlieb called out.

"Going defensive—stay on my wing!" Mason yelled, aborting his attack on the skimmer as he pulled a hard right turn.

His seat tilted back as the gs from the hard turn fell on him. The hard

180 gave him time to think and to get a better look at what the skimmer had just thrown at them.

It only took a moment for Mason to realize they weren't missiles. Their acceleration wasn't high enough for missiles running on solid propellant. When the sensor AI gave him a magnified image, he saw a sleek, aerodynamic object.

Fighters. The skimmers carried fighters. And they were gaining fast.

Before he knew what he was doing, Mason had instructed his communications AI to send a burst transmission up to *Independence*. In a fraction of a second, a pulse of microwaves shot up into Neptune's sky. He hoped their communications personnel would relay his warning to the rest of his squadron in time.

"What do we do, Hauler? Bug out for orbit?" Gottlieb asked.

"They're gaining too fast. We'll make easy targets if we climb," Mason said. "Stay on my wing—we're going down."

"Into the storm?"

"Where else?" Mason said. "Follow me. We're about to get missiles launched our way."

Indeed, Mason's launch alarm sounded as the ten contacts each launched a pair of air-to-air missiles at him and Gottlieb. The swarm of missiles climbed high into the atmosphere before descending towards the fleeing Lightnings.

Mason increased his throttle and turned hard right into the direction of the storm's wall. Neptune's winds shook his fighter hard, the frame groaning under the abuse. But his engine kept his speed up even as the air got thicker and more violent.

The missiles continued on their course, following Mason and Gottlieb into the storm. They would have to fight the same winds as the Lightnings did, but they didn't have engines to continue fighting the drag. The higher the winds, the more the missiles had to fight to stay on target, thus expending more and more of their kinetic energy until they started to lag.

Mason sighed in relief as the missiles dropped off the threat board. He returned his attention to the Cendy aero fighters and discovered them high above, setting up a missile shot from high altitude.

"Skids, pick targets and engage!" Mason ordered. He locked all ten enemy fighters and fired one Skylancer each, Gottlieb matching his volley.

The Cendies fired more of their own missiles at the same time, and Mason wrenched his fighter into a diving turn. Having to fight both gravity and the high winds, he was certain that none of the missiles he'd just fired would hit, but they would keep the Cendies busy while he dealt with their missiles.

The Cendies dove almost straight down on Mason and Gottlieb, and as the pressure increased, the winds buffeting his fighter became more violent. He was quickly running out of altitude to use.

"Drop decoys!" Mason called as he started dropping a line of burning decoys behind him.

In trying to draw the missile away, Gottlieb left a fiery trail of her own.

Just as Mason was about to reach minimum altitude, he pulled up hard. The wings of his Lightning flexed upward as aerodynamic forces tried to rip them off.

The missiles were too fast to follow the turn. They pursued the decoys instead, flying straight down into the abyss of the storm.

The hard climb also brought the Cendy fighters back into view. They had all survived the first volley but were scattered now from having to go defensive.

"Same as before, Skids. Engage!"

"Roger."

Mason fired another volley of Skylances, one for each fighter. Then he immediately turned hard and went defensive, even before the Cendies fired more missiles of their own.

The twenty Skylances Mason and Gottlieb had fired climbed up toward the Cendies, forcing them to dive and turn to try to shake them in the thicker lower atmosphere.

Mason's turn forced the Cendy missiles to turn with him, fighting progressively thicker air and stronger winds as they did so. Again, the Cendy missiles expended their energy before they could reach his fighter. None of his or Gottlieb's missiles hit either, but they further scattered the Cendies and forced them down to the same altitude as the Lightnings.

"Stay on my wing, Skids. We're going to pick them off one at a time," Mason said.

The nearest Cendy fighter was just twenty kilometers away when Mason and Gottlieb both launched a pair of Skylances at them.

The Cendy fighter reacted instantly, turning hard away from the incoming Federal missiles, but the missile closed the distance quickly, and two of them detonated near the fighter, turning it into a black splotch against the blue sky. Neptune's powerful winds quickly scattered the debris.

Mason immediately engaged another nearby Cendy, striking it down with another volley of Skylances. The remaining eight Cendy fighters re-formed to attack the two Federal fighters.

No missiles came his way; Mason suspected they were out of missiles. The small fighters couldn't have carried that many. But the large size that allowed Lightnings to carry far more missiles could be a detriment in a close-in fight with smaller, lighter fighters.

"I think they're out of missiles, Skids. Don't let them sucker you into a dogfight," Mason warned.

"Wouldn't dream of it, Hauler," Gottlieb said.

Mason fired another volley of missiles, half his remaining supply, to scatter the Cendies. Gottlieb did the same. All the Cendy fighters managed to evade the missiles but were further scattered.

Mason turned hard and fired a missile at the first one that he got his nose on. The Skylance dropped from his fighter's belly and rocketed toward the Cendy fighter, reaching it in a couple of seconds before blotting it out of the sky with its fragmentation warhead.

Mason targeted another Cendy. "This one's yours, Skids."

"I'll get 'em," she said as a Skylance leaped from one of her wing stations. It crashed into the Cendy fighter seconds later.

The six remaining fighters vectored straight in for Mason and Gottlieb, turning hard as the Lightnings flew past, and fired streams of penetrators after them. Mason pulled hard to keep out of the stream of projectiles that cut through the air behind him. The little Cendy parasite fighters could turn fast, that was for sure.

The Cendy stayed tight on Gottlieb and Mason's tails.

"Skids, break hard right. I'll break hard left, then turn around and fly toward me."

"Just give the word."

"Break!" Mason yelled as he wrenched his control as far to the left as it would go, banking his fighter left before he pulled up hard, not putting his fighter into a high-g turn. Four parasite fighters followed him, with the remaining two following Gottlieb.

A few seconds later, Mason reversed his turn until he was flying straight toward Gottlieb and the fighters pursuing her.

The combat AI had already locked Skylances onto the parasite fighters following Gottlieb. Mason launched a volley of three missiles each, with Gottlieb firing missiles of her own. An instant later, the fighters chasing Gottlieb exploded, while those behind Mason died at almost the same instant.

"Good work, Skids. That's going to be one for the textbooks," Mason said.

"Don't have many missiles left for the skimmer," Gottlieb said.

"Let's not give them a chance to throw another surprise our way. Split up and attack the skimmer off their right wing. I'll approach from the left."

"Roger that, Hauler."

Mason flew his fighter in a long, high-speed loop that took him around the far side of the Cendy skimmer, while Gottlieb took up position off the right wing.

The massive skimmer loomed like some great flying beast, cornered by two smaller predators. In perilous danger but still a threat.

"Engage!" Mason called, turning toward the skimmer.

Gottlieb matched his maneuver on the other side of the skimmer, and at the same time, they fired their remaining Skylances before breaking off. The Skylances closed the distance quickly, covering the thirty-kilometer distance within seconds.

The skimmer erupted with point defense from at least two turrets that attempted to pick off the missiles before they hit, but four missiles closing from either side were too much for the skimmer's point defenses.

The skimmer shot down five Skylances, while the remaining three detonated just off the its nose, showering it with shrapnel. The skimmer must have been full of super-compressed helium, because the moment it was hit, it disappeared into a massive cloud of expanding gas.

"Woah!" Mason breathed, just before the shockwave reached his fighter and shook him hard enough to cause his teeth to chatter.

"Never saw helium explode like that before," Gottlieb said.

"Anything will explode like that if you put it under enough pressure," Mason said. "Let's return to orbit and see if the rest of Osiris Squadron has had as much trouble as we've had."

"You think they ran into the same trouble?"

"That's what I want to find out."

Returning to orbit was a simple matter of climbing at full power until the atmosphere became too thin for the turbines to breathe and then closing the intakes and transitioning to longburn drives. As he broke atmosphere, he was relieved to see his squadron appear on his sensor display.

"Saw you had quite the fight down there, Hauler," Dominic said.

"You could say that," Mason said. "You have any trouble, Silverback?"

"No. You gave us fair warning, so we dealt with the parasite fighters before dealing with the skimmer," Dominic said. "You were the only one to be taken by surprise."

"Lucky me," Mason said dryly.

Far above, the battle in space was wrapping up. The warships were broken wrecks left in the wake of Taskforce Delta's cruisers and destroyers, while another wave of strikecraft with fresh munitions was burning for the Cendy refinery ships and gas mining infrastructure.

Pair by pair, Osiris Squadron returned to orbit around Mason. All his pilots and their craft had avoided damage from the Cendy parasite fighters, but there were only four missiles shared between sixteen fighters. Mason felt good that he had insisted on bringing as many missiles as possible with them. "Better to have too many missiles and not need them than need them and not have them," he recalled one of his instructors saying back in combat flight school.

"We're done here," Mason said. "Set a vector for *Independence* and commence full cruising burn. With luck, *Independence* will jump out for Pluto before Cendy reinforcements arrive."

"Speak for yourself, Hauler. I'd love to get some more action against the Cendies," Sabal said.

"Well, I would like a hot meal and a shower," Mason said. "Begin burn now."

Longburn drives flared up as the fighters started thrusting out of Neptune's orbit. Mason throttled up to fly after them, enduring the multiple gs falling on him as he ascended away from Neptune.

On the flight back to *Independence*, he watched Neptune fall away behind him, looking at the dark-blue spot where he once again had nearly died because of a Cendy surprise. He wondered if he would run out of luck before the Cendies ran out of ways to try to kill him. He wasn't optimistic.

CHAPTER 6

JESSICA SAT DOWN in the seat next to Miriam, wires running from her suit to Miriam's mobility rig. Isobel stood nearby, observing Jessica.

"So, this is how you hacked into her virtual before?" Isobel asked.

"I didn't hack," Jessica said. "I made a discreet hardware connection and then requested her audience. I was lucky enough to get her attention."

"So you intend to do the same now," Isobel said. "How exactly?"

"I figured I'd rely on the rapport I've built with her since we first met."

"So you're friends with her?"

"As a matter of fact, I am," Jessica said. "Which hopefully means she won't be too cross with me."

"Well, good luck, then. I'll just wait here until you come back."

Jessica nodded and lay back in her seat, relaxing her body while she opened a menu in her HUD. Because her body was artificial, she could switch off all articulation, making sure she didn't reflexively fly out of her seat in reacting to whatever she saw on the other side.

Then, like the first time she had met Miriam, she requested a connection.

Almost instantly, Miriam accepted.

Jessica saw that as a good sign. She accepted the connection, and the real world faded away.

The first thing she noticed was the sound of a crackling fireplace as a plush parlor filled with antique wood furniture faded into view. She found herself standing on a rich carpet, facing the fire. A familiar pair of long, toned legs were visible from the large cushioned seat that faced the fireplace.

Walking around, Jessica found Miriam lying back wearing a maroon silk robe with a black sash that barely covered the upper half of her thighs and open at the chest to give Jessica an easy view of her cleavage. In a perfectly manicured hand rested a snifter of brandy, while dark, almond-shaped eyes regarded Jessica with lazy interest.

A heat rose into Jessica's cheeks that had nothing to do with the fire.

"Why, hello, Jessica," Miriam said. "I see you still have that drab uniform as your default. No one can see us in here, you realize?"

"I'm afraid I'm here for work, and I do have some sense of professionalism," Jessica said.

"You mean this isn't a social visit?" Miriam asked.

"I'm sorry if I disappoint you," Jessica said.

"Oh, hardly, darling. I'm happy to see you regardless," Miriam said. "It's a nice change of pace from the Ascended."

"Have they not been nice?"

"No, they've been excessively pleasant with me, with an emphasis on the 'excessively' part," Miriam said. "You have my gratitude for giving me an excuse to take a break from them for a while."

"So they've been keeping you busy?" Jessica asked.

"Oh, yes. They've been showing me all kinds of interesting constructs within their Consensus—basically, interactive art pieces made by individual Ascended. I've been so occupied with them that I haven't noticed how many days I've been under."

"It's been weeks, actually," Jessica told her.

Miriam tipped her glass to Jessica. "You see my point." She took a long sip and then gestured to Jessica. "Please sit, darling. You're not speaking with your Colonel Shimura here."

"Oh, I know," Jessica said, settling herself in an identical chair adjacent to Miriam. She leaned over the armrest toward Miriam. "We have visitors from the League who are very curious about what you've been up to."

Miriam swirled her brandy with a dramatic flourish. "I suppose we are technically in their territory. Like I said, I've been inundated with Ascended who want to show me all their precious constructs."

"What can you tell me about them?" Jessica asked.

Miriam took a long sip of her brandy. "Well, there are two basic categories: individual and communal. The individual ones are, of course, abstractions of each Ascended's life experience, while the communal ones are built by the crew in general.

"The communal construct seems to be something of a very abstract log of the mothership. The individual construct follows patterns similar to the various types of Ascended. Workers have constructs interpreting their jobs maintaining the ship, while the soldiers have ones that are unsurprisingly martial in nature. The emissaries are filled with interpretations of their encounters with humanity."

"The communal construct—you said it's something of a ship's log. Does that include where the ship has been?" Jessica asked.

"Probably," Miriam said. "But I don't know where to begin interpreting it. It's like a giant twisted ribbon. Best guess is the ribbon starts where the mothership was built while the end is where the mothership currently resides. But beyond that, I couldn't begin to translate it into actual places in space."

"I don't suppose you could re-create it for us?" Jessica asked.

Miriam smiled. "That, I think I can do. A benefit of being a digitized mind is that I have perfect recall …"

The parlor fell away, leaving Jessica and Miriam seated in an infinite white space.

Miriam pointed up, and Jessica looked up to see the beginnings of a ribbon drawing itself out of space, starting at one point and turning and twisting in a seemingly random fashion, often curving back on itself or reaching off a long way before making more sudden twists and turns. Its end stretched beyond where Jessica could see.

"Seems a bit bare for a communal art piece," Jessica observed.

"You're thinking in human scales. In the virtual world, things can be about as big or as granular as you wish," Miriam said.

The ribbon expanded toward the center. No, not expanded. Zoomed in. It turned from a monolithic color to a collage of images.

"Each patch is a snippet of the experience of all the mothership's crew going back to the beginning," Miriam explained. "Lots of images of star systems and planets or the manufacturing of tools. But as you get closer to the end, the patches take on a more militant tone."

The ribbon moved, and the patches all blurred together as they raced past until they came to a sudden stop toward the end. There were still many images of stars, planets, and space, but there were also patches featuring the recognizable hulls of Cendy warships being built—the manufacturing of weapons and images of battle and carnage.

These images included scenes of the Battle of 30 Skeksis, such as soldiers leaping down to the access tunnel to fight off the Federal invasion and Lightnings bursting out and throwing out flares while being chewed up by small-arms fire. There was even a scene of the drone swarm Jessica had sent into the mothership to map out the interior before Mason's fighters had entered the ship to neutralize the operation of the Turtlebacks defending the interior.

"My God," Jessica whispered. "I'm going to have to share this."

"Please do," Miriam said. "If you or your colleagues can make sense of this mess, I would be very much interested to learn."

※

Colonel Shimura, Colonel Miller, Isobel, and Jessica stood around the holotank back at base camp, staring at the ribbon floating inside it. Zoomed out to fit within the diameter of the holotank, the innumerable individual patches that made up the ribbon all blended into a single shimmering strip. Some quick math showed that if the individual images were blown up to the size of a postcard, the ribbon would be millions of kilometers long.

The data download from Miriam had taken hours. It might have been an abstraction of the accumulated experience of the mothership's crew, but it was also a massive data dump.

"Well, this is quite the insight into Cendy culture," Colonel Miller said. "Is this indicative of how the Cendies record their experiences on all their ships?"

"Unknown, sir," Jessica said. "We would have to capture more of their vessels before drawing such conclusions."

"Easier said than done," Miller said. "I would like a copy to send to my data miners down on Triumph."

Colonel Shimura nodded. "I've already booked you time with our tight beam to send down to Triumph at your leisure, Colonel."

"Thank you, Colonel Shimura," Miller said. "It will probably take weeks at the earliest for our data miners to get useful intel from this."

"Maybe not, sir," Isobel said.

All eyes turned to her.

"How so, Major Hesme?" Colonel Shimura asked.

Isobel traced the ribbon with her finger. "If you draw straight lines between each bend in the ribbon, it looks a lot like the route of a starship jumping from system to system."

"That's an interesting theory," Colonel Shimura said. "It would certainly explain why that ribbon has been laid out in such a deceptively random fashion."

"My astrogation training coming into use," Isobel said. "I've seen enough lifetime tracks of various starships' FTL journeys to recognize the pattern."

"So how do we reference it?" Colonel Shimura asked.

"Well, we know where the endpoint of the ribbon is," Isobel said. "Could you superimpose the ribbon over a star map? I don't know how to work a Federal holotank."

Colonel Shimura nodded and stared at the holotank, commanding it through her brainset to add a three-dimensional star map.

"Now, can we replace the ribbon with a simple point and line?" Isobel asked.

The ribbon disappeared and was replaced by a segmented line, with each segment varying wildly in length and angle.

Isobel pointed to one end of the ribbon. "This represents the far end of the ribbon. So, let's place that on 61 Virginis."

The end of the last segment snapped over 61 Virginis, with the rest of the segments stretching off into the cosmos like sticks joined together end to end.

"And now to give the AI instructions to try to match the points to known stars," Isobel said.

The star map was replaced by a progress bar as the AI got to work, filling up in the space of a few seconds.

Then the progress bar disappeared and the star map returned, the points of each vertex lined up with the current position of known stars. Toward the end, however, the many points, including what would be the very first, did not seem to line up with any system in particular.

"Ninety-five percent match," Isobel said.

"So what about the remaining five percent?" Colonel Shimura asked.

"Either points in space that don't line up with any stars or systems that aren't on the star map," Isobel said.

"There's a lot of stuff out there that won't show up on our maps. Brown dwarves or rogue planets," Jessica said. "Given that a mothership can latch onto an asteroid and start making ships, I wouldn't be surprised if the Cendies make a habit of seeking out unbound planetary bodies. Good way to build up their forces without attracting notice."

"Not to mention the further out you get from the center of settled space, the more uncharted objects there are going to be," Colonel Shimura said. She tapped on the controls of the holotank, and a simple line went directly between 61 Virginis and the end of the segmented line, out seemingly in the middle of empty space, fifty light-years from 61 Virginis. "If Major Hesme's assumption about the ribbon being a timeline is correct, then this is where the mothership came from."

"Fifty light-years? That's about a month's trip via a stardrive," Colonel Miller said.

"Outside the range of most of our ships without refueling along the way," Colonel Shimura said. "And with our ships focused on trying to relieve Earth, we are short on ships to scout that location."

"Fortunately, we might have something that could work," Colonel Miller said.

"What do you propose?" Colonel Shimura asked.

"Well, I know for a fact that IID has a scout vessel that would be well suited to a discreet inspection of origin points of the Cendy mothership," Colonel Miller said. "And it would be a trivial matter for my people to requisition a tender vessel to provide the additional fuel needed."

"That's still talking over thirty days in transit," Colonel Shimura said. "Unless your people's ships have gotten faster since I last checked."

"Alas, the vessel that we'd use wouldn't be any faster but would be otherwise well suited to what I'm proposing," Colonel Miller said.

"Then explain—starting with the ship in question," Colonel Shimura said.

"The ship's codename is *Midnight Diamond*—a purpose-built recon vessel that's currently berthed at our base on Scirocco," Colonel Miller said. "She'd be able to make it out there without attracting attention to herself."

"What are the ship's capabilities?" Colone Shimura asked.

"I can't go into detail, I'm afraid," Colonel Miller said. "Unless you're willing to share the details of how the Special Purpose Branch's mimic arrays work?"

Colonel Shimura did not answer.

"I thought not," Colonel Miller said. "What I can say is that *Midnight Diamond* is a starship that does not produce the highly detectable arrival and departure flash of conventional vessels. I won't explain how she does that, but I'm sure it's clear how she might be useful for a long-range reconnaissance mission."

"Pop into existence at the edge of the system with no jump flash to give you away?" Jessica said. "Yes, I can see how that could be useful."

"How quickly can you get such an operation underway?" Colonel Shimura asked.

"Almost immediately," Colonel Miller answered. "*Midnight Diamond* is ready to launch, and I can requisition a ship from the battlefleet in the time it takes me to fly down to Scirocco to pick her up."

"You'd go yourself? What about your assignment to study the mothership?"

"My assignment was to find actionable intelligence, which Major Hesme just did for me," Colonel Miller said. "My subordinates can handle a coordinated study of the mothership with your people."

"I want one of my people to join any expedition out there," Colonel Shimura said firmly.

"I thought you would," Colonel Miller said. "I hope that person will be someone who will contribute to the success of our mission and not just someone wanting to get an up-close look at one of our best intelligence ships."

"Lieutenant Sinclair is the obvious choice," Colonel Shimura said. "And Miriam Xia should go with her. Her insights may prove valuable out there."

Colonel Miller nodded. "An interesting proposal. I'll send it up the chain of command to see what my superiors think, but I think it will prove acceptable."

Later, in Colonel Shimura's office, Jessica closed the door. "So, have I just been volunteered to go with the Leaguers?" she asked.

"My preference would be to send you with a staff and a squad of Raiders, but I doubt Colonel Miller would allow that," Colonel Shimura said. "Not enough room aboard *Midnight Diamond*."

"You know about her?"

"Only dimensionally," Colonel Shimura said. "About as small as a starship can get while still carrying a useful payload, with a squeeze. We knew the IID had their own brand of stealth technology. Our worry was their own variant of the mimic arrays our recon ships use, but that does not appear to be the case."

"I can certainly see how having a ship that doesn't emit a jump flash would be useful for reconnaissance," Jessica said. "Still, if *Midnight Diamond* is so small, I wonder how much capability it can really have."

"Enough for scouting out the Cendy origin systems," Colonel Shimura said. "Though fifty light-years is going to be a stretch for a ship so small."

※

"Hello again, Jessica," Miriam said. The parlor had been exchanged for the exterior of a slate-stone mansion, surrounded by rolling hills covered in bright grass.

Miriam wore blue striped trousers, a white blouse, and a tan vest. Draped over her forearm was an ornately engraved antique firearm, the twin barrels separated from the stock at a hinge.

"Hello, Miriam. Shooting?" Jessica asked.

"I've been feeling the need to turn some clay pigeons into dust," Miriam said.

"Pardon?"

"Skeet, darling. Have you never heard of it?"

"I'm afraid I'm not familiar with shooting sports," Jessica said. "Are you really going to shoot clay pigeons?"

Miriam smirked as she loaded two plastic shells into the breech of each barrel and then closed the weapon with a snap. She shouldered the stock, aimed into the sky, and shouted, "Pull!" A pair of red disks flew out over the lawn from either side of Miriam. Both disks turned into clouds of red dust with two rapid shots from Miriam's gun.

In VR, hearing protection wasn't necessary, but the blast from the shots startled Jessica.

With a smug grin, Miriam broke open the weapon, and two spent shells flew out with a hollow pop, leaving trails of smoke as they fell to the ground. She walked over to one of the launchers that had thrown one of the unfortunate disks into the air, grabbed an identical orange disk from a hopper, and tossed it to Jessica like a frisbee.

Jessica caught the disk and stared down at it.

"That's a clay pigeon. Not as literal as you imagine," Miriam said. "I believe back in the day, centuries before even my time, skeet was played with live pigeons."

"How gruesome," Jessica said.

"Someone thought so, hence the replacement of birds with clay disks," Miriam said. "Do they not play skeet anymore?"

Jessica shrugged. "I don't know. I might be clever, but I don't know everything."

"Well, I'll show you. I've always found the sport a good way to let off steam," Miriam said, handing the weapon over to Jessica. "You do know what a shotgun is, yes?"

Jessica accepted the weapon, feeling its heft and the texture of the fine checkering of the stock. "I do, but I'm not familiar with ones as old as this. Do you really have to break it open to load it?'

"Yes, darling," Miriam said. "Much more engaging than modern firearms."

Miriam handed Jessica two shells made of red plastic with brass bases. Jessica looked at the shells, noting the crimped plastic at the front of them. She could see the dozens of tiny pellets through the translucent plastic.

Loading was easy to figure out; she just pushed the shells in until the brass bases were flush with the breech of each barrel. She closed the weapon, which made a satisfying click. Bringing it up to her shoulder, it felt odd to have the grip integrated into the stock rather than have a separate pistol grip, but the weapon pointed naturally.

"Are you ready, darling?" Miriam asked.

"I am. Fire when ready," Jessica said.

Miriam chuckled. "Shout 'pull,' darling."

"Oh, right. Umm. Pull!"

A clay pigeon went spinning into the air. Jessica lined up the bead at the front of the barrel with the pigeon and pulled the trigger.

The shotgun recoiled in her shoulder, and the pigeon seemed untroubled.

Jessica snapped off her second shot to similar effect. The pigeon landed safely in the grass fifty meters away.

Miriam walked up to Jessica and handed her two more shells. "You must lead the targets, darling. Those pellets fly slow compared to what you're used to."

"How much lead should I give?" Jessica asked.

"Aim slightly ahead of the disk and you should hit it."

Jessica nodded and reloaded her shotgun. "Pull!" she shouted, and a second pigeon went flying. She aimed for a spot in the sky just ahead of the pigeon and fired just before it crossed her sights.

The pigeon shattered into pieces.

"Wow!" Jessica cried as she let the shotgun fall from her shoulder. Miriam clapped behind her.

Opening the action, Jessica was surprised when just the spent shell flew out the back. "Clever design."

"Oh, yes. It often goes unappreciated that people in the past were just as smart as they are today. Modern people just know more."

"I've never thought you weren't smart," Jessica said.

"I wasn't referring to you," Miriam said. "I've worked with many people who had a dismissive attitude toward people of the past."

"That include the Ascension Foundation?" Jessica asked.

"No, actually," Miriam said. "Julian and his followers had a different read on the past."

"Which was?"

"That people don't change," Miriam said.

"Is that what you believe?" Jessica asked.

"It is," Miriam said. "Humanity might be a space-faring civilization. But they're still not all that different from the subsistence hunters that migrated out of Africa not all that long ago, cosmologically speaking."

"You speak of humanity like you're an outsider," Jessica said. "Like you don't see yourself as human."

"I'm not, really," Miriam said. "I'm a person, yes. But at the end of the day, there's nothing biological about me. What humanity I have is simply an echo of a dead woman."

"That seems like a bleak outlook," Jessica said. "Is there something about the Ascended that's upset you?'

Miriam walked over to a table, where a pair of tall glasses rested next to an ice bucket containing a bottle of champagne. She took one of the glasses and drank a generous gulp from it.

"The Ascended do change," Miriam said. "That's what I've learned."

"And that's a bad thing?" Jessica asked.

"It can be if the wrong decisions are made," Miriam said. "I've gotten a feel for their history. They haven't revealed anything directly about their motivations for the war. But I know for certain that when they first started out, they were explorers. This ship was meant as an exploration vessel before it became part of their war machine."

"It does bear a striking resemblance to the original *Ascension*," Jessica remarked.

"*Ascension* served as a template, yes," Miriam said. "This mothership was meant to go out to a system and find useful resources to build another mothership, which would then proceed to another system to repeat the process."

"Like a von Neumann probe," Jessica said.

"Exactly that," Miriam said. "I think Julian intended for the Ascended to spread across the entire galaxy over millions of years, each mothership leapfrogging the rest. I remember talking with him about his extreme long-term plans, and I do mean extreme. Discussing how what would become the Ascended might survive the eventual heat death of the Universe. How to preserve intelligence far into the post-stellar era of the Universe."

"Not lacking in ambition, that one," Jessica said. "But obviously that changed."

Miriam nodded. "Yes. As far as I can tell, the Ascended operated as explorers for about fifty years. They explored dozens of systems further out but then suddenly stopped, instead hunkering down to build up the war machine they are today." Miriam set her glass down on the table with a click. "And I have no fucking idea why."

"Do you think they're hiding it from you?" Jessica asked.

Miriam nodded. "There's something they aren't willing to tell me. But I don't know what it is. I just know their decision to attack humans was a sudden one."

Jessica leaned against the ornate stone railing of the balcony, staring off toward the virtual landscape.

"You said this mothership was originally an exploration ship," Jessica said. "Which means it was built before the Cendies made their switch from exploration."

"That's correct," Miriam said. "I would guess this is an early-generation mothership, though I doubt it's one of the first generation."

"Which means there are newer-generation motherships out there," Jessica said. "Ones that were built from the start with war in mind."

"Yes."

"Bloody hell!" Jessica breathed.

Miriam walked up to Jessica after refilling her glass, setting it down on the railing next to Jessica. She was technically on the job, but it was just simulated alcohol. So she took a sip and let the bubbly beverage trickle down her throat.

"Well, we might know where this ship started. Seems the ribbon is, in fact, a literal interpretation of the lifetime journey of this ship," Jessica said.

"Where does it start?" Miriam asked.

"Middle of nowhere, fifty light-years from here. Probably around some faint object that's not on the charts."

"That's what I expected," Miriam said. "Julian was keen on doing his work without being stumbled upon. How certain are you that there's something out there?"

"I'm not," Jessica said. "The only way to find out is to get a ship out there to investigate."

"Fifty light-years sounds like a long trip, even with current stardrive technology," Miriam mused.

"Any ship would have to refuel in flight to make the journey there and back," Jessica said. "Our colleagues in the League IID are currently working out that problem."

"You're letting the League handle that?" Miriam asked with faint surprise.

"No choice," Jessica said. "All Federal ships are currently busy with the relief efforts for Earth. And besides, it looks like the League might have the perfect ship for this mission, assuming what they claim about it works."

"Which is?"

"No jump flash," Jessica said. "I'm sure you can see the value in that."

"I can. So, I take it you are telling me this because you want me to come along?"

"I figured you'd be interested," Jessica said. "You want to know what happened to your friends—well, here's the next step."

Miriam smiled. "Indeed. I'll see about making my goodbyes to the locals. I think they will be very sad to see me go, but the fact is, I'm starting to get bored with them."

Jessica nodded. "Well, that settles that."

"Indeed." Miriam hefted her shotgun. "Now. Shall we do more shooting?"

CHAPTER 7

MASON WASN'T ALLOWED out of his fighter upon returning to *Independence*. Being the only fighter on station while *Independence*'s other squadrons were occupied, as soon as he touched down on the deck, the hangar crew appeared to start rearming and refueling his fighter. All he could do was sleep in his cockpit, resting in the relatively gentle 1 g pull of *Independence* as she accelerated deeper into Neptune's jump limit.

Though being deep inside the jump limit would prevent a fast escape, it would also prevent the Cendies from jumping right on top of *Independence*. It was simply a question of when and in what force the Cendies would respond to Earth Fed's attack.

With the Cendy warships and fighters destroyed, the bombers made short work of the Cendy refinery ships and tankers, with no further surprises showing up to threaten Federal forces.

When an alert came, Mason woke up with a start, but it wasn't an attack. It was Chief Rabin, dressed in a simple jumpsuit, staring down at Mason through his open cockpit.

"Did we win?" Mason asked.

Rabin nodded. "So far. You looked so peaceful that I decided to let you rest while we repressurized the hangar."

"Well, thanks. I needed the sleep," Mason said. "How does my fighter look?"

"Like it's seen some hard flying."

"Turns out the Cendies carry parasite fighters on their gas skimmers," Mason told him. "Nimble little bastards."

"You came out better than they did. Marshal Singh said you should see him as soon as you get out."

"Nice of him to let me rest before the debrief. We're still in Neptune space, right?"

Rabin nodded. "The other squadrons just got back, and the taskforces are burning to depart now."

"Any sign of the Cendy response?"

Rabin shrugged. "You ask Marshal Singh. My job is to make sure your fighter is ready when they do show up."

"Fair enough," Mason said, climbing out of the cockpit with Rabin's help. A ladder had been rolled up to the side of his fighter, making climbing down in the full 1 g acceleration easier.

Mason took off his helmet and enjoyed the sweet kiss of cool air against his skin as he walked through the airlock. He stopped in the suit storage to pull himself out of his hardsuit and put on the spare jumpsuit he kept in his locker.

Pinging *Independence*'s network for Marshal Singh's location, he found he was in the flag bridge in the main hull of the starship, a deck above the main bridge. It made sense. The flag bridge was inside the most heavily armored part of the ship.

Mason boarded an elevator that took him up to the command level, located between the main gun turrets above the habitat ring. The command level was familiar to him, as he had spent days there as part of the ad hoc crew that had got *Independence* out of Jovian space and to Alpha Centauri. Mason smiled at the fond memories of operating *Independence*'s gunnery controls. As much as he loved flying Lightnings, getting to use all of *Independence*'s multitude of guns had been the power trip of a lifetime.

The troopers guarding the single entrance to the flag bridge stopped him to verify his identity before letting him through.

Marshal Singh was not the only brass on the flag bridge. Admiral Moebius stood next to him at the main holotank. Both were deep in conversation with Rear Admiral Park Ji-Woo, commanding officer of Taskforce Charlie.

Admiral Park had a lean, angular face, her straight black hair bound into a tight bun behind her head. As Mason approached to introduce himself, she smiled and spoke. "I see Squadron Leader Grey has decided to join us."

Marshal Singh and Admiral Moebius both turned to look at him as he saluted. He could feel the weight of three flag officers looking at him.

"At ease, Squadron Leader," Marshal Singh said. "Your squadron did fine work with the skimmers on Neptune."

"Thank you, sir," Mason said. "Looks like our assumptions that the Cendies would have a surprise waiting for us were accurate."

"Indeed. I think we might be starting to get wise to their tricks," Marshal Singh said.

"Just means they'll come up with better tricks eventually," Admiral Moebius said pessimistically. "All the more reason to keep the pressure on."

"So how long do we have until they come up with better tricks, Admiral?" Mason asked.

"Hopefully after the convoy gets here," Admiral Moebius replied.

"Anything you can tell us about those parasite fighters, Squadron Leader?" Marshal Singh asked.

"Small, fast. Like dedicated aero-fighters, sir. They don't carry anywhere near as many missiles as a Lightning can, a fact my pilots were able to leverage to their advantage."

"When you get the chance," Marshal Singh said, "I'd like you to make a detailed report on what you fought in Neptune. I doubt this will be the only time our pilots will have to face Cendy skimmers and their parasite fighters."

"The pilots over Uranus are probably dealing with the same problem," Mason said.

"Most likely, but we can only hope they fared as well as Osiris Squadron."

"I'll get right on it, sir," Mason said. "I admit I'm glad to be done with Neptune."

"You may not be finished with Neptune just yet, Squadron Leader. And regardless, what we did here today was just the start," Admiral Moebius said. "By hitting their gas mining operations, we've made their position within Sol more tenuous. They'll have to assign more ships to protect their gas mining, which will mean fewer for us to deal with when the time comes to run the blockade."

"Is it too much to hope they'll just retreat if it becomes clear they can't hold Outer Sol?" Mason speculated.

Admiral Moebius chuckled. "I don't think that will happen until the Cendies have to face the prospect of fighting a fully fueled First Fleet along with us."

"So, what's next for Osiris Squadron?" Mason asked.

"For now, just be ready to jump back into your fighters in case the Cendies try to attack us before we jump out," Marshall Singh said. "Then we'll return to Pluto to rearm and resupply. Then, off to our next target."

"And what will that be?"

"We're still narrowing our options," Marshal Singh said. "It probably won't be a large strike like we did today but a mission befitting a special operations squadron."

"Sounds ominous, sir," Mason said.

"Not eager to get back into action, Squadron Leader?" Admiral Moebius asked.

"I'm absolutely eager, Admiral. I just like to know what I need to prepare my pilots for ahead of time."

"A luxury I think we all wish we could have," Admiral Park said from the holotank. "Unfortunately, we're as much subject to our enemy's decisions as we are to our own."

"As true a statement as I have ever heard," Admiral Moebius said.

An alarm sounded, and Admiral Park's image shrank on the holotank, revealing a projection of the Neptune system and the arrival of a Cendy taskforce at the edge of the jump limit—right along the path of escape for the Federal warships.

"Looks like the Cendy response is here," Admiral Moebius said. "Seems we're not done with Neptune just yet, Squadron Leader. Prepare your fighters for launch."

"Yes, Admiral!" Mason said, turning and running for the hatch.

The Cendy intercept was much larger than the force that had defended Neptune—a dozen Cendy warships and nine Fusiliers along with three Katyushas in support. Ninety Outriders formed a fighter screen just ahead of the warships, ready to savage any bomber or torpedo attacks from the Federal ships.

Independence occupied the tip of the wedge between the cruisers of taskforces Charlie and Delta arrayed to either side of her, the taskforces' combined destroyer squadrons spread out ahead of the main force. *Cassowary* remained far behind, with a pair of destroyers in close escort.

Mason had a nervous feeling as he looked down at nine spinal-mounted guns. If the Fusiliers could use their main guns without interference, they'd shoot *Independence* and the cruisers to pieces before the latter could bring their main guns to bear. It would be up to the strikecraft to disrupt the Fusiliers—which meant running the gauntlet of Outriders and the vast numbers of interceptors the arsenal ships could throw out.

Osiris Squadron was in full space-combat configuration. Each fighter carried four Stiletto pods on the inner hardpoints and interceptors on the outer hardpoints. Eight more interceptors filled the weapons bays in their bellies.

The key would be the bombers—this time outfitted with freefall space bombs. The stealthy weapons were difficult for even the best point defenses to defeat. But they required getting in close to be effective. The long, thin hulls of the Cendy warships meant they couldn't turn very fast, but they could pull three gs of acceleration, a fast enough change in velocity to make getting the bombs into detonation range challenging.

Osiris Squadron's job was the same as that of *Independence*'s other two fighter squadrons: keep the Conqueror bombers of Nova Squadron alive until they delivered their ordnance.

The Cendies remained outside the jump limit, close enough to fire upon any Federal ships that made it to the jump limit and far enough away to simply jump in front of them again if the Federals attempted to turn away.

In other words, there was no way out of Neptune but through the Cendies.

The Federal ships continued to accelerate at a steady 1 g, the highest acceleration *Independence* and *Cassowary* could maintain. The closing velocity was already measured in several kilometers per second, limiting the amount of time the Cendies would have to fire upon the Federal forces, but they would still have plenty of time to kill every Federal ship if the timing of the strikecraft attack wasn't just right.

"All destroyer divisions—begin attack runs," Admiral Moebius ordered over the command channel. "All strikecraft—keep pace with the destroyers."

"Here goes," Mason said as he throttled up with the destroyers.

FSFV *Hagerty* was the nearest destroyer, and her drives lit up like five tiny suns as her acceleration climbed to six gs.

The destroyers were the quickest warships in the Federal service, and their crews needed special training to function during the sustained six-g burns they were capable of. But six gs was mild to Mason, even compared to the gs he had pulled just during the previous mission. However, these mild gs were not going to last.

Mason checked the squadron status display and saw the vital signs of his pilots and the telemetry of their fighters all coming in green.

It wasn't often that a Federal fighter pilot stroked out, even when they pushed twenty gs. Modern cybernetics made those kinds of pulls much more survivable. But that didn't mean it didn't happen or that a part of Mason wasn't a little worried every time he had to accelerate so hard that a little vein in his brain would burst.

Of course, he was much more likely to die from a Cendy interceptor, regardless of how hard he pushed his Lightning.

"Silverback, Hardball, Otter—how are your pilots doing?" Mason asked.

"Ready," Dominic replied.

"Eager to kick some ass," Sabal said.

"Ready and willing," Seymore said.

"Skids, you ready?" Mason asked.

"Just as ready as I was the first time you asked, Hauler," she said.

"Good," Mason said. "Marbles, Slap—ready?"

"Just waiting for the word," Armitage said.

"I'm always ready," Dash said.

He had to give it to his pilots. They invariably sounded more optimistic than he felt.

Thousands of kilometers ahead, the Outriders started accelerating, not content to remain close to their starships. The Cendies had probably guessed what it meant to have destroyers and strikecraft accelerate together and were moving to stop them.

"Fighter squadrons—advance ahead of the destroyers and engage enemy fighters," Marshal Singh ordered.

"That's our cue," Mason said, pushing his throttles forward. *Hagerty* fell away as he more than doubled his acceleration.

The distance to the enemy fighter started counting down with terrifying speed as the combined closing acceleration added up to over thirty gs. Mason armed his interceptors and started selecting targets. The combat AIs of each fighter shared data and automatically designated optimal targets for each fighter, taking much of the decision-making out of Mason's hands.

Mason locked six interceptors on a single fighter, maximizing his chance of a kill. The knowledge that more than one Cendy was probably doing the same for him didn't escape him. Hopefully the Stilettos would do their work.

The Cendies launched first, firing a mass volley of over eight hundred missiles. Seemingly their entire loads.

Belts and zones, Mason thought.

Mason fired his interceptors a few seconds later, adding his firepower to that of the seventy-six Lightnings around him. The Federal volley was just over half the size of the Cendy one. Unlike the Cendies, the Federals had to save interceptors for fighting the warships behind the Cendy outriders.

As the missiles closed the range, an invisible battle conducted across the electromagnetic spectrum played out faster than the speed of thought. Interceptors by the dozen went stupid, flying aimlessly either into the void or down toward Neptune.

Mason's sensor AI tracked twenty Cendy interceptors homing in on him, stimulating his heart to beat even harder as it struggled to pump blood against several times normal gravity. He tried to calm himself, placing his faith in his Lightning's automated countermeasures, particularly the Stiletto interceptors that had proven so effective.

That faith shattered when the twenty interceptors tracking him suddenly became eighty.

Belts and zones! Motivated by pure instinct, Mason pushed his long-burn drives to emergency power, assaulting his body with twenty gs.

Stilettos rippled off as Cendy interceptors entered range. Mason's entire arsenal of Stilettos was depleted in a couple of seconds.

Seconds before impact, the space to Mason's right lit up with dozens of impact flashes as Stilettos impacted Cendy missiles.

Mason maintained a steady trail of decoys burning like little suns behind him, trying to tempt away the tiny submunitions the Cendy interceptors had dropped. At the last moment, he rolled hard to present the thinnest possible profile to the incoming missiles.

A *thunk* shook his fighter as he flew through the gaseous remains of a Cendy missile intercepted by one of his Stilettos.

Cutting his thrust by half, down to a more sustainable ten gs, he took a moment to survey the damage.

The hit wasn't serious. All systems reported normal.

Gottlieb: <*What the hell were those?*>

Mason: <*Cendy counter to our Stilettos, I would guess.*>

The squadron display showed two fighters destroyed, and the rest of his squadron was critically low, if not empty, of Stilettos.

Mason: <*All fighters—conserve interceptors. We're back to old-school missile defense.*>

Mason took a moment to restore his situational awareness. His target was down, along with more than half the Cendy Outriders. Though their new missiles were more effective, the Cendies themselves didn't have any special defense against Federal interceptors. The remaining Outriders were scattered and isolated, even as they approached close range.

Mason picked a target and throttled back up to twenty gs to put himself on a course that would take him within gun range of an Outrider.

<*Skids, focus on my target!*>

<*Roger.*>

Mason's remaining pilots all went after Cendy Outriders on their own initiative while he bore down on his target. The Outrider, far from trying to evade Mason's attack, burned to meet it head-on.

Firing his lateral thrusters to confuse the Cendy's aim, Mason pressed down the trigger, giving the combat AI temporary control of his fighter as it aimed and fired the cannon. His Lightning shuddered beneath him, and the Outrider shuddered less than a second later. An expanding cloud of dead Outrider receded rapidly behind him as Mason reoriented toward the Cendy starships.

His remaining pilots had survived the brief gun battle that saw the remaining Outriders mostly wiped out, with a few stragglers burning hard to re-engage. But their trajectories had taken them within interceptor range of the destroyers burning behind Osiris Squadron. The two bomber squadrons had remained unmolested as they prepared their bombing runs.

As Mason burned to keep out of engagement range of the arsenal ships, the bombers released their payloads simultaneously.

The freefall space bombs were not visible on the tactical display. The precooled bombs and their stealthy coatings made them almost impossible to track. All Mason had was a timer counting down to the expected time to impact.

The Cendies did not remain idle while the nearly invisible bombs drifted toward them. The formation started to scatter as all the ships erupted with RADAR and LIDAR to try to detect and kill the bombs before they detonated.

Interceptors went flying and point-defense guns opened fire in the last second before impact, knocking down over a dozen bombs. It wasn't enough.

All at once, the space around the Cendy warships lit up with nuclear fire as several hundred megatons' worth of shaped-charge fusion warheads detonated within a second of each other.

Mason's sensors went dark to protect themselves from the glare, gradually coming back online to reveal the devastation the bombs had left behind. Most of the Cendy warships were drifting wrecks with large sections of the hulls vaporized by the columns of nuclear fire the bombs had generated. Four Fusiliers still appeared to have power, but they all had varying degrees of damage.

Minutes later, the surviving Fusiliers came under fire from *Independence* as the battlecarrier reached effective range before they could bring their spinal guns to bear. Though the spinal guns of Cendy ships gave them an advantage in range and penetration, they couldn't match the brute firepower of *Independence*'s eight main guns, each firing a kinetic kill vehicle every thirty seconds.

Each remaining Fusilier got the attention of one of *Independence*'s main gun turrets as the battlecarrier fired seven volleys in the time it took the first KKV to reach its target.

The point-defense guns of at least two of the Fusiliers failed to fire before *Independence*'s KKVs reached them and punched clean through their hulls, shooting out the other side as jets of plasma.

The other two managed to vaporize the first KKVs before they hit. But destroying a KKV didn't render it harmless. The cloud of metallic gas left behind had the same momentum as the KKV itself, and that cloud impacted the hulls of the Fusiliers, causing widespread surface damage and knocking out more point defenses and sensors.

By the time the second volley arrived, the remaining two Fusiliers were defenseless. One went dark after a KKV punched through its hull, while the other exploded into a cloud of expanding gas as its metastable deuterium fuel transitioned to gas with extreme force.

And with that, the battle was over.

The remaining Outriders continued on their outbound course while the surviving Federal strikecraft began to gather up and return to their carriers.

Search and rescue shuttles launched from *Cassowary* and the cruisers. Meanwhile, destroyers homed in on the beacons of pilots who had ejected from crippled fighters and were set adrift on an escape trajectory out of Neptune.

The two pilots Mason lost, Flight Lieutenant Ortiz and Flying Officer Pohl, did not have active rescue beacons. Search and rescue shuttles still vectored in on the drifting wrecks of their fighters, the fear of leaving someone behind overriding the extreme unlikelihood of a pilot surviving without a rescue beacon.

"All right, folks. Vector back to *Independence*—we're done with Neptune."

CHAPTER 8

Two hours after the last shots were fired over Neptune, *Independence* jumped back into space over Pluto.

Mason should have been asleep in his quarters, resting for the next mission, but he had stayed awake in the futile hope that the rescue shuttles would return with his two missing pilots.

All they returned with was confirmation of their deaths, two more pilots added to the growing list of spacers who had died under his command.

Now he watched through his access to *Independence*'s sensors and saw that the space over Pluto was more crowded than when they had left. There were fully a dozen destroyers escorting a convoy of twenty freighters, with shuttles busily transferring cargo from orbit to New Lowell.

Further, a pair of assault ships, *Hoplite* and *Cataphract*, were offloading more reinforcements to Pluto's surface, primarily in the form of multiple carryalls ferrying Pele superheavies to the surface.

Having taken Pluto, Earth Fed was keen on keeping it.

"A moment of your time, Squadron Leader," Marshal Singh asked.

Mason closed the connection and looked up at Marshal Singh towering over him. "Of course, sir."

"I know you're probably eager to return to your quarters, but I think since you're here, we have a matter to discuss."

"The pilots I lost over Neptune," Mason said.

His face grim, Marshal Singh nodded. "You have my condolences, but I wish to get Osiris Squadron back to full strength within forty-eight hours. You'll have your pick of the pilots at the replacement depot on Pluto, though the sooner you can get them integrated with your squadron, the better."

Mason sighed. "I'll get on it, sir. Wasn't going to get much sleep tonight anyway."

"Be sure to do something about that, Squadron Leader," Marshal Singh said. "I can't have the leader of my special operations squadron burning himself out."

"I'll take care of that too, sir," Mason said.

"Be sure that you do, Squadron Leader. You don't want someone like me mothering you."

"Given you're occupied with helping coordinate the liberation of Outer Sol, I won't make you do that, sir," Mason said.

"Then be on your way, Squadron Leader. Next time I see you, I expect to see you rested and with a full-strength squadron."

"Yes, sir," Mason said, saluting before departing.

He headed straight for his quarters, which functioned as both office and cabin, and sat down at his desk, booting up the screen on his personal console.

Accessing the manifest of available pilots at the replacement depot, he found there were thirty-six pilots, enough to fully equip three regular squadrons. The simplest method of choosing replacement pilots was to list them by order of performance metrics. This revealed the pilots who consistently made top marks in training and deployment.

But that was not what Mason did. Though he had a good record by every metric, it was not exceptional in any way beyond his kill score. Any pilot who survived what he had would have racked up an impressive kill count.

If there was one thing Mason had learned leading Osiris Squadron, it was that the most important metric was not someone's kill score or flying hours or grades from flight school.

It was perseverance through adversity.

Mason was disappointed most of the pilots in the replacement depot were fresh out of combat flight school and waiting for their first assignments. But there were a few from squadrons that had been disbanded after suffering severe losses.

Flight Lieutenant Quentin "Max Q" Ellis was an easy choice. He had participated in the Battle of Triumph, where the 132nd "Gargoyles" had lost half their pilots. Most of the remaining pilots had been transferred to reinforce other squadrons, while Ellis had been left unassigned in anticipation of future losses.

Mason marked him for recruitment and moved on.

The next pilot that drew his eye had not seen combat against the Ascendancy yet. She had not been assigned to a combat squadron for over a year because she was a casualty of the previous war with the League. Lucinda "Splinter" Arroyo had spent almost a year in the hospital after getting shot down in combat with the League. Her report didn't specify her injuries, but the time she had spent in recovery meant she'd probably had to have something regrown.

Mason opened a connection to Dominic.

"Yeah, Hauler?"

"I've got two pilots at the replacement depot I'd like you to review," Mason said.

"Replacements for Sledge and Diode?"

"Yep," Mason said simply.

"All right, I'll take a look."

Mason waited on the line as his XO checked their records.

"Seems a good fit for Osiris Squadron, though Arroyo's out of practice."

"Are you saying we should skip her?" Mason asked.

"No. I'm guessing she'll be very eager to get back into the thick of things after spending a year out of action. Her enthusiasm should compensate."

"All right, I'll send the orders," Mason said. "Thanks, Silverback."

"What's an XO for? Take care, Hauler," Dominic said before closing the connection.

Mason drafted his request to transfer Ellis and Arroyo to *Independence* and then transmitted it down to Pluto's surface. Finally, he slid into his cot and let himself drift off to sleep.

The Edge of Nowhere

❧

Mason woke up with a notification on his brainset telling him his new pilots were inbound.

"That didn't take long," he muttered as he got up. He checked the time and realized *Independence* had slotted into orbit over Pluto, halfway between the surface and Charon's orbit.

He had slept through orbital insertion.

Mason got himself cleaned up and put on a fresh uniform before leaving his quarters. The replacement pilots were already docking when he reached the hangar, taking the empty spots left by Ortiz and Pohl. He waited for them to take off their hardsuits before greeting them.

Flight Lieutenant Ellis was the smaller of the two. He was a short, slight man with a boyish face that looked too young for the age printed on his record.

Flying Officer Arroyo was taller but not by much. Just by looking at her float down the corridor, Mason couldn't make out any sign of what had left her convalescent for a year.

Both new pilots saluted Mason as they came to a stop in front of him.

"Welcome aboard *Independence*," Mason said "I'm Squadron Leader Mason Grey of the 77th Special Operations Squadron."

"You're our new boss, eh, sir?" Ellis asked.

"Yes, I'd be the one. You both can call me Hauler."

"Max Q," Ellis said.

"Splinter," Arroyo said.

Mason nodded. "Max Q, Splinter, come with me and I'll introduce you to the squadron." The replacements followed him, and Mason felt a twinge of shame at thinking of them as replacements.

After a weightless journey through *Independence*'s corridors and a transfer to the spinning habitation ring, Mason led the replacements to Osiris Squadron's berthing. Most of the squadron was present in the ready room, gathered by Dominic to greet the new arrivals.

"Max Q, Splinter—your new squadron. Max Q, you'll berth with Cooler; Splinter will share her quarters with Slap."

"I was just getting used to having quarters to myself," Flying Officer

Octavia Dash grumbled, provoking a backhanded slap to the shoulder from Sabal.

"Show some respect," Sabal said.

It wasn't the warmest reception, and Mason knew why. With the turnover Osiris Squadron had had since its inception, no one wanted to get too attached to new arrivals.

"This is my XO, Flight Lieutenant Dominic Tanner," Mason said.

"You can just call me Silverback. You two need anything, come to me first."

"Yes, sir," Flight Lieutenant Ellis said. "What will be our flying assignment?"

Mason cleared his throat. "Already taken care of. Just worry about getting settled in. I doubt we'll have to wait long for our next mission."

"That I don't doubt, Hauler," Ellis said. "Saw a bunch of shuttles full of supplies loading up *Independence* while we were docking."

"We used up a bunch of missiles during the last fight," Mason told him. "It looks like the Cendies developed a counter to our Stilettos."

"Yes, sir—the multiceptors," Ellis said.

"The what?"

"That's what people were calling them on Pluto, sir," Ellis explained.

"Belts and zones, beaten to the punch naming those things," Mason said. "You know who coined the term?"

"I don't, sir."

"Well, in any case, don't expect Stilettos to be the same impenetrable defense they were before," Mason said. "It will be more like old times when we had to use Javelins to defend ourselves from hostile interceptors."

"Old times being a year ago, sir?" Flying Officer Arroyo said.

"Time flies," Mason said.

"Maybe for you, sir," she said.

"Apologies, Flying Officer," Mason said. "I'm sure it wasn't easy sitting out the last few months."

"I mean, between my last combat assignment and now, the Ascendency attacks have come out of nowhere, and the League is now our friend," she said. "It has been quite an adjustment."

"Have you studied up on combat with the Cendies, Splinter?" Mason asked.

"Yes, sir. I kept myself busy during my recovery studying every after-action report and combat recording I could get my hands on. I look forward to getting to put that knowledge to use."

Mason nodded. "You'll have plenty of opportunity. I'll leave you two to settle in."

The two new pilots nodded and saluted Mason before turning to mingle with the rest of the squadron in the common area.

Mason sighed. It had only taken just over a day for his squadron to return to full strength. He doubted that would last very long.

Retiring to his cabin, he sat down at his desk and got to work dealing with the administrative parts of his job, such as sending reports up the chain informing Marshal Singh that Osiris Squadron was back to full strength, then the report of the attack on Uranus.

Like Neptune, the Cendy skimmers harvesting gas from the skies of Uranus carried parasite fighters that had surprised the fighters sent down to kill them. A couple of Lightnings had been lost because of that, though the skimmers were destroyed.

Goshawk's and *Hyena*'s taskforces had not been intercepted on the way out of Neptune like *Independence*'s and *Cassowary*'s were. Mason guessed the Cendies had decided to concentrate on one Federal attack rather than dividing their forces. Thus the pilots flying off *Goshawk* and *Hyena* had not encountered the new Cendy multiceptors. All the intelligence gathered about them came only from the battle over Neptune.

There wasn't anything too surprising. Based on combat recordings, the multiceptor was a missile bus with four small interceptors housed in the front. It appeared they had been launched in the last five seconds prior to impact, attempting to penetrate the defense provided by the Stilettos through saturation.

The recommendations were what Mason had expected—reserve a few larger Javelins for dealing with the multiceptors before they released their submunitions. Stopgap solutions until Earth Fed could gain the upper hand in the arms race.

At least until the Cendies leapfrogged them again.

And that was just with one weapons system.

Mason supposed he should brainstorm tactics for dealing with the multiceptors with the hardware he had, but that was best done in collaboration with his senior pilots, who were currently busy with the new pilots.

Instead he drafted a message for Jessica. In all the excitement since arriving in Sol, he had not had a chance to send any messages her way.

The message was short and to the point. There weren't too many details he could give that would get past the censors. He just let her know he was safe and that he loved her.

With that done, he put his message in the queue for the next courier drone out to 61 Virginis. It would be two weeks before Jessica received it. Mason was very aware of the fact he could be dead by then.

Just another grim reality of interstellar warfare.

With that, he could no longer resist the call to return to his bunk. He still had a few hours before he had to attend a briefing by Marshal Singh, likely for the next mission for Osiris Squadron.

He pulled off his jumpsuit and slipped into his bunk, falling fast asleep before his mind could further ponder his troubles.

CHAPTER 9

The assault shuttle's pilots cut the main drive and flipped the craft over, revealing Scirocco's horizon through the cockpit canopy.

Ember's second-largest moon orbited just three hundred thousand kilometers above the surface of the hot gas giant, the surface invisible beneath the thick tan atmosphere, broken only by wisps of white cloud.

The moon superficially resembled Saturn's moon Titan in both color and size. But Scirocco was far hotter, denser, and dryer than Titan. The average temperature around the equator hovered around the 100 degrees Celsius mark. Where Titan had scattered hydrocarbon lakes, Scirocco had vast deserts of wind-blasted rock. That rock was constantly replenished by Scirocco's volcanic activity, fed by the tidal interactions between Scirocco and Ember.

Fortunately for Jessica, her destination was nowhere near the hellscape of the equator but the relatively mild north pole. The poles averaged 30 degrees Centigrade, with far gentler winds, broken up by the mountains that dominated both poles because the volcanic activity built them up faster than the abrasive winds could grind them down.

Scirocco had three settlements—a mining settlement at each pole extracting valuable metals deposited on the surface by the moon's volcanic activity, plus one sprawling military installation at the northern pole.

The League used Scirocco for clandestine technology development because the thick, hot atmosphere blocked the view of any Federal observers loitering at the edge of the system. The Special Purpose Branch knew almost nothing about the base beyond what the League had stated publicly. Everything else was purely speculative.

And Jessica would be the first member of the Special Purpose Branch to set foot inside the base, as well as lay eyes on *Midnight Diamond*.

The opportunity to get a look at the mysterious little ship's stealth technology was of particular interest to Jessica. Clandestine surveillance of an enemy system was far easier when you didn't have to worry about your arrival flash announcing your presence to everyone with half-decent sensors.

"We're about to hit turbulence, Lieutenant Sinclair," Colonel Miller warned. "Scirocco is not gentle with its visitors."

"I'm sure it will be an exciting descent," Jessica replied.

She occupied one of the two jump seats behind the assault shuttle's two pilots, Colonel Miller in the other, with an almost unobstructed view out the front. Where Federal assault shuttles had small windows looking over the nose, the League assault shuttle had a full bubble canopy.

Turbulence marked the beginning of entry into Scirocco's atmosphere, and Jessica heard the whine of the descent thrusters fighting Scirocco's gravity to maintain a safe approach speed.

The assault shuttle flew parallel to the day–night terminator, with the bulk of Ember itself dominating the horizon. The whine of the descent thrusters faded as the atmosphere became thick enough to arrest the descent and allow the assault shuttle's wings and lifting body to work. The shuttle rattled under the turbulence, and Jessica barely heard the air-breathing turbines spool up as the shuttle leveled out at cruising altitude. They were still above the cloud layer, but Jessica could see the peaks of Scirocco's polar mountains sticking out from beneath the haze.

The assault shuttle continued to descend, flying between the peaks, the pilots chattering between each other and traffic control as they approached the base. It continued to descend, now below the altitude of the tallest peaks. She saw one peak, a jagged spike of black rock at least twenty kilometers tall, swing by. She started to feel a little anxious as the assault shuttle plunged into the mist below. She knew the pilots could see through the haze just fine with the assault shuttle's sensors, but she couldn't shake off the worry about all the other mountains lurking below the cloud layer.

When the assault shuttle broke through the cloud layer, Jessica found herself flying above a vast lava river.

"Blimey!" she breathed.

Colonel Miller leaned forward. "Yes, Mount Devastation has been quite active for the last decade."

"Good name," Jessica said as she traced the lava river to its source, a round dome spewing a fountain of magma into the sky.

The assault shuttle shook as it flew over the lava river. "Is it safe to have an approach over a volcano?" Jessica asked.

"Volcanos on Scirocco's northern pole tend to have effusive eruptions that just seep out lava," Colonel Miller said. "The southern pole volcanos tend to be more explosive."

"I guess that's another reason to put your military base on the north pole, then," Jessica said. "It would be embarrassing to have an expensive military base and all its valuable assets buried under a pyroclastic flow."

"Yes, indeed."

Jessica could see more plumes of smoke in the distance disappearing into the cloud layer above. "This place must be a volcanologist's idea of heaven," she remarked.

"It's certainly one of the more economically productive moons in 61 Virginis," Colonel Miller said. "Much of the metal in this very assault shuttle probably came from here."

"So no shortage of raw materials for prototyping," Jessica said.

The assault shuttle continued its flight between the mountains until it reached a wide-open area. Jessica realized it was the caldera of an—hopefully—extinct volcano.

A massive installation filled the caldera, complete with runways, landing pads, and squat, robust buildings. Jessica could see how the surrounding mountains and the ridge of the caldera could shelter the base from Scirocco's vicious winds.

The assault shuttle banked for one of the runways to make a conventional landing approach. Along the tarmac, she could see various League craft—tiltrotors, trans-atmospheric shuttles, and enough Asp fighters to outfit a squadron.

And there were more than a few massive silo doors to cover the entrance to buried shipyards.

Wheels squeaked as they touched the tarmac, and hard deceleration pulled Jessica into her seatbelt. On the ground, she saw automated plows standing next to piles of gray dust. "Volcanic ash from the last ash fall," Colonel Miller explained.

"You get that a lot?"

"It's part of the regular weather here."

"This moon is truly awful."

"No argument from me, Lieutenant."

The assault shuttle rolled off the runway and onto a taxiway, heading directly for one of the many hangars attached to the base's central terminal. One of the hangars was already open, beckoning the assault shuttle to come in from the wind and ash. It rolled into the hangar, and the massive doors slid shut as soon as the tail cleared the threshold. As the shuttle's engines spooled down, their whine was replaced by the sound of powerful blowers that expelled Scirocco's toxic atmosphere for something more amenable to human life.

Colonel Miller unbuckled his seatbelt and gestured for Jessica to follow. "The air should be safe to breathe by the time we get our gear."

Jessica nodded, not mentioning that she could hold her breath for hours thanks to her artificial body's stored reserves. What made Scirocco's atmosphere dangerous for her was not the toxins but the heat. Without a pressure suit to assist with cooling, her body would quickly overheat and cook her brain inside its protective casing.

Jessica turned and walked through the hatch that connected the cockpit with the cargo bay. Inside were Isobel and Miriam, seated next to each other, while the rest of the cargo bay was filled with samples of Cendy equipment sent to Scirocco for study.

Miriam looked up at Jessica. "Quite the bumpy flight down. I'm glad I'm no longer capable of becoming nauseous."

"It's considered a rite of passage for someone to puke while flying over Scirocco," Isobel said.

"Yes, I'm sure it would have been quite the honor to have the half-digested remains of whatever I had last eaten splattered over the deck," Miriam said.

Isobel and Miriam shared a chuckle as they both stood up. Isobel grabbed her duffel bag while Miriam headed for the tail. She hadn't brought any luggage along. Jessica grabbed her own bag from the storage rack and followed Miriam to the back of the cargo bay.

Colonel Miller joined them a moment later, hoisting his luggage over one shoulder. "Did you enjoy your flight, Miss Xia?" he asked.

"Hrmph, these military flights are a bit spartan for my taste," Miriam complained. "It's a good thing I checked out for most of it."

"You looked like you were having a lovely nap," Isobel said.

"Nap? I was swimming laps in my pool in VR," Miriam told her.

Seals hissed and hydraulics whined as the tail ramp descended. Warm air tinged with the smell of sulfur rushed into the assault shuttle.

League personnel were there to greet Colonel Miller, and they all did a double-take when they noticed a Federal officer and a feminine mobility rig standing with Colonel Miller.

Jessica gave them her best smile and said, "Oh? Did I get on the wrong shuttle?"

That elicited a chuckle from Colonel Miller. "I could see how one could think so." In Exo, he said, "Don't be so chilly with our guests. I'll make sure she doesn't see more than she needs to."

The officer nodded glumly and replied in Exo, "I would hope so, Colonel Miller. And I hope she doesn't abuse your trust." To Jessica, he said in accented Federal, "Welcome to Scirocco, Lieutenant."

"Fortunately, I won't be here long enough for sightseeing," Jessica said airily, revealing she understood Exo. "I have a connecting flight to catch."

"Is *Midnight Diamond* ready?" Colonel Miller asked.

"Crewed and powered up, Colonel."

"Then let's not delay any longer."

It was a short walk through a subterranean tunnel from the hangar to the central terminal. All the while, League Espatiers watched Jessica like hawks.

Her passive sensors picked up more than a few scans as she entered the terminal, likely confirming for the umpteenth time the synthetic nature of her body.

Inside the terminal, they headed directly for the nearest elevators. Jessica noted the sterility of the terminal, with no windows looking out onto the vast expanse of the caldera outside. It seemed to reinforce the secretive nature of the base—its very design prevented secrets from leaking out. The elevator was large enough to fit Colonel Miller's entire team, including Jessica, before the doors sealed shut and it started to descend.

Jessica detected two more scans on the way down. One was an ultrasonic scan meant to peer through her clothes—as if she would try to hide anything under this jumpsuit. She hoped the AI enjoyed what it saw.

The second was a high-frequency radar scan.

"If your people are going to keep blasting me with active scans, I'm going to need a dosimeter," Jessica said.

"My apologies, Lieutenant," Colonel Miller said. His eyes went distant for a moment, and there were no further scans afterward.

The lobby at the bottom was as sterile as the terminal above. Jessica's internal accelerometers indicated they were five hundred meters below the surface.

"So how close are we to the magma chamber?" she asked.

"Oh, don't worry, Lieutenant, this volcano has been dormant for millions of years," Colonel Miller assured her.

"I would hope so," Jessica said.

They proceed down the tunnels, passing shut doors with labels that had been taped over because of Jessica's visit. *They really want to keep what I learn about the base to an absolute minimum,* she thought.

They arrived at a beefy airlock door with its labels helpfully taped over.

"This our stop?"

Colonel Miller nodded and pressed the button on the panel next to the hatch. The airlock opened both inner and outer hatches and presented a large empty volume behind.

Colonel Miller led his team through, and Jessica followed. She came to a stop when she saw what was inside.

It was a sleek vessel that looked superficially like a League assault shuttle but much larger, almost two hundred meters from its sharp nose to its engine bells. And it rested on the ground horizontally like an assault shuttle, rather than vertically like most starships.

From the craft's aerodynamic shape and robust landing gear, it was clear it was designed for landing directly on the surface of planets with substantial atmospheres.

"Is this *Midnight Diamond*?"

"Yes. We were going to give her a proper name at some point, but the codename has stuck."

"This must be the largest spaceplane ever built," Jessica said. She stared up at *Midnight Diamond*. The hull didn't seem entirely optimized for atmospheric flight. There were several strange angles and shapes around it. The hull itself was a dark gray verging on black, with a texture that reminded Jessica of sandpaper. She wondered if they were part of whatever technology allowed *Midnight Diamond* to make flashless jumps.

She also wondered how the interior was laid out, given the ship had to account for the fact gravity could be pulling in two different directions depending on whether it was accelerating through space or landing on the surface of a planet.

"Reminds me of some space yachts my contemporaries used," Miriam said as she took in the tiny starship.

"I'm afraid she's not very luxurious, Miss Xia," Colonel Miller said. "Crew quarters are a pair of gimbaled modules inside the main hull."

"Beneath those bulges at the ring roots?" Jessica asked.

Colonel Miller nodded. "Yes. The crew modules will rotate to keep gravity pointed in the same direction, either under acceleration or when landing on a planetary body."

"How many people are we going to cram into that thing?" Jessica asked.

"The ship has a crew of fifty, including the four of us and a squad of Espatiers," Colonel Miller said. "I'm afraid there's no room for private quarters aboard ship. Everyone will get a capsule bed, and that's about it."

"So we're going to be cozy is what you're saying?" Jessica said.

"Cozy is one word to describe it," Colonel Miller said.

They continued to walk toward *Midnight Diamond*, the .3 gravity just strong enough to make walking somewhat normal.

A large ramp descended from the nose, leading into a large cargo bay like the one inside an assault shuttle. Inside were several crates, drones of various kinds, and personal thruster rigs. It looked like *Midnight Diamond* was equipped for exploration in deep space.

Tucked away in one corner was a pair of partly disassembled rovers, apparently there just in case they did end up landing on a planet.

Jessica looked up and saw a housing area running parallel to the line of the ship. She guessed the area covered the drive keel that ran through the center. At least in this way, *Midnight Diamond* was no different from any other starship.

"Welcome aboard *Midnight Diamond*, Colonel Miller," said an unfamiliar voice.

Jessica looked down to see a dark-skinned man, his short black hair blending seamlessly into his beard, wearing the uniform of the League battlefleet. He looked a bit young for the full commander rank pinned on his uniform.

"Thank you, Commander Ngata," Colonel Miller said. "Thank you for getting your ship ready for us on such short notice."

"I should be thanking you, Colonel," Commander Ngata said. "My crew and I are sick and tired of waiting."

"You can thank Lieutenant Sinclair and Miss Miriam Xia," Colonel Miller said.

Commander Ngata looked at Jessica and gave her a polite smile. "Welcome aboard my ship, Lieutenant. I'm Commander Milton Ngata. It's my privilege to be the commanding officer of *Midnight Diamond*."

"I noticed no one has used the LCS prefix for *Midnight Diamond*," Jessica remarked.

Commander Ngata chuckled. "Despite being crewed by battlefleet personnel, *Midnight Diamond*'s not a commissioned warship in the battlefleet."

"Not surprising, given the clandestine nature of this vessel," Jessica said.

"I'm sure the Special Purpose Branch does the same," Commander Ngata said.

Jessica just smiled and said nothing else.

"I have pods reserved for you in the starboard crew module," Commander Ngata said. "Officers get some special luxuries on this ship. You won't have to hot bunk with anyone."

"Nice to have a bit of privacy," Jessica said.

A small elevator carried them up to a narrow corridor that ran parallel to the drive keel. Jessica had to follow behind Colonel Miller, as there was only enough space for one lane of traffic going in either direction.

She noted the horizontal handholds running along the walls.

They arrived at a hatch leading into the habitat module, and the bearing around the hatch made it clear the hab module was designed to rotate to keep the decks aligned with whatever direction was down during flight.

Through the hatch, they could see the crew quarters consisted of a long corridor going the length of the module, with rows of sleeping capsules recessed into the walls. There was also a ladder well at the center.

"Upper deck is where the officers' wardroom is," Colonel Miller explained. "Showers are in the level below." He pointed toward the corridor heading toward the bow. "Our quarters are over there."

"Dibs," Miriam said as she half-leaped, half-climbed onto a top pod.

"Really? You have to be on top?" Jessica asked.

"Always, darling," Miriam said.

"Not interested in a tour of *Midnight Diamond*, Miss Xia?" Colonel Miller asked.

"Not particularly, no," Miriam said. "I'm content to lounge here until we reach our destination."

Colonel Miller glanced at Jessica. She shrugged. "I don't think the austerity of a ship like *Midnight Diamond* is to her taste," Jessica said.

"You are not wrong there," Miriam said.

Colonel Miller and Isobel claimed the top and bottom pods respectively on the opposite side. As soon as Isobel had stored her gear, she departed without comment.

Jessica examined the pod; it had enough length and width that she wouldn't have to curl up to fit in. And it looked like there was just enough height to sit up without banging her head. Luxurious. There were, of course, straps for holding a sleeper down while in zero gravity.

When she pressed on the mattress, it felt like it was filled with a viscous gel.

"How much acceleration does *Midnight Diamond* have?" Jessica asked.

"She's rated for six gs of sustained acceleration," Colonel Miller said. "More in short bursts, but then you run the risk of the habitat modules damaging their bearings."

"Hopefully that won't be necessary," Jessica said. "So, where are the workspaces on this ship?"

"The command section is a tube that runs parallel to the top of the drive keel," Colonel Miller said. "There are also smaller engineering spaces scattered around the ship. The cargo bay is the single largest pressurized compartment."

This was a cramped ship, Jessica realized. It made the cozy confines of a Federal destroyer appear generous. The idea of spending three months crammed inside did not appeal to her. She suspected she'd be spending a lot of time hanging out with Miriam in virtual.

Jessica stowed her belongings away in the cubby adjacent to her pod. She'd see about unpacking after *Midnight Diamond* had launched.

"So, when do we launch?" she asked.

"Any moment," Colonel Miller said. "We can watch from the command section. There are workspaces up there that I think you might find useful."

"You interested in the launch?" Jessica asked Miriam, but Miriam didn't answer. Jessica could tell by the unnatural stillness of her mobility rig that she had retreated into the virtual, likely underclocked to pass the time more quickly. Lucky her.

"I'll take that as a no, then," Jessica said. "Lead the way, Colonel."

It was a short trip through narrow corridors and up a tubular ladder well before they reached the command section. Though the ship was horizontal, it was clear the command section was laid out with vertical acceleration in mind. It was divided into circular decks, like a narrow tower with a corridor that doubled as a ladder well when the ship was under acceleration.

Jessica noted that the workstations were laid out so that the acceleration seats could rotate ninety degrees to allow the crew to work in relative comfort.

Midnight Diamond seemed to require a lot of complex mechanisms for transitioning from horizontal to vertical gravity and back again. She wasn't sure if the ability to land horizontally was worth the tradeoffs.

They walked down the narrow corridor until they reached *Midnight Diamond*'s tiny bridge, where Isobel and Commander Ngata were both seated.

All the crew positions were on gimbals, including seats, displays, and controls, with the captain's seat at the center and the pilot directly in front. Flanking the captain's seat were positions for the astrogator, sensor officer, and comms. Jessica assumed the other necessary crew positions were located in the compartments behind her.

Colonel Miller gestured to a pair of fold-out jump seats. "Please take a seat, Lieutenant."

"Not much of a view," Jessica commented, noting the bridge was windowless.

"I can fix that for you," Commander Ngata said.

The smooth ceiling suddenly became transparent as false windows fed by external cameras projected over the sides and ceiling, giving Jessica a clear view of the docks *Midnight Diamond* rested in. The doors above were already open, revealing Scirocco's golden sky.

Speaking in Exo, Commander Ngata traded comms with the base's air traffic control. Jessica felt a tremor as the hangar elevators started lifting the small starship to the surface.

As *Midnight Diamond* ascended, Jessica watched the crew go through the startup procedures, preparing for flight. Glancing at each station, she read labels with the assistance of her telescopic vision and fluency in Exo to get a better feel of the starship's capabilities.

There was nothing too surprising. The pilot had controls for transitioning from horizontal to vertical flight, as well as for changing the engines from airbreathing to pure fusion thrust.

To the captain's right, she noted a weapons station occupied by a young officer. As she had not seen any weapons externally, she presumed they must be retractable. The controls seemed geared toward point defense, with space on the screens for at least four gun turrets. A small pair of missile launchers was also highlighted on the wireframe of the ship's outline.

Midnight Diamond was not unarmed, but Jessica wouldn't want to get into a fight aboard her. She'd be outclassed by just about anything out there. A fully loaded Lightning would have more firepower than *Midnight Diamond* did.

Commander Ngata began calling out to the various stations, asking if they were ready for launch. All acknowledged in sequence, and Jessica could hear something inside the ship spooling up.

Ash clouded the external view as *Midnight Diamond*'s lifting thrusters throttled up until the starship lifted off the ground. The deep crater of the base slowly fell away as they gained altitude and horizontal speed.

Jessica heard the lifting engines shut down as they gained enough speed for the wings to provide lift, and then the pilot put the starship into a shallow climb as they continued to gain speed. Turbulence rattled the ship as they fought their way through the lower reaches of Scirocco's violent atmosphere until they broke out of the cloud layer and into the clear skies of the upper atmosphere.

For several minutes, *Midnight Diamond* continued to climb gently as she broke the sound barrier and gradually started running up the Mach numbers.

"Transitioning to closed cycle," the pilot said, and *Midnight Diamond*'s acceleration increased as the longburn drives came on.

Jessica's seat tilted as the direction of down transitioned ninety degrees toward the ship's tail. *Midnight Diamond* quickly reached orbital velocity but did not cut her drives; she continued to accelerate at a steady 1 g as she climbed away from Scirocco. A glance at the plotted course showed a direct transit to the edge of the system.

"Nonstop flight, I see," Jessica said.

"No point in hanging out in orbit," Colonel Miller said.

"And now I'll have to get used to this ship with gravity pulling ninety degrees from where it was before."

"You'll get used to it," Colonel Miller said. "It's not too unlike riding an assault shuttle."

"I generally didn't walk around an assault shuttle during acceleration," Jessica said. "At least the habitation modules are gimbaled. A concession to creature comforts."

"One of the few," Colonel Miller said. "But if it makes you feel better, we won't be limited to just *Midnight Diamond* for the first half of our flight."

"What? Are we going to hitch a ride?"

"So to speak," Colonel Miller said cryptically.

CHAPTER 10

MASON STOOD AT the holotank with the leaders of each of *Independence*'s strikecraft squadrons, awaiting a briefing from Marshal Singh, who towered over all of them. The war room's lights were turned down so as not to wash out the holotank, casting everything in a green hue that gave everyone a sickly appearance.

The points of interest on the holotank were several seemingly empty points in space scattered like stars in a constellation above and below the orbital plane of the outer Solar System. Those points, however, were not stars.

"Ladies and gentlemen, by now the convoy from 61 Virginis carrying the fuel we need to supply the First Fleet is inbound, which means we need to begin clearing the way for them." Singh traced a finger through each point. "These are the confirmed locations of Cendy picket ships waiting to jump in and engage any Federal ships that appear at the edge of Sol's jump limit. I intend to destroy all of them over the next twenty-four hours.

"That mission falls to *Independence* and Taskforce Delta. Because the operation will require jumping right on top of the enemy, it will be too dangerous for conventional carriers, so instead, taskforces Alpha, Bravo, and Charlie will depart Pluto for Checkpoint Wilson to rendezvous with the tanker convoy.

"With that said, it will be up to the strikecraft to destroy the enemy before they have a chance to jump out, which means each attack will be hard and fast. *Independence* jumps in, strikecraft engage and destroy the enemy, then return to *Independence* to rearm before *Independence* jumps to the next target. Thanks to the data we've gathered from Pluto's observatories, we've been able to mark the precise orbit of each Cendy taskforce, but even with that, the range from the target upon jumping in will be highly variable due to the vagaries of FTL jumps. Expect to arrive anywhere from over ten thousand klicks to within visual range.

"If it's the latter, the guns of the warships should make short work of the Cendies, but outside of that, expect to be kicked out of the hangar and making a hard burn for the enemy. Each strikecraft attack will be further augmented by torpedo volleys launched from the warships.

"The bombers will carry freefall bombs, while fighters will carry a mix of interceptors and shortburn torpedoes. Enemy fighters will be the responsibility of our destroyers to deal with; our fighters are just to keep them off the bombers' backs and assist them in their attacks against the Cendy starships.

"Each attack is simple in concept, but we're going to be launching thirteen such attacks in sequence, with less than an hour budgeted for each attack. We must be finished with each attack before the light reaches the nearest Cendy picket. That means fast docking and loading and no chance to take a break between missions, so make sure you get a good rest before the mission starts and you have fresh uppers in your hardsuit's medical systems. You and your pilots can expect to be in the cockpit for the next twelve to twenty hours."

"We regularly spend longer than that in flight, sir," said one squadron leader.

"Not in combat, Squadron Leader," Marshal Singh responded. "It will be one combat jump after another. Time in combat lasts a lot longer than the equivalent time at cruising burn. Keep an eye on your pilots, and make sure they're keeping an eye on their fighters. This mission will be hard on both people and machines."

Marshal Singh looked around at each of the pilots in turn, seeing if there were any questions that they wanted to ask. When he fixed his gaze on Mason, he arched a bushy eyebrow.

Mason cleared his throat. "We're going to take casualties, sir. How have we accounted for that?"

"Based on my staff's high confidence estimate of losses, all squadrons should remain at combat readiness through the whole operation," Marshal Singh said. "And there should be enough replacements on Pluto to replace losses as we arrive."

Faint nausea twisted Mason's gut. There was something ghoulish about talking of replacements for pilots who had yet to die.

But such was the reality of war.

Mason forced himself to nod. "Thank you, sir. I have no other questions."

"Then return to your squadrons and prepare them as best you can," Marshal Singh said. "Good luck and happy hunting."

※

The first attack went smoothly. *Independence* and her taskforce jumped within five thousand kilometers of the hidden Cendy force of two Fusiliers and one Katyusha. The catapult kicked Mason out into space, where he immediately turned and fired his drives at full power.

His squadron formed up with the bombers as they made their attack runs. The Fusiliers launched Outriders and turned toward *Independence* to meet the attack head-on. The opportunity to damage a Federal capital ship was more desirable than attempting to escape.

Independence and the cruisers launched their torpedoes while the strikecraft were on approach, their launch timed to arrive at the same time the bombers were supposed to release their loads. The Katyusha replied with a massive launch of its own, emptying every launch tube along the flanks of its hull.

The Outriders remained close to their launch ships to augment their defenses.

Mason flew past the Cendy torpedo volley, not bothering to engage them. It was the job of the destroyers to screen against torpedoes. He had to save his interceptors for defending the bombers.

The Outriders started accelerating as the Conquerors neared their release point, attempting to disrupt the Federal strikecraft before they could drop their ordnance.

All at once, the Lightnings pushed ahead of the bombers. Mason picked his targets and armed his interceptors. It wasn't important to kill all the Outriders, just to keep them from disrupting the bombers. Killing the starships was the priority.

The Outriders fired their missiles first, and an electronic duel between belligerents erupted.

Mason's combat AI identified the likely targets of each Cendy interceptor and coordinated with the combat AIs of the other fighters to prioritize enemy interceptors for destruction. Some incoming interceptors dropped off the threat list before Mason fired his first counter-volley, rendered blind and stupid by the dazzler lasers lashing out to burn out seeker heads.

The only way to tell a multiceptor from a conventional interceptor was when the multiceptor released its submunitions, so the plan was based on the assumption that all the Cendy interceptors were multiceptors.

Mason fired the externally mounted interceptors first, his fighter shuddering under the sudden loss of weight. A second later, his internal rotary launcher started kicking more interceptors out into space, all of them locked on the Cendy interceptors deemed most likely to survive the electronic barrage.

More Cendy interceptors dropped off the threat list as they were soft-killed by dazzle lasers.

Those that survived crashed into the Federal counter-volley, lighting up space between Federal and Cendy forces for an instant. The surviving Cendy interceptors pushed through, and Mason prepared for his Stilettos to come into play.

The assumption that all the Cendy missiles were multiceptors proved true when they all split and released their submunitions, but the attrition inflicted on them had reduced them to a manageable number. Stilettos rippled out of their pods and streaked for the Cendy submunitions, vaporizing them an instant later. Mason wrenched his Lightning to the left to avoid the expanding cloud of gas and debris left by the mutual destruction of a Stiletto and multiceptor submunitions.

The Outriders continued to approach, clearly intent on reaching gun range, but they were too late. As the torpedoes launched by the starships were just about to pass the strikecraft, the Conquerors released their bombs and flared their drives to emergency power to pull their vectors away from the warships.

Mason and the rest of Osiris Squadron followed, and the whole mass of Federal strikecraft turned away like a flock of birds evading a predator. The change in vector prevented the Outriders from closing into gun range before they zipped by their vector, taking them toward the Federal destroyers waiting to kill them.

The Katyusha erupted with interceptors as the *Independence*'s torpedoes entered range. Torpedoes died by the dozen, but all the while, the nearly invisible bombs continued their approach.

A few seconds later, each Cendy starship was bracketed by standoff fusion detonations that superheated their hulls and left three glowing wrecks behind.

The destroyers had cleaned up the Outriders by the time the Federal strikecraft were on their return vector to *Independence*. Rather than the usual sequential docking, all the strikecraft did a simultaneous combat docking, a task that made Mason feel sorry for the space traffic controllers who had to coordinate it.

As soon as Mason and Gottlieb had touched down in their shared hangar, the doors closed and the hangar crews appeared out of their hiding places, with robot helpers carrying new weapons. In a coordinated dance, the hangar crews loaded new interceptors into his fighter and refiled his Stiletto pods while topping up fuel at the same time. By the time *Independence* started counting down to her next jump, Mason had a fully armed and fueled fighter again, less than an hour after launching the first time.

The second attack went off much like the first, as did the third. The Cendy pickets, caught by surprise by an overwhelming force, were unable to mount an effective defense before being destroyed.

The fourth jump had *Independence* arrive almost on top of the Cendy starships. Mason had a fright when he saw three Cendy warships barely more than a hundred kilometers away. But the Fusiliers were pointed the wrong way to use their deadly spinal guns, while *Independence* and the cruisers had turrets that allowed for their guns to be brought to bear much faster.

The Cendy warships jettisoned their cloaks while their hulls lit up with maneuvering thrusters in a futile attempt to face the Federal ships.

The cruisers got their lighter guns into action first and started saturating the Cendy warships with their rapid-fire guns, focusing fire on a Katyusha. The Katyusha barely got off a volley of torpedoes before it started taking multiple hits from KKVs and was blown in half when one of its missile batteries exploded. As the Katyusha died, *Independence* brought her main guns to bear on the Fusiliers.

Mason's fighter shook as the deck below trembled under the recoil of *Independence*'s massive guns, flinging quarter-ton KKVs at the Fusiliers that punched clear through the sides of their hulls.

Fusiliers were specialized long-range capital ship killers, making them vulnerable when one of those said capital ships appeared right next to them. Both Fusiliers were knocked out in the first volley, though *Independence* put a second volley into them for good measure.

No fighters or bombers had launched in that time.

"Never thought I'd get an up-close sight of *Independence* kicking ass," Gottlieb said.

"Enjoy the show. I doubt we'll get to sit out the next fight," Mason said.

Indeed, when *Independence* jumped next, the Cendy warships were thousands of kilometers away, far enough not to immediately fall victim to *Independence*'s guns.

Mason flew down the short catapult track and into space, turning and burning hard for the Cendies as soon as he cleared the carrier. Again, the combined firepower of the Federal starships and the bombers overwhelmed the Cendy picket force, and within minutes he was flying back to the carrier with an empty fighter. He repeated the sequence nine more times as *Independence* cut a trail of destruction across Outer Sol.

When Mason landed the last time, he felt himself trembling inside his hardsuit, burned out from constant adrenaline drops and regular doses of stimulants. He had a metallic taste in his mouth, and his body was numb from the repeated cycles of high acceleration and sudden weightlessness.

Opening the cockpit, Mason carefully climbed out. If there had been any appreciable gravity, he would have needed to crawl across the deck to the airlock. Instead he just floated slowly toward the airlock while the hangar crew got to work tending to his Lightning after the abuse she had just gone through.

There were no such crews trying to attend to him. Earth Fed expected its pilots to take care of themselves.

Gottlieb was waiting for him in the airlock.

"Thanks for waiting for me, Skids," Mason told her.

"Gave me a couple of minutes where I don't have to move around," Gottlieb said.

"Smart," Mason said.

After the airlock had cycled, Mason proceeded to the suit room with Gottlieb, where he encountered the other pilots of Osiris Squadron in various stages of getting out of their hardsuits.

Armitage was floating in a corner of the suit room curled into a ball, her blue hair fanning out in the microgravity as she wept into her knees. Dominic waited near her with a concerned look on his face. He gave Mason a nod and gestured to let him know he was handling Armitage.

Locking his hardsuit's feet to the deck of its storage alcove, Mason signaled the suit to open, and it peeled its plates away from his body, allowing cool air to come flooding into contact with the thin layer of sweat his hardsuit couldn't wick away. He shivered at the sudden chill as he pulled himself out.

Armitage had pulled herself together by the time Mason had finished extracting himself from his hardsuit. Dominic had kept the other pilots from crowding around, giving her the space that she needed.

"You all right, Marbles?" Mason asked.

"Eh, I think so," Armitage said. "That was just … intense, you know? Most missions are dull, with a few moments of terror. This one? It just didn't stop."

"Well, it's over—for now, Marbles," Mason said.

"Yeah, until the next one," Armitage said.

Mason nodded. "Until the next one. Silverback, can you get the kids to bed while I speak with the brass?"

Dominic nodded. "I will, Hauler. But don't forget to get yourself tucked in."

"I'll try," Mason said.

As Mason made his way through the ship, it was clear it wasn't just his pilots who were suffering under the strain of the multiple running battles. All the crew he ran across on his way to the flag bridge looked drained, the long hours at battle stations in nearly constant combat having taken a toll on the ship.

Admiral Moebius and Marshal Singh had directed the mission from the flag bridge deep within *Independence*'s armored citadel at the front of the ship, sandwiched between the forwardmost pair of main gun turrets.

Singh and Moebius looked as tired and worn as everyone else. Admiral Moebius's pale skin made the bags under her eyes all the more obvious, while Marshal Singh's turban looked like it had started to come loose after hours of neglect.

"You look like hell, Squadron Leader," Admiral Moebius said.

"You should see the other guys, Admiral," Mason said.

She smiled. "Indeed. The last day has been a horrible grind, but we've neutralized most, if not all, of the Cendy picket ships. Next up, we will be receiving the convoy."

"When can we expect them to arrive, Admiral?" Mason asked.

"In a couple of days," she said. "Time enough for us to restock our ships and make necessary repairs. Also, I think your pilots have earned some rest."

"I won't argue with that," Mason said.

"I didn't think you would. Marshal Singh and I feel that *Independence* can do without her pilots for a couple of days. Therefore, upon our return to Pluto, you'll be transferred down to Pluto to have some leave time in New Lowell."

"I'm sure my pilots will appreciate the downtime," Mason said. "What kind of amenities can we expect down there?"

"It's not a resort town, but New Lowell does have all the things you can expect from a city of a few hundred thousand," Admiral Moebius said. "And since we liberated Pluto, we've restocked many of their luxury consumables from our own inventories, much to the delight of the scientists living off of hydroponic coffee."

"I'm sure they appreciate that, Admiral," Mason said.

"Well, it's not just for them," she admitted. "New Lowell is the only settlement in Sol we currently have access to until we can re-establish our lines of communication with Inner Sol."

"And what can we expect the Cendies to do in the meantime?" Mason asked. "We've been kicking the hornet's nest pretty hard since we got here. Are we sure they're not going to try to push us out of Pluto while my squadron is on leave planetside?"

"We've thought of that and have taken precautions," Marshal Singh said. "The area around New Lowell is being fortified with anti-starship missile batteries as we speak, supported by troopers and the Pele superheavies we landed in the initial invasion. New Lowell's spaceport has also been repurposed as a base for strikecraft."

"So, while on leave, my pilots should be ready to get in the cockpit on short notice?"

"Yes, Squadron Leader," Marshal Singh said. "Be sure to tell your pilots to watch their drinking and keep their brainsets connected. The squadron won't be on alert, but you'll still be on call."

"Hopefully the Cendies will be considerate enough not to interrupt our leave, sir," Mason said.

"*Independence* will remain on station, along with her escorts. Attacking Pluto would require the Cendies to commit a large force—likely by cannibalizing their blockade force," the marshal said. "We won't hold you any longer, Squadron Leader."

Mason nodded. "I'll give my pilots the good news, sir."

CHAPTER 11

It took *Midnight Diamond* six days under cruising burn, including a turnover at the midpoint, to slow down and reach the edge of 61 Virginis's jump limit.

Commander Ngata had chosen a course that took *Midnight Diamond* out of the system's orbital plane to a particularly empty region of the 61 Virginis system, which was very deliberately not in the direction of their planned destination.

As preparations were made for the first jump, Jessica couldn't shake a profound feeling of vulnerability inside the cramped little starship drifting alone at the edge of 61 Virginis's jump limit.

Outside the jump limit, a Cendy starship could jump right on top of them, and there would be little they could do to survive an attack. To a Fusilier-class battlecruiser, *Midnight Diamond* was little more than a gnat waiting to be crushed.

Jessica rested in her bunk, with the crew at precautionary action stations. There was nowhere else on the ship she could stay, though she noted that Colonel Miller was not in his bunk. Presumably he was up in the command module with Commander Ngata.

Miriam rested in the bunk above her, while Isobel occupied the bunk directly adjacent to Jessica.

"You look nervous," Isobel observed.

Jessica nodded. "I'm a bit out of my comfort zone with this one."

"I would think it would be exciting to travel to the Origin System aboard a top-secret League vessel," Isobel said.

"Six days on this thing has already made it clear that the next three months are going to be tough," Jessica said. "I hope whatever ship we meet is comfortable. Colonel Miller hasn't elaborated what that ship is."

Isobel shrugged. "You won't have long to wait to find out."

Jessica snorted. "I'd rather know plans in detail well ahead of time."

"I gather you're usually involved in crafting them," Isobel said.

"I often am," Jessica admitted. "It's nice to keep my mind occupied."

A faint buzz edged into the range of hearing, slowly growing as *Midnight Diamond* started charging her capacitors.

"Any Cendy recon ship at the edge of the system is going to find it rather curious when it sees *Midnight Diamond* jump without leaving a departure flash," Jessica predicted.

"The signature-reduction measures won't be activated for the first jump," Isobel said. "She'll leave a departure flash just like any vessel her mass would."

"So the system can be switched on and off? Interesting. Well, that's good to know. Would hate to spoil the surprise for the Cendies."

The buzz gradually grew into a growl, and then Jessica felt a stout vibration travel through the deck. "Is the ship supposed to be trembling so much?" she asked a little nervously.

"It's a function of her small size," Isobel explained. "*Midnight Diamond* doesn't have the mass to smooth out the vibrations that a larger vessel would."

"Sounds like you've been aboard her before," Jessica said.

"No, but I have served on small starships before," Isobel said. "You'll get used to it."

Jessica wasn't sure about that. The noises of a larger starship cycling its stardrive had always grated on her nerves, and her years in the Federal Space Forces had done nothing to change that.

"So, any tips on not going mad while stuck on a small starship for months?" Jessica asked.

Isobel turned her head to face Jessica, keeping her back flat against the bunk. "Really, much the same as on a big ship, just with less space. A stable daily routine, plenty of exercise, and getting enough sleep. Having access to a good entertainment library helps as well. Oh, and there's a noise-isolation feature in the sleeping pods."

Jessica flipped through the options menu on her pod's built-in monitor and noted the noise-isolation option. "Does this keep noise in or out?"

"Both," Isobel said. "That way you won't be disturbed by anything going on outside or disturb anyone with whatever you might be up to in the privacy of your pod."

"Oh, do people fuck in these?" Jessica asked.

Isobel chuckled. "Yes, they do. Though it's hard to carry on illicit relationships within the confines of a ship this size."

"Speaking from experience?"

"Oh, no. I make sure all my relationships are consistent with regulations," Isobel said piously.

"The battlefleet has formal rules for that sort of thing?" Jessica asked, surprised.

"Of course. Don't the Space Forces?"

"Nothing written down besides prohibitions on sleeping with people within your chain of command," Jessica said. "Mostly there are a lot of informal norms governing sexual relationships among Space Forces personnel that boil down to not allowing it to interfere with your duties or the duties of those outside the relationship."

"How well does it work?" Isobel asked.

"It's messy, kind of like how relationships normally are," Jessica said.

"So how do you navigate those relationships?" Isobel persisted.

"You first," Jessica said.

"Easy. I got married," Isobel said.

Jessica snorted. "Boring."

"Well?"

Jessica sighed. "You find someone you have good chemistry with, budget time during off-duty hours, and understand that the relationship can end abruptly at any moment depending on where the participants' duties take them."

"So you've never tried a long-distance relationship?" Isobel asked.

"I'm actually giving it a try right now," Jessica said.

"And?"

"I'll let you know."

An alarm sounded, marking a minute until the jump.

"Well, I guess this is it," Jessica said, bracing herself against the non-existent acceleration of FTL travel. Leaping across a hundred billion kilometers of space ought to feel like something. But Jessica didn't feel anything beyond the vibration of her bunk. She checked her brainset and confirmed that *Midnight Diamond* had indeed jumped a hundred billion kilometers away from 61 Virginis, placing them somewhere between the system's Kuiper Belt and the Oort Cloud.

They were not alone.

Two friendly contacts loitered ten thousand kilometers high off *Midnight Diamond*'s starboard side. One contact was a League fleet tanker, while the other was a Dragon-class cruiser with a familiar name.

Fafnir, the cruiser that had surrendered to Mason in order to get safe passage to Federal territory after the initial Ascendancy attacks on League commence raiding bases had left her stranded without enough fuel to return home.

"Small Universe," Jessica said.

"I was wondering if you would recognize *Fafnir*," Isobel said.

"I was in Procyon when she arrived," Jessica said. "Quite the talk of the town."

"Fresh out of drydock repairs," Isobel said. "Captain Baye and her crew were eager for a mission after missing out on the Battle of Triumph."

"She's still in charge?"

"Yes. Did you meet her?"

"No, not personally. I just knew someone who did."

"Would that happen to be the Federal pilot she captured?"

"And then surrendered to?" Jessica said with a smile. "I was there for his debriefing."

"The surrender was a matter of convenience," Isobel said. "I hope that didn't go to his head."

"I think Mason was just grateful for the ride home," Jessica said before she realized she had just used Mason's first name.

"Mason, is it? You know him well?" Isobel asked.

Jessica felt a heat in her rise up in her cheeks. "We worked together."

"I see," Isobel said. "I understand he participated in the Siege of Triumph."

"Yes. He tends to end up where the action is," Jessica said. "He's deployed to Sol now."

"Well, I hope he proves as successful at liberating Sol as he did in helping defend Triumph," Isobel said.

"Me too," Jessica said. "So, the tanker and cruiser—I take it they're going to escort us out to Origin?"

"Now that we're here, there's no harm in telling you—the tanker is just going to top up our tanks. We're then going to piggyback on *Fafnir* about halfway to the system. Then we'll proceed the remaining distance. She'll wait for us to return and carry us back to 61 Virginis."

"Wouldn't it be easier just to have the tanker fly with us all the way there?"

"Battlefleet can't spare a fleet tanker for the duration of the mission," Isobel explained. "It's only luck that we had *Fafnir* available."

"Resources are tight for everyone right now," Jessica conceded.

"Very true."

A request popped into Jessica's brainset, and the way Isobel's expression became distant stated that she had also received a notification.

"Looks like Colonel Miller has something he wants to talk to us about," Jessica said.

"Let's not keep him waiting," Isobel said as she undid the straps holding her to her bed.

They floated out of the hab module and down the corridor, running parallel to the drive keel until they floated up into the command section.

Colonel Miller was waiting for them at the holotank two levels below the bridge, the holotank displaying *Fafnir* and the tanker.

"Thank you two for being so prompt," Colonel Miller said. "Commander, you may start your burn."

Gentle thrust gravity pulled Jessica to the deck as *Midnight Diamond* began maneuvering toward the friendly ships.

"We'll be docking with *Fafnir* in two hours," Colonel Miller told them. "Afterward, most of the crew and passengers will disembark to take advantage of *Fafnir*'s comparative luxuries for the first half of our voyage. After that, we'll be back to stuffing ourselves inside this tin can. We'll then proceed to Origin and upon completion of our mission, return to *Fafnir* to dock and ride her the rest of the way home."

"How long is *Fafnir* going to wait for us?" Jessica asked.

"Forty days without contact," Colonel Miller said. "But we'll be carrying a pair of courier drones with us to send updates to *Fafnir*."

"This ship can carry courier drones?" Jessica asked.

"They're with *Fafnir* right now. They're the smallest ones we have. Single use," Colonel Miller said.

"So, two shots to send messages back to *Fafnir*, and then we have to be back within forty days of our last transmission, otherwise we're stranded?" Jessica checked.

"That's right, Lieutenant," Colonel Miller said. "I suppose if we do fail to meet our rendezvous in time, someone will eventually come looking for us, although I suspect anything that delays our return will not leave any survivors behind."

"Probably not," Jessica said. "So, I take it *Fafnir* will be sending courier drones of her own to 61 Virginis?"

Colonel Miller nodded. "*Fafnir* will update 61 Virginis on what they get from us. But there will be no return traffic. The jump flashes of courier drones would give us away."

"I'm surprised you haven't adapted your flashless stardrive technology to courier drones yet," Jessica said.

"It's inconvenient, yes," Colonel Miller admitted.

"Well then, we'll be on our own when we arrive, so nothing unexpected there."

"No," Colonel Miller said.

"There is something I'm not completely clear on," Jessica continued.

"I may be able to clear that up for you, Lieutenant," Colonel Miller offered.

"What do we do if we find something on Origin? Are we just going to report our findings and leave, or are we going to stay and observe?"

"That depends on what's there," Colonel Miller said. "And the risks involved in staying. We don't want to risk the Cendies acquiring *Midnight Diamond*'s technology."

"That's reasonable," Jessica said. "I noticed a lot of equipment aboard that's not just for distant observation.'"

"We don't know what to expect, so we're making sure we've covered as many bases as *Midnight Diamond*'s payload capacity allows," Colonel Miller said. "I take it you're hoping to get up close with whatever we find?"

"As long as it's not likely to shoot at me, yes," Jessica said. "Studying whatever's there in person would reap far more intelligence than just sitting back reading their emissions. And with Miriam Xia, we have an invaluable resource to call upon."

"How is Miss Xia?" Colonel Miller asked.

"Still underclocked in VR. She doesn't like being bored, and there's nothing much to keep her attention in the real world while we're in transit," Jessica said.

"Fair enough," Colonel Miller said. "I'll leave it to you to keep an eye on her status."

Jessica understood that as far as Colonel Miller was concerned, Miriam wasn't worth thinking about until she became useful to him and his mission.

∼

Fafnir, and the tanker she was attached to, was a study in the contrasts of starship design. The League cruiser—a sharply pointed cone with a cluster of engine bells sticking out the bottom—reminded Jessica of a bouquet flipped upside down. The tanker, by contrast, looked like a lozenge that flared at the base for the engine bells, with a habitat ring mounted at the top.

Though the tanker was one of the smaller fleet tankers in the League's inventory, it still dwarfed the cruiser. A pair of long bridges attached the cruiser to the tanker, one for fuel and the other for bulk cargo.

Midnight Diamond approached from behind and above the linked cruiser and tanker, moving with deliberate slowness as she approached the cruiser's ventral docking port.

Jessica could see on the feeds that a cradle had been added to the cruiser's hull for *Midnight Diamond*. It told her that *Fafnir* had been prepared for ferrying the spy ship, or other vessels like her, before they had discovered the candidate for the Cendy home system.

Docking clamps rang *Midnight Diamond*'s hull like a bell as she attached herself atop *Fafnir*'s drive section. The tiny starship was less than half the length of the cruiser, fitting easily in the space between the cruiser's drive and the spinning habitat rotor.

Jessica had been looking forward to transferring to the habitat rotor. She always preferred to have a definitive direction of down, even when provided by the fictitious force of spin gravity. She pondered why it was considered fictitious. It might not be one of the fundamental forces of the Universe, but if a centrifuge spun up fast enough, it would crush her just as effectively as real gravity would. The force might be fictitious, but the effects certainly weren't.

Jessica shook her head and dismissed the idle thoughts. She had forty days to prepare for whatever they found on Origin. While she had theories, in the rush after they got the lead, she hadn't had time to make educated guesses about what Origin might be.

When the docking bridge from *Fafnir* sealed against *Midnight Diamond*'s primary airlock, Jessica, with a bag full of her basic belongings, was ready to transfer. Miriam was still in the sleeping pod, underclocked and largely oblivious to the world. Jessica left Miriam a text message to read at her leisure. With her brainset synced to *Midnight Diamond*'s network, she'd know when Miriam sped up to real time.

Jessica followed Colonel Miller and Isobel across the bridge. It was a reinforced bridge that allowed the safe transfer of people and cargo while under acceleration. It hung from a telescoping arm, with a pair of cables suspending each segment.

On the other side, Captain Eva Baye waited to greet them.

"Welcome aboard *Fafnir*, Colonel Miller," Captain Baye said.

Colonel Miller exchanged salutes with Captain Baye. "Thank you for welcoming us aboard. This is my subordinate, Major Hesme, and our guest from the Special Purpose Branch, Lieutenant Jessica Sinclair."

Captain Baye's eyes swept over the three of them. "A pleasure. I've already assigned you your quarters. You will have a cabin with the senior officers, Colonel, but I'm afraid the two of you are going to have to share a cabin."

"That won't be a problem," Jessica said. "Can't be cozier than our quarters on *Midnight Diamond*."

Captain Baye nodded. "Once the tanker finishes us off, we'll jump out for Origin."

After Jessica had synced her brainset to *Fafnir*'s internal network, it provided her with guidance to her quarters on the habitation rotor. When she arrived at her quarters, she fell onto her new bed, letting one-third standard gravity pull her down onto the gel mattress. She gave a contented sigh. She was going to savor every second of gravity she could get for the next twenty days.

Isobel stowed her belongings under her bed, but instead of lying on it, she unfolded a seat with a desk and sat down.

"Already working?" Jessica asked.

"No. I'm going to record a message for my husband," Isobel said. "This will be the last chance we'll have to send personal messages."

"Oh, would you like some privacy?" Jessica asked.

"I'd appreciate that," Isobel said. "You can pull down the privacy screen and activate your noise canceling. You might want to take this chance to send a message to someone."

Jessica nodded and pulled down the screen, activating the pod's privacy mode.

All noise from outside abruptly vanished. It was so quiet, Jessica could hear her artificial heart pumping equally artificial blood through her body.

Taking Isobel's advice, she drafted two messages. The first was a quick report to Colonel Shimura to update her on her arrival aboard *Fafnir*.

The next was a message for Mason.

She spent a while pondering where to start. She had misgivings about trying to maintain a relationship over a long distance during a war, but the thought of not trying at all seemed worse than breaking things off entirely.

"Hey there, Mason," Jessica wrote. "Hope you're not getting into too much trouble. I've got a thing I must do and won't be able to send you anything for a while. It's all very hush-hush, so I can't go into details. I'm sure you understand.

"I want you to know that whenever I haven't been fully occupied with my work, I've been thinking about you and how much I miss you. But I don't want you to worry about me. You've got plenty to worry about already. I can't say when I'll send you another message, but I can promise I'll send one as soon as I can.

"Stay safe—and know I will be thinking about you."

Jessica reviewed the message and felt a bit of trepidation at the last statement. Was it too soon to talk about love stuff? Would it place too much of a burden on him? They'd known each other for a while, but they'd only had a relationship for a short time.

"Bollocks," Jessica said. She hesitated a while longer before forcing herself to send the message.

It would be the last time she'd be able to send a message to Mason for weeks. Perhaps forever if things went poorly out at the edge of nowhere.

CHAPTER 12

"Wow, the engineers have been busy!" Dominic said in undisguised admiration as the strikecraft from *Independence* approached New Lowell.

The wrecked Turtlebacks were still there, seemingly ignored as the engineers did their work. In the days since Pluto's liberation, they had built a spaceport directly south of New Lowell.

The Sputnik Planitia had plenty of flat open space to construct a spaceport, and the engineers had managed to lay out a landing field as large as any major spaceport on Earth. Dozens of landing pads, each with its own flame trench and walls made from piled-up ice, were arranged in neat rows stretching across several square kilometers. Adjacent to the landing pads was a large collection of prefabricated buildings, including hangars, barracks, and a control tower. The ice between the landing pads, and between the spaceport and New Lowell, was streaked with the tracks of ground vehicles, both large and small.

At each corner of the base, the Pele superheavies were dug into defensive positions, leaving just their turrets exposed above the ice, while multiple missile launchers, mobile point-defense guns, and control radars dotted the landscape around New Lowell. After going to the trouble of taking Pluto, it was clear Admiral Moebius intended to keep it.

Mason opened a channel with the tower. "New Lowell Tower, Osiris Leader. Requesting landing clearance."

"Osiris Leader, New Lowell Tower. You're cleared to land on Pad 49."

A large number 49 projected onto Mason's HUD over his assigned landing pad, complete with an arrow pointing to exactly where it was.

"Pad 49, copy. Beginning approach."

In the low gravity of Pluto, landing was not hard, and the pad was more than large enough for a single Lightning. Mason didn't even bother folding his wings as he approached.

Lowering his landing gear, Mason superimposed his vertical velocity vector symbol over the landing pad, using just enough thrust from his landing thrusters to keep from gaining speed as he descended. A few meters above the pad, he throttled up the thrusters to kill the last of his speed and landed gently on the grating covering the landing pad.

Mason quickly shut down his Lightning as the ground crew approached. He popped open the cockpit and climbed out, jumping off the side of his fighter and landing softly in the low gravity.

One of the ground crew in an orange jumpsuit approached and saluted him. "There's a rover waiting to take you to New Lowell, sir. It's just off the ramp."

Mason returned the salute. "Thanks. Take care of my bird."

"We will, sir."

Mason walked off the landing pad and came to a dead stop upon seeing the vast expanse of the Sputnik Planitia.

Memories of being stranded on an ice world not unlike Pluto, light-years away in Ross 128, came flooding into his awareness. He had flashes of a crashed Lightning being pulverized by Cendy strafing runs, broken League cruisers lying on their sides. Memories of stepping over the frozen bodies of League spacers who didn't know they were under attack until fire came raining down from above.

He snapped back to the present when another Lightning came down on the pad next to him, the exhaust from its landing thrusters blowing dust over him.

Mason took a long steady breath, letting the traumatic memories pass like a storm. If the gravity had been high, he was certain he would've collapsed to his knees. Instead, he started skipping toward the rover, taking careful, gentle jumps so as not to upset his balance.

The waiting rover was a four-seat, open-topped vehicle, one of several dispersed around the spaceport. He climbed into the driver's seat, though the vehicles were under automatic control.

A figure approached him, his HUD identifying it as Flight Lieutenant Gottlieb.

"Are you driving us into the city, Hauler?" Gottlieb asked.

"I guess I'm the designated driver," Mason said.

Armitage and her wingmate soon appeared, walking toward the rover while Gottlieb took the front passenger seat.

"My, what nice wheels," Armitage said. "It's even got seatbelts. Fancy!"

"Only the finest for us pilots," Mason said.

After Armitage and her wingmate had stowed their packs in the cargo basket, they climbed into the rear passenger seats. Once everyone was buckled in, Mason tapped on the rover's console screen and directed the auto-driver to follow the pre-programmed course to New Lowell. Without further input from Mason, the rover gently accelerated over the ice, the wheels throwing up short arcs of ice behind them.

The rover followed the road between rows of landing pads, passing other members of the Osiris Squadron as they disembarked their fighters. Mason waved at Dominic as he drove by and watched the skies as other strikecraft from *Independence* continued to land.

One of the Conqueror bombers came in to land on one of the landing pads ahead of him. Though roughly the same size as a Lightning, the Conqueror bore no resemblance to its stablemate. No considerations were made for aerodynamics with the Conqueror's design. It was a box with engines and hardpoints for heavy ordnance. That was about it—a craft specialized in killing things much larger than itself. It was something their pilots took with pride. While Lightning pilots tended to get the attention, bomber pilots got the work done.

Or so they liked to tell themselves. Mason had flown plenty of missions in his Lightning that were seemingly the boring drudgery of strike missions.

They passed through the spaceport's northern gate, the troopers guarding the gate giving them a wave as they passed. Mason waved back while observing the simple chain-link fence erected around the spaceport. The fence wasn't tall enough to prove much of an obstacle in Pluto's low gravity. Even without suit thrusters, a person could easily jump over it. Clearly it was there as a psychological barrier rather than a physical one—a way of deterring curious civilians.

Mason turned his attention away from the fence and toward New Lowell, or at least the above-ground part.

All that was visible of New Lowell was the blinking lights atop the communication towers that stuck out from the shallow dome covering the city. Most of the city extended several kilometers down into the ice. All that lay between the spaceport and the city was an empty expanse of ice.

Again, memories of Ross 128 intruded on his mind, the ruins of a League base superimposed over his vision.

Mason closed his eyes and waited for the thoughts to pass.

"You all right, Hauler?" Armitage asked. "If this rover wasn't self-driving, I would be worried."

"Bad memories. I don't have the best history with ice dwarves," Mason said.

"You need to talk about it?" Armitage asked.

"No. I just need to get inside," Mason said.

After all that had happened with the grinding combat on Triumph and the pilots lost under his command, it annoyed Mason that the thing that had stuck with him was his time stranded upon the ice dwarf in Ross 128. He didn't understand why. Other than the initial attack that had stranded him, he had not been fighting against anything other than time—an issue he had resolved by salvaging League equipment.

But again, the sight of frozen bodies appeared in his head, and his stomach churned.

Mason shook his head and focused his attention on New Lowell. The dome grew taller and taller as the rover approached.

A Pele superheavy tank guarded the entrance outside the dome, its massive main gun trained skyward in preparation for turning back a Cendy assault. The armored behemoth paid Mason and his pilots no mind as they rolled past the tank and into the dome.

The rover pulled into a parking area near one of the personnel airlocks. Mason released his restraints and stood up out of the rover, skipping off toward the airlock.

Inside the dome, with concrete below his feet and metal over his head, he felt his anxiety fade.

An airlock cycle later, they were inside the dome proper. Mason unlatched his helmet and pulled it off, and the other pilots did the same. Gottlieb ran a hand through her short hair while Armitage shook her head, causing her blue locks to whip wildly in the low gravity.

Markers along the corridor pointed the way to the elevators that would take them into New Lowell. "Anyone ever been in a city like this before?" Armitage asked.

"What do you mean?" Gottlieb asked.

"You know, a tapered cylinder dug straight into the ground."

"I haven't," Gottlieb admitted. "What about you, Hauler?"

"Yes, but not really," Mason said.

"But not really?"

"The shipyard where *Independence* was built. It was disguised as a buried cylinder habitat, a supposed high-end resort in low-Jovian orbit," Mason elaborated. "Of course, that wasn't the case. The tunnel that would've housed the cylinder instead housed the battlecarrier we now serve on."

"So the short answer is no," Gottlieb said.

"The short answer is no," Mason said.

The rest of Osiris Squadron passed through the airlock, and all sixteen pilots barely filled the volume of the corridor. It was clear that in normal times New Lowell hosted far more traffic than it currently did.

A vast concourse expanded before them, with just a scattering of Federal personnel walking among dozens of abandoned shops and kiosks. At the center of the concourse was a massive sculpture of Pluto. Around it, its system of moons seemingly floated several meters above the floor of the concourse, Charon by far the largest, with the smaller moons, Styx, Nix, Kerberos, and Hydra, just lumpy rocks floating over Mason's head.

As they crossed the concourse and got closer, he could see fine wires suspending the models from the ceiling. "Wow!" Mason breathed, stopping to take in the massive model.

"Yep, I think we're on Pluto," said Dominic.

"Stunning deduction, Silverback," Sabal said. "So, are we going to stare at this thing all day?"

"Just appreciating the sights," Mason said. "Come on, let's see what else is waiting for us in New Lowell."

They passed through a hundred meters of corridor until they transitioned into a catwalk inside the dome. The inner surface of the opaque dome was illuminated by strips of LEDs, but Mason's attention was drawn downward.

Before he knew what he was doing, he had walked to the railing and was looking down on a brightly lit cylinder with greenery and civilization wrapped around the interior. The city of New Lowell stretched for several kilometers straight down, and the slight taper of the cylinder exaggerated the feeling of depth. The sight was surreal.

"Belts and zones," Mason muttered.

"Wow, now that's a sight!" Armitage exclaimed.

"Not something you get to see in a space habitat," Dominic agreed.

Warm, moist wind ran through Mason's hair as he stared down into the depths of New Lowell. The smell of it reminded him of every planet he had ever stood on—a sharp contrast to the cold airlessness outside the dome.

Like a gigantic skyscraper, a tower ran down the center of the cylinder, terminating at the base.

"I bet the view from the elevator's going to be something else," Mason said. He started walking down the catwalk toward the elevator lobby at the top of the tower, but he ran his hand over the railing as he looked down, unable to take his eyes off the sight of the city below.

They passed into the elevator lobby, a large room that felt more like a hotel lobby than the entrance to a cylindrical city. There were empty kiosks for shops and cafes, while in the center of the lobby was a visitor center staffed by four civilians.

A pair of civilian police officers waited by one kiosk. The more senior of them waved to get Mason's attention. "Welcome to New Lowell," greeted the police officer. "I'm Officer Munroe. I take it you're the first of our new guests?"

"Yeah. We've got a few dozen more pilots behind us," Mason told him.

"There's plenty of elevators for you all," Officer Munroe said. "Hell, you could each take one individually."

"Tempting," Mason said. "Any suggestions where we can relax?"

Officer Munroe chuckled. "Do I look like a tour guide? The hotels should be full of brochures. Though most of our tourist industry is closed for obvious reasons."

"Guess we'll just have to go where the locals like to have fun," Mason said.

"Shouldn't be too hard. Enjoy your stay," Officer Munroe said.

They boarded the nearest elevator. "Wow!" Armitage said again.

Mason shared her awe as he stepped onto the glass floor of the elevator, looking straight down the rotating cylinder of New Lowell. The walls on three sides were also glass, giving a full view of the dome at the top of the cylinder.

"They really know how to make an impression," Armitage said.

The doors closed behind them, and after a musical chime, the elevator started descending. The acceleration was enough to overcome Pluto's gravity, and Mason had to hold the railing to keep his boots on the floor. Pluto's weak gravity returned as the elevator reached its maximum descent speed, but Mason kept a firm hold on the railing as he watched New Lowell rise toward him. Green light spilled into the elevator, reflecting off the multitude of grass lawns and forest parks. It looked a lot like any space habitat cylinder Mason had ever been inside, just turned on its side.

New Lowell rotated once every two minutes as the elevator rode down the long tower that ran through the center of the cylinder. Mason looked to one side and saw the large shade covering the massive LED lights illuminating New Lowell's interior with a near-perfect simulation of natural light. Between each elevator bank ran strips of LED arrays that provided the city's simulated daylight. A screen next to the elevator door showed the temperature and local time. The cylinder's climate simulated the temperate climate on Earth in early spring—just enough humidity to prevent skin from drying out and just warm enough to go outside without the need for a sweater.

Mason wondered whether the seasons in New Lowell changed over the year. It was something that wasn't consistently done on habitats. The choice was cultural. Most just kept a single moderate climate year-round, but some habitats simulated a gentle version of a four-season cycle.

He probably wasn't going to be in New Lowell long enough to find out.

As the elevator continued its descent, they saw vehicles driving through the streets. From Mason's vantage point they looked like toys. In fact, the entire city didn't look real from inside the elevator but like a meticulously created diorama wrapped around itself. He imagined a model maker using a pair of tweezers to set down each tree, building, vehicle, and tiny human figure.

The cityscape disappeared as the elevator descended to the receiving building at the bottom of the cylinder. The slowing of the elevator multiplied the pull of gravity, and for a moment Mason could almost stand normally.

The elevator stopped with a gentle bounce and the doors parted, revealing the conical bowl at the bottom of the cylinder.

"I feel like I'm inside a mixing bowl," Dominic said.

"At least there are lots of signs with directions," Armitage noted.

"Plenty of warning signs too," Mason said. "Guess they have low expectations of the average intelligence of their visitors."

Mason walked up to the edge of the elevator platform at the bottom of the cylinder, where a yellow line, evenly divided by diagonal black stripes, marked where the stationary platform at the base of the bowl transitioned to the rotating part of the cylinder. The gap between moving and nonmoving parts looked barely large enough to slip a playing card through.

Mason had spent his entire life transitioning to non-spinning and spinning parts of a station. The only difference here was that it was on Pluto. He stepped over the partition and proceeded toward the conveyor that followed the gentle curve of the bowl. Grabbing the moving railing, he stood in place as the conveyor carried him to the outer edge of the cylinder, gravity gradually increasing as it arched upwards.

It could be a disorienting sensation for people who weren't used to varying gravity, but every pilot from *Independence* experienced it every time they took an elevator from their quarters to the disparate parts of the ship.

The conveyor deposited him at the cylinder's edge, with a full g pulling him to the ground. Mason felt the weight of his hardsuit bear down on him, only partly offset by the hardsuit's actuators. A raised train station, identical to any Mason had seen on any habitat station, lay adjacent to the conveyor. It took his brain a moment to reorient the station from being above him to in front instead.

As the rest of Osiris Squadron arrived, Mason turned to greet them. "All right, kids, you have your hotel assignments, so from now until our leave ends, your time is yours."

"Awesome. Let's see what fun we can have," Sabal said, leaving directly for the train station. Some pilots followed, but Dominic didn't; instead, he looked off into the distance, trying to take it all in.

As Mason turned, he noticed the locals were staring at them. Amused, he waved, and some waved back, but most just continued to stare. Sabal walked past the civilians on her way to the station, seemingly oblivious to them. Her bulky dark-gray hardsuit contrasted sharply with the shirt-sleeves of the locals.

"It's like they've never seen spacers before," Dominic remarked.

"I doubt pilots stomping around in hardsuits is a common sight around here," Mason said. "We don't look like scientists."

"You don't say?" Dominic said. "Should have put on lab coats and goggles if we wanted to blend in."

Mason snorted. "Right."

Dominic scratched his chin as they observed the gawking civilians. "I do wonder how much interaction the locals have had with the Cendies."

"I suppose we'll soon find out."

CHAPTER 13

Mason thanked his lucky stars that New Lowell followed the same standardized day–night cycle that Federal starships and stations did. When it was local night, the lights dimmed to a warm circadian-rhythm-friendly amber color. Even if New Lowell wasn't buried in a several-thousand-meter-deep shaft, Pluto's sidereal day wouldn't have been very useful, given that it lasted six Earth days. And despite the distance from the Sun, it was more than bright enough to disrupt people's sleep.

He woke up in the morning alone in a hotel bed at least four times the size of his cot aboard *Independence*, feeling more refreshed than he had in months. He sat up and looked at the headless form of his empty hardsuit standing in the corner of his hotel room. "Good morning. You sleep well?" he asked the empty suit.

Sensing his movement, the window shades opened and simulated late-morning light spilled in.

Mason got up and walked to the window to admire the view of New Lowell arcing up in the distance. To his left, the cylinder tapered out toward the surface.

Then he noticed something just across the street from his hotel room. A playground. With children.

Belts and zones, I haven't seen children since Earth Fed was still fighting the League.

Mason stared out of the window in wonder, watching as children darted through the playground under the watchful eyes of their parents, oblivious to the wider world. They probably didn't even think about the fact that they were living inside a spinning cone buried under the ice of Pluto.

All they cared about was that they were at the playground with their friends.

Mason walked away from the window and changed out of the T-shirt and shorts he wore to sleep, putting on some of the few civilian clothes he owned—a reminder that outside of the Space Forces, he was essentially homeless.

After taking advantage of the complimentary breakfast, he walked out of the hotel. Children were still playing across the street, and Mason couldn't take his eyes away from the sight. It was so far from what he had experienced in the last year: all the fighting and the isolation from the larger Federal society. He realized the closest he'd been to children since the war with the League started was a pair of teenagers who had tried to rob him while he was on Dagon Freeport in Fomalhaut. The memories of that time hit him like a wave of cold water.

He sat down on a bench and rested his head in his hands.

The sight of something as mundane and innocent as children playing put his life over the last year into stark relief. He considered his life as nothing even close to normal, even accounting for the war that was going on. He was only leading Osiris Squadron by accident. There simply wasn't anyone else available to do the job.

The last time he had been on a planet was during the middle of a large-scale invasion—the only large-scale invasion of a developed planet in history. And now here he was in the most remote settlement in the Solar System having an epiphany after seeing children play.

"Belts and zones, I need a break," Mason muttered to himself, then chuckled. Technically he was having a break right now.

But on leave or not, he was still in a warzone. A warzone that included children.

"You okay there?"

Mason looked up at a middle-aged woman with brown hair and brown skin a darker shade than her hair. She was clutching the hand of a small girl who bore an unmistakable resemblance to her.

"Oh, uh, yeah. I'm just adjusting," Mason said.

"Space Forces?" she asked.

"That obvious?"

"You're a new face sitting in front of a hotel that hasn't had guests in over a year," she said. "I didn't exactly need a running start to make that deductive leap."

Mason stood up. "I'm Squadron Leader Mason Grey."

She gave him a lopsided smile. "Do you usually introduce yourself with your rank?"

"Uh, force of habit," Mason said apologetically. "Just Mason's fine."

"Carrie," she said. "Or Doctor Carrie Finegold, if you prefer."

Mason looked down at the young girl with Carrie, who hugged herself close to Carrie's leg.

Carrie stroked the girl's hair. "This is my daughter, Catelyn. She's a bit shy. She hasn't met new adults in a while."

"How old?"

"Four."

"Belts and zones!"

"Never seen a four-year-old?"

"It just hit me that she's been living under occupation for a year," Mason said. "I can't imagine what it's like to raise a kid like that."

"It's been challenging, but that's the nice thing about kids. They're pretty oblivious to anything happening outside of their little worlds," Carrie said. "As for occupation, it's not like the Ascendancy had soldiers marching through the streets. I've never seen one, though I know people who have spoken with their emissaries."

"Well, I can understand why Catelyn is feeling shy," Mason said.

"Catelyn needs to get over it," Carrie said. "You won't be the last stranger she's going to have to interact with. So, Squadron Leader, that mean what it says on the tin?"

Mason nodded. "I command a fighter squadron."

"A fighter squadron! How neat!" Carrie kneeled beside her daughter. "You hear that, Catelyn? He's a fighter pilot."

Catelyn's eyes lit up with interest. "He is?"

Mason nodded. "I am."

"She's currently in a fighter pilot phase of what she wants to be when she grows up."

"My parents thought it was just a phase too," Mason said.

"You a recruiter too?"

"No, ma'am," Mason said.

"Carrie's fine," she said. "If you do insist on being overly formal, at least call me Doctor."

"You got it, Doctor," Mason said. "So, Catelyn, what do you want to know?"

"What do you fly?"

"Lightning Mark V," Mason told her.

Catelyn nodded. "New build or upgraded?"

Mason was surprised she knew there was a difference. "The one I'm flying is a new build. Though the one I used to fly started as a Mark I."

"Wow. What happened to it?"

"I … had to leave it behind during a mission," Mason said. "I don't know what's happened to it."

"Will you try to get it back?" Catelyn asked.

"You know, I've been so busy that it hasn't occurred to me," Mason said. "I suppose if it's still there, I'll give it a try."

"Nice. I want to fly Lightnings when I grow up."

Mason glanced up at Carrie and could tell from the look on her face that she didn't want him to encourage Catelyn.

When he thought back to all the danger, all the death he had both seen and inflicted in his career, the idea of encouraging the little girl in front of him to follow the same path repulsed him.

"You know, it's cool to be the person flying fighters, but d'you know what's even cooler?" Mason asked.

Catelyn gave him a suspicious side-eye. "What, like being an astronomer? Mom has already said that line."

"Not a bad career path, but that wasn't what I was getting at," Mason said. "Anyone can fly a Lightning with enough training and augmentation. But it takes someone special to build one. You know who makes Lightnings?"

"Xia-McIntyre Space Works," Catelyn said. Her awareness of one of the major players in Earth Fed's military–industrial complex was a bit disturbing.

"Yeah. Well, Lightnings are very complex machines that take a lot of very smart people working together to make fly," Mason said. "That could be you one day."

"I want to blow things up," Catelyn said.

"Well, you'd be making the things that blow things up, so in a way, you would be," Mason pointed out.

Catelyn shrugged. "Mommy, can I go to the playground now?"

"Sure, honey. But look both ways as you cross the street."

The road was deserted, and Mason had not seen a single vehicle cross while standing with Carrie and her daughter. Still, Catelyn did stop at the curb to look both ways before scampering across the street to the playground.

"I'm not sure I like it that you tried to encourage my daughter to join the arms industry, but I do appreciate you trying to steer her away from the military," Carrie said.

"You can never have too many engineers, and she could put those skills to more peaceful uses than designing fighters," Mason said.

"I suppose you're right," Carrie said. "And the idea of her working on Luna is a much more comfortable one than thinking of my little girl flinging herself into danger inside a fighter."

"You're not wrong to worry," Mason said.

"That bad out there?"

"You haven't kept up with the news?"

"The Ascendancy cut our communication links with Inner Sol during their occupation, and getting them back online has not been a priority for your people," Carrie said. "So I'm a bit out of date with the war."

"Well, the League is our ally now—I suppose I should start with that," Mason said. "We lost hard over Jupiter, won big over Triumph. Now we're trying to establish a supply line between Inner Sol and 61 Virginis before Earth and the First Fleet run out of fuel."

"And Pluto's part of that plan?" Carrie asked.

"Yes."

"Curious they would choose Pluto."

Mason swept his hand across the tubular vista. "This is the only place in the Kuiper Belt with a city as big as New Lowell."

"I suppose I can see the logic in that," Carrie said.

"You don't seem very happy about us being here," Mason remarked.

"No offense, Mason, but with you here, my home is now a target for the Ascendancy." Carrie gestured toward the playground. "You've brought the war to them."

Mason wanted to disagree, to reassure Carrie that she and her daughter were safe. But the dread welling up in his guts said otherwise. "I'm sorry."

"An apology?"

"Would you rather I lied?"

"No, thank you," Carrie said. "If you will forgive the impertinence, I don't suppose you know when they'll start evacuating civilians?"

"I don't," Mason said. "But I can ask."

"You'd do that for me?"

"Yes."

Carrie pulled out a business card. "Here's my contact information."

Mason accepted the card and pocketed it. "I'll let you know when I know the answer to your question."

Carrie nodded. "Thank you, Mason. I know you're not here to work, but I would really appreciate it if you found out sooner rather than later."

"I'll get on it as soon as I can," Mason said. "I can't make any promises, but I'll be happy to help however I can."

"Well, this has turned out to be a fortuitous meeting," Carrie said. "I'll leave you to enjoy your day and look forward to hearing from you later."

Mason smiled and nodded as Carrie crossed the street to join the other adults watching the children play. The leaden weight of dread in his stomach lightened a bit at the prospect of doing some good. He went back to his hotel room.

He kicked the door shut and pulled out Carrie's card. He locked his eyes on the reference code long enough for his brainset to read it and save Carrie's contact information. Sitting down in one of the hotel's fake wood seats, Mason made a secure connection through New Lowell's network to *Independence* in orbit.

To his surprise, Marshal Singh answered. "Yes, Squadron Leader Grey?"

Mason sat up and straightened his posture as if Marshal Singh were in the room with him. "Good morning, sir," he said. "Thank you for taking my call."

"I keep my promises, Squadron Leader. How can I help you?"

"I was wondering when we'll start evacuating civilians from New Lowell," Mason said. "I'm asking for a friend."

Marshal Singh sighed through the connection. "Yours is not the first request in regard to civilian evacuation. Admiral Moebius's staff has been inundated with queries to that effect by New Lowell's government. As of right now, no transport capacity is being set aside for civilian use, and I cannot speak as to when that will change."

"I understand, sir," Mason said. "I won't occupy your time any longer. Thank you."

"Enjoy your leave, Squadron Leader." Marshal Singh closed the connection.

Carrie was going to be disappointed to hear that. Mason was disappointed to hear it. And she was bound not to be the only parent waiting for news on when they could evacuate themselves and their children from New Lowell.

If the thought of this place being in a warzone terrified Mason, he could only imagine what it would be like for people who had much more to lose here and no way to protect themselves.

There was a knock at his door. Mason got up. Through the door's camera feed, he saw Gottlieb standing outside.

He opened the door. "Hey, Skids," he greeted her.

"Hey, Hauler. I just saw you got back to your hotel room, and I was wondering if you wanted to join me and Marbles and Silverback for lunch."

"Sure. Where?"

"There's a taco place down the way that's managed to stay open through the occupation. Apparently they've become pretty creative with what they can get through hydroponics and vitro-meats."

"Sounds appetizing," Mason said. "I'll come along."

Armitage and Dominic were waiting in front of the hotel, where Dominic leaned against the fender of a four-door ground car.

"Where did you get that?" Mason asked, impressed.

"Rented it," Dominic said. "New Lowell has a fully automated car rental service still operating. I just transferred some stellars and now we have a ride."

"How about that?" Mason said. "So, I understand there's a taco place?"

"There is indeed. Shall we?"

"Shotgun!" Mason called.

"I already called it," Armitage said.

"I'm pulling rank and overruling you," Mason said.

Armitage snorted but opened a door to enter the rear passenger seat. Mason climbed into the front passenger seat and buckled in while Dominic took the driver's seat. After buckling his seatbelt, Dominic grabbed the wheel and the car took off.

"You're driving yourself?'

"I haven't had a chance to drive a car in months. I'm not missing this opportunity," Dominic said.

"You're a fighter pilot," Mason said.

"What? You think just because I fly Lightnings, I shouldn't enjoy the simple freedom of driving a car?" Dominic retorted.

"I can't say I ever understood the appeal of driving a car," Mason admitted.

"That's because you grew up on a space station too small to accommodate road traffic."

"I know how to drive," Mason protested.

"I never said you didn't. But you never had a chance to learn how to enjoy driving—how much fun it could be."

Dominic made a hard right turn. Mason braced himself against the center console as lateral gs pulled him hard to the right. Armitage giggled in the back seat.

Dominic's joy ride was a short one before he brought the car to a stop in front of a shopping center, where a building with a digital sign over the door projected "Far Out Tacos!"

"They're confident in their product," Mason said.

"I believe it's a reference to being the most remote taco restaurant in Sol." Dominic unbuckled his seatbelt and exited the vehicle.

Mason got out and stepped onto the sidewalk. Once everyone had exited the car, the vehicle pinged and then drove off to park itself somewhere out of the way.

Mason followed Dominic into the restaurant, where he was surprised to see patrons occupying most of the tables. Dominic claimed a booth, and Mason slid in next to him, Armitage and Gottlieb sliding onto the bench across from them.

Mason grabbed a menu, which came to life as he opened it, highlighting the daily special. "That's a lot of options," he remarked.

"Yeah. Not bad for a place that was cut off from Sol a year ago," Dominic said.

Every item on the menu had its ingredients listed. Mason glanced through them and noticed that everything on the menu was made from things that could easily be grown in a hydroponic farm or inside a vitro tank. He suspected that any dishes made with imported ingredients, such as meat from actual animals or plants grown in soils of specific regions, had been deleted. It piqued his curiosity to find out how good the food was with no premium items, just stuff grown locally.

He tapped the vitro-chicken tacos with sour cream and spicy salsa, with water as his beverage, and tapped again to confirm his order.

A robot waiter trundled up to their table, its wheels squeaking on the tile floor. It carried a tray of glasses on top of its squat, cylindrical body and placed four glasses on the table, one in front of each occupant, with a pincer arm. Another arm with a nozzle on the end filled the glasses with their chosen drinks: water for Mason and Gottlieb, something dark and fizzy for Armitage, and a clear amber beverage for Dominic.

"Your orders will be out shortly!" the robot said in a cheery pre-recorded voice before trundling off to clear plates from a newly vacated table.

"Well, that saves on labor costs," Mason said.

"Don't like robot waiters?" Armitage asked.

"Guess I like the human touch," Mason said. "But given the average education here, I doubt it would be easy to find waiters."

When their food came, it was not delivered by a robot, however, but by a smiling potbellied man in denim pants and a mint-green T-shirt.

"Welcome to Far Out Tacos. I'm your host, Emil Kuma!" he said as he transferred their plates from his tray with practiced ease. "Here are your orders. Feel free to ask me for anything you like. It's been too long since I've had new customers."

"How did you stay open during the occupation?" Gottlieb asked.

"People gotta eat!" Emil said.

"Inelastic demand," Dominic said.

"This man knows business," Emil said.

"From my past life," Dominic said.

"I'll leave you to your food."

Mason looked down at his tacos, salivating. He picked one up. The hard corn tortilla felt and looked substantial—more than up to the task of holding its contents together until he brought it to his mouth. Biting down with a satisfying crunch, he was greeted by an explosion of hot flavor.

"Belts and zones!" Mason said around a mouthful.

The salsa was proper spicy. He needed to take generous sips of his water with each bite to keep his tongue from burning off.

"This is some good shit," Armitage said between bites.

"If this is what they have with just locally grown ingredients, just imagine what this must have tasted like when they could add imported ingredients," Gottlieb said.

Mason chewed through his second and then a third taco and was disappointed to be left with an empty plate afterward. The spicy chicken left a pleasant warmth in his belly.

The waiter robot collected their plates when they were all finished, and Emil appeared soon afterward. "How was it?" he asked.

"Excellent," Mason said. "Haven't had a meal this good in months. How did you manage this with just hydroponics and vitro-meat?"

"There's nothing that says hydroponically grown vegetables and spices can't be just as good as soil-grown, and there are tricks you can use to cover up the texture issues with vitro-meat."

"I'll need to learn those tricks," Mason said.

"I'm afraid I don't give lessons," Emil said.

"Tell me, Emil, what possessed you to open a taco joint here out on the edge of Sol?" Dominic asked.

"Opportunity," Emil said. "New Lowell is full of hungry scientists too busy to cook their own meals. And the city government has incentives for small business owners like me to relocate out here."

"Where did you come from originally?" Dominic asked.

"Earth. Los Angeles mostly. Got started working a stand in the arcologies," Emil said.

"This is quite the change of scenery from LA," Armitage remarked.

"Yes—the weather is nicer, the people are more civilized. I haven't had anyone try to rob me or throw garbage in my face once in the years I've lived here."

"And you're not bothered by the fact that we're in a warzone?" Armitage asked.

Emil shrugged. "I have customers. I have food to sell them. It's all the same to me. All that's different now is I get to feed hungry spacers and get paid from their food allowance."

Dominic smiled and nodded. "Always a pleasure to meet another entrepreneur."

"You in business?"

"Formerly. I retired and joined the Space Forces," Dominic said. "Hence why I'm old for my rank."

"Oh, I just assumed you were younger than you looked," Emil said.

"Thanks …" Dominic said.

"Shall I tempt you with dessert? If you like my tacos, you will love my *tres leches* cake."

"You got yourself a deal there, mister," Dominic said.

"I'll get right on it, then." Emil departed.

"He's eager to please," Gottlieb said.

"You heard what he said—we're the first new customers he's had in a year," Dominic said. "Must have gotten tired of seeing the same old faces."

"Well, he isn't the only one paying attention to the newcomers," Armitage said, pointing behind Mason.

Mason looked over his right shoulder and saw customers in the next booth struggling unsuccessfully not to stare at Mason and his pilots.

"I guess we shouldn't be surprised if we draw attention from everyone here," Mason said. "I suspect the novelty of new faces will wear off pretty fast once more spacers start cycling through here on leave."

"I'm sure the people who live here will be ecstatic about that," Armitage said dryly.

"I don't follow," Mason said.

"New Lowell's a science town," Armitage said. "Most of the people who live here work the vast arrays of telescopes that cover hundreds of square kilometers of ice around this city. They haven't been able to do that for a year, and it doesn't look like they'll be able to use their scopes again, since we commandeered them."

Mason shrugged. "You have to admit, using Pluto's observatories to spot cloaked Cendy ships from interplanetary distances is a genius move. I wonder where Admiral Moebius got the idea."

"It wasn't your girlfriend?" Armitage asked.

"Why would you think that?"

"I flew her around Inner Sol before I joined up with you. She seemed pretty smart."

"As much as I'd like to attribute every smart move made by Admiral Moebius to Jessica, I'm going to assume it came from somewhere else," Mason said. "Jessica's not an astronomer."

"If anything, it was Admiral Moebius's idea," Gottlieb said.

"What makes you think that?" Mason asked.

"You know what her specialty was when she was just a regular officer?"

"I've honestly never given it a thought," Mason said.

"She came up the ranks as an astrogator. Studying astronomy is a mandatory part of every astrogator's training," Gottlieb said.

"Where did you learn so much about astrogation?" Dominic asked.

"My older sister is a senior astrogator aboard *Veracruz*. We trade stories when we see each other. I bet she knows more about piloting Lightnings than your average astrogator."

"Well, that makes sense, both how Admiral Moebius would think of using Pluto's telescopes and why astrogators would study astronomy," Mason said.

"Well, looks like we've solved the big mystery as to why Pluto was picked as our staging ground in Sol," Dominic said. "Now it's just a question of what we do from here."

"Right now? Enjoy our leave," Mason said. "Best guess is after we're done, we'll be tasked with escorting the convoy when it arrives."

Emil arrived bearing a tray carrying four generous slices of cake. He set down a plate in front of each pilot, complete with a clean fork.

"Oh boy, this looks good," Armitage said. She quickly took a bite and nodded in satisfaction. "Oh yeah, way better than the prepackaged crap they offer on *Independence*."

Mason sliced a piece of cake off and scooped it into his mouth. The cake dissolved into a sweet delight of vanilla flavor, and in mere moments, he had reduced the piece to scattered crumbs on his plate. He quickly went about shoveling all the crumbs he could into his mouth.

"Well, I've blown through my calorie budget for the day," Gottlieb said.

"My solution to that problem is to disable my calorie tracker," Dominic said.

"Your waistline keeps track of your calorie intake just fine, Silverback," Gottlieb said.

"You calling me fat, Skids?" Dominic asked.

"Yes," Gottlieb said.

Dominic patted his belly, which bulged slightly under his shirt. "Fair enough. So, Hauler, Marbles, how do you keep yourselves so trim?"

"Exercise," Mason said.

"Cheating," Armitage said.

"How do you do that, and can you teach me?" Dominic asked her.

"Before big meals, I take blockers that prevent me from digesting carbohydrates," she said.

"Don't those cause terrible gas?" Gottlieb asked.

"Yes, yes they do, Skids," Armitage said with a smile.

Gottlieb eased out of her seat. "In that case, I think we should head back to the hotel before Marbles' microbiome goes to town on all the sugars she's about to feed them."

"I'm with you on that," Dominic said.

"How was everything?" Emil asked.

"Excellent," Dominic said. "I'll tell everyone I know in the fleet to come by here." Emil nodded his thanks as Mason and the others turned for the exit.

Dominic's rental arrived like a loyal animal when summoned, and everyone got inside. All windows were opened in expectation of the consequences of Armitage's calorie-control strategy. Fortunately, the drive ended before any gaseous emissions started to fill the cabin, and Armitage made a quick goodbye before heading toward her hotel room at a brisk walk.

"What do you think the chances are that the side effects of those carb blockers aren't just gaseous?" Dominic asked.

"Not a question I want answered," Mason said. "Thanks for inviting us out, XO."

"My pleasure, boss," Dominic said. "New Lowell may seem like a stuffy academic town, and it is, but that doesn't mean there aren't things to enjoy here if you look for them."

"As you have demonstrated," Mason said.

Dominic turned to his rental.

"You're not done yet?" Mason asked.

"Like I said, Hauler, there are good times to be had if you look for them." He shut the door, and the rental rolled off.

"Well, he's on a mission to get laid," Gottlieb said.

"What gives you that impression?" Mason asked.

"He might have said something about trying to pick up a lonely astronomer or two when we were eating breakfast together," Gottlieb said.

"I guess now that he's done his part in maintaining squadron morale, he's off to take care of his needs," Mason said.

"And what about your needs, Hauler?" Gottlieb asked.

"That's private," Mason said. "And I don't shit where I eat."

"Say no more, Hauler," Gottlieb said. She turned and sauntered away. "Enjoy your day."

Having one of his pilots—his wingmate, no less—unsubtly proposition him was both disturbing and a little flattering. It also spoke to how bold, or reckless, Gottlieb was.

Mason shook his head—at least she'd had the sense to backtrack when it was clear he wasn't the type to break fraternization rules.

More importantly, he didn't want to violate Jessica's trust. There hadn't been time to discuss issues of exclusivity in their relationship. But Mason found the idea of pursuing more than one romantic relationship at a time exhausting.

That left him wondering what he could do while in New Lowell. A part of him just wanted to park himself in his hotel room and spend the rest of his leave sleeping, but he decided that wasn't the healthiest use of his time.

He had gotten some quality time socializing with some of his squadron mates. Maybe it was time now to do something for himself.

With the decision made, Mason elected not to go back to his hotel room but head instead to the train station to see what adventures awaited him.

CHAPTER 14

Most of the points of interest suggested by New Lowell's tourist guide were closed due to the ongoing war. But to Mason's surprise, there was a place still open—the Clyde Tombaugh Museum of Astronomy and Cosmology.

After a short walk from the train station, he approached the front entrance of the museum. The doors opened on their own, revealing a life-sized statue of Clyde Tombaugh staring into the eyepiece of a telescope.

Mason walked into the main hallway, noticing the empty visitor center. A sign displayed the day's docent tours. Mason looked around but didn't see anyone wandering about. As far as he could tell, he was the only person in the museum.

Curious if the docent tours were still a thing, Mason filled the waiting time by studying a detailed scale model of the Lowell Observatory in Flagstaff, Arizona.

Five minutes before the tour was about to begin, he heard the click of hard-soled shoes against the museum's polished granite floor. An older man approached in an equally old-looking suit. A lanyard hanging about his neck declared him to be a museum docent. He was smiling at Mason, arms open as if to embrace him.

The docent stopped a couple of meters from Mason, clasped his hands, and rubbed them together. "Ah, you must be one of our new visitors from the Space Forces," he said.

"I am. How can you tell?"

"I was given a heads-up there were pilots on leave in New Lowell, so I figured any new faces would probably be them."

"You figured right," Mason said. "Squadron Leader Mason Grey."

"Doctor Carlton Wynn, retired."

"This is your retirement?"

"It's a volunteer position. Before retirement, I was the head astronomer leading the Sagittarius Telescope Array," Doctor Wynn explained. "I worked there for thirty years and retired after the last major upgrade."

"That's a black hole observatory, right?"

"Yes. You know of it?"

"Just from articles I've read. Observes the supergiant black hole at the center of our galaxy."

"Primarily—though it also makes observations of intermediate and stellar mass black holes," Doctor Wynn said.

"So, I take it I'm going to learn a lot about Clyde Tombaugh here?"

"You'll want to head to Flagstaff, Arizona for that, Squadron Leader. Though this place bears the name of Pluto's discoverer, its focus is not on the man himself but on the history of astronomy from the surface of Pluto. Would you like to start the tour?"

"That's what I'm here for," Mason said.

"Excellent. The museum's galleries are organized by time, beginning with Pluto's discovery through to the establishment of the first surface telescopes and the founding of New Lowell."

Doctor Wynn proceeded to the gallery, Mason following behind. They passed through the entrance to the exhibit, where hanging from the ceiling was an ancient space probe with a triangular body and a massive antenna dish.

Doctor Wynn glanced up at the probe. "That is New Horizons, the first space probe to visit Pluto. It took the very first images of the Tombaugh Regio where New Lowell is situated now."

"Is that the actual probe?" Mason asked.

"It is," Doctor Wynn said. "One of several old space probes recovered after stardrives were invented. Though this is the only one in the outer Solar System. Most of them are on Earth."

"Must have been quite the fight keeping New Horizons here."

"The team that recovered New Horizons stipulated that the probe should be displayed on New Lowell," Doctor Wynn said. "It carries a portion of Clyde Tombaugh's ashes, so bringing them to Earth was seen as disrespectful to his remains."

"There's a dead guy in that?"

"Just a pinch of ashes." Doctor Wynn held his thumb and forefinger together for emphasis.

"I suppose it's appropriate that a portion of his remains should be on the world he discovered," Mason said.

"It is."

"So, what else is in here?" Mason asked.

Doctor Wynn pointed to a mockup of a pre-space office filled with unfamiliar brass and glass instruments. "That is a re-creation of the workspace Clyde Tombaugh worked in when he was studying photo plates."

"I have no clue what I'm looking at," Mason admitted.

"Not much experience with artifacts of the pre-digital age?" Doctor Wynn asked.

"I was raised on a space station over Jupiter," Mason told him.

"I thought I heard a Jovian accent," Doctor Wynn said. "See that orange tube right there? That's a reproduction of the astrograph that Tombaugh used to take photographs of the part of the night sky where Pluto was."

"And that thing with the eyepiece?" Mason asked.

"That's a blink comparator," Doctor Wynn said. "Before the digital age, if you wanted to switch quickly between two images, you had to look through a scope with two objective lenses and then flip a switch to rapidly change which one you were looking for. Tombaugh would use that to switch between plates taken days apart to detect any objects that might have moved."

"Must have been tedious."

"Tombaugh worked with what he had and did a fine job of it," Doctor Wynn said. "Back then, astronomers had to actually look for things, rather than just feed raw data into an AI to do the work for them."

"So, after this is New Horizons?" Mason asked.

"There's also the debate at the end of the twentieth century over whether or not Pluto was a planet," Doctor Wynn said.

"Yeah, I know about that," Mason said. "Pluto was considered the ninth planet until they started discovering other dwarf planets in the Kuiper Belt."

"Indeed, though the modern definition is a bit simpler than the one they used back in the day," Doctor Wynn said.

"How so?"

"The old definition included having to clear out the orbit, though how cleared out always seemed arbitrary, especially when you consider extra-solar worlds such as super-Earths in crowded orbits or round bodies smaller than Ceres in otherwise deserted orbits. So instead, dwarf planets are classified based on their mass."

Mason looked at the data displayed in the exhibit. "Seems like quite the gap between New Horizons and the next visit."

"Yes—the next major milestone was an orbiter, which required the use of an ion engine powered by a fusion reactor," Doctor Wynn said. "The first manned expedition wasn't until almost two hundred years after Pluto's discovery."

Doctor Wynn pointed to the picture of a figure in an old pressure suit standing next to a pole bearing multiple flags of the nations that had contributed to the mission.

The exhibit ended at the start of the twenty-fifth century.

"And now we have the invention of faster-than-light travel, which is where things will really pick up in the next exhibit," Doctor Wynn said.

"Kind of hard to believe Pluto wasn't visited more before the development of the stardrive," Mason mused.

"You're talking long transit times even with the best fusion drives you had pre-FTL," Doctor Wynn said. "And the gas giants were always more attractive targets for colonization."

"My ancestors thought the same."

"Indeed," Doctor Wynn said. "I'm sorry about what happened to your homes."

"It's the people who matter, and they're now safe around Earth space," Mason said. "For now, at least."

"Which is why you're here in New Lowell—to ensure their safety," Doctor Wynn said.

"It would be hard to win the war without Earth."

"I suppose it would," Doctor Wynn said. "Now, where were we? Ah! Yes, the invention of faster-than-light-travel and the first settlement on Pluto."

Mason pointed to a model in a glass case. "That the first one?"

"Yes, a privately funded research station. Intra-system traffic increased rapidly during the early colonization period when national alliances and private ventures scrambled to claim as many worlds as possible. All those drives burning in deep space did no favors for observatories in the inner Solar System trying to peer through the clutter into the Universe beyond. So some astronomers came out here, where there was basically no traffic, no light pollution from thousands of fusion drives. Here, the first observatories were built—New Lowell's reason for being established."

"But the city itself came after?"

"Yes. Unfortunately the first attempts at settling Pluto were hampered by the General Conflict," Doctor Wynn said. "With the disruption of interstellar traffic, the original settlers had to evacuate back to Earth. No one returned for many years while the nascent Earth Federation was busy rebuilding space-based infrastructure after the war."

"But you did rebuild." Mason pointed to the first permanent settlement in Tombaugh Regio, a covered ring that provided rotational gravity for New Lowell residents.

"Yes, we rebuilt," Doctor Wynn said. "Pluto's promise as a place for uninterrupted observation of the Universe has not changed. And as you can see, that continued to expand as more and more telescopes were built, and more and more people came to live here until a hundred years ago, when a truly self-sufficient colony was formed and the city that you're standing in was founded."

"And now it's a military staging ground," Mason said. "Funny how things work out."

"Yes. Well, not to sound ungrateful, but I do hope that this phase of our history ends soon so we can get back to studying the cosmos," Doctor Wynn said.

"I couldn't agree more, Doctor."

At the end of the tour, Mason wandered the museum by himself, looking over exhibits, reading placards, and studying the development of the current New Lowell colony. By the time he was finished with the museum, New Lowell's lighting was starting to turn amber, simulating the first stages of sunset.

Mason stood and took in the view. It didn't feel like he was standing kilometers beneath the surface of Pluto inside a spinning cylinder. There were no references to suggest he wasn't in one of the thousands of habitats that filled cislunar space or co-orbited the Sun in Earth's orbit.

Of course, New Lowell would be small compared to most habitats downorbit. It was the most distant settlement in the Solar System, but it wouldn't rank in even the top one hundred habitats near Earth.

Mason boarded the train to return to his hotel. Halfway there, an alert appeared on his brainset, and the message chilled his bones. A large hostile force had jumped in. The Cendies were back.

CHAPTER 15

ALARMS ECHOED OFF New Lowell's interior as panicked civilians scrambled in random directions.

Mason reached his hotel room and put on his uniform, then climbed into his hardsuit. From there, he headed back to the lobby to wait for his pilots. Osiris Squadron was supposed to gather at the hotel in such an emergency, but with his pilots scattered around the city, it would take time.

In the meantime, Mason busied himself trying to connect to the external sensors to get an idea of what was going on. Unfortunately, New Lowell's civilian network was not connected to any military data link, so Mason was blind to what was happening beyond that there was an attack of some kind.

Sabal was the first to arrive, her stride indicating her eagerness to get back into action. "You know what's going on, Hauler?"

Mason shook his head. "I don't think there's anything we can learn down here. We'll need to get to the surface and figure out what good we can do."

The rest of Mason's pilots arrived within thirty minutes and got to work putting their hardsuits on. From there, they headed directly for the elevator shaft that ran up the center of the New Lowell cylinder.

Elevator cars were moving up and down the shaft as they approached, much to Mason's relief. Chief Monroe stood at the base of the elevator station. "I take it you're looking for a ride up?" he asked.

"That's right, Chief," Mason said. "Any word about what's going on up there?"

"Nope. Just orders to help evacuate civilians from the surface and assist Space Forces personnel to make it up," Chief Monroe said. "As soon as I deboard the next car, your people can take it up."

"Thanks, Chief," Mason said.

When the next elevator car arrived, the doors opened and a group of frightened civilians were taken away by Chief Monroe's officers, making room for Mason's pilots to board.

The doors closed and the elevator started to ascend, New Lowell's interior scrolling down as they did so.

For several minutes as the elevator ascended, Mason waited with no way of knowing what was happening on the surface. He dreaded his squadron arriving on the surface only to find the battle lost, their fighters destroyed on the ground before they had even had the chance to put their hardsuits on.

Upon arrival, the lobby was cleared of civilians, now occupied only by fully armed and armored troopers.

Mason's brainset automatically connected to the data link, and he paused to take in the information.

He didn't like what he saw. "Dammit!"

"Squadron Leader Grey?" one of the troopers enquired.

"Yes?"

"General Asif wishes to speak with you at the command post, sir," said the trooper.

"I won't keep the general waiting."

General Asif's command post occupied a wing of New Lowell's surface station, laid out like a camp inside one of New Lowell's surface warehouses. Mason and his pilots were allowed through the security fence, and Mason soon spotted General Asif and her staff standing around a mobile holotank.

"General Asif," Mason greeted her.

General Asif was a thin, solidly built woman with grey streaks running through tightly bound black hair. "Squadron Leader Grey, I'm sorry we're not meeting under better circumstances, but I'm going to be in need of your help."

"You have it, General," Mason said.

"*Independence*'s retirement from Pluto space has left a major gap in our orbital defenses," she explained. "Admiral Moebius believes that our surface defenses would be up to the task of defending from a Cendy counterattack, and it looks like that assumption is going to be put to the test."

"What's our mission, General?" Mason asked.

"Fighter screen. The torpedo batteries can keep the Cendy warships from attacking us directly, but the big threat will be from strikecraft approaching from below the horizon to take out our defenses from close range."

"Just like we did when we took this place," Mason said.

"Exactly," General Asif said. "I've set up a perimeter of early-warning stations all across the Tombaugh Regio, but our close-range defenses amount to just the Pele superheavies and infantry-borne missiles. Our best bet for holding out is to keep any enemy strikecraft from closing in on New Lowell, and the best tools I have for that are the fighters *Independence* left behind."

"Then that's what we'll do, General," Mason said. "When can we expect relief from Admiral Moebius?"

General Asif sighed. "That's to be determined. Her last message sounded like she wanted Pluto to come under siege, as it would mean tying up Cendy warships that could otherwise be used to threaten the relief convoy from 61 Virginis. And no, I don't know when that's supposed to arrive."

"So we hold out until then, whenever that is," Mason said.

"That's about the size of it, Squadron Leader," General Asif said.

The floor rumbled, almost causing Mason to float off the ground in the low gravity. "What was that?" he asked.

"That was one of my Peles firing its main gun at targets in orbit," General Asif told him. "You're dismissed, Squadron Leader. Suit up and get to your fighters."

"Yes, General." Mason saluted and departed.

Their suits were waiting for them at the airlock, hunched over and open in the back. Mason slipped into his hardsuit feet first and closed it around him. He immediately sealed his helmet over his head and led his pilots into the airlock.

Once the airlock had cycled, the outer hatch opened, revealing a pair of open-topped rovers waiting for them. They piled into the rovers and drove directly toward Charon as it floated, suspended, just above the horizon.

There was a flash and the rover shook again. Mason turned and saw one of the superheavies with its massive gun trained on the sky, its barrel glowing from the heat of the previous shot.

"How long can those tanks keep firing?" Armitage asked.

"Indefinitely." Gottlieb pointed at the superheavy. "See those hoses sprouting from the back? They're pumping coolant into Pluto's crust. They're basically using the whole planet as a giant heat sink."

"Won't that cause the ice to melt?" Armitage asked.

"There's too much ice," Gottlieb said. "If the engineers did the job right, the heat from each shot will be dissipated across several cubic kilometers of ice. Just look at the piles of dug-up ice surrounding the base. Where do you think they came from?"

"Of course, if those tanks move, then they lose their cooling advantage," Mason said.

"Yes, sir," Gottlieb said. "They're basically gun turrets now."

There was a flash of another Pele unleashing her fury against the Cendies in space, followed seconds later by a gentler shaking that Mason could barely feel through the suspension of the rover.

They rolled into the flight line, each landing pad surrounded by mounds of dug-up ice. The rover came to a stop right where Mason's fighter had landed. Getting out, he bounded toward his fighter, jumping up to the cockpit in a single bound.

He climbed in and started the boot-up process while buckling himself in. With the reactors shut down, he needed external power to get the reactors up to operating temperatures. All the while, more tremors disturbed his fighter. He hoped the Peles were finding their marks.

"Osiris Leader powered and ready for takeoff," Mason said.

"Roger, Osiris Leader. Take off and enter the holding pattern at one thousand meters," instructed the air traffic control officer.

"Understood," Mason said. With the low gravity, he didn't need to use the main landing engines. Just a gentle puff from the maneuvering thrusters was enough to lift off from the landing pad.

The assigned holding pattern was a circle over one of the nearby telescopes, outside the firing arcs of the Peles and torpedo batteries. Once Mason had reached his assigned altitude, he put his fighter into a lazy circle, letting the low thrust of his longburn drives maintain his relative position.

The rest of the Osiris Squadron lifted off soon after, forming up with him in the circle.

"Osiris Leader, early warning stations are detecting bandits inbound from directly east of New Lowell," said the ground control officer.

"Roger that, vectoring to engage," Mason said. "Silverback, Hardball—take holding positions around New Lowell. I'll take my flight to investigate the contact."

"Roger that, Hauler," Dominic said.

"Get 'em, Hauler," Sabal said.

Mason turned to the east, putting his nose toward Charon as it floated just above the horizon, and accelerated. He only used ten percent of his fighter's thrust to accelerate up to speed, as full power would put him on an elliptical orbit far above the protection afforded by Pluto's terrain and the defenses around New Lowell.

The data link from the early warning stations showed intermittent contacts, likely Outriders flying low and using the rugged terrain east of the Sputnik Planitia to mask their approach.

As Mason approached, stations started going dark.

"They're going after the early warning sensors," Mason said.

"Guess we know where they intend to attack from," Armitage said.

"Stay slow and hug the terrain. We might have to double back to New Lowell in a hurry," Mason said.

One by one, stations went dark, and Mason started to see a pattern.

"Follow my lead," he said as he maneuvered his fighter between the mountains of water ice.

"What's the plan, Hauler?" Armitage asked.

"Ambush. We'll hit them when they attack the next station," Mason said.

Though the speed was relatively slow for Mason, with water-ice mountains looming kilometers above him on each side, the sensation of speed was intimidating. He kept his focus on the gaps between them, intent on not blundering into the side of an ice mountain.

As he made a turn, the early warning station came into view. It was an automated sensor tower placed on the summit of one of the taller mountains to scan the horizon for threats. It didn't show any hostiles, but Mason was certain that just meant the enemy was hiding below the line of sight of the tower.

"I'll take the southern flank. Marbles, go north," Mason said.

"Roger," Armitage said.

Mason made his turn around the mountain's southern edge, threading between it and one of its neighbors, one eye on his scopes and the other on the data link from the sensor station.

On his topographical map, he saw a valley that led right up to the sensor tower. If he was attacking a tower using the terrain to mask his approach, that would be the valley he would use.

Mason followed the bend of the mountain, intent on hovering just around the corner, ready to take the Cendies by surprise.

As he made the bend, however, he encountered four Outriders on fast approach.

"Shit!" Mason reflexively fired his cannon, spewing a stream of projectiles that missed his target and traced a line of impacts against the ice mountain beyond.

Then the Cendies zipped past.

Mason wrenched his fighter around, maneuvering thrusters roaring as they fought to keep his Lightning from slamming into the mountain.

The four Cendies broke into two pairs. One pair turned to engage Mason while the other maintained its approach toward the sensor tower.

"Skids, loft interceptors after the runners," Mason ordered.

"Roger. Interceptors away," she said. Four Javelins dropped from her Lightning in rapid succession and rocketed up over the lip of the canyon.

Mason launched four interceptors of his own, two each against the Outriders. The tight confines of the canyon were not ideal environments for interceptors, and both Outriders evaded them. They impacted against the walls of the valley.

Gottlieb's interceptors apexed their arcing trajectory and dove onto the Cendies that were making their run on the sensor tower. One of the Cendies released its missiles before the plunging interceptors smashed into it and smeared its wreckage across the side of the mountain. The other Outrider managed to evade Gottlieb's missiles.

The sensor tower disappeared from the data link as the Cendy missile reached it, but defending it wasn't the priority. Killing the Outriders was.

The Cendy fighters split to try to flank Mason and Gottlieb.

"I got the leader—you deal with their wingmate," Mason said.

The Cendy fighter blossomed with maneuvering thruster exhaust as it fought to bring its guns around. Mason did the same, resulting in both craft spiraling around each other within the confines of the valley.

It quickly became clear that the Outrider had the advantage in a circular turning fight, its lighter weight giving it the edge. But Mason couldn't break off without giving the Cendy a missile shot.

Then he realized he was surrounded by mountains of water ice, and he was flying a machine with two longburn drives.

Mason reversed his turn and then pointed his nose straight up toward space. Just as the Outrider came around to lay its sights on him, Mason ignited his longburn drives at full power.

Nearly twenty gs slammed into Mason as he launched out of the canyon, leaving a cloud of dust and steam behind as the hot exhaust from his drives instantly turned several tons of ice into vapor. He cut his drives and flipped over barely a second later, firing his drives again to break his momentum.

Below, the Cendy fighter was still low and turning, not yet realizing Mason was now above it. Mason launched an interceptor, and it took less than a second for the missile to streak from above and strike the Outrider through its center.

Still loaded with most of its fuel, the interceptor exploded on impact, blasting the Outrider and scattering the pieces across the valley.

Then an alarm warned Mason that a powerful radar had just locked onto his fighter. The sensor AI marked the source of the radar, and Mason turned his attention to it. "Belts and zones!" he called out as the sensor AI identified the contact.

Or contacts, more precisely. Three large contacts. Two Fusiliers and one Katyusha, moving at extremely low altitudes, barely cleared the peaks of the mountains.

"New Lowell Control, we have a big problem," Mason said, relaying his data back to New Lowell.

"Stand by, Osiris Leader," New Lowell said.

Missile alarms sounded as the Katyusha launched interceptors.

"Not likely," Mason said. "Osiris Leader, defensive!"

He dived for the floor of the valley, accelerating as fast as he dared. "Skids, stay low!" he shouted.

Gottlieb had finished off her opponent and was climbing to join Mason when he detected the warships. "Roger that," she said as she reversed her climb to follow Mason into his dive.

"Now we know why they're going after the sensor towers," Mason said.

"Those Fusiliers are going to make short work of our base if they get in firing range," Gottlieb warned.

"One problem at a time," Mason said. "Let's find Marbles and form up with the rest of the squadron."

Armitage and her wingmate were flying around the side of the mountain after presumably not encountering any enemy fighters on their leg. "So, we're going back to base, right?" Armitage asked. "Because we're not equipped for taking on big ships."

"We're not returning to base," Mason said. "We stay on station until we know how General Asif intends to defend against the Cendy starships."

Mason kept his pilots low to the surface, flying between mountain peaks, staying out of the line of sight of the Cendy starships, particularly the Katyusha and her missiles.

Dominic's, Sabal's, and Sawyer's flights were waiting for them just where the mountains turned into the flat expanse of the Sputnik Planitia, staying below a thousand meters altitude.

And approaching from the direction of New Lowell were several carryalls skimming over the ice, each bearing a Pele superheavy.

"So, what are the tanks for, Silverback?" Mason asked.

"General Asif's got a plan for them," Dominic said. "They're going to position themselves between the mountains and strike the Cendies from below when they fly over 'em. Our job is to keep the Cendy Outriders from finding them."

"What about the bombers?" Mason asked.

"She's keeping the Conquerors in reserve. I guess she thinks with the Cendies so low, they'll be vulnerable to attack from the surface," Dominic said.

Pele superheavies were designed to fire on starships but from hundreds or even thousands of kilometers away, not from a few thousand meters, practically in the shadow of the ships they were engaging.

"That Katyusha's going to complicate matters," Mason said.

"General Asif's going to engage it with New Lowell's torpedo batteries," Dominic told him. "That should keep the Katyusha's interceptors occupied."

"I hope so. Because we'll be next on the priority list."

The carryalls flew low over the surface, their thrusters throwing up plumes of vapor and dust behind them. When they reached their drop zone, they came to an abrupt stop and released the Peles. The superheavy tanks used their own thrusters to slow their descent and come to a landing at the foot of the mountains.

Mason placed his fighters into a patrolling screen low over the mountains to the west of where the Peles had landed.

The tanks started rolling up the shallower mountains, placing themselves on either side of a valley that opened onto the Sputnik Planitia, right along the projected path of the Cendy warships. Troopers started spilling out of the Peles, setting up defensive positions around the tanks, some bearing large shoulder launchers.

The idea of the infantry engaging starships seemed ludicrous to Mason, but that was the situation unfolding before him.

Drones launched from the Peles gave a high overview of the battlefield, showing the approaching Cendy warships and the Outriders moving ahead of them.

"All right—let's keep the Cendies blind," Mason said. He assigned targets and moved to engage, keeping below the line of sight of the Katyusha.

This time, he was prepared to engage the Cendies in extremely close quarters. As he rounded the bend of a mountain, four Cendy fighters appeared in front of him.

He snapped his pipper over the first one and fired his cannon. The projectiles shot through the Outrider and impacted the ice mountain beyond it, turning the Outrider into a wreck that crashed into the mountainside. The other pilots of his flight lashed out with their guns, taking down the unprepared Outriders in rapid succession. On the data link, the sole remaining Cendy fighter doubled back, afraid of more engagements with Lightnings in the tight confines of the mountains.

The warships continued their approach toward New Lowell, which would take them directly over the Peles.

The torpedoes launched from New Lowell's torpedo batteries flew straight up for several kilometers before turning and burning directly for the Cendy warships. The Katyusha fired a barrage of interceptors at the torpedoes as they entered range while still over the smooth planes of the Sputnik Planitia.

Interceptors vaporized the torpedoes above, and the resulting debris fell to the ice in a hard rain of shattered metal. None of the torpedoes got through, but they were keeping the Katyusha occupied as they continued to approach, seemingly unaware of the Peles waiting in ambush.

Over the data link, the thermal imagers of the surveillance drones showed the temperatures of the Fusiliers spiking as they charged up their main guns. They were going to fire their kinetic kill vehicle on New Lowell as soon as they had line of sight. Mason didn't know what a KKV fired at an oblique angle would do to the base built around New Lowell, but he doubted the results would be pleasant.

Peles dug into either side of the valley, the low gravity allowing the massive vehicles to climb the steep slopes. Then they waited as the Cendy warships drifted toward them.

Held aloft by their maneuvering thrusters, the three massive warships dipped into the valley, throwing steam up and dust from the surface, making it look like they were riding clouds.

Mason flew down the other side of the mountain, keeping the mountains of water ice between his fighter and the warships. He didn't have the weapons needed for dealing with warships at close range.

The Peles waited until all three Cendy warships were fully inside the valley. The Cendies showed no signs of being aware of the superheavy tanks waiting for them.

Then the Peles fired.

The first volley from the main guns of the Peles slammed into the sides of the Katyusha. With the range so close, their shots could be precisely aimed, and the penetrators fired from the Pele's main guns punched through the missile batteries that covered the sides of the warship.

The hits caused a chain reaction of missiles to explode in their tubes, blasting large holes in the sides of the Katyusha.

The Fusiliers opened fire with their point-defense guns, peppering the Peles with rapid-fire projectiles. The Peles quickly turned their attention to the Fusiliers and started punching holes through the sides of their hulls.

All Mason could do was watch and marvel as superheavy tanks and warships traded blows at extremely close range.

As point defenses lashed out, the Peles started knocking out turrets with precise shots, gradually rendering the Fusiliers defenseless.

More precise fire from the Peles struck the longburn drives of all three Cendy warships. The powerful guns of the Peles were more than capable of penetrating the thin armor along the flanks of the Cendy warships.

Explosions erupted from the rear of each Cendy warship as damaged containment rings released their energy, and all three starships soon started bleeding fuel. Outriders made runs on the Peles only to leave themselves vulnerable to Mason's fighters. Mason himself climbed over the ridge of the mountain and engaged with the interceptors. The interceptors and guns cut the Outriders down, forcing them away as the Peles continued to savage the two Fusiliers and one Katyusha.

The Katyusha was the first to fall. As it lost the ability to keep itself aloft, it drifted down to the valley floor. Though slow, the million-ton Katyusha had tremendous momentum as it crashed into the valley floor, cutting a long trench into the ice.

The Fusiliers continued to push toward New Lowell, determined to bring their main guns to bear no matter the cost. But while the Cendies were determined to press their attack, the crews of the Peles were just as determined to bring them down, continuing to pour fire into the flanks of the Cendy warships, concentrating their fire along the spinal guns.

Gas and debris poured out the sides of the ships as they pressed their attack, but the damage soon started to overtake them. Thrusters died and the main guns ceased charging as they drifted out of the valley and over the flat ice of the Sputnik Planitia.

Both Cendy warships crashed into the ground at sharp angles, carving deep ruts into the nitrogen ice and throwing dust and gas high into the sky.

"All forces, retreat to a safe distance. Nuclear weapons incoming," came an announcement over the command channel. "General Asif's not screwing around. All fighters—put a mountain between you and those warships."

The troopers gathered into the Peles before the superheavies started rolling, moving to shelter behind mountains. A dozen torpedoes were launched from New Lowell and arched toward the helpless Cendy warships.

Flying quickly out of the blast radius, Mason brought his fighter to a hover a few hundred meters above the surface of the Sputnik Planitia and waited for the fireworks to start.

The torpedoes detonated simultaneously several kilometers above the surface, their directional warheads blasting straight down on the wrecks of the Cendy warships. Mason's sensors darkened to protect him from the flash of high-energy radiation. When they recovered, all that was left were shallow craters where the warships used to be, surrounded by clouds of vaporized ice that almost instantly refroze and fell to the ground as snow.

"Osiris Squadron, maintain overwatch for the Peles as they return to base."

"Understood, New Lowell," Mason said. "We'll keep them safe."

"Well, that's not something you see every day," Dominic remarked.

CHAPTER 16

Osiris Squadron was relieved by the Wildcards when the carryalls arrived to transport the Peles back to New Lowell.

Mason bid the tank crews goodbye before flying off to New Lowell. The Cendy forces had remained around Charon during that time, no doubt considering their next move after their attempt to sneak warships into firing range of New Lowell had failed.

The Peles had proved their worth, which meant that they were now a priority target for the Cendies.

Night had fallen over New Lowell by the time Osiris Squadron approached for landing, the base illuminated by pools of light against the inky black darkness of the outer Solar System. Mason settled his Lightning down on the same protected landing pad he had taken off from. By the time he had depressurized and opened the cockpit, ground crew were already attaching fuel lines and power cables to his fighter as they readied his strikecraft for the next fight.

Rovers waited to pick up Mason and his pilots and bring them back to New Lowell's surface hub.

Inside, Mason could pull off his helmet and enjoy the cool, fresh air. He already missed the spin gravity of New Lowell's habitat cylinder, but there was no chance of returning while the Cendies were in Pluto's orbit. Leave was indefinitely suspended.

It didn't take long for a summons to General Asif's headquarters to appear on Mason's HUD.

"Guess figuring out our quarters will be your job, Silverback," Mason said. "General Asif wants to see me."

"I'll make sure we get something nice," Dominic said.

It was a brisk skip toward headquarters. The once sterile and empty surface station now bustled with the activity of spacers and troopers milling about, carrying out the more mundane activities of war.

All around, Mason found neatly grouped blocks of tents centered on public restrooms or mobile toilets, along with the odd canteen serving hot food in covered dishes. The smell of hot food tempted Mason to make a detour and help himself, but he was not one to make generals wait.

He arrived at headquarters, where General Asif and her staff were continuing to work around the holotank projecting the Sputnik Planitia. Three icons representing the crash sites of the Cendy warships glowed along the western edge.

General Asif looked at Mason. "Squadron Leader Grey, good work spotting the Cendy attack. It gave me just enough time to reposition the Peles into an ambush position."

"It was impressive watching the Peles get to work, General," Mason said.

"Ground vehicles can punch well above their weight under the right circumstances, but I'm afraid that trick is only going to work once," General Asif said. "The Cendies aren't going to try something like that again."

"What makes you so sure?" Mason asked.

"Because they know we'll be looking out for it," General Asif said. "Flying starships so low to the ground? That only works if your enemy assumes you wouldn't be reckless enough to do that. Something that I'm afraid I am guilty of."

Mason nodded. "The Cendies aren't bound by our conventions, General. They've come up with their own way of fighting wars."

"Which is all the more infuriating. I spent decades learning how to fight other humans, especially the League. A lot of what I know is no longer applicable," General Asif said. "Speaking of things that we didn't expect, the Cendies setting up shop around Charon rather than directly challenging New Lowell has complicated my defense plans."

"In what way, General?" Mason asked.

"While the Cendies occupy Charon, our staging ground on Pluto's surface won't be available for the arrival of the convoy. And the longer they're there, the more dug in they'll get."

"How do you propose we dig them out?"

"We can't," General Asif admitted. "With our ships in orbit either destroyed or driven off, the only power projection I have is in the form of the strikecraft here on Pluto. All the rest of my forces are geared toward repelling a direct assault."

"So we need to wait until *Independence* returns," Mason said.

"No, we need to prepare for *Independence*'s return, whenever that might be, which means disrupting the Cendies as much as we can, preventing them from creating an effective foothold on Charon. If they just sit there, Pluto is effectively neutralized as a staging ground."

"What do you need Osiris Squadron to do, General?"

"I don't know, Squadron Leader. What can you do? I've never had a special operations fighter squadron at my disposal before."

Mason scratched his chin as he thought about it. On the surface, there wasn't much that was different about Osiris Squadron from other fighter squadrons. Just a bit larger, with more experience in ground attack and higher risk tolerance.

"If we can reach Charon, we can probably fly close to the surface and reach the Cendy base to deliver a nuke or two to keep them from digging in," he finally said. "But we'd have to make the trip without getting annihilated by the enemy."

"That's the tricky part," General Asif acknowledged. "Right now, the Cendies have pretty much locked down any space that's not directly over New Lowell."

Mason pinched the bridge of his nose. "I'll need time to figure out what our options are, General."

General Asif nodded. "You've just come back from a mission, I understand. After you get some rest, I'll want you to give me some preliminary plans. My staff will furnish whatever intelligence you need."

"Thank you, General," Mason said.

"No, thank you, Squadron Leader. If we hadn't stopped those warships in time, we wouldn't be having this conversation."

"Be a shame, too. I was just starting to like this place."

"I'll leave you to your free time, Squadron Leader."

Mason saluted General Asif and departed headquarters.

A group of empty tents had been laid out for Mason's pilots, each one a basic shelter held to the deck with adhesive strips. Inside each was a simple mesh sleeping cot. Mason slid out of his hardsuit and slowly collapsed into his cot in the low gravity. He quickly fell asleep.

∽

Things were quiet the following day. The Cendies, apparently still reeling from the loss of three warships, had elected to keep their distance from New Lowell. That suited Mason—his workflow always suffered if he had to be ready to jump into the cockpit at a moment's notice.

General Asif kept a steady stream of drones flying out toward Charon, each capturing a glimpse of Cendy operations before being detected and destroyed. The intelligence they gathered revealed that the Cendies were building a base on the Pluto-facing side of Charon. Three Turtleback landing ships on the surface were disembarking supplies for the construction effort.

If that base became operational, Cendy control over Pluto would become exponentially harder to pry away, leaving Federal forces on Pluto trapped, unable to assist in protecting the convoy. They had to strike the base—and soon. But with the Cendy fleet orbiting Charon ready to pounce on any forces rising from Pluto, any attack was bound to result in a lot of dead pilots and nothing to show for it.

Outside the privacy screen of his makeshift quarters, voices and footfalls echoed through the large enclosed space of New Lowell's surface station. Thousands of spacers milled about, conducting the business of war, which for most of them involved trying to stay busy until the next fight.

"Dammit," Mason swore, standing up from his cot and walking out of his quarters. He saw Sabal, Tarkovsky, Dash, and Pohl sitting around a board game, trying to relax while waiting for the next mission. He left them to their game and walked toward the canteen setup inside the surface station food courts, passing the sculpture of Pluto and its moons that dominated the central concourse.

Among the gathering of anonymous troopers and spacers, Mason spotted familiar faces—Dominic, Gottlieb, and Armitage—at one of the tables in the center of the food court. They were enjoying meals of freshly cooked low-gravity food. Armitage was the first to see Mason approaching. She pulled the plastic spoon out of her mouth and called, "Hauler, you want to join us?"

Mason held up his coffee packet. "Just here for a refill. What are you all up to?"

Dominic shrugged. "Waiting, just like everyone else. How about you? Come up with a brilliant plan yet to stick it to the Cendies?"

"Not yet—need more coffee first."

"I need a refill too," Dominic said, standing up from the table and bouncing into the air slightly in the low gravity.

They joined the line for the coffee dispenser, where spacers lined up with practiced precision, waiting their turn.

"You know, Hauler, it isn't your fault if you can't think of something. Maybe there is no safe way to get to Charon," Dominic said.

"You're not confident that I can think of something?"

"I'm saying you shouldn't come up with something extremely risky just to satisfy General Asif."

"If we don't keep the Cendies from finishing that base on Charon, we can't help the convoy reach Earth. If that happens …"

"… the war's likely lost, I know," Dominic finished. "So, no pressure."

"Nope, none," Mason said. "Got any ideas of your own?"

"Oh, that's your job," Dominic said. "But I do have advice."

"Shoot."

"Back in my civilian career, whenever I was presented with a problem that I could not immediately solve, I found it helpful to step back and consider the problem in a larger context," Dominic said. "To see solutions that might not be immediately evident under the microscope."

"Hrmm," Mason said. "I'm not sure how that would help."

"It's better than banging your head against a wall until you make mushy noises," Dominic said.

Mason departed with his coffee, retracing his path back to his quarters. As he reached the sculpture depicting Pluto and its moons, he came to a stop.

In the time he had been on Pluto, he had not paid much attention to the sculpture. He now noted that it depicted Pluto and Charon balanced on the barycenter where both bodies orbited, while further out, Pluto's smaller moons—Styx, Nix, Kerberos, and Hydra—moved around them in almost perfectly circular orbits. They were so tiny compared to their larger siblings that their existence was easy to overlook. These relatively small moons hung far above the dominant objects in the system, watching them circle each other below.

"Oh," Mason said as a thought hit him. He summoned a display on his HUD showing the current position of Pluto's moons. Styx, the next closest of Pluto's moons, was almost directly above the anti-Charon side of Pluto and almost directly above New Lowell.

The first tendrils of a plan started to worm their way into Mason's mind.

He got into motion, startling an enlisted spacer he almost ran into. "Sorry," he said without giving the spacer a second thought.

He skipped past Sabal and the three other pilots still playing the board game and burst through the flap of his privacy screen, sending the flaps high over his head in the low gravity.

He sat back down in his seat and started making trajectories.

Styx orbited 42,656 kilometers from the barycenter between Pluto and Charon. The barycenter was 900 kilometers above the surface of Pluto, plus Pluto's almost 2,400 kilometers diameter. That put New Lowell 3,300 kilometers closer to Styx than the barycenter, which meant Nix would pass less than 40,000 kilometers over New Lowell at the closest approach. Not a great distance in space terms, but enough that it might make a difference based on how much a strikecraft moving toward Styx would have to burn.

"Belts and zones!" Mason muttered under his breath. He had forgotten how compact Pluto's system was. A life around Jupiter had not prepared him well for smaller scales. Some rough math put a full 20 g burn at fifteen minutes constant acceleration, including the flip-over for braking burn. More than enough time for a Lightning to reach Styx before it became visible from the ships orbiting Charon.

To the surprise of his pilots, Mason burst from his tent and marched to General Asif's headquarters. His plan was undercooked, but he thought it could work to get a Federal strike down to Charon and hit the base before the Cendies got it operational.

He breezed past the guards at headquarters and found General Asif speaking with one of her subordinates. When she glanced Mason's way, she dismissed the subordinate and waved him over.

"What do you have for me, Squadron Leader?"

"I have an idea."

"Let's hear it."

Mason pointed to the holotank. "May I?"

"As you please, Squadron Leader."

Mason walked over to the holotank, which was displaying Pluto, Charon, and enemy contacts in orbit off Charon. Manipulating the holotanks, Mason zoomed out until it displayed the entire Pluto system.

Mason pointed to Styx. "In the next thirty hours, Styx is going to pass over New Lowell, or to put it another way, we're going to pass under it. What I'm proposing is for my squadron to fly up to Styx under maximum acceleration and land on the moon while it's concealed from Charon by Pluto."

"Go on," General Asif prompted.

"So, roughly three days later, Pluto and Charon will swap places relative to Styx, giving my fighters a straight shot down to Charon's anti-Pluto side. Flying low over Charon's surface, we can hit the Cendy base while avoiding most of their defenses."

General Asif stared at Mason with a thoughtful expression, rubbing her chin for a moment. "Using the orbital mechanics of the Pluto system to conceal your movements is clever. But can your pilots handle several days in the cockpit like that?"

"We've trained for longer, General, and we'll be spending most of it loitering in a crater on Styx," Mason told her.

"It's a start. We'll need to dig up some detailed topographical knowledge of Styx to get a better idea of where to hide your fighters. And we'll need to make sure there aren't any Cendy ships poking their heads over the horizon."

"And that's just getting to Styx, sir," Mason continued. "We're going to need a distraction to pull away the Cendies' attention from an attack on the anti-Pluto side of Charon."

"That's something I think we can accomplish with the remaining strikecraft and torpedoes we have on the base," General Asif said. "My staff and I will plan out the diversion. You need to study up on the topography of Styx and Charon to find the best place to hide on the former and the best attack path to follow on the latter."

"It's a good thing we happen to be right on top of a city full of scientists with in-depth knowledge of Pluto and its moons," Mason said.

"Most of the scientists down there are specialized in studying objects much further away than Pluto's moons, but I see the wisdom in speaking with the locals," General Asif said. "Would you like my people to make inquiries?"

"I can do that myself, General," Mason said. "I think I know who to ask."

"Then we have the start of a plan, Squadron Leader," General Asif said. "Get to work. I want Osiris Squadron ready to launch as soon as Styx is above us."

"Yes, General."

CHAPTER 17

"Ah, Squadron Leader, I'm glad you are well," Doctor Wynn said over the video call. "How can I be of service?"

"I need the most detailed topographical knowledge on Styx and Charon currently available, and you were the first person I thought to call," Mason said.

"Do the Space Forces not already have that data, Squadron Leader?"

"Data's not the problem, Doctor. Knowledge is. New Lowell must have people who have actually been to Styx and Charon."

"You're speaking to one of them," Doctor Wynn said. "Back in my graduate days, I surveyed Styx for locations of possible telescopes."

"What did you find?"

"That there's nothing about Styx that would make it a better location for observatories than Pluto's surface," Doctor Wynn said. "Really, it's just a mountain of water ice—something Pluto has plenty of on the surface. But it does have a very rough surface. Lots of craters and deep crevasses. I'll send you the coordinates."

"Thanks, Doctor," Mason said. "And what about Charon?"

"I'm afraid there's nothing I can add that's not readily available."

"That'll have to do, I guess," Mason said. "Thank you, Doctor."

"I'm going to refrain from asking what exactly you're planning, but I'm certain it will be dangerous, so good luck, Squadron Leader."

"Thanks, Doctor," Mason said, then closed the connection.

Minutes later, Mason got the coordinates from Doctor Wynn. Each set of coordinates marked a particularly deep crater or crevasse. Mason looked over them all individually, eliminating those that were too small or exposed until he had his list of candidates. There was no single location that would safely hide all sixteen Lightnings of the Osiris Squadron. But there were more than enough to hide a four-ship flight in each.

There was the problem that each flight would be cut off from communicating with each other, but it was an easy tradeoff for finding good hiding spots for his pilots.

The next issue was how to hit the base.

The Cendies were building their base on the moon's northern hemisphere, just south of the dark patch of the Mordor Macula. The most direct route from Styx on the closest approach would be to fly low over Charon's north pole, staying low enough to keep out of the line of sight of the base's defenses. Hopefully whatever diversion General Asif's people cooked up would draw away any Cendy forces in orbit.

After a few more hours, Mason had enough of a plan to summon his pilots for a briefing. He appropriated one of the lounges meant for travelers as an improvised briefing room.

"What do you have for us, Hauler?" Sabal asked.

"General Asif's asked me to come up with a mission for hitting the base the Cendies are building on Charon, and this is the fruit of my labors," Mason said, uploading the mission data.

"We'll be launching for Styx in twenty-seven hours, where we'll execute a hard burn and turnover. Once we reach Styx, each flight will hide in a location I've assigned and wait approximately three days for Charon's orbit to bring it directly under Styx. Once Charon's below Styx, we'll launch. At the same time, General Asif will launch a diversionary attack from New Lowell. That should draw away most of the fighters and warships guarding Charon and give us a chance to strike the base from behind.

"I've already doled out the roles for each flight. First and Second Flights will be our strike packages, carrying nukes for dealing with the base. Third and Fourth flights will be our escorts."

"Why do you and Silverback get to be the ones carrying nukes?" Sabal asked.

"I'll make sure you get a turn next time, Hardball," Mason said. There was a chorus of chuckles from the assembled pilots.

"In the meantime, ensure your fighters are ready and you are ready. That means checkups with the flight surgeons," Mason said. "There will be a lot of sitting and waiting in this mission, so I don't want to lose anyone to malfunctions or medical issues if I can avoid it."

∽

The makeshift clinic was in an area off the main concourse sectioned off by curtains. Inside was a fully equipped and staffed field hospital.

A physician's assistant was waiting for him—a thick-limbed, square-jawed woman in a white jumpsuit. "Please lie down on the table, Squadron Leader, and I'll get the diagnostics started presently," the PA said.

"Thank, Lieutenant," Mason said, lying down.

Moments later, the scanner arm started moving down the bed, starting with his head and moving down toward his feet, scanning the network of cyberware implanted in his body early in his flight career. Sensors in Mason's bio-monitoring system detected the blast of radiation coming from the scanner and helpfully informed him of the dose he was taking.

When the scan was complete, the PA walked up. "Looks like most of your cybernetics is in good shape, but I'm getting error codes from your cardio regulator."

"I don't see any issues on my internal diagnostics," Mason said.

"Those aren't as sensitive as the scanner," the PA pointed out. "Your internal diagnostics are good at picking up implants that are about to fail. The scanner will pick things up with more warning."

"What's the solution?" Mason asked.

"Lie back and let the autodoc replace it," the PA told him. "Open the top of your jumpsuit and take off any undershirt."

"I'm going to be pulling twenty gs in about a day, Lieutenant. Is surgery such a good idea?"

"Better idea than a faulty cardio regulator, Squadron Leader. It's part of the system that keeps you from stroking out when you're pulling hard gs."

"Guess you have a point," Mason said as he unzipped his jumpsuit and draped the top around his waist, then pulled his T-shirt off and let it float down to the floor.

The PA caught the shirt and hung it over the back of a chair. "Now just lie back and stay still." Mason did so, lying back and forcing himself to relax.

Thin arms from the autodoc unfolded from above and reached down. One sprayed down Mason's chest with an antiseptic, while another with a needle injected a local anesthetic.

Cold numbness spread across his chest just over his heart while the arms reached up and exchanged instruments—one arm with a padded ring and the other with another, larger needle. The autodoc pressed the ring over where his cardio regulator implant was located while the other arm inserted the needle. Mason felt nothing but a slight pressure against his chest. He kept his breaths shallow and regular.

His bio-monitor instantly noted the removal of the cardio regulator implant just as the probe withdrew. It came out holding a blood-covered capsule the size of a small pill in wire-like pincers and deposited the capsule while an identical arm, clean of blood, lined up to install the fresh implant. It went in through the same hole in Mason's chest, and his bio-monitor recognized the installation of a new cardio regulator. Both arms retracted, and the PA walked up, pressing a sterile pad against the tiny hole in Mason's chest to absorb the blood seeping out.

Mason's bio-monitor instantly detected and integrated the new cardio regulator, showing it working normally.

"Looks like the new implant's working," Mason said.

"I can see it on my end too." The PA plucked away the gauze and placed an adhesive bandage over the injection site. "The anesthetic will start wearing off in about twenty minutes. You might feel some aches afterward."

"And when I'm pulling twenty gs?" Mason asked.

"It will more than ache, but it should be manageable," the PA said.

Mason pulled on his shirt and started pushing his arms through the sleeves of his hardsuit. "There anything else I should worry about?"

"You're coming up on some routine firmware updates, but nothing that needs to be dealt with now," the PA said. "Good luck with your mission, sir."

"Thanks," Mason said.

After departing the clinic, he spotted Dominic walking out as well. "What's the verdict?" Mason asked him.

"I'm old but in good shape," Dominic said. "What about you, Hauler?"

Mason tapped his chest. "Needed a new cardio regulator, apparently."

"Ouch," Dominic said. "Sometimes I feel like I'm more a machine than a man with all the bits they need to replace."

"You're not too far off with that analogy," Mason said. "I even have a firmware update in my future."

Dominic chuckled. "Got to make sure your implants know how to talk to each other. Where are you headed next?"

"I've got a meeting with General Asif to see what she and her staff have cooked up to divert the Cendies' attention. You going out to supervise the loading?"

"Loading nuclear weapons is best done under adult supervision," Dominic said.

"Can't think of a better adult for the job," Mason said.

Dominic nodded and headed back toward the billet, presumably to put on his hardsuit, while Mason strode toward headquarters.

General Asif was waiting for him, along with the leaders of *Independence*'s other stranded strikecraft squadrons.

"Good afternoon, Squadron Leader Grey," General Asif greeted him.

"Afternoon, General," Mason said. "I take it you have come up with a diversionary attack?"

"We have," she said. "It's nothing too complicated. The Conquerors will launch an attack against Cendy space assets in conjunction with a mass torpedo launch from the surface."

"That'll get the Cendies' attention all right."

"You said you needed a distraction."

"And you delivered, General," Mason said. "Will this be just a distraction or will you be trying to inflict real damage?"

The bomber squadron leader scoffed. "You think we'd go to all this trouble and not kill something?"

"Fair enough," Mason said. "So, is everything good to go? Because if we don't launch within the next day, we're going to have to wait another three for the next launch window."

"By that time it will be too late," General Asif said. "Everything's good to go on our end, Squadron Leader. Make sure you're on Styx, and I'll make sure you get a distraction three days later."

"That'll do," Mason said. "So, it's just a question of exfiltration."

"Hopefully the fighters from New Lowell will keep any Outriders occupied enough to let you get back to Pluto in one piece," General Asif said. "But our strikecraft will be fully engaged. If you run into any trouble trying to get out of Charon, you're going to be on your own."

"Operating without support's part of the job," Mason said. "I guess now it's just making sure everything's ready."

"I'll leave you to that, Squadron Leader."

"Thank you, General."

Mason departed the briefing and returned to his squadron's billet. Most of the pilots were there when he arrived.

"What's the word, Hauler?" Sabal asked.

"Nothing left but to make sure we're ready for go-time," Mason said. "Silverback still outside?"

Sabal nodded. "Yeah. He's been wrangling technicians to make sure all our fighters are ready. Probably won't be back for a couple of hours."

"Well, there's just enough time left for me to get eight hours of sleep and still have time to troubleshoot any problems that arise before launch," Mason said. "There anything that needs my attention before then?"

Sabal shook her head. "I think we're all about to do the same, Hauler. Get your beauty sleep."

"I'll get to it," Mason said.

Pushing through the flap of his tent, Mason sat down on his cot and fished out a bottle of downers from one of his jumpsuit's pockets, popped a pill, and washed it down with water. Then he pulled his jumpsuit off. Down to his T-shirt and boxers, he lay down on his cot to wait for the downers to take effect.

As he felt the first cold fingers of drowsiness starting to caress his brain, Mason started thinking about the things that could go wrong. On the surface, the plan was simple—just get up to Styx and wait for Charon to swing around. But things could change a lot while his squadron was isolated and radio silent. The Cendies could invade New Lowell, and he and his pilots would be unaware.

Those worries faded away as drug-assisted sleep washed over him.

CHAPTER 18

The ground buzzed with activity as Mason's rover rolled onto the flight line. It seemed all Federal personnel on Pluto were there to see Osiris Squadron off on its flight to Styx.

Mason looked up. Styx was the brightest star in Pluto's night sky, forty thousand kilometers overhead.

The rover gradually slowed to a stop near Mason's fighter, and he carefully slid out of his seat to keep from bouncing off the ground in the low gravity.

"See you in the air," Armitage called over her shoulder as she walked in the other direction toward her fighter. Mason waved to her and proceeded to his Lightning.

The cockpit was already open as Mason approached. In the low gravity, he climbed up the retractable ladder, using just his hands and letting his legs dangle below him. At the top of the ladder, he used his arms to launch himself up and let Pluto's low gravity pull his feet down onto the wing's leading edge. When he climbed into his open cockpit, the displays showed everything was already powered up. The fighter was just waiting for a pilot.

Mason initiated his brainset connection while buckling himself in, sensor data flooding into his awareness as the Lightning's sensors became his eyes, making the cockpit transparent and letting him look at the smooth ground below him.

He closed the cockpit with a command through his brainset.

As the canopy closed and the cockpit started to fill with inert gas, Mason went through his preflight checklist, making sure everything was in order, especially the four shortburn torpedoes with their nuclear warheads inside the weapons bay. Four interceptors shared the weapons bay with the torpedoes, and two Stiletto pods were mounted on each wing, one on top and one on the bottom.

It appeared that his fighter was in good working order and ready for the flight to Styx and, hopefully, the attack on Charon three days after.

"Osiris Leader, New Lowell Control—request liftoff clearance," Mason said.

"New Lowell Control, Osiris Leader—request granted. You may begin liftoff."

"Roger," Mason said, firing the ventral thrusters.

Vapor and dust crashed into the walls surrounding the launchpad as his fighter slowly ascended straight up. Other fighters from Osiris Squadron also took off from their launchpads, using a fraction of the power of their maneuvering thrusters to overpower Pluto's gravity.

Once he was a few hundred meters above the surface, Mason transitioned to horizontal flight, still using low-power maneuvering thrusters. The longburn drives were too powerful to use so close to New Lowell, especially with personnel in pressure suits hopping around.

Mason continued to gain altitude, slowly opening the distance from New Lowell, following a preplanned route over the flat expanse of the Sputnik Planitia, away from any telescopes or other delicate infrastructure that dotted the surface. Over the empty expanse of ice, he plotted his course, almost straight up, toward Styx. The little moon was just a dot on the scope.

"New Lowell, Osiris Leader—we're over the designated departure zone, and our spacing is good. Request final clearance for main drive ignition," Mason said.

"Osiris Leader, you're clear for ignition. You may begin at your discretion. Good luck."

"Thanks, New Lowell Control," Mason said. "Osiris Squadron, lock approach vectors to Styx and proceed directly to assigned landing sites."

Mason's pilots acknowledged, and with that, there was nothing left but to execute his orders. He locked onto his chosen landing site and pitched his nose up, centering the moon on his HUD.

Then he ignited his longburn drives. Twin plumes of exhaust spewed out the back of his fighter, vaporizing the nitrogen ice below. The twin exhaust plumes of fifteen additional Lightnings joined his, adding to the cloud of vapor obscuring the ground as it fell away.

As he gained altitude, Mason started adding more power, increasing his acceleration and the consequent g forces on his body. His weight multiplied by two, then three, then four times and continued to build up, the gel layer of his hardsuit cushioning the pressure. Meanwhile, his bio-monitor showed his vitals and implants were normal, including his new cardio regulator.

At full military power, Mason was pulling fifteen gs. And that wasn't the end of it. He disengaged the safeties and pushed the throttles further into emergency power, not stopping until he was crushed under twenty times his own weight.

Mason's augmentations allowed him to sustain ten gs indefinitely, fifteen gs for hours, and twenty gs for mere minutes. His ribcage felt like it was made of depleted uranium, far too heavy for normal in-and-out breathing.

Sharp inhale, hold, sharp exhale, repeat.

Snatching and holding each precious breath and getting just barely enough oxygen to maintain full consciousness, his chest muscles burned, and each inhalation felt like he would tear his diaphragm.

Pluto fell away like it had been thrown, while tiny Styx remained a point of light on the HUD. Mason gained a kilometer a second of velocity every five seconds, dumping fusion fuel into the longburn drives.

Sharp inhale, hold, sharp exhale, repeat.

Mason glanced at his fighter's status displays. The digital gauges showed everything pushed to the limit but holding. Twenty gs was hard on the fighter, especially on the joints and weapon mounts. If something broke free, even the near-instant reaction time of the flight AI wouldn't be able to shut down the longburn drives quickly enough to prevent catastrophic damage. Twenty gs was well in the range where a Lightning's own weight could cause the engines to rip off the wings, tearing the fighter apart like a sheet of paper.

But all the sensors indicated everything was holding. Both Lightning and pilot. Hopefully that would hold true for the whole flight.

Five minutes into his flight, just as the turnover time dipped below two and a half minutes, an alarm sounded and a red icon flashed on his HUD. But it wasn't an alert for a problem with his body or fighter but with one of his pilots.

Mason contacted Marbles: <*Marbles, your bio-monitor's flashing alerts at me. What's happening?*>

<*Nothing I won't survive, Hauler. Just a leaky artery. Bio's already working on it.*>

<*Marbles, cut your drives now and return to base.*>

<*Hauler—*>

<*That's an order, Flight Lieutenant. I won't have you stroke out on me. We'll continue the mission without you.*>

Armitage cut her drives, and her Lightning fell away rapidly like a taut line just snapped. Her medical alert disappeared as the gs on her body fell to zero.

<*I'm sorry, guys.*>

<*It can happen to anyone, Marbles. Fly gently back to base. As for everyone else, if your bio-monitor flashes an alert, you cut your drives! Don't do the Cendies' work for them!*>

The turnover was violent. He didn't cut the drives to turn but kept the burning the whole time until he was flying tail-first toward Styx.

After another fifteen minutes of torturous, crushing acceleration, Osiris Squadron arrived over Styx.

The little moon looked like any other irregularly shaped body too small to pull itself into a sphere—a potato made mostly of water ice, seasoned with a dusting of tholins, giving it a dark reddish color.

It was smaller than 30 Skeksis, the asteroid back in 61 Virginis the Cendies had used as their base for the invasion of Triumph. The events that led to Styx's creation had left it filled with many deep crevasses big enough to hide multiple Lightnings. Thanks to the data from Doctor Wynn, Mason had already selected suitable locations. "All fighters, sync your clocks to mine. This will be the last time for a few days that we'll have communications with the outside Universe," Mason said.

"Clocks synced, proceeding to the landing zone," Dominic said. "See you over Charon, Hauler."

"You too, Silverback," Mason said.

With Marbles gone, Osiris Squadron split into three four-ship flights and one three-ship flight as it proceeded to its assigned hiding spots. Mason wanted to keep each flight together so that if its pilot had a problem, there was at least some help at the ready.

The site Mason chose for his flight was on the far side of Styx. He passed slowly over the center of Styx's axis of rotation, following the contours of its surface, crossing the jagged edge of the moon's day–night terminator.

Night, even the deep night of the outer Solar System, was no impediment to the sensors of Mason's Lightning. High-frequency radar gave him a clear view of the surface as he came up on his landing site.

Styx was not devoid of signs of human visitation. Mason spotted the landing site where Doctor Wynn's survey had blasted off decades ago. There were also odd bits of debris left from previous visits, held down by the moon's weak gravity. The crevasse was a deep valley between what had probably been two separate bodies eons ago that had gently merged.

Mason came to a stop just above the crevasse and turned his fighter tail-first toward the entrance. And with a gentle push from the maneuvering thrusters, he backed into the crevasse and lowered his landing gear as the crevasse walls rose around him. Once deep enough, he pushed his thrusters again to come to a stop and fired harpoons from the belly of his fighter into the ice. Then his Lightning winched herself down to the ice until the wheels touched down and held firm.

There was a light jostle as his fighter secured herself into place.

One by one, the other three fighters of his flight backed in and secured themselves to the ice like moths clinging to the walls of a cave. Lightnings were big fighters, but the size of the crevasse gave them the illusion of being much smaller, with dozens of meters between each strikecraft.

Mason began powering down to a minimal operative state, lowering the reactor to idle power, where they would sip just enough fuel to keep themselves running. Extraneous things like active sensors, the identify-friend-or-foe system, jammers, and long-range comms were shut down to minimize the emissions that could leak out of the crevasse.

Short-range communications were kept on, each fighter linked by a line-of-sight comm laser that wouldn't leak out into open space.

In the darkness of the crevasse, the starlight was bright and clear in the visual spectrum, easily visible to the naked eye for anyone who ventured out of their fighter.

Mason released his restraints and let himself float. Styx only had enough gravity to tell him which direction down was. That weak gravity gradually pulled him toward the back of his cockpit, past the stowed passenger seat, until he landed on the back wall. He stretched his limbs, working out the stiffness left from the hard burn.

"It's been a spell since I've last spent whole days in my fighter," Mason said to Gottlieb.

"Yeah. I'm sure it'll be fun peeling our diapers off after three days," she said.

"If that's the most unpleasant thing we have to deal with on this mission, I'll call it a win," Mason said.

"I don't know. I think the Cendies would be doing me a favor if they killed me before I had to deal with three days of piss and shit."

"We're here for five minutes and you're already talking about bodily waste?" Mason said. "Aren't there better topics to discuss? Like literally anything else?"

Mason stretched out his arms, noting that he could almost fully extend them by placing his palms flat on the walls. "I forget how much room we get inside our cockpits."

"That works," Gottlieb said. "I see your point, Hauler. Being locked into our seat, with our attention focused outwards, it's not always evident we have a lot of space."

Mason bounced off his toes, finding himself flying past his seat toward the minimalist instrument panel. He settled down at the back of the cockpit, bracing his back against the canopy. Despite the lack of padding and the fact he was wearing a hardsuit, it was quite comfortable because of the hardsuit's inner gel layer.

Opening the stored media on his brainset, he browsed through the selection of entertainment. With all of the games, books, movies, and shows stored in his brainset, there was no shortage of options. Rather, the mind-numbing number of options was somewhat paralyzing.

Mason decided to pick something educational. More information about Pluto and its system of moons. People chose to live out here in Pluto's tiny system. New Lowell's reason for being was scientific research, but that didn't explain why a hundred thousand people came here to live, work, and raise families.

New Lowell was the tiniest speck of civilization at the edge of Outer Sol. A place that, until the Ascendancy showed up, had never known war.

Maybe that was part of the reason people came out here. None of the old national conflicts had reached this far, even during the free-for-all of the General Conflict. And the League had never once launched a raid against Pluto despite its relative vulnerability to raids. It was a scientific outpost of dubious military value.

Even pirates never attacked New Lowell. Those daring enough to hunt in Sol kept their activities focused on the gas giants, where prey was more abundant and likely to carry valuable cargo.

Then the Cendies conquered Outer Sol and gave it military value.

Now Pluto was Earth Fed's toehold in Outer Sol—the latest focal point in a war that followed no conventions because no one could have predicted the Ascendancy showing up.

Mason looked forward to driving the Cendies out and moving the war away from Pluto and New Lowell. Hopefully the Plutonians could get back to work observing the most distant objects in the Universe that humanity had yet to reach—objects that, even with faster-than-light travel, would probably be forever out of reach.

Looking up through the front of his cockpit, rendered transparent by his connection to his sensors, Mason observed the stars, watching them slowly pan across his view as Styx rotated. His brainset helpfully detailed each star that came into view. Not all of them were stars.

Some of the brighter stars were Pluto's other irregular moons. Kerberos and Nix were in view but slowly panned out of view, replaced by Hydra. When Hydra disappeared, Pluto and Charon came into view.

Three days. In three days, he would be burning hard for Charon and whatever dangers awaited him and his squadron. He hoped General Asif's diversion happened on time. Otherwise his squadron would die isolated and alone.

CHAPTER 19

The minutes to the start of the mission felt longer than the previous three days of waiting. With Pluto completely eclipsed by Charon, Mason couldn't see if General Asif's diversionary attack was happening.

His Lightning was fully warmed up and ready to launch. Detection at this stage would not make a difference. In a few minutes his squadron would be out in space and burning at full power for Charon, lighting up the sky brighter than any star other than the distant sun behind them.

The base was on Charon's night side, though darkness would do little to hinder the sensors of either Mason's squadron or the Cendies.

The status display of the three other fighters in his flight showed them all powered up and running normally. He hoped the other flights, isolated from him while hiding on Styx, were also ready.

"Thirty seconds," Mason said. "I'm detaching from the ice."

He severed the harpoon cables that held his fighter in place and pushed his fighter off the wall with a pulse from the maneuvering thrusters. By the time he had drifted to the center of the crevasse, the timer had hit zero, and he pushed himself forward with a longer pulse from the rear maneuvering thrusters.

As Mason crossed into open space, Gottlieb detached from the wall and followed him out, followed by Armitage and her wingmate.

The light pulse of the maneuvering thrusters was enough to put Mason's fighter on an escape trajectory from Styx. He quickly established connections with Dominic's, Sabal's, and Sawyer's fighters.

"Good to see everyone up. What's your status?" Mason asked.

"My pilots all survived the wait," Sabal said, irritation evident in her voice. She evidently had not enjoyed spending three days hiding on Styx.

"All my pilots and fighters are ready for action, Hauler," Dominic said.

"We're all ready and eager here in Fourth Flight," Sawyer said.

"In that case, spread out into transit formation and prepare to initiate burn," Mason ordered.

Osiris Squadron split into a long left-echelon formation, with the distance between Mason's fighter and the last fighter in formation twice the diameter of Styx.

Mason locked his destination and prepared his vector. The predicted line of flight moved toward Charon's north pole before curving below the horizon.

"Beginning countdown," Mason said, grabbing the throttle handle.

As the countdown to launch proceeded, Mason had the sensor AI do a sweep. No contacts were on the scopes. Everything was under the shadow of Charon.

The countdown hit zero. Mason slammed the throttle forward, and the Lightning crashed into his back.

❧

Fifteen minutes later, Mason completed his braking burn ten kilometers above the surface of Charon's north pole.

"This is it. Everyone on the deck!" Mason called as he dove for Charon's surface. He leveled out dangerously low, hugging just a few meters above the surface at a thousand kilometers an hour—slow by comparison to open space but terrifyingly fast with rough dark ice zipping below.

It would take longer to fly the 500-kilometer distance to the Cendy base on the southern tip of Mordor Macula than it did to fly the 40,000-kilometer distance from Styx. But they had to stay low, relying on minimal thrust to maximize their chance of surprise.

Each Lightning followed its own discrete track to the Cendy base to give maximum flexibility in navigating so low.

Mason dipped in and out of craters as he flew over the north pole.

The ground transitioned from dark gray to rusty red as he entered Mordor Macula. Ahead, Pluto started rising above the horizon, and Mason detected the first signs of combat thousands of kilometers away in the space between Pluto and Charon.

The emissions of six starships and dozens of fighters shone brightly against Pluto's cold background as Federal strikecraft sparred with Cendy forces. It looked like General Asif's distraction had worked in pulling away the warships and fighters defending the Cendy base, leaving it open for Mason's attack.

Thus far no threats had appeared on the tactical display, but Mason was certain that would change as he got closer to the Cendy base. It was only a question of when that would be and how much warning the Cendies would have before his fighters appeared over the horizon. Memories of the murderous effectiveness of the Turtlebacks' point defenses were forever seared into his brain.

Combat continued to rage over Pluto as it rose higher over the horizon. Mason hoped the Cendies' attention was so focused on what was happening in front of them that none would notice the fifteen Lightnings creeping up on their base from behind.

As Mason crested the ridge, he got illuminated by search radar.

"I'm lit up—they know we're incoming!" Mason yelled as he pushed his fighter back down to the deck and out of the view of the Turtleback's search radar.

Interceptors launched from the base climbed up before turning to dive down. The missiles were under self-guidance, with the Turtlebacks unable to track the Lightnings flying so low to the ground—which meant they were at a disadvantage against the multiple layers of anti-missile defense that a Lightning came with.

The dazzle laser turret on the top of his fuselage lashed out first, burning out the seeker heads of each interceptor in sequence. But the dazzle laser couldn't neutralize all the incoming interceptors.

The combat AI automatically started ejecting decoys, leaving twin trails of brightly burning devices behind his fighter and lighting up the ice below. The first interceptors swooped past Mason's fighter to crash into the ice, becoming one more crater among the multitudes that covered Charon's surface.

But even the dazzle lasers and decoys were not enough to deal with the sheer volume of interceptors crashing down. The lucky few that survived the harassment of the dazzle lasers and avoided the temptation of decoys met one last line of defense.

While Mason concentrated on staying slow and following the contours of the Mordor Macula, the combat AI tracked, locked, and fired Stiletto interceptors. The sky above Mason flashed as the tiny Stilettoes collided with their larger prey, briefly illuminating the dark ice with flashes of light. If any interceptor slipped through the defenses, Mason would be dead before he knew it.

But he didn't die, even as more waves of interceptors dove toward him.

Flying low, he could not maintain a line of sight or have a real-time data link with all his pilots. He didn't know if anyone had been shot down or if they were in a position to fire.

All he had was faith in his pilots that they would complete their mission.

He approached the launch zone, which was the imaginary circle drawn over the ice where he would launch his torpedoes. The nice thing about attacking a base on a planet was that there was no need to lock onto the target. You just had to assign coordinates and let the torpedo guide itself to the target.

A minute out, Mason armed his torpedoes and opened the weapons bay, the first torpedo lowering into launch position.

Then, as he crossed into the launch zone, he held down the firing button on the back of his control stick and began the firing sequence. One, two, three, four, and the torpedoes were away, skimming close to the surface.

Mason immediately turned away and burned hard to start moving from the Cendy base even while he maintained his low altitude.

The first sign that the Cendies had noticed the torpedoes came when the interceptors stopped dropping on Mason and instead dropped on targets over the horizon. It appeared the Cendies were having as much trouble engaging the low-flying torpedoes as they had the Lightnings.

Mason stayed low as he watched the timer count down to the predicted time to impact.

An enormous flash shone like a brief sunrise from the direction of the Cendy base, casting long shadows across Mordor Macula before fading out, leaving behind an expanding plume of superheated gas rising from the surface.

Mason started to climb as he proceeded along his departure vector and saw the results of his squadron's bloody work.

"Yes!" He pumped his fist as he saw the glowing wreckage of what was left of the Turtlebacks and the mostly completed Cendy base.

The directional warheads of the torpedoes had acted like gargantuan cutting torches, slashing across the southern tip of Mordor Macula, cutting through the hulls of landed Turtlebacks, and crisscrossing the center of the base. The reddish surface had been blown away, exposing the pristine ice below.

Mason's jubilation quickly sobered as he realized he had just left a permanent scar on the surface of Charon that would last billions of years.

It was a hell of a legacy.

Much to his relief, fourteen Lightnings appeared on his tactical display. All his pilots had survived the approach to the Cendy base. Now it was just a matter of surviving the return journey.

"Good to see you all. Form up with me so we can get the hell out of here!"

CHAPTER 20

As Mason set his Lightning down for a gentle landing on the pad at New Lowell, a small crowd of ground crew plus troopers in armored hardsuits gathered to greet Osiris Squadron. Some clapped silently in the vacuum as Mason climbed from the cockpit, while others threw thumbs-ups or other signs of approval.

The mission had worked, and he hadn't lost any pilots. The biggest threat, for now, had been neutralized.

But Mason didn't share the jubilation of the crowd coming to greet him. He just felt tired. Days waiting on Styx, followed by half an hour of hard acceleration with a dash of combat, had drained him physically and emotionally.

His hardsuit and Pluto's low gravity hid any signs of fatigue. The skipping movements of a tired man in a hardsuit were indistinguishable from those of a rested one. Mason returned a few of the hand waves and thumbs-up signals as he moved toward the rovers left to ferry his pilots to New Lowell's surface station.

A lone figure stood among the rovers. Even before his HUD identified her, Mason knew it was Armitage waiting to greet her squadron mates.

"Welcome back, Hauler."

"Thanks, Marbles. It's good to see you."

"I can't tell you how relieved I am to see you all back."

"You and me both, Marbles," Mason said. "Thanks for bringing us our rides."

Armitage scoffed. "The rovers drove themselves. I just hopped in before anyone could stop me."

"Well, let's not waste any more time out here." He climbed into the driver's seat of the first rover, Armitage taking the seat next to him.

"Belts and zones, this feels like a parade," he said.

Armitage stood in her seat, waving back enthusiastically. "I know. Isn't it great?"

The rovers rolled up to one of New Lowell's main airlocks, and Mason led Osiris Squadron into it. When the airlock had cycled, he pulled off his helmet for the first time in over three days and immediately felt the sweat on his face cool on contact with the clean, dry air of New Lowell.

Sabal pulled her helmet off with such force that beads of sweat arched across the airlock. "I need a fucking shower."

Dominic dodged the globules of sweat that splattered on the wall behind him. "Well, don't try to give us a shower at the same time, Hardball."

"Don't act like you're any cleaner, Silverback," Sabal snapped.

"Oh, no argument there, but I would prefer to marinate in my own juices," Dominic said.

When the inner hatch of the airlock opened, General Asif was waiting on the other side, flanked by some of her staff. She smiled at Mason. "Welcome back, Squadron Leader. I'm glad to see Osiris Squadron lives up to its glowing reputation."

"We're happy to please, General," Mason said.

"You've done much more than please, Squadron Leader. You've helped salvage the entire campaign. I've dispatched a courier drone to inform Admiral Moebius that we've driven the Cendies from Pluto's space."

"When can we expect our fleet to arrive, General?"

"We'll find out soon, Squadron Leader. The fleet should only be one jump out."

"If you don't mind, then, I would like to wait with you at headquarters for the reply."

"You don't want to get some rest?"

"Desperately, but I'm not going to be able to sleep until I know what's going on with the convoy."

General Asif nodded. "In that case, you're welcome to come along."

Mason turned to his pilots. "Feel free to get your showers and rest. I'm not going to drag you along with me."

The assembled pilots immediately departed, leaving just Osiris Squadron's XO with Mason.

"Not waiting for you to change your mind, I see," Dominic said.

"They have the right idea," Mason said. "Best you do the same before I do."

Dominic gave Mason a mock salute and departed with the rest of his pilots.

Headquarters was quieter than usual, with the main holotank showing Pluto clear of hostile contacts. "Take a seat, Squadron Leader," General Asif invited, gesturing to an empty chair next to the holotank.

"Thank you, General," Mason said, settling his weight into the seat, which had little trouble supporting him in the low gravity despite his heavy hardsuit.

"How do you like your coffee?"

"Uh, black, sir," Mason said. General Asif nodded to a spacer, who darted off.

The general settled down next to Mason. "And now we wait."

"For the coffee or Admiral Moebius's reply?" Mason asked.

"For both," General Asif said.

The assistant returned, bearing two swollen drinking packets. "Black coffee for you, sir," the assistant said. "And green tea with honey for you, General."

"Thank you, Sergeant." The general nodded to Mason. "The perks of rank."

"Yes, General," Mason said, taking a sip of his coffee. He recognized the flavor as that of New Lowell's hydroponically grown blend. "See we're using the local stock."

"Having a self-sustainable city below us does simplify some of our supply issues."

"I suppose it does. We should liberate cities more often."

"Just wait until we liberate the rest of Sol, Squadron Leader," General Asif said, taking a long sip of her tea.

The Edge of Nowhere

Mason enjoyed more of his coffee as he waited for the tiny flash of a courier drone jumping in. As the minutes passed, he started to worry. A lot could happen in the vast expanse of space outside of a jump limit.

He finished his packet and still no courier drone carrying Admiral Moebius's expected reply had appeared.

Mason looked at General Asif, who merely shrugged. "I guess I should get a refill of my coffee," he said.

Before he could look around for General Asif's assistant, a staccato of flashes erupted in the space sixty thousand kilometers over New Lowell, close enough that anyone on the surface would be in for a light show.

The holotank instantly identified the new arrivals as friendlies. It was the convoy of dozens of massive tankers escorted by a small fleet of warships, with *Independence* at the head.

"Belts and zones!" Mason exclaimed.

"I suppose that's one way to send a reply," General Asif said as she stood up, setting her packet aside and straightening her uniform. "Contact *Independence*."

"They're already contacting us, General."

"Then put them on the holotank. You might want to stand up, Squadron Leader."

"Yes, General," Mason said, standing up carefully to keep from bouncing in the low gravity.

Moments later, a window showing Admiral Moebius's face appeared in the holotank. "General Asif, it's good to see you managed to clear the Cendies from Pluto."

"Thank you, Admiral. Your pilots provided a lot of help."

"As I gathered from your report, General," Admiral Moebius said. "Squadron Leader Grey, you continue to get outsized results."

"Thank you, Admiral," Mason said. "I see you were busy."

Admiral Moebius chuckled. "I suppose I have been. Once you and your pilots are rested, I expect you to return to *Independence*. I plan on departing Pluto within the next forty-eight hours. We're in the final stretch, and I don't want to give the Cendies more time to react to our movements."

Mason nodded. "I'll get my pilots back to *Independence* in the next twelve hours."

"I look forward to your return, Squadron Leader," Admiral Moebius said. "General Asif, fine work keeping what we fought for. Now I need to start shooting tight beams downorbit to coordinate with the First Fleet."

Admiral Moebius disappeared from the holotank.

General Asif turned to Mason. "You should get to your cot, Squadron Leader. I think you have a very busy time ahead of you."

"Nothing new about that, General." He gave General Asif a salute and departed headquarters.

At his squadron's billet, Mason found Dominic sitting in the improvised common area, dressed down to a shirt and shorts after a fresh shower.

"So Admiral Moebius is back, and she brought friends with her," Dominic said.

Mason set himself down across from Dominic. "Seems so. Fifty fleet tankers ready to make the run for Earth."

"And we'll be right in the thick of it again," Dominic said.

"As always," Mason said.

"I hope they let us have a nice long leave when we make it to Earth," Dominic said. "There are some nice beaches in Australia that I very much look forward to lounging on. What about you, Hauler?"

"Eh, I haven't thought that far ahead," Mason said. "Seems a bit optimistic to plan my vacation when survival isn't a given."

"What can I say? I like to think positively," Dominic said.

"I wish I could do that," Mason said. "I keep thinking about what the Cendies are going to do to try and stop us. They're not just going to sit back and let us ruin their blockade, no matter how many warships we have covering the convoy."

"If they kill the convoy, they might very well win the war, I know," Dominic said. "But what's going to happen is going to happen. No point in torturing ourselves worrying about it."

"I suppose," Mason said, though Dominic's advice did nothing to alleviate his worries. "I should get out of this hardsuit and take a shower."

"Might help with the gloomy mood," Dominic said. "Get yourself a good meal while you're at it. We've all been pushed hard since we arrived on Pluto, and our interrupted leave didn't help."

"I will. Thanks, Silverback."

"I do what I can, Hauler."

Mason marched over to the cleared area where his pilots stowed their hardsuits, taking a position at the end of the row and commanding the suit to open. Seals popped as the shell separated, allowing him to pull himself out the back. He then yanked out the power cell and slotted it into a charging station. Gathering a change of fresh clothes, he proceeded to the shower tent and activated the shower. Water droplets fell in a lazy cascade in the low gravity.

Mason didn't waste any more time washing off the last three days trapped inside his hardsuit. When he stepped out of the shower in a clean shirt and shorts, he felt human again.

He returned to the squadron billet and noted that Dominic had disappeared, presumably to his tent. He headed to his own tent and sat on the bed to activate his HUD and check his communications. With *Independence*'s return, he hoped there would be some messages or updates from Jessica, but there was nothing.

Mason rubbed the bridge of his nose. He knew she would have only sporadic chances to contact him on whatever secret mission she was on. But it would've been nice if she'd had time to let him know she was doing all right. He had enough worries weighing down on him.

For his part, he drafted a short message to Jessica, letting her know he was in good health, if not in good spirits, and sent it off to the communications queue. He hoped she wasn't getting herself into anything too dangerous.

CHAPTER 21

The first half of the flight to Origin had been comfortable and uneventful aboard *Fafnir*. Just the slow rhythm of a starship traversing the vast nothing between the stars. But the time came for Jessica to return to her cramped quarters back aboard *Midnight Diamond* with the rest of the tiny starship's crew.

The release of the docking clamps rumbled through the starship's hull, and they drifted away from the cruiser.

"Colonel Miller, how long until we make our first jump?" Jessica asked.

"Thirty minutes while the crew makes final inspections, Lieutenant. Why?"

"I would like to deploy *Midnight Diamond*'s scopes to see if we can't detect Origin now that we're closer to its presumed location."

Colonel Miller nodded. "That shouldn't interfere with our schedule, but don't take too long."

"A few minutes should be more than sufficient," Jessica assured him.

While *Midnight Diamond* deployed her sensitive scopes, Jessica programmed the sensor AI to filter out all stars and known brown dwarves and other known sub-stellar objects unbound from any star system. The starship's scopes soaked up raw data for ten minutes and fed them into the sensor AI. When the scopes retracted to prepare for the jump and the countdown to the first jump started, Jessica got her first results.

There were no objects that matched Origin. Not that she expected it—they were still thirty light-years away. But it did rule out a brown dwarf as the location of the Origin system. Even failed stars would give off enough infrared light to stand out on *Midnight Diamond*'s sensors.

The sensor AI did flag candidates for nearby sub-stellar objects. There was even what looked like a comet hurtling through space just a few billion kilometers away on its eons-long journey.

After the first jump, Jessica settled in for the long journey to a destination the ship's sensor still could not see.

As the days passed and they got closer to the presumed destination, Jessica would repeat her search with *Midnight Diamond*'s sensors. Each time, it would find new sub-stellar objects, but none that could be Origin.

As more time went on without discovering Origin, Jessica started to worry that Origin was not there—that her hypothesis was wrong and she had just wasted a month chasing a phantom. Her anxiety continued to grow until, mercifully, five days out from their destination, she finally detected something.

Even with *Midnight Diamond*'s powerful scopes, the sub-stellar candidate barely stood out against the black background of space.

Jessica sent a message over the network to Colonel Miller. Within moments, the colonel and Isobel appeared at her workstation, with Commander Ngata in tow.

"You have something, Lieutenant Sinclair?" Colonel Miller enquired.

Wearing a theatrically large smile, Jessica swiveled her seat to face her floating audience. "There's something there, Colonel!"

"You're sure?"

"Well, it will be awfully embarrassing if there isn't," Jessica said.

"What can you tell us about our destination, Lieutenant?" Commander Ngata asked.

"Mostly what it's not," Jessica said. "It's sub-stellar, but we already assumed that. Now we can rule out brown dwarves or rogue gas giants. What we're seeing is somewhere between the mass of Mars at the low end and super-Earth at the high end."

"That's quite a size range," Colonel Miller remarked.

"It's the best I can give you at this distance," Jessica said. "And I'm not sure if it really matters. Even something as small as Mars would have more than enough resources for *Ascension* to do its work, assuming it's a silicate body."

"Well, it's good to know there's something there," Colonel Miller said. "Hopefully we'll learn more over the next week."

Over the next week, they did learn more. Every day, between jumps, Jessica opened *Midnight Diamond*'s scopes to get another snapshot of Origin, and the size and mass estimates of the object narrowed.

One thing that became abundantly clear as she got more data was that the object had a pronounced wobble. She wasn't an astronomer by trade, but she didn't have to be to know what a wobble could mean.

It wasn't just one object but two. A planet and its moon, or perhaps even a double planet.

By the time they were just two days out, the sensor AI had gathered enough data to give a detailed view of the object.

"And voila! Origin!" Jessica announced with a flourish as a representation of the rogue planet and its moon appeared inside the holotank.

Colonel Miller pointed at the planet. "Is that an atmosphere?"

"It is, Colonel," Jessica said. "I don't yet have details of the composition. What the sensor AI estimates is that the primary is shrouded in a thick nitrogen atmosphere. Something like a massive version of Saturn's moon, Titan."

"So it's a big ball of ice," Colonel Miller said. "What can you tell me about the moon?"

"That it's an airless ball of metal, possibly the core of a ruined rocky planet destroyed in whatever cataclysm that threw both out of their home star system," Jessica replied.

Colonel Miller gave her a skeptical glance. "You can learn all that from three light-years out?"

"Not from direct observation but from interpreting the orbits," Jessica said. "The moon is at least a quarter of the mass of the primary body but is far smaller in volume. Assuming the primary is mostly ice, the satellite would have to be mostly metal. Nickle-iron."

"A ball of metal that size would be more than enough to build a fleet," Colonel Miller said. "Vastly more. Any technological signatures?"

"Not yet," Jessica said. "I suppose we'll find out as we get closer."

The following day and a light-year and a half closer, there were still no signs of technological activity around Origin—just more details about the composition of the two bodies.

Origin A was, indeed, a gigantic analog of Titan, close to the mass of Earth, shrouded in a thick nitrogen atmosphere. Its companion, Origin Ab, was more massive than Mars but roughly the diameter of Mercury—a metal sphere orbiting a snowball closer than Luna orbiting Earth.

The tidal interactions probably caused some interesting cryovolcanic activity on Origin A's surface. There was almost certainly a subsurface ocean as well.

It was interesting to speculate on how Origin A and its iron moon had ended up ejected from their home system and how they had ended up together in the first place. It seemed unlikely they had formed together. A metallic body like Origin Ab would have needed to form close to its parent star—so close that Origin A would have vaporized down to its rocky core.

But that wasn't relevant to why she was out here. Maybe years from now, some exogeologists would come by to study the strange double planet.

It wasn't until *Midnight Diamond* was one jump away, a hundred billion kilometers, that the starship's sensors picked up the first signs of artificial construction.

"There's something orbiting Origin Ab," Jessica said. "A large structure in a synchronous orbit."

"An indication of anything on the surface it might be orbiting over?" Colonel Miller asked.

"Not from this distance," Jessica said. "We'll need to get closer to figure out why the structure is in a synchronous orbit. And to figure out what it is."

"Any guesses?"

"It's a station of some kind, non-rotating and irregular in shape," Jessica said.

"I suppose we'll figure out more in the next jump." Colonel Miller rubbed his chin. "Commander Ngata, set the ship to battle stations. We're going in."

"Yes, Colonel," Commander Ngata snapped.

"Make sure you're strapped in, Lieutenant. Just in case we must pull hard gs," Colonel Miller warned. Jessica nodded and pulled her straps tight, making sure she was held securely to the acceleration gel.

The familiar buzz of *Midnight Diamond* charging her drive keel reverberated through the hull as the countdown to the final jump began. Jessica hoped that whatever magic attenuated the arrival flash of *Midnight Diamond*'s jump would keep her off the scopes of any Cendy sensors.

More crew entered the command section when those who weren't already on duty went to their action stations. The ship was preparing for battle.

When the jump came, Origin A and its companion resolved from a faint point of light only visible on the scopes to a pair of planets just a million kilometers away.

In the darkness between the stars, there wasn't much to see in the visible spectrum. The silhouettes of both worlds were outlined by the stars they blocked.

Under image intensification, the details of the worlds were resolved. If there was a sun to illuminate the worlds, Origin A would be an Earth-sized planet shrouded in a blue-gray atmosphere decorated with wispy white clouds in the upper atmosphere.

Origin Ab, on the other hand, was an airless dark-gray object that looked like it had been scorched by whatever cataclysm had stripped it down to its metal core.

As before, *Midnight Diamond*'s passive sensor arrays fed raw data to the sensor AI, and the sensor AI translated the data into information Jessica could understand. Both Origin A and Origin Ab were cold but still significantly warmer than the background of space. Tidal interactions heated both objects. The thermal radiation coming off Origin Ab served to illuminate the cold structure orbiting it.

The sensor AI built a detailed model of the structure and projected it onto the holotank. Colonel Miller and Isobel returned from the bridge in time to see the projection.

The structure was minuscule compared to the bulk of Origin Ab. But it was still large in absolute terms—over ten thousand meters across its longest axis.

"That looks like quite the kludge," Isobel said.

"Probably just added modules as needed," Jessica said. "Though it doesn't look like there's anything active. The whole structure is cold. Same temperature as the planets."

"Any hot spots?" Colonel Miller asked.

"I wouldn't call them hot spots. But there are points that are a bit warmer," Jessica said. "My guess would be heaters to protect sensitive electronics from getting too cold."

"So whoever built the structure intended to preserve it for future use," Colonel Miller said. "What's that skinny structure coming out of it?"

Jessica shifted the view. A filament of metal, slightly warmer than the background, extended from the structure. She zoomed out the image to see how far it extended. And it just seemed to keep going and going.

On a hunch, Jessica programmed the AI to highlight the filament from the structure and then zoomed the image out until Origin Ab was fully visible. From the location of the structure, the filament stretched all the way down to the surface.

"A space elevator," Colonel Miller said.

Isobel nodded. "Explains why the structure is in a synchronous orbit."

"Also explains why there are warm spots," Jessica added. "Something like this would need active station keeping for it to remain in place."

"Any signs of defensive systems?" Colonel Miller asked.

"Nothing obvious, but we should assume so," Jessica said.

"But why is no one home?" Isobel asked. "If this is indeed the Ascendancy's origin system, then why is it abandoned?"

"Focus on the orbital station," Colonel Miller advised. "Look for any signs of docked Cendy warships."

Jessica instructed the sensor AI to run the detected emission through its database of known Cendy warships. It came up dry.

"That doesn't mean there's nothing there," Colonel Miller said.

"But why go to the effort of hiding warships when the base is detectable?" Jessica wondered.

"Not that detectable," Isobel said. "We only found it because we knew where to look."

Jessica glanced over the model of the orbital base projected onto the holotank. It wasn't quite the random kludge of modules she had initially thought it was. It appeared everything radiated from a central spine, with the cables running up into the bottom of the central spin.

Something about the spine tickled something in the back of her brain. Jessica checked it against *Midnight Diamond*'s database, but it didn't match the central module of the station to known objects.

"Colonel Miller, would you mind if I uploaded something into the database?" Jessica asked.

"What is it you're trying to upload?"

"The schematics of a ship that's not on *Midnight Diamond*'s system," Jessica told him.

"You understand we will need to check it?"

"I'll upload it as plain text. I just need the sensor AI to match the schematics against what we're seeing."

Colonel Miller nodded. "You have my authorization."

Jessica uploaded the text file, which was just a list of values representing the schematics of a ship. When the sensor AI matched them against the station's modules, the central spine came back as a perfect match.

"What ship were you looking for, Lieutenant?" Colonel Miller asked.

"*Ascension*—the colony ship of the Ascendancy's creators," Jessica said. "And I think we've found her."

"It seems they built a station around it," Isobel said.

Jessica nodded. "I think it's time we wake up Miriam. She'll want to see this."

⚜

A few minutes later, Jessica woke Miriam and brought her to the command module.

Miriam looked around the module with scant interest until she saw the holotank and the station with *Ascension*'s silhouette superimposed.

"You found her!"

"Yes, I think so," Jessica said. "This is where your friends decided to begin their project."

"They're running a space elevator all the way down to the surface of the moon," Miriam said. "I never imagined they would build something of this scale."

"Origin Ab has plentiful resources," Jessica said. "Based on what I'm seeing, they probably spent years using those resources to build more and more automated manufacturing infrastructure."

"And then the Ascended just abandoned it."

"That appears to be the case."

"We need to explore that station."

Jessica was surprised by Miriam's sudden enthusiasm. She normally had a detached view of the living world.

"That's a given," Colonel Miller said. "But we need to be careful. We don't know if there are automatic defenses. Or if that station is as abandoned as it looks."

"When we get to the point where we can explore that station, I want to get aboard it," Miriam said.

"You seem rather eager," Colonel Miller remarked.

Miriam fixed Colonel Miller with a hard look. "Wouldn't you want to know the fate of your friends after two hundred years?"

"It's not something I've really thought about," Colonel Miller said. "We'll launch probes and begin our approach under low thrust. Keep our eyes open for signs of any automated system detecting us. We're hoping you could share some insights."

"What? About defenses? No idea," Miriam said. "Julian's whole goal was to remain undiscovered and unbothered by the rest of humanity while he and his team went about their great work. He succeeded, as is no doubt clear." She gestured to the holotank and its projection of the orbital station. "That has served its purpose. To the Ascended I believe it's little more than a historical curiosity. They probably decided to preserve it in the hope that its remoteness would be its defense. I doubt they would put much effort into anything more than simple meteoroid defenses. So long as you can keep us from looking like a rock, I think we'll be fine."

"Can you be sure the Cen— the Ascended wouldn't have left something more robust?" Colonel Miller asked.

"No," Miriam said. "I never knew the Ascended personally. I just know how Julian and his people thought. Origin's remoteness was the defense. I doubt they thought for a moment about fending off a League spy ship two centuries later."

"I'll return to the bridge and tell Commander Ngata to begin our approach," Colonel Miller said. "Assuming nothing tries to kill us, we can enter orbit near the station within twelve hours."

"I'll wait in my cabin, then," Miriam said. She departed without asking if she was dismissed, though no one seemed willing to take issue with her. It wasn't like she was a member of any armed forces. Only so much authority could be exercised over a dead and digitized woman.

Jessica remained at her station for a few hours more, going over the sensor readings of the station with Isobel and watching to see if there was any reaction when *Midnight Diamond* ignited her longburn drive and started accelerating toward Origin Ab at a gentle one-third g.

The station didn't react. Nor did the probes launched ahead of *Midnight Diamond* provoke any response. As far as the sensor AI could tell, Ascension Station, as Jessica had started calling it, and the Ascension Base at the bottom of the elevator were both completely dormant.

She did wonder what, if anything, they could do that would trigger a response. If there was anything that could respond.

By the time *Midnight Diamond* slotted into the synchronous orbit of Origin Ab, two thousand kilometers trailing Ascension Station, everything remained as quiet as when they had arrived.

Jessica wasn't quite sure why, but *Ascension*'s crew had decided to build their station and its attached space elevator on the side of Origin Ab that permanently faced Origin A, which placed the station forever between the two tidally locked worlds. Above was the cold and cloudy ice world of Origin A. Below was the scorched metal ball of Origin Ab. She was struck by a profound sense of loneliness. Sandwiched between two cold, orphaned planets, Ascension Station was alone in the dark. The nearest natural light source was over five light-years away.

She had to wonder how that had affected the crew. While they plied their work, they were the most isolated population of humans in the Universe at that time. Perhaps ever.

When she returned to her quarters after *Midnight Diamond* had finished entering orbit, Jessica found Miriam still awake and seated on a fold-out seat between bunks in the small common area.

"We've taken position off Ascension Station," Jessica said. "I have to say, your friends picked just about the most isolated corner of the galaxy that I think any person has ever occupied."

"Julian was quite serious about avoiding interruptions," Miriam said. "Learn anything new about the station?"

"A close inspection by the probes reveals a lot of orbital manufacturing. There are some massive docks on either side of the station that look like they might have been shipyards. I did some measurements, and they match the captured mothership's dimensions perfectly."

"So this might be where Julian built the first motherships, crewed by the first Ascended," Miriam said.

"Makes me wonder why they stopped," Jessica mused.

"Probably after building the first few motherships, Julian felt they had accomplished their tasks and decommissioned the station," Miriam suggested. "Each mothership can build another mothership on its own. This station had served its purpose."

"Does make me wonder why the Ascended didn't repurpose the station for their war effort, though," Jessica persisted. "Between Origin Ab's resources and the infrastructure already in place, it would be a valuable contribution to the war machine."

"Perhaps Origin is not needed for their purposes. Or maybe on some level, the Ascended knew their creators would not approve of them making war with the human race," Miriam said. "When does Colonel Miller intend to send people aboard the station?"

"I think he wants to let probes take care of poking around, at least for the next couple of days," Jessica said. "After that, I intend to be among the first to board. I take it you want to come along?"

"Of course," Miriam said. "I want to know first-hand what happened to my friends."

"What do you think happened to them?"

"I think that at some point in the last two hundred years, they all died."

CHAPTER 22

As Mason floated through the inner hatch of the airlock, he sighed with relief to be back aboard *Independence* rather than trapped on the surface of Pluto.

He found Chief Rabin in his grease-stained orange pressure suit waiting for him, detached helmet floating tethered to his belt. "Welcome back, sir," Rabin greeted him.

"Glad to be back, Chief. I missed having you looking over my fighters."

"I admit I got more than a bit bored not having strikecraft to work on. Had to keep my people busy assisting with *Independence*'s repairs."

"How did that go?" Mason asked.

"Faster than I'd expect for a ship as big as *Independence*. Admiral Moebius arranged quite the operation at Checkpoint Ares. A pair of fleet tenders and freighters filled with spare parts. I think the crews set a record for turnaround speed."

"Being that *Independence* is the only one of her kind does put her at the top of any repair priorities."

"That's true, and it looks like Admiral Moebius wants to throw us back into the fray."

"Well, our fighters got plenty of work fighting over Pluto. We had some sustained twenty-g acceleration."

"Which means I need my people to crawl around inside looking for cracks in the structure. It'll be nice to get them back to the work they're specialized in. Now, if you will excuse me, sir, I need to see how badly you abused my birds."

Mason gestured to the hatch. "Be my guest."

"Your guest? I work here. If anything, you pilots are the guests ... sir," Rabin said before snapping his helmet over the collar of his pressure suit.

Mason proceeded to the suit storage room, where the other pilots of Osiris Squadron were already busy removing their suits and stowing them away. Aiming for his assigned alcove, he grabbed the sides of the open hatch and launched himself. His trajectory was good as he floated directly for the alcove.

But then Armitage pushed herself out of her hardsuit with too much force and launched herself on a collision course with Mason. Mason reached out and caught her shoulder with one outstretched arm, pushing her away from him before her head collided with the plates of his hardsuit. The action propelled him toward an occupied alcove.

"Hardball, look out!"

Sabal saw Mason and pushed herself away, the blades of her prosthetic feet barely clearing the way before Mason crushed her.

Mason reached out and grabbed the handhold, arresting his movement but causing his body to pivot around the handhold and slam into Sabal's empty hardsuit. The loud thump of composite plating banging against each other echoed through his helmet.

"Dammit, is everyone okay?"

"I'm fine, Hauler," Armitage said. "Sorry about that."

"And you, Hardball?" Mason checked.

"I'm fine," she said with clear annoyance. "Just a bit surprised is all."

"Sorry," Mason said as he moved, handhold to handhold, back to his alcove and jammed his boots into the clamps at the bottom. The hardsuit split apart, allowing him to pull himself out the back. From there, he headed directly for his assigned quarters aboard *Independence*.

Arriving in the hab ring, Mason enjoyed the comforting weight of .3 g pulling down on him. Living in the minuscule gravity of Pluto's surface had quickly lost its luster.

His cabin was much as it was when he left it, with all the carefully stored personal items he had not taken to New Lowell still in place. He let himself settle into his cot; the cushion still adjusted to his preferences. There he lay, listening to the sound of the living starships around him—the buzz of the air recycler blowing cool fresh air into his living space, unintelligible voices echoing through the thin plastic walls of his cabin, and the thumps of boots on the deck conducted through the decking.

To many people, the sounds of life on a starship were an annoying cacophony to be filtered out with earplugs or implanted noise filters. But to Mason, it was a lullaby. In space, noise meant life. If all you heard was silence, that meant something was very, very wrong.

Just as he started to drift off to sleep, he was interrupted by a notification on his HUD. It was a summons to *Independence*'s war room.

"Belts and zones!" Mason muttered, getting up from his cot. He took a moment to straighten himself, putting on a fresh jumpsuit from his belongings and washing his face. Then he headed back out.

"Where you headed, Hauler?" Sabal asked as she saw him leave the quarters.

"Got business in the war room," Mason answered. "I'll let you know if there's anything you need to worry about."

"So don't get too comfortable? Got it."

Mason marched anti-spinward through the segments of *Independence*'s internal habitat ring, passing along the narrow corridor that ran through the center of each segment until he arrived in the flag officers' module.

The war room was full of busy people, but Mason didn't see either Admiral Moebius or Marshal Singh. The holotank they usually stood next to was dark and abandoned.

"Marshal Singh's in his office, Squadron Leader," said one of the flag staff.

"Thank you," Mason said and proceeded to Marshal Singh's office in a compartment adjacent to the war room.

Mason saluted automatically as he walked in. Marshal Singh loomed comically large behind his small desk, though the massive pilot didn't seem to care. He simply returned Mason's salute and gestured to one of the chairs in front of his desk. "Take a seat, Squadron Leader."

"Thank you, sir."

"General Asif was very complimentary about your efforts in helping

The Edge of Nowhere

drive the Cendies from Pluto, Squadron Leader," Marshal Singh began. "Using Styx as cover for a backdoor attack was clever."

"Just using the terrain to our advantage," Mason said. "Lucky for us the Cendies didn't seem to grasp how the dynamics of Pluto's moons could be used to create avenues for attack."

"Yes, lucky for us," Marshal Singh agreed. "Hopefully we haven't exhausted our supply of luck just yet."

"Yeah. There's still the small matter of getting the convoy through without getting shot to pieces."

"Which is why I wanted to speak with you, Squadron Leader. We're about ninety percent sure there is a Monolith-class mothership hiding at the edge of the Kuiper Belt."

Mason's blood chilled at the mention of a mothership. The battle to capture the Cendy mothership in 61 Virginis had been the deadliest mission he had ever led.

"I hope this doesn't require flying inside it," Mason said.

"Hopefully not."

"So I take it—it was the telescope on Pluto that discovered it?"

Marshal Singh nodded. "There's a rock out at the edge of the Kuiper Belt that's just a bit warmer than it should be. Our analysts suspect it's a mothership hidden behind a cloak mining the asteroid and using the resources to make war material to support the blockade."

"Has there been confirmation beyond the telescope?" Mason asked.

"No—there's a worry trying to get a closer look will spook the mothership into retreating," Marshal Singh said. "If the suspected contact is, in fact, a mothership, Admiral Moebius wants it dead, and so do I. Something that can pump out new starships and fighters for the Cendies is too dangerous to be left on the board while the convoy's trying to run the blockade."

"So what's the plan for taking the mothership down?" Mason asked.

"Thanks to the capture of the mothership in 61 Virginis, we have a good idea of their defensive capabilities. They're ... considerable. Covered in point defense and with a hull thicker than any other known starship. But they do have weaknesses."

Marshal Singh gestured, and a projection of the mothership appeared on Mason's HUD. Parts of the hull started blinking red on the side and front.

"The highlighted areas are doors in the outer hull that can potentially be exploited as weak points," Marshal Singh elaborated. "The preliminary plan is to strike the mothership from the front, concentrating fire on the forward construction bays. At the very least, that fire will prevent any ships that might be docked inside the mothership from launching and defending her."

"And what about escorts?" Mason asked. "I doubt the Cendies would leave a mothership undefended."

"That will be for *Independence* and the other embarked squadrons to deal with," Marshal Singh said. "I want Osiris Squadron to incapacitate the mothership."

Mason looked up at the projection. "By striking the front hangar?"

"Correct," Marshal Singh said. "From what we learned from the mothership we captured, the forward bay is the only way for large vessels to enter and exit the hull. The secondary doors are only large enough to accommodate strikecraft."

"So when we jump in, we'll launch and try to chuck a few nukes down the mothership's throat?"

Marshal Singh nodded, the movement exaggerated by his peaked turban. "That is the size of it, yes. The construction bay is a single contiguous volume that runs halfway down the hull of the mothership with no compartmentalization to speak of—which means if we can line up a torpedo's directional warhead with the construction bay, it ought to disable or destroy any craft inside the mothership, particularly her strikecraft."

"But we're going to be short on time," Mason pointed out. "The mothership's going to close that bay as soon as they're under attack."

"Which is why I'm tasking Osiris Squadron with the mission," Marshal Singh said. "We don't know where the mothership is pointed, and it's unlikely *Independence* will jump in with a clear shot down her front. So it will be up to the speed of your fighters, combined with your familiarity with the mothership's design, to land the critical strike before the Cendies inside her have a chance to react. Once that's done, it should be a simple task for *Independence* and her escorts to finish the mothership off."

"Yes, sir," Mason said, though he was dubious that the Cendies would let things go the way they "should."

※

After Mason had briefed his squadron, the mood was as diverse as their personalities.

Dominic's frown deepened the wrinkles on his face, projecting his foreboding at once again facing the Cendies' biggest starship. Sabal's smile, by contrast, displayed her joyful anticipation at getting into another big fight with the Cendies. Armitage's eyes were distant; she was nodding her head slightly as if listening to a conversation that only she could hear.

Overall, the mood of the fifteen pilots seated before him was about equal parts anxiety and anticipation. With a sprinkling of fear thrown in.

"You have thirty minutes to get suited up and into your fighters. I suggest you get to it."

Twenty minutes later, Mason floated through the airlock, approaching his fighter directly from behind. The hangar crew passed him as they started to evacuate the hangar after making their last-minute inspections.

All of Osiris Squadron's fighters had accumulated serious wear and tear, but all systems and structural components were still within spec, according to Chief Rabin's reports. They would need to get a full overhaul in the near future after the convoy reached Earth. Even machines needed to rest eventually.

Mason's Lightning was fully loaded, with four Stiletto pods mounted on the inner hardpoints and four shortburn torpedoes on the outer hardpoints. The weapons bay was closed, concealing the eight interceptors within.

All told, his squadron would have sixty-four torpedoes available to fling into the mothership's maw. Just one of them should be enough to disable the hangar, assuming it had a clear line of sight for its directional warhead.

It was just a matter of launching the torpedoes before the Cendies could close the massive armored doors that protected the construction bay. It was unknown how fast those doors could close, but given each one massed tens of thousands of tons, it was expected to take several minutes.

Mason floated around his fighter to do his own final preflight inspection, as much to pass the time as to make sure there wasn't anything the hangar crew had missed. All he found were signs of wear—scratches and scuffs on the paint, scorch marks around the maneuvering thruster nozzles that the crew had not had time to clean, and carbon deposits around the muzzle of the main gun. The fighter looked worn and tired, much like how Mason felt.

Mason gave the fighter a pat on the nose as he floated into the cockpit.

The control systems were already powered up and the reactor warmed up. All Mason had to do was strap himself in and sync his brainset with the fighter's AI systems.

Flight, sensor, and combat AIs each reported normal as he connected to his fighter. He settled himself in and connected to *Independence*'s external sensors.

Independence and her escorts detached from the convoy. Two Vancouver-class cruisers and four Churchill-class destroyers rounded out *Independence*'s battlegroup.

It seemed a small force to take on a mothership, but *Independence* had shown she could punch above her considerable weight more than once in her short career since Mason had helped pull her from the tiny Jovian moon of Amalthea.

The clock ticked down inexorably to zero, when *Independence* would jump toward the suspected location of the mothership. He hoped the massive arrays of infrared telescopes on Pluto's surface had given an accurate reading.

Minutes ticked down to seconds, and the seconds counted down with excruciating slowness.

A familiar muted vibration traveled through Mason's butt as capacitors discharged into the drive keel in the last second before the jump.

And suddenly Pluto, Charon, and the convoy disappeared, leaving *Independence* floating in the deep space of Sol's Kuiper Belt with the Sun little more than a bright star at her back. Before her was nothing. No mothership or Cendy escorts—just a vast emptiness devoid of even stars.

Mason didn't have time to process what he was seeing before the hangar doors opened and the catapult kicked his fighter free. A flood of information poured into his awareness as he was fed data from his own fighter's sensors.

Independence occupied the center of a wedge of Federal starships, with two cruisers flanking her and wedges of destroyer squadrons stacked atop the formation of larger ships. The battlecarrier continued to launch strike-craft, even as the entire fleet faced a massive wall of blackness.

Over the general comm, Admiral Moebius's voice said what Mason was just starting to realize. "All ships—we jumped on the dark side of the mothership's cloak. We're launching torpedoes to clear it away."

Just then a volley of torpedoes launched from *Independence*, forming into a ring as they burned toward the volume of empty space.

Minutes later, they detonated, blinding Mason's sensors with their glare.

When the blast faded, a blob of hostile contacts appeared with the enormous mothership at the center, dwarfing even *Independence*. It was surrounded by battlecruisers, which were already turning to engage the Federal starships while the mothership spewed a stream of Outrider fighters into the void.

They had arrived at the stern of the mothership, on the wrong side to engage the hangar bay. And every second, more and more Cendy fighters were launching to fill the space between Mason's fighters and their target.

Mason realized they weren't going to make it. The jump had placed them too far away and on the wrong side of the mothership.

"*Independence* Control, Osiris Leader—we're not going to be able to attack the mothership's construction bay before it closes its doors. Please advise."

"I acknowledge you, Osiris Leader," Marshal Singh replied. "Engage Cendy escorts. New objective is to protect *Independence*."

"Roger that," Mason said. "All fighters, follow me." With that, he throttled his engines up to full power, and twenty gs piled on top of him like a rockslide as he burned for his target.

The Cendy fighter screen was still forming and leaving the Cendy battlecruisers on the near side of the mothership exposed.

Mason selected four battlecruisers, one for each flight, to concentrate his squadron's torpedoes on. There were no verbal orders, just cues sent through the data link.

Dominic, Sabal, and Sawyer split their flights off to engage their assigned targets, while Mason's flight stayed with him as they burned for their target. The battlecruiser's maneuvering thrusters burned bright as the warship turned to bring its spinal gun to bear.

Contacts split off as the battlecruiser launched its own fighters, and the Outriders started burning on a hard intercept course as soon as they left their racks.

<*Launch interceptors at maximum range. Give those Outriders something to think about while we make our runs,*> Mason told his pilots.

His pilots acknowledged, and Mason started picking targets. He selected four Outriders and locked two interceptors on each. He wasn't trying to maximize his probability of a kill; he just wanted to disrupt the Cendy fighters while he made his run on his primary target.

Mason pressed *weapons release*, and his fighter shuddered as the ejectors started kicking interceptors out in rapid succession, depleting his eight weapons in four seconds.

Interceptors streaked away toward their targets. The Outriders changed course to evade, delaying their own intercept of Mason's fighters.

Hopefully he had bought enough time to make his runs on the battlecruisers.

<*Program your torpedoes to focus on the bow of the Fusiliers. Even if we don't kill them, knocking out their main guns will be enough.*>

His pilots acknowledged.

All Mason had to do was follow the course dictated by his AI weapon for optimal release of the shortburn torpedoes just before turnover, when he would turn his fighter ninety degrees to his current course to bend his vector away from the Fusilier and stay out of range of its point-defense guns.

The Outriders either evaded or shot down his interceptors with their own. Of the forty going after his squadron, only three were knocked out. But the delay was enough.

As soon as Mason reached the launch point, he held down his weapons release, triggering the simultaneous launch of all four externally mounted torpedoes.

He then turned toward his escape vector, maintaining the punishing acceleration as the torpedoes burned for their targets. They were close enough to accelerate the entire way. The only way the Cendies could stop them would be to either shoot them down or spoof their seekers.

The Fusiliers erupted with heavy jamming, blasting the torpedoes with dazzle lasers and electronic noise to try to break their lock.

Mason directed his own jammers against the Fusiliers. His fighter's jammers could not match the wattage a starship could put out, but any little bit of interference could improve the chances of at least one torpedo getting through.

Attrition started eating away at the torpedo volley. A few torpedoes broke lock, flying off toward nothing with dead seeker heads. Others were vaporized as they hit the wall of point-defense fire unleashed by the Fusiliers in the last seconds before impact.

The first detonations blinded Mason's sensors, and for a moment, all hostile contacts were lost behind the glow of a nuclear fire. But the glow quickly faded as the gas expanded and cooled, revealing the damage.

The sensor AI confirmed all four battlecruisers had taken at least a standoff-range hit. Two of the four were drifting hulks with their engines dead and guns silent. The remaining two were still active but showed severe damage to the frontal sections, almost guaranteeing their primary weapons were disabled.

Momentum carried Mason's fighters past the enemy as they continued to burn away, with no enemy fighters in pursuit. The Cendy Outriders had other problems to deal with.

Independence and her escorts launched a mass wave of torpedoes just after Mason had delivered his own ordnance. Conqueror bombers from Nova Squadron were burning behind the wave of torpedoes under the escort of Dagger Squadron.

Mason ordered: <*All fighters, make the fastest possible vector to* Independence *to restock on munitions and fuel.*>

Dominic replied: <*You think they'll let us dock while under fire, Hauler?*>
<*We'll find out when we get there, Silverback.*>

Armitage commented: <*Has anyone noticed that the big ship isn't doing anything?*>

Mason checked the tactical screen. All hostile fire and fighters were coming from the mothership's escorts, not the mothership herself.

Checking the thermals, it was clear why the mothership wasn't fighting. She was running.

Mason announced: <*Mothership's trying to jump out.*>

Sabal asked: <*Can we stop her?*>

Mason answered: <*Won't be up to us.*>

The first volley of torpedoes would reach the mothership before she finished charging her drive keel, but the escorting Katyushas launched a withering barrage of interceptors that crashed into the torpedo volley and wiped them out. The bombers released their weapons early to stay out of range, their freefall space bombs almost invisible as they drifted on a ballistic trajectory toward their target.

And *Independence*'s emissions spiked as she fired her main guns, lobbing eight kinetic kill vehicles at the mothership.

The Cendies concentrated on finding and destroying the bombs while the KKVs streaked through space. Point-defense guns, fewer than Mason was expecting, opened fire, cutting through the space before the KKVs. Some were vaporized in the last moments before impact, turning into fast-moving clouds of metal gas.

But a few got through, making clean hits, though the impacts they left on the hull of the massive starship seemed minuscule. Pinpricks in the side of a leviathan. Whatever internal damage they might have caused, it didn't stop the mothership from charging her drive keel.

"All ships—concentrate fire on *Independence*'s impacts!" Admiral Moebius called through the general comms.

The cruisers opened fire with their main guns. Though normally outside their effective range, the mothership was a massive target.

KKVs started impacting at about the same point. Admiral Moebius was trying to use her ships' guns to dig through the mothership's thick hull and hit something vital. If there had been just a little more time, it might have succeeded. But there wasn't enough time. Even as *Independence* and her cruiser escort launched volley after volley, the mothership disappeared in a massive flash of light.

For a moment, Mason hoped something had exploded inside the

mothership. But that was a fool's hope. The flash and sudden redshift was only caused by a departure jump, albeit a massive one.

The Cendy ships closest to the mothership were scorched by the flash, their hulls showing damage on the sensors.

The mothership had left her escorts behind to die. But it didn't matter. She could just build more.

CHAPTER 23

Independence returned to Plutonian space after recovering her strikecraft. Only then did Mason dismount his fighter and float out of the hangar. The hangar techs wasted no time swarming his Lightning to prepare it for the next mission.

Mason arrived at Osiris Squadron's suit storage room in time to see Sabal rip the helmet off her hardsuit and hurl it at the far wall. The momentum of her throw sent her tumbling backward while the helmet bounced off the wall with an audible crack.

Grabbing a handhold and bracing his foot against the wall, Mason caught the collar of Sabal's hardsuit to stop her rotation. "What's the problem, Hardball?"

"The bitch got away!"

"Yeah, she did. That doesn't mean you get to take your frustration out on vital equipment," Mason said, gesturing toward Sabal's helmet as it floated about the compartment. A scuff was visible just above the visor.

Sabal sighed. "I needed to throw something."

"What you need to do is get your helmet examined by a tech before the next mission," Mason said.

Sabal nodded. "Yes, sir."

When they had finished removing their hardsuits and securing them in their alcoves, Armitage approached him. "She's really angry, isn't she?"

"She's just expressing what we're all feeling," Mason said. "Things are going to get much harder for her with that monster still out there."

"Yeah," Armitage said. "What do you think caused the mis-jump?"

"There was no mis-jump," Mason said. "We just popped out in the wrong spot due to random chance."

"Bad luck, then?"

"Yeah. Can't expect to get dealt a winning hand every time."

"Doesn't make me feel any better."

"Nor I, Marbles," Mason said.

A notification appeared in Mason's HUD, a summons to the war room. "And that's my cue," he said. "Get yourself squared away, Marbles. I can't say how much downtime we'll have before our next mission."

Minutes later, Mason was in the war room, along with the leaders of *Independence*'s three other strikecraft squadrons.

Marshal Singh and Admiral Moebius were there as well, standing next to the holotank. Both their faces were illuminated by the light coming off the holotank, revealing Marshal Singh's solidly neutral expression and Admiral Moebius's scowl. Moebius looked just about as angry as Sabal had without having a helmet to chuck at the nearest wall.

As the pilots took their places around the holotank, Admiral Moebius leaned against the rim as if weighed down by far more than the .3 spin gravity of *Independence*'s internal ring.

"The mission was a failure, but the failure was no one's fault but mine for making a bad bet," Admiral Moebius said. "Because of that failure, our primary objective is going to be that much harder. We can expect to be under constant attack while we escort the convoy to Inner Sol." She manipulated the controls of the holotank, showing a representation of the space between the edge of the Solar System's jump limit and Earth.

"The bulk of the First Fleet is deployed around Earth-Sun L2. That will be the endpoint for the convoy's run to Sol. Until then, we shouldn't expect much support. And that's not the worst part. The whole point of this mission is to deliver fuel, which means we can't just burn it all making a continuous burn all the way to Sol. Instead, it will be a two-week flight, with fourteen hours of burning at either end. That means the Cendies will have two weeks to destroy as many of our tankers as they can before we reach the protection of the First Fleet."

The holotank changed, this time displaying a convoy of fifty massive fleet tankers arranged into ten chevrons of five ships each, with each chevron stacked atop the other. A scale inside the holotank showed the wedge to be over a thousand kilometers tall and five hundred kilometers wide.

The holotank zoomed out, revealing four escorting battlegroups, including *Independence*.

"We'll be working with the carriers *Goshawk*, *Cassowary*, and *Hyena* to protect the convoy, along with sixteen cruisers and twenty destroyers," Admiral Moebius continued. "We'll be relying on strikecraft as the first line of defense, with warships forming the close escort. Marshal Singh will be in overall command of the combined strikecraft." She nodded to the tallest man in the room.

Marshal Singh stood a bit straighter, using his full two meters of height to command the attention of the assembled pilots. He touched a button on the holotank and the projection of the convoy was replaced by a list of the squadrons that would be participating in the convoy—four from each carrier, including *Independence*.

"In total, we'll have a hundred and forty-eight strikecraft available for defending the convoy," Marshal Singh said. "It's unknown what exactly the Cendies will do to attack the convoy, but we do know that the most dangerous time for our ships will be during the acceleration and deceleration phases of our flight. All the Cendies will have to do is damage a tanker enough to cause it to fall out of formation for them to destroy at their leisure.

"And there's the matter of the Cendy mothership. It will almost certainly be deployed against the convoy when we make our run. And with its production capacity, the Cendies will have an indefinite supply of weapons and strikecraft to throw at us."

"Sir, would it be possible to attack the mothership when she appears?" asked Squadron Leader Masterson, the commander of *Independence*'s bomber squadron, the Novas. "The Cendies might put a higher priority on defending her rather than attacking our tankers."

"That presupposes we'd be able to threaten her, Squadron Leader Masterson," Marshal Singh said. "As it is, I think it best to concentrate our forces, including our bombers, on defending the convoy. Thus I want all bombers, including yours, to carry full loads of interceptors. You'll augment the firepower of the fighter screen."

The look on Masterson's face made it clear she did not like the idea of her bombers being used as glorified interceptor batteries, but she didn't challenge Marshal Singh.

Marshal Singh nodded to his superior officer and stepped back from the holotank while she stepped forward.

"*Independence* and the other carriers will be formed up separately from the tankers," Admiral Moebius said. "That should give the pilots a clear docking approach without having to mind your way around a few dozen tankers. The flight crews of every carrier will be ready to rearm and refuel your strikecraft as soon as your wheels touch the deck. I expect no more than a ten-minute turnaround time."

※

There was an air of anticipation in the briefing room as Mason laid out the plan cooked up by Marshal Singh's staff. Mason gestured to the display behind him. "Bombers from Nova, Blockbusters, Executioners, and Demolishers squadrons will be split into pairs and interspersed between the tankers. They'll be the last layer of defense, aside from the tankers' own point defenses. The next layer will be provided by cruisers and destroyers forming a wall behind the tankers. And then the first line of defense will be us and the other fighter squadrons.

"Our job's a simple one. We'll maintain a distance of a thousand kilometers behind the cruisers and fire on anything the Cendies try to send through. We'll be fully loaded with Stiletto pods and Javelin interceptors for that job.

"Because the Cendies have an indefinite supply of fighters and we don't, Marshal Singh wants me to impress on all of you that you should avoid getting into close combat with the enemy if avoidable. We've got a two-week fight ahead of us and can't afford to let the Cendies attrite us down so they can kill the tankers on Earth's doorstep.

"To put it simply, when you're out of interceptors, return to *Independence* for rearmament and return to your screening positions at the best possible speed. No closing into gun range after you run out of missiles—as much as you might want to. Let the big ships deal with anything that gets past us."

※

Mason launched as soon as *Independence* had completed her jump. Flying free in the void, he got his first unobstructed view of the convoy in all its glory.

It was one thing to see the convoy laid out inside a holotank. It was quite another to see it through the sensors of his fighter, where he could appreciate the full scale: fifty massive tankers arranged in a wedge, spread out to fill a volume of space over a thousand kilometers across.

Not long after Mason had launched, the tankers lit their longburn drives and started their burn for Earth. Mason let the tankers accelerate away as his squadron formed up, waiting for them to open the distance until he was in an escort position.

Cruisers and destroyers formed up behind the tankers, taking positions between the drive trails of each tanker. The bombers flew among the tankers, the close formation acting as mobile interceptor batteries, adding another layer of protection for the tankers.

Independence and the carriers were not part of the tanker formation, instead flying a parallel course in a formation of their own, the four capital ships flying line abreast some fifty kilometers between each ship, with *Independence* on the leftmost point, closest to the tankers. A squadron of destroyers in close formation provided their escort.

Mason kept his attention on the tactical screen, waiting for the inevitable Cendy response. They knew the Cendies were coming and had a good idea of where they would jump in. It was just a question of when the light from the jump would reach their sensors.

For several minutes, nothing happened as the tankers continued their burn, but that wasn't surprising. The Cendies would wait until all the Federal ships were well inside the jump limit, making escape via FTL impossible.

The first flashes of arriving Cendies lit up the sensor display half an hour into the convoy's acceleration burn. Six ships—four Fusiliers and two Katyushas—jumped in. The Fusiliers immediately deployed their strikecraft and all six hostile starships started burning after the convoy.

"Not much of a fleet," Sabal commented.

"They're a picket force here to confirm we're here," Mason said. "They'll call their friends over soon."

The departure flash of a courier drone confirmed Mason's assumption. The Cendies were probably worried that the convoy was a diversion or an ambush, but Earth Fed did not have the resources for such tricks.

Minutes later, a much larger collection of arrival flashes lit up Mason's sensors. Mason counted thirty warships, with the same two-to-one ratio of Fusiliers to Katyushas that typified Cendy fleet formation.

The arrival of the main Cendy force was punctuated by the gargantuan arrival flash of the mothership herself, flashing into existence well away from the rest of the ships so the light of her arrival didn't damage any smaller ships. The mothership lit her longburn drives, and an enormous plume of fusion exhaust spewed out the back of the cylindrical vessel like a gout of flame from a flare.

"Good God, look at the power output of that thing!" Dominic said.

The vast quantities of waste heat dumped from the massive radiators along the mothership's hull highlighted the mind-boggling amounts of power the mothership generated just to move—more power generation than any ship ever built by human hands.

The mothership captured in 61 Virginis, even crippled and immobile, was an engineering marvel. Seeing one that was fully operational and in hot pursuit inspired awe and dread in equal measure, especially when it started launching strikecraft.

The only analogy Mason could bring to mind was bees swarming from the hive. So many Outriders appeared on the tactical display that the sensor AI didn't bother trying to display them individually but as squadrons.

After the last Outriders had launched, over four hundred of them formed into a tight formation, like a closed fist raised to strike, and started burning hard for the convoy. The Outriders accelerated up to twenty gs, and the collective output of their hundreds of small longburn drives partially obscured the massive emissions of the mothership behind them.

Mason flipped his Lightning around to face the incoming attack.

"All right, folks, you know the drill. Launch interceptors at maximum effective range and then bug out. We're not going to win trading punches with that many Cendies. Prepare for hard gs on my mark."

Fifteen pilots acknowledged with non-verbal notifications of the data link.

"Mark!" Mason yelled as he pushed the drives to full power. Acceleration quickly built up to fifteen gs as the Lightning slammed into Mason's back.

All around him, Lightning squadrons from four carriers burned as a unit on intercept with the oncoming assault. Amid the assembled forces moving to engage each other, Mason started to feel small—a solitary man in a small fighter among hundreds.

But it was only a feeling. He had a job to do.

The combat AI drew up firing solutions for his selected targets and sharing telemetry between the fighters in his squadron. The tightly balled fist of Cendy fighters grew as their formation loosened.

As soon as Mason reached effective range, he pressed down on his launch button, giving the combat AI authorization to fire. The four Javelins on his wings ejected from their hardpoints and fell back behind Mason's fighter a couple of dozen meters before their shortburn drives lit and shot off toward the enemy.

The rotary launch in the belly of his fighter kicked interceptors out in half-second intervals. As soon as the last missile had fallen out of the weapons bay and ignited its drive, Mason turned away from the Cendies and pushed his acceleration to twenty gs. The force of acceleration went from uncomfortable to outright painful as he used all the power his fighter could give without killing him to pull his flight vector away from the enemy.

All the other Lightnings, including those of Osiris Squadron, did the same, breaking away to let the mass volley of interceptors fend for themselves.

The ball of Cendy fighters continued on their path as if they intended to smash through the wall of interceptors bearing down on them. Cendy jamming caused some of the interceptors to lose lock and go stupid, breaking off from the rest of the interceptors that maintained their guidance.

The Cendies launched interceptors of their own, a mass volley—some three thousand of their interceptors against the seventeen hundred Javelins.

When the clouds of missiles met, there was a staccato of flashes, and the Federal volley thinned out to fewer than a thousand interceptors. The Outriders maintained their attack vector, making no effort to evade, relying on their numbers instead.

The remaining interceptors tore into the Cendy formations. Mason's sensor AI cataloged dozens of hits. Almost half the Cendy Outriders dropped off the display, but the rest continued.

The cruisers and destroyers escorting the convoy had already cut their drives and turned to face the incoming threat, bringing their thickest armor, best sensors, and heaviest firepower to bear. The bombers scattered among the tankers remained as a last layer of defense.

The Outriders few past the scattering Lightnings, none breaking off to engage the Federal fighters.

Mason had already fully turned around and was burning hard to start moving back toward *Independence*, cutting his acceleration to a more sustainable fifteen gs.

<*Hauler, I don't think the Outriders are going after the tankers.*>

It looked like the Outriders were burning for the convoy, but Dominic wouldn't have said anything if he hadn't seen something odd.

<*Hold on, Silverback. I'm checking their vectors myself.*>

The sensor AI ran the numbers and confirmed Dominic's warning. The predicted vector of the enemy fighters was not optimal for attacking the tankers. Their new predicted vector traced directly toward the carriers.

Mason immediately opened a tight beam to *Independence*.

<*Independence Control, Osiris Leader—enemy strikecraft are on an attack vector with you and the other carriers. They're not going after the tankers.*>

A few seconds later, time enough for light lag and human processing, Mason got a reply from one of *Independence*'s comm officers. "Roger that, Osiris Leader. Our sensors match what you're seeing. Thanks for the heads-up."

Mason hoped it was enough, otherwise he had a long flight ahead of him.

The destroyers and cruisers escorting *Independence* and the carriers cut their thrust and fell behind to put themselves between the carriers and the incoming Cendy strikecraft. The carriers changed formation as well. *Goshawk*, *Hyena*, and *Cassowary* pushed their drives to increase their acceleration, getting ahead of *Independence*.

The Cendies would have to get past *Independence* to attack the more vulnerable carriers. Of course, that was supposing *Independence* herself wasn't the target.

The battlecarrier was a tough ship. She had fought her way out of occupied Jovian space practically on her own and weathered the first shots of the Cendy fleet over Triumph.

But that didn't mean she was invulnerable. A torpedo hit to her drive section and she'd fall out of formation and be left to the mercy of the Cendy pursuers.

Trapped by the physics of space flight, all Mason could do was watch. By the time the Lightnings reached the carriers, the Cendies would be finished with their attack.

The cruisers *Bangalore* and *Reykjavik* maneuvered directly into the path of the ball of Outriders, each flanked by a pair of destroyers: *Zaitsev* and *Cincinnatus* with *Bangalore*, *Boudicca* and *Segimer* with *Reykjavik*. Their actions were both brave and coldly rational. The combined crew complement of both cruisers and all four destroyers was less than that of a single carrier. The crews of the escorts knew they were expendable. It turned Mason's stomach to see it.

The Outriders launched their torpedoes outside of effective interceptor range and immediately started to stay out of the point-defense range of the starships.

There was no subtlety to the attack, just the brute force of a mass volley to penetrate Federal defenses. The torpedoes were organized into attack formations under pre-programmed commands. The intent was clear: to strike all at the same time in order to overwhelm the defenses of the starships.

The Federal starships started launching interceptors as soon as the torpedoes entered range. A constant stream from each warship launched to engage the wall of torpedoes.

Contacts became blurry on the display as all the starships started blasting the torpedoes with jamming, the strongest emissions coming from *Independence* as she dumped her immense power reserves into her emitters. Torpedoes started losing lock as their seeker heads burned out, but it was a trickle compared to those that flew true.

Interceptors started striking torpedoes, ripping holes in the formation. But the torpedoes simply reorganized their formation to fill in the gaps.

The last few seconds before impact saw the heaviest attrition as point-defense guns came to bear. Torpedoes by the dozen winked out of existence, thinning out the wall missiles.

Despite being far from the danger, Mason braced himself as the torpedoes reached the cruisers ... and then passed by them. The Cendies weren't concerned with taking out escorts.

The bulk of the torpedoes moved to engage *Independence* as the battlecarrier point defenses filled space with tungsten and jamming. She punched a hole into the torpedoes so wide, they didn't have time to reorganize before reaching detonation range.

All at once, several remaining torpedoes detonated simultaneously, triggered by some AI algorithm that decided that moment was the best chance the torpedoes had of damaging *Independence*.

The flash obscured *Independence* for several seconds, leaving a rock-hard knot in Mason's stomach as he waited to see if there would be a carrier for him to return to.

When the glare faded, *Independence* was still there, the forward armor of her hull scorched and glowing from the blast of multiple directional warheads.

But she was still there and still intact.

Then another burst of detonations signaled when the rest of the torpedoes reached the three other carriers.

As the glare faded, *Cassowary* and *Hyena* were dark and falling out of formation. Only *Goshawk*'s drives were still burning.

In their first attack, the Cendies had knocked out half the convoy's carrier strength.

CHAPTER 24

After two days of drones exploring the abandoned Ascension Station, nothing came out to bite them.

That seemed to satisfy Colonel Miller enough to take *Midnight Diamond* in close to begin a physical exploration of the station.

Midnight Diamond hovered above Ascension Station, with Origin A directly above and Origin Ab directly below. But Jessica couldn't tell through the visor of her pressure suit. It was too dark even for her eyes. The only illumination came from *Midnight Diamond*'s spotlights.

The tiny starship could only illuminate a small portion of Ascension Station's hull. The cast of the spotlights looked like an island of light amid a sea of absolute blackness.

The knowledge of how much more station there was than her eyes could see caused shivers to run up her spine. The tip of an artificial iceberg floating in darkness.

The old colony ship was the largest starship of her day, and its scale was still impressive even in modern times. Larger than *Independence*, she was outsized only by the largest of starliners, mega freighters, and Ascendancy motherships that shared her design. The modules attached to the sides of the former colony ship made her even bigger.

"One hundred meters to the hull," the Espatier sergeant said in Exo. "No sign of movement around the airlock."

"Understood, Sergeant. Stay alert," Colonel Miller replied in Exo.

The hardsuits of the Espatiers lit up as they flew into the beams cast by *Midnight Diamond*'s searchlights. Moments later, thrusters on their maneuvering rigs ignited to slow the Espatiers down to landing speed.

"Contact!" the Espatier sergeant announced.

The eight Espatiers formed points of an octagon around the hatch, four facing toward and the other four facing away from the hatch.

"Major Hesme, Lieutenant Sinclair, Miss Xia—you're clear to approach."

"Acknowledged," Jessica said. She glanced at Miriam, who wore the same type of borrowed League pressure suit she did. "Ready?"

Miriam nodded behind her visor. "Yes. Let's go."

Jessica pushed herself out of the airlock and found herself hanging over the island of light with nothing between her and Ascension Station other than a squad of Espatiers guarding the airlock. She pulsed her suit thrusters and started moving toward the station with Miriam and Isobel.

Shadows slid across the hull as Jessica approached. She picked out hers as it moved toward her landing spot, growing ever larger. She flipped on her helmet lights to cut through her own shadow, but even with those on, the bright floodlights from *Midnight Diamond* overpowered her lights enough that she still had a faint shadow as she got close.

Just like on modern Federal ships, the airlock on Ascension Station had handholds and hardpoints around the outer hatch. Jessica slowed herself to less-than-walking speed—slow enough that grabbing a handhold was enough to arrest her movement. Isobel landed next to her, and Miriam joined them almost immediately after.

"Any advice for opening you would like to tell us, Miss Xia?" Isobel asked.

"Airlocks haven't changed very much in the last couple of hundred years," Miriam answered. "There should be a panel you can pull open to the right." Miriam pointed to the panel in question.

"I got it," Jessica said as she pushed herself across the airlock to the panel.

There was a lever in a painted yellow recess next to the panel. Jessica yanked the lever and the panel popped open like the trunk of a car. Bracing herself against a handhold, Jessica pulled the panel open, latching it in place after uncovering the airlock controls. The screen of the control console was as dark as the rest of the ship.

"No power," Jessica said. "We can risk powering up the airlock, or we could open it manually."

"Go with the manual option, Lieutenant. I don't want to risk waking something up trying to power it," Colonel Miller advised.

"Got it," Jessica said. She tightened the line holding her to *Ascension*'s hull and examined the emergency pump. It was a simple handle with a safety pin in place. Jessica pulled the cross pin out and let it float, attached to the panel by just a thin wire, then started pumping.

"The airlock's starting to crack open," Isobel said. "No signs of gas escaping."

"No big surprise that," Jessica said as she continued to pump. The effort wasn't tiring due to her artificial body, but it was tedious, and it did start to raise her body temperature, though her pressure suit kept her from overheating from the effort.

The door swung open a couple of degrees with each stroke of the pump handle. After forty-five pumps, it was fully open.

"All done," Jessica said.

Isobel and Miriam had already floated inside by the time Jessica moved to enter the airlock. She found the IID officer shining a light through the viewport of the inner hatch. "See anything?" Jessica asked.

"Just dark empty corridor, like something out of a ghost story," Isobel said. "I don't even see dust floating about. I'm willing to bet there's no air on the other side of the inner hatch either."

"One way to confirm that," Miriam said. She floated over to one side of the airlock and pulled open a small panel, exposing a small valve. She pulled a lever on the top of the valve, and nothing happened. "No air on the other side," she said. "Looks like the Ascended depressurized the station before they abandoned it."

Miriam opened another, larger panel. "I'll disconnect the safety interlock so we can open the inner hatch."

The safety interlock was just a simple bar that mechanically connected the inner and outer hatches of the airlock—a mechanism that predated the interstellar era. Miriam removed the safety pin and pulled the lever to free the inner hatch's locking mechanism from the outer hatch.

The inner hatch was lighter in construction than the outer hatch and did not require opening with a hydraulic pump. Miriam simply pulled a release lever and the inner door popped open just enough for Jessica and Isobel to fit their fingers through and pull the inner hatch open, locking it to one side.

Isobel then shone her helmet lights down the empty corridor. "No signs of activity," she said.

"Let's make sure," Colonel Miller said. "The Espatiers are going in."

Jessica moved to one side with Isobel and Miriam as the Espatiers filed in, flying through the airlock under the power of their hardsuits' thruster rigs, weapons held ready before them. The Espatier team moved intersection by intersection, corridor by corridor, making cursory sweeps, creating a safe corridor from the airlock to the intersection.

"Every hatch we've come across is open," the Espatier sergeant informed them.

"I'm getting the sense they might have depressurized the whole station," Isobel said.

"The add-on modules were probably left unpressurized from the start," Miriam said. "The crew would've worked remotely using robots."

"So they probably depressurized the interior of the former colony ship to preserve it," Isobel said. "What do you think they're saving it for?"

"It's a monument," Jessica said. "It's the Ascendancy's Garden of Eden."

"Curious that they would abandon it, then," Isobel said.

"I'm not sure the Ascended were that sentimental," Miriam said. "They might have preserved it for posterity, but I doubt they would have much interest in tourism."

The Espatiers continued their search as Jessica waited in the airlock. After forty minutes of slow progress, they made their way from the airlock to what used to be *Ascension*'s bridge.

"What does the bridge look like?" Colonel Miller asked.

"Empty, sir. Just a bunch of chairs and dark displays. We'll need to power these up if we want to get anything useful from them."

"Colonel Miller, are we clear to proceed to the habitat module?" Miriam asked.

"Yes, but stick to routes cleared by the Espatiers," Colonel Miller advised. "I'm going to send another squad in to conduct more searching."

"Understood," Jessica said. "Who wants to go first?"

"I will," Miriam said, shoving her way through the airlock.

Isobel looked at Jessica and shrugged. "We should follow her. Yes?" Jessica nodded and pushed her way through.

The Espatiers had left glow sticks taped to the walls of the corridor every few meters to illuminate the corridor with a dull green light, giving *Ascension*'s interior a sickly appearance that did nothing to make it look any less haunted. Her helmet light illuminated details left hidden in the dim green chemiluminescence: handholds worn by decades of hands, scuffs on walls from bodies slipping past, and faded stains spotting the paneling.

Haunted or not, *Ascension* felt lived in.

They arrived at the hub of one of *Ascension*'s two contra-rotating habitat rings. The foremost one was where the ship's bridge was located.

The hatches that divided the sections were wide open.

"I don't think there're enough glowsticks aboard *Midnight Diamond* to light up the habitat rings," Isobel said.

"This place looks like it's in pretty good condition," Jessica said. "Assuming the backup batteries are still functional, we could try powering up emergency lighting from the bridge."

"Would it still work after two hundred years?"

"Of course," Miriam said. "My company built this ship, and she was built to last."

"Let's do it, then," Isobel said.

They floated down one of the spokes that connected the ring hub to the actual living spaces of the starship, continuing to follow the trail of glowsticks the Espatiers had placed leading to the bridge.

Just as the Espatiers had said, there was nothing on the bridge but unoccupied chairs and dark screens. Jessica ignored them and proceeded to a locked panel with high-voltage warnings painted on it. She got to work on the lock. The purpose of the lock was to deter someone casually opening the panel rather than stopping a determined attack, and she picked it open in less than a minute.

"Special Purpose Branch teaches their officers how to pick locks?" Miriam asked.

"They did this one," Jessica said as she replaced her tools and opened the panel.

As she suspected, the main breaker was open. That meant someone had opened the breaker, cut the connection to the battery backup, and then locked the access panel afterward. She wondered who had taken the keys with them.

"Colonel Miller, I've found the breakers for the first habitation ring. I can engage it presently," Jessica said.

"What will you end up powering?" Colonel Miller asked.

"This breaker controls emergency lighting," Jessica said. "Shouldn't wake anything else up."

"Go for it, Lieutenant."

Jessica pulled the breaker and was bathed in cool LED light.

"Well, the batteries still have power," she said. "A small screen inside the breaker box displays the batteries have sixty percent charge—more than enough juice to run the lights for a long while. Probably could run life support off these for a few days if we got that working."

"We'll stick to pressure suits for the time being," Colonel Miller said. "I'll start sending techs over to figure out how to get power to the computer systems. What will you do in the meantime?"

"We should start with the laboratories," Miriam said. "They're inside this ring along with the bridge."

"Then that's what we'll do." Jessica turned to Isobel. "You want to come along or stay here and chaperone the techs?"

"The techs can take care of themselves. I want to explore this ship," Isobel said.

It was a long float up the shaft illuminated by strings of LEDs until they reached the top.

With proper lighting, the evidence of life aboard *Ascension* became all the clearer: traction coating almost worn down to the deck plating, scuffed paint on the wall paneling. But it was all very tidy. No trash or debris floating in the microgravity. No dust clinging to the walls by static electricity. Care had been taken to secure any loose objects before the rotation of the habitat rings was stopped.

Miriam turned left in the main corridor. "Nearest labs are this way."

"We'll follow your lead," Jessica said.

The three of them floated along the wall, moving from one handhold to the next along the circumference of the ring.

The laboratories were marked by overhead signs. The doors were open.

Jessica followed Miriam into the first lab and saw an immediately familiar sight—a more primitive, less refined version of the birthing tanks aboard the captured mothership.

"Well, I think I know where the first Cendies were created," Jessica said.

"I count at least a dozen in this lab," Isobel said.

"Likely more in the rest of this ring. There are a hundred compartments just like the one in this section," Jessica said.

"So they didn't just develop the Cendies here. They mass produced them," Isobel said.

"That was the plan," Miriam said. "Build up enough infrastructure and create Ascended until they had a self-sustaining population."

"So what happened to the human crew? To Doctor Marr and his people?" Isobel pondered.

"That's what I'm here to find out," Miriam said. "I suspect we'll find the answers in the second ring. Until then, we should check the other labs."

An investigation of the other labs confirmed Jessica's assumption. Lab after lab was filled with early birthing tanks, all dry and empty. The labs were clean and organized. Signs of wear were the only evidence that they were ever used.

"We've reached the crew quarters," the Espatier sergeant said. "All the doors are closed and locked."

"Why would they close the individual crew quarters?" Isobel asked.

"I doubt it was for privacy," Jessica said.

"Tell them not to try to open the quarters," Miriam said. Then she pushed herself out of the lab. Jessica moved to follow her.

"What about the labs?" Isobel asked.

"They're not going anywhere," Jessica said. "Come along."

It took half an hour to transfer back into *Ascension*'s main hull, then into the second habitat ring where the crew quarters were located. The Espatiers had remained in position, dutifully refraining from trying to open any of the closed doors that ran along both sides of the corridor.

Each door bore the name of the person who had occupied the room. *Ascension*'s massive size and relatively small crew afforded the crew a level of personal luxury usually only afforded to starliners.

But *Ascension*'s crew hadn't come all the way out here for a pleasure cruise. They had come to make their great work. Their final work.

Jessica followed Miriam until she stopped at the door with the name Julian Marr stenciled in sharp black lettering across the off-white paintwork.

Miriam ran her fingers over Julian Marr's name.

"Do you want to open it?" Jessica asked.

Wordlessly, Miriam grabbed the door latch and turned it without apparent resistance. She then swung the door into the quarters.

Inside was a well-appointed, tidy living space consisting of a central living area with a couch, carpeting, and a kitchen. Some effort must have been made to secure all the small objects to prevent them from floating about in microgravity.

Miriam floated inside. Jessica followed with Isobel in tow.

"If I didn't know any better, I would think someone still lived here," Isobel said.

"They might still do, after a fashion," Miriam said. "The bedroom's this way."

Jessica felt a sense of foreboding as she followed Miriam into the bedroom. The door was lightly made, meant for privacy and little else.

Miriam grabbed the latch and hesitated.

"Afraid of what we're going to find in there?" Isobel asked her.

"I'm not looking forward to seeing what's on the other side," Miriam admitted. With that, she threw the door open.

Illuminated by a combination of emergency lighting and helmet lights, Julian Marr's body lay peacefully in the middle of the bed, his hands clasped on his chest.

He was much older than he looked in his files. His hair and beard were bleached nearly white, and his skin was deeply wrinkled around his hands and face.

Whatever the Cendies had done to preserve his body made him look uncannily alive. There were no signs of the desiccation one would expect from long-term vacuum exposure.

"Entombed with all their worldly possessions like the Pharaohs," Isobel breathed.

"I'm surprised the Ascended would make an effort to preserve the bodies of Julian Marr and his crew," Jessica said.

"Why would you be?" Miriam asked. "These are their creators. A bit of reverence is not surprising. If anything, I'm surprised how restrained it is."

"What were you expecting?" Jessica asked.

"Something more ... interactive."

"You mean ... like you. Digitized consciousness."

Miriam nodded. "That's why I'm out here. I'm the ghost of one of the Ascension Foundation's principal financiers. I'd like to ask the ghosts of my old friends what they did."

"Are you worried they lied to you?" Jessica asked.

"I'm worried that I don't know," Miriam said.

"Well, I doubt there's much to learn in here," Isobel said. "We can have medics come in to examine the bodies—see how exactly they're preserved against vacuum."

Miriam glanced at Julian's body. "That is just a curiosity. We should figure out how to get some portion of the computer systems operational."

"Given all the add-ons on the outsides, I suspect the computer systems have deviated quite a bit from where they were when *Ascension* departed Sol," Jessica speculated. "Where would the main cores be?"

"The main computer cores would be housed in a torus wrapped around the drive-keel aft of the habitat ring," Miriam said. "If there's any data aboard this ship, it will be there."

Jessica passed the word along to Colonel Miller.

"I'll route a team there now to secure it," Colonel Miller said.

Miriam left Marr's quarters.

"Miriam, wait," Jessica said, following. "What's the hurry?"

"I need to know," Miriam said. "I need to know if there's something left of my friends other than preserved flesh."

"Well, slow down a bit. Let the Espatiers make sure it's safe."

"Oh, Jessica, there aren't any traps here. This isn't some old military base filled with secrets. It's a memorial. A museum. A tomb. It's clear as day that the Ascended meant to visit this place."

"Even museums have security systems," Jessica pointed out. "And it's not unheard of for tombs to have traps."

"You've watched too many movies," Miriam said.

Jessica followed Miriam down the spoke, into the hub, and then down toward the computer core.

Espatiers were just starting to clear the compartment when they arrived. One tried to stop Miriam, but she just brushed by the soldier. Isobel spoke to the soldiers in Exo to get them to stand down while Jessica followed Miriam inside.

"Miriam, what are you planning on?" Jessica asked.

"I helped design these computers," Miriam said. "I know how to power them on, assuming their backup power supplies are online."

"Miriam, we don't know what else powering up the computer core will activate on this station," Jessica warned.

Miriam moved to a panel, opened it, and pulled a lever before anyone could stop her.

"There," Miriam said. "I just physically isolated the computer core from the rest of the ship's network." She glanced at Jessica. "My company built this ship, remember?"

"I know that, Miriam. But maybe slow down," Jessica said. "Your friends had decades to modify *Ascension* from its original design. This ship's already been radically modified from the outside. There's nothing to say the same hasn't happened to the interior."

Miriam gestured to the dark banks of hardware. "The answers are in these computers, Jessica. Would you have me wait while they're right here?"

"For a few more minutes, yes, Miriam," Jessica said firmly. "At least until we can be certain that flipping these things on isn't going to activate anything we'd regret waking up."

Miriam huffed. "Fine. But as soon as you're satisfied, I'm flipping these machines on."

CHAPTER 25

The loss of *Cassowary* and *Hyena* evoked images of seagoing ships of old sinking beneath the waves. Both carriers were largely intact beyond their crippled longburn drives. Thus they fell away from the convoy toward the implacable Cendy mothership and her escorts.

Bangalore and *Reykjavik* each moved toward one of the stricken carriers to take on their crews, reaching the carriers at about the same time as Mason reached the final docking approach with *Independence*. He couldn't help but notice how the space around *Independence* and *Goshawk* was crowded with orphaned fighter squadrons. He couldn't begin to think how they were going to manage four carriers' worth of strikecraft with half that number of carriers.

"Belts and zones," Mason muttered as he approached the open hangar.

The battlecarrier's armored nose was blackened by the concentrated blasts of the few torpedoes that had gotten through her defensive screen. On the thermal imaging, the front of the ship still glowed as the armor continued to radiate heat.

Otherwise, the damage to the battlecarrier herself had been minimal. The warheads had detonated too far away to penetrate *Independence*'s frontal armor.

Independence was still under acceleration, burning to join formation with *Goshawk*, necessitating docking under power. Mason guided his Lightning under the thrust of its lifting engines, slipping it into the hangar. Engine exhaust hit the actively cool floor of the hangar, where blast deflectors guided the exhaust back into space.

Mason set his fighter down gently, cutting the engines as soon as the wheels touched. The fighter settled under the weight of *Independence*'s acceleration.

Moments later, the hangar crew appeared, along with loader robots trundling toward his fighter bearing bundles of interceptors in their arms.

The crews set about attaching tubes and cables to his fighter. One loader robot fed interceptors into his empty weapons bay while another exchanged expended Stiletto pods for fresh ones. In the space of ten minutes, Mason's Lightning, fully restocked with fuel and weapons, was ready to launch.

The hangar crew turned his fighter around on its wheels until it faced space again and attached the nose gear to the catapult. After a rote communication with *Independence*'s traffic controller, the catapult kicked Mason back into space.

He immediately vectored for the crippled carriers—not that the Cendies seemed eager to finish their work. Their remaining Outriders, barely a quarter of what they'd started with, were on a return vector to the mothership.

Bangalore positioned herself next to *Cassowary* and *Reykjavik* next to *Hyena*. Multiple lines attached each carrier to the cruisers, and streams of spacers in pressure suits moved across the lines to the cruisers.

Most of the crews had survived, though now the fleet had four thousand extra spacers they would need to house. Accommodation was going to get tight.

Behind him, *Independence* and *Goshawk* had finished servicing their own strikecraft and were now taking on the former complements of *Cassowary* and *Hyena*. There wasn't enough room aboard both carriers for all those strikecraft, which meant half of all the convoy's strikecraft would have to be in flight for the whole time.

Things were going to get a lot more uncomfortable for the pilots of the convoy's strikecraft.

The evacuation of the crippled carriers proceeded quickly, and when *Bangalore* and *Reykjavik* were stuffed full of rescued spacers, they detached from the drifting hulks and lit their drives to catch up with *Independence*. Once far enough away, both cruisers launched one torpedo each at the abandoned carriers, denying the Cendies the satisfaction of finishing off the carriers themselves.

The Cendies seemed content to watch as both carriers exploded into clouds of gas and debris. Mason had no doubt the mothership was busy converting raw materials stored within its massive holds into more Outriders to fling at the convoy.

A communications query appeared in Mason's notifications display. It was a general request from Marshal Singh to all squadron leaders, including the eight who'd just lost their carriers.

"Silverback, I'll be in communications with Marshal Singh. Hold down the fort while I'm on autopilot," Mason said.

"I'll try to make sure no one goes astray while you're busy, Hauler," Dominic answered.

Mason opened a communications channel with *Independence*, and the communications officer quickly placed him on a joint call with sixteen other pilots. There was no small talk between pilots in the queue. Just lists of names quietly waiting for the virtual meeting to start.

Marshal Singh's face appeared in the window with his name projected below in green letters.

"The loss of *Cassowary* and *Hyena* severely complicates our mission to protect the convoy. But I'll say that this was despite the best efforts of our pilots. The fault lies with me for failing to anticipate that the Cendies would focus on attacking our carriers rather than the tankers.

"With that said, despite losing two carriers, we still have the same number of strikecraft we started with. The challenge will be to keep things that way with just two carriers.

"Obviously, we can't fit *Cassowary*'s and *Hyena*'s strikecraft groups aboard *Independence* and *Goshawk*, but we can hot swap hangar space to allow pilots and strikecraft to at least get some respite.

"We'll be transferring *Cassowary*'s and *Hyena*'s hangar crew to help take up the work of maintaining fighters while in flight. Unfortunately, there are some sacrifices pilots will have to make.

"Don't expect to see your beds for the remainder of your flights

The Edge of Nowhere

downorbit. Pilots will be sleeping in their fighters while under the direction of their flight AIs. While not in combat, we'll be rotating squadrons every four hours to give pilots a chance to stretch their legs. But otherwise, everyone's going to learn to get very familiar with the interior of their strikecraft.

"Once *Reykjavik* and *Bangalore* return to the formation, we'll move *Independence* and *Goshawk* into the middle of the convoy so they won't be caught isolated again. Fighters will continue to deploy as part of the fighter screen, while bomber squadrons will maintain their close escort of the tankers to act as mobile interceptor batteries.

"It's unknown when the Cendies will attack again, but it's assumed it will be while the convoy is still accelerating. For the remainder of the approach burn, all strikecraft are to remain in space, save for docking to rearm and refuel.

"I'll leave you to pass the word on to your pilots. Marshal Singh, out."

The connection closed, and Mason was left alone in his cockpit with just the whine of his Lightning's drives for company. He broke his solitude by opening his squadron channel to pass the word on to his pilots.

"Well, so much for relaxing in my cabin between flights," Dominic said. "Twenty hours a day in the cockpit is going to wear pretty hard on us."

"Speak for yourself, Silverback," Sabal said. "We've all had long flights before. I don't see how this is any different."

"The constant threat of attack is one difference," Dominic pointed out.

"We'll deal with whatever the Cendies throw our way," Mason said. "They're going to need time to recover from their last attack, but we should be ready to deal with further attacks while the convoy is still accelerating."

"And then we'll be spending most of the next two weeks in zero gravity," Dominic said. "And there isn't enough room in our cockpits for normal exercise."

"That's what the breaks aboard *Independence* are for," Mason said. "But we still have seven hours until the convoy finishes its approach burn. Let's stay alert until then."

CHAPTER 26

AFTER THE LEAGUE techs had confirmed they were isolated from the rest of the ship, Miriam started waking up the old computers.

In the vacuum, there was no air to carry the sound of electronics coming to life. Lights simply blinked on while screens activated, showing the bootup process.

Despite being over two hundred years old, the computers didn't take long to boot up. Screens lit up to identical login screens, each one speckled with a unique mosaic of stuck pixels.

"Anyone want to guess the password?" Isobel asked.

Miriam moved up to the station and rapidly typed the login information. A second prompt appeared, asking for biometric verification.

"Jessica, I'm going to need you for this part," Miriam said.

"I'll need your biometric data if you want me to match your eyes," Jessica said.

"I'm uploading it now," Miriam said.

"Wait—you can change your eyes?" Isobel asked.

"You wouldn't notice, but Miriam used to have the same eye color I do," Jessica said as she reconfigured the artificial retinas in her eyes to match those of Miriam's old biological eyes.

"Why would they save Miriam Xia's biometrics?" Isobel asked.

"Because I had full access to *Ascension*'s systems when I was alive," Miriam answered. "And it does not appear that Julian ever got around to deleting my credentials."

Jessica placed her face up to the scanner, and lasers pierced her face plate to scan her irises. It took less than a second for the computer to decide Jessica's eyes matched Miriam's, and the login screen was replaced by the main menu.

Swiping through menus with obvious familiarity, Miriam soon found what she was looking for. "There," she said. On the screen was a file marked as the digitized consciousness of Doctor Julian Marr.

"I see," Jessica said. "So, uh, how do we spin him up?"

"We'll need to construct a proper virtual environment," Miriam said. "Right now, all we have is a gray box. If he were awake, he wouldn't be aware of what's going on outside."

"So how do you propose we do that?" Jessica asked.

"We'll need to pressurize the compartment. I can't make hardwire connections through this suit, and my mobility rig can't operate in a vacuum," Miriam said.

"I'll see about getting this compartment pressurized," Isobel said.

Miriam turned to Jessica. "You and I are the only two with the hardware to dive directly into a VR environment. So it stands to reason that we'll be the ones to talk to Julian."

"How do you think it will go?" Jessica asked.

"I suggest you make sure your default appearance is not set to your uniform," Miriam said. "Seeing someone in a military uniform when he wakes up will give him the wrong impression."

"I'll make sure to dress for the occasion," Jessica said.

The League technicians started getting the compartment ready for pressurization by checking seals and running checks on the environmental systems. There was no spare gas stored in *Ascension*'s tanks, so air had to be brought in from *Midnight Diamond*. Once the air bottles were in place and the compartment's atmospheric systems were online, the techs sealed the doors, leaving Jessica, Isobel, and Miriam alone inside.

As air flooded in, the sound of computers gradually entered hearing range and grew in volume until the ambiance settled into a beehive-style buzz. An air check showed one atmosphere of pressure and a safe breathing mix.

Jessica popped the seal on her helmet and pulled it off, straightaway feeling cool air kiss her face. Miriam pulled off her helmet and the cap underneath, causing her artificial hair to fan out behind her head. Isobel also removed her helmet but kept her cap on.

Miriam was already at work connecting wires to ports on the computers. Adaptors fabricated aboard *Midnight Diamond* bridged the 200-year gap in the interface technology, allowing Miriam to slot a wire behind her right ear. She handed the end of another wire to Jessica.

Jessica pulled off her cap and grabbed her hair to keep it from floating over her connection port. She placed the end of the cable behind her ear and felt it snap into place by a magnetic connection. Her HUD immediately displayed a warning that she was connecting to an unsecured system.

"So, what kind of VR are we going for?" Jessica asked. "Beach? Tropical pool?"

Miriam shook her head, smiling. "No, just my old parlor. It will be familiar to Julian."

"Many an evening sipping brandy while contemplating the future?" Jessica asked.

"Yes, actually," Miriam said. "You should get comfortable. I'm going to spin up the VR."

Jessica clipped herself to a handhold to keep from floating about and waited for Miriam's connection request. As soon as the icon appeared on her HUD, she accepted, and the *Ascension* computer core faded away, replaced by Miriam's parlor, complete with a fire crackling in the fireplace.

Looking down, Jessica was satisfied with the clothes she had selected: black pants and a white jacket over a purple blouse.

"Not a bad outfit," Miriam approved. Jessica looked up to find Miriam standing by the liquor cabinet, dressed in a sleeveless blue blouse and cream pants. She had three glasses set out and poured a couple of fingers of Scotch whisky into each of them.

Miriam waved Jessica over and handed her a glass, then took the two remaining glasses and walked over to the three chairs arranged in a semicircle in front of the fireplace. She placed one glass on a small table in front of the center chair and settled into the seat to the right of the fireplace.

"Take a seat, Jessica. Julian's going to be startled enough waking up without seeing someone looming over him."

Jessica sat down, clasping her glass in both hands.

"I'm spinning him up now," Miriam said. "Try to smile. You'll only get one chance to make a good first impression with him."

Jessica relaxed and waited.

An old man appeared. His skin was wrinkled and liver-spotted, and his hair was bleached white by age. His eyes were closed, and his breathing was slow like he was napping. He was dressed in casual work clothes: a button-down shirt and khaki pants teamed with moccasin-like shoes.

His eyes snapped open, and he launched himself out of his seat, looking around as he desperately tried to take in his surroundings. His eyes fixed on Jessica.

"Where am I, and who in the bloody fuck are you?" Julian Marr demanded in a pronounced Scottish accent.

Jessica tried to maintain her most pleasant smile as she opened her mouth to introduce herself, but Miriam beat her to it. "That's Jessica, Julian," Miriam said. "Don't tell me you've forgotten my old parlor?"

Julian's eyes snapped to Miriam, looking her up and down. "Ah, you look well, Miriam. Much younger than the last time we met."

"Can't say the same about you, Julian," Miriam said. "I'm going to have to teach you how to alter your VR appearance."

Julian looked down at his wrinkled hand. "Spent much more time as an old man than anything else. So, what's gone wrong?"

"What makes you think something's gone wrong?" Miriam asked.

"Because you're the one waking me up rather than the Ascended." Julian turned to Jessica. "And you have a stranger with you."

Jessica stood up. "I'm Jessica Sinclair. It's a pleasure to meet you, Doctor Marr."

"Aye," Julian said but made no move to greet her. "Your accent sounds a bit funny. Almost but not quite like London."

"Born and raised," Jessica affirmed.

Julian shook his head. "This is wrong." He turned to Miriam. "This wasn't the plan. How long have I been dead?"

"A hundred and fifty years," Miriam told him.

"Only a century and a half? That's not even close to long enough. What has happened?"

"I'll get straight to the point, Julian," Miriam said. "The Ascended are waging war against humanity, and I am here with Jessica to figure out why."

"War? Impossible!" Julian spluttered. He turned to Jessica. "And what's your purpose in being here, Jessica?"

Jessica cleared her throat. "I'm with the Federal Space Forces Special Purpose Branch."

"A bloody spy? Brilliant," Julian said. He turned to Miriam. "Are you really Miriam? Or another Federal spy made to look like her in virtual reality?"

"Try that whisky and find out," Miriam said.

Julian picked up the glass from the table and, after a precautionary sniff, took a sip.

The sourest expression Jessica had ever seen blossomed on his face as he shook his head like he was trying to shake away the memory of what he'd just experienced. "Oh, you scabrous bitch!" Julian said. "I thought I was free of this shite when I left Earth."

"I made sure I had the flavor profile digitized," Miriam said. "I thought it would be a serviceable proof of my identity."

"Of course you of all people would remember that," Julian said.

"I'm sorry, what did I miss?" Jessica held up her glass. "Is this bad Scotch or something?"

"It's very good Scotch," Miriam said.

"Tastes like a fucking bog," Julian said.

Jessica took a sip. The Scotch was indeed very peaty but still quite palatable.

"Julian hates peaty whisky," Miriam told her.

"I'll just mix some ashes in vodka and get the same flavor," Julian said. "You have any Irish whiskey? Something to wash the dirt off my tongue?"

"You remember where I keep it in the liquor cabinet?"

"Let's see," Julian said. He marched over to the liquor cabinet and quickly found what he was looking for, as evidenced by the smile on his face.

He took out a glass, dropped a ball of ice in it, and poured himself a drink. Taking a sip, relief washed through his body.

"Aye, that's better," he said. "All right. I believe you're the real Miriam, or at least close enough. Anyone who did a little research could have known my favorite whiskey."

"But only a true friend would know what you hated," Miriam said.

Julian deposited himself in his seat, whiskey in hand, and glanced at Jessica and Miriam. "So, the Ascended have been causing trouble."

"Yes," Jessica said. "We came out here trying to find out why."

"Out here? Are we still aboard *Ascension*?" Julian asked.

"That's right," Jessica said.

"Came a long bloody way, then," Julian said. "Unless stardrives have gotten much faster since I left Sol."

"Not especially," Jessica said. "Biggest advances have been in efficiency."

"Aye? Interesting."

"Also beside the point," Miriam said. "Julian, what's happened to the Ascended? What they're doing isn't what you told me they would do."

Julian sighed. "I wish I knew. This is the first I've heard of it. I'm as confused as you are."

"So you really did intend for the Ascended to be explorers?" Jessica asked.

"Aye, lass. Why would you think otherwise?"

"The results."

"How bad is it?" Julian asked.

Jessica looked at Miriam. "Would you like to tell him, or should I?"

"Oh, please do the honors, Jessica. I insist," Miriam said.

"Just over a year ago, the Cendies … err … I mean, the Ascended launched a surprise attack across several systems. They captured the outer Solar System, wiping out almost an entire Federal fleet in the process, and since then have had Earth under siege. They also launched an invasion of Triumph that only barely failed."

Julian was quiet for a moment and took another sip of his virtual whiskey. "Bloody hell! I don't know if I should be horrified or proud that my creations have become powerful enough after a hundred and fifty years to challenge the Earth Federation and the League at the same time."

"They certainly have the capacity," Jessica said. "What we don't know is their true motivation. We only know their stated reasons."

"Which are?"

"They say they wish to pacify us," Jessica said. "They want to forcibly disarm all human systems and ultimately achieve sole control over interstellar space travel."

"Hrmph. I admit I can see the logic in that," Julian said. "But it does not appear that their plan is working if Earth Fed and the League are still fighting them."

"We've been able to deal them some setbacks," Jessica said. "But winning the war will be difficult if we don't know why the Ascended started the war in the first place."

"And why do you think I would help you fight my creations?" Julian asked. "If they decided war was the only option, they must have a good reason."

"Or they deviated from your original intent," Jessica suggested.

"Lass, I spent decades perfecting the Ascended," Julian said. "Their entire psychology was specifically engineered to avoid human pitfalls."

"That sounds like your pride's doing the talking, not logic," Miriam said. "Even you can't predict every possibility with the Ascended. As evidenced by the forces they were able to build up, they must have decided to prepare for war not long after your death."

Julian set his drink down and rubbed his face with both hands. "I wish I knew what to tell you, Miriam. None of this makes any sense. The Ascended aren't supposed to need territory or to compete with human civilization for resources. Even after two hundred years, I doubt settled space has expanded that much."

"I don't think this war is about resources or territory, Doctor Marr," Jessica said. "It's my belief that the Ascended's motivation for the war is rooted in their desire to accumulate knowledge. I think there's something they're worried about us finding out and want to stop us before that happens."

Julian was quiet for a few seconds, pondering Jessica's statement. "Aye, that would make more sense. It would have to be something that isn't easily moved or fungible. Simple data can just be copied."

"What do you think it could be?" Jessica asked.

"Aliens," Julian said.

There were several seconds of silence as Julian let that word sink in.

Miriam broke the silence first. "Julian, my dear, you're going to have to be more specific than that."

"Are we talking simple primordial life or a civilization?" Jessica asked.

"Civilization. Any critters the Ascended found interesting would simply be sampled and cataloged, even if they were certain humans would wipe them out. But as to the nature of the civilization, its size and technological capability, that would be purely speculative."

"An advanced civilization probably wouldn't be too threatened by humanity," Jessica mused.

"Has contact been made with an alien civilization in the past two hundred years?" Julian asked.

"No," Jessica said.

"I suppose if anyone was going to make contact, it would be the Ascended," Julian said. "Maybe a pre-industrial civilization that hasn't yet developed to the point where they would change their planet in ways that are easily detected—though I have a hard time believing the Ascended risked war to protect an underdeveloped civilization. They'd take records, try to sample the culture without disrupting them, and then move on."

"So maybe it's the remains of an advanced civilization," Jessica suggested.

"I suppose," Julian said. "We are a greedy species. Discovering the ruins of an advanced civilization would spark a gold rush that would likely destroy more artifacts than it discovered. It doesn't explain why the Ascended would wage an offensive war, but I suppose it's a start."

"At the very least, it will be one more breadcrumb for us to follow," Jessica said.

"So, what happens when you reach the end of that trail, Lieutenant?" Julian asked. "What happens when you find out what's motivating the Ascended?"

"That's 'above my paygrade,' as my colleagues would say," Jessica said. "Personally, my hope is that if we learn why the Ascended are waging war on us, then we can find a way to end the war without further loss of life."

"You want a peaceful solution to the war after they attacked you?" Julian asked.

Jessica shrugged. "The alternative is more death."

"You're not as bloodthirsty as most military types," Julian observed.

"How many 'military types' have you met?" Jessica countered.

"Enough," Julian said. "Perhaps the intervening years have mellowed out the Earth Federation's jingoism."

Jessica gave a one-shouldered shrug. "I wasn't around back then. Of the three of us, I'm the only one here whose age isn't measured in triple digits."

Miriam made a pained expression. "Way to make me feel old."

"As if you would forget." Jessica smiled at Miriam, then returned her attention to Julian. "We need your help, Doctor Marr."

"It's the Ascended who need my help," Julian said. "And I'm not sure how helping Earth Fed win does that."

"Have you not listened to what I said, Doctor Marr?" Jessica said. "I'm not asking you to help Earth Fed win the war. I'm asking you to help me end it."

"You might be, but I doubt Earth Fed would settle for anything less than victory. A victory that would end the Ascended."

"And what if the Ascended win?" Jessica asked. "Assume they overcome both Earth Fed and the League, becoming overlords of space. You think they'll do much exploring if they have to keep an eye on billions of humans waiting for the moment to rise up and overthrow them?"

Julian took another sip of his simulated Irish whiskey, his eyes lost in thought.

"She has a point, Julian," Miriam said. "The Ascended are trying to build an empire, even if they refuse to use that word. The same thing Earth Fed did that provoked you into coming out here."

He looked at Miriam, and Jessica could see the wordless exchange that only old friends could share. "I'll need to know everything about what the Ascended have done in this war so far."

Jessica rubbed her hands together. "Well, would you like me to put together a presentation or just tell you here and now?"

Julian walked over to the liquor cabinet and refilled his glass. "I have nothing but time, Lieutenant. And I'm a fair man. If you clear things up for me, I can point out what you have wrong about the Ascended."

⚜

Three hours later, Julian reclined in his seat as Miriam added more logs to the fire.

"Emissaries are a fascinating addition to the Ascended's forms," Julian said.

"You didn't expect the Ascended to need to talk to humans?" Jessica asked.

"No, actually," Julian said. "I had intended for them to just venture off into the deepest reaches of the galaxy and beyond, never to interact with humanity again. Clearly they decided differently."

"The Ascended do seem to be interested in human culture," Jessica said. "One Emissary was quite interested in the human literature written in the years since *Ascension*'s departure. It was the first clue I found about the Ascended's origins."

"Curious. I can't say that we ever encouraged an interest in human literature and culture."

"Just because you never appreciated the arts doesn't mean your creations wouldn't, Julian," Miriam pointed out.

"Yes, well, if an interest in old stories was the only deviation, the two of you wouldn't be here," Julian said.

"But they did deviate, Julian," Miriam said. "And they're going to destroy everything we dreamed of if we don't get them to correct their course."

"And how do you suppose we do that?" Julian asked.

"We find out what's motivating them," Jessica said. "Tell me, Doctor Marr, how much have the Ascended deviated from your original intentions?"

Julian put his glass down and rubbed his forehead. "Not very much, other than the whole war thing. And the way they're approaching warfare is consistent with how we intended them to solve their problems."

"So if we figure out what's motivating them to make war and remove it, then they should stop, right?" Jessica asked.

"Unless they're more like humans than I meant them to be, yes," Julian said. "If the reason ends, so will the war. But that assumes Earth Fed agrees to end the war."

"I'm not the one who gets to make that decision," Jessica said. "But if we can at least give everyone a less violent alternative ..."

"And you don't think it's too late?" Julian asked. "After all the death and destruction?"

"It's never too late to reduce harm," Jessica said. "But first we need to find out what's motivating the Ascendency's attack."

"I guess I will ask them," Julian said.

Jessica paused for a moment. "Like what? Send them a letter? There aren't any Ascended on this station. We've looked."

"I'll just summon them here," Julian said.

"You can do that?" Jessica asked.

"Of course. I built this station. I know what it's capable of. And if the Ascended have been as good at preserving this station as you say they are, there should be some pre-programmed courier drones ready to jump to the nearest Ascended communications hub."

"What are these communications hubs?" Jessica asked.

"Predetermined locations in space with automated relay stations containing fleets of courier drones," Julian elaborated. "It's a way to allow the Ascended motherships to remain in contact with each other, even across the galaxy."

"How do you know this?" Jessica asked.

"My team designed it," Julian said. "Though I'm sure the Ascended have made improvements to the system in the last two centuries."

Jessica started massaging her temples. "Of bloody course. That's how they've been able to coordinate across multiple systems. You wouldn't happen to have technical data on the relay stations?"

"My knowledge is a bit out of date, lass," Julian said. "As originally designed, the relay stations maintain constant contact with each other through their courier drones. If a mothership wanted to contact another, it would send a courier to one relay station, which would then share that information with all the others. Thus the receiving mothership would just need to send a courier drone to whatever relay was nearest to receive the message."

"If what you're saying is true, then if we captured one, we'd find out everything the Cendies know," Jessica said.

"If you could break the encryption," Julian said. "And that's assuming they don't have a deadly failsafe. I'm sure the Ascended have made such accommodations, given they're at war now."

"So how long would it take for the Ascended to reply?" Miriam asked.

"I don't know. Days at least. Weeks at most. But I am confident that if I send a message, the Ascended will come."

"I'm going to need to log out," Jessica said. "I need to discuss this with our allies."

Miriam dismissed Jessica with a wave. "Then off you go, my dear. Julian and I will catch up."

CHAPTER 27

"Pardon me for being dense, Lieutenant, but did you just suggest that we contact the Ascendancy?" Colonel Miller asked, seated aboard *Midnight Diamond*'s small bridge while Jessica floated before him.

Jessica nodded. "Yes, sir. Doctor Marr seems keen on getting an explanation from his creations, and he's confident they will tell him if he asks."

"That's one hell of an assumption, Lieutenant. I'd rather find one of those relay stations and pry information from it," Colonel Miller said.

"That is certainly a possibility, but there are risks with that as well," Jessica said. "I've no doubt the Cendies would have measures to protect the information on those relays. And besides, I doubt we'd be able to break Cendy encryption fast enough to extract actionable intelligence."

"There's still the small matter that when the Cendies arrive, they'll kill us before answering any questions from Doctor Marr," Colonel Miller said.

"That's where we have an advantage, sir," Jessica said. "The Ascended don't know we're here. *Midnight Diamond* could land on the surface of Origin A. Under those clouds, the Cendies aren't going to be able to see us."

"Assuming Doctor Marr doesn't give us up," Colonel Miller said.

"He doesn't know about *Midnight Diamond* or her capabilities, sir," Jessica said. "Even if he gives up our presence, he won't know where to point the Cendies."

"Still a hell of a risk."

"A worthwhile one, I think, sir," Jessica persisted.

The Edge of Nowhere

Colonel Miller tapped on his armrest, a slow rhythm evoking the pace of his thoughts. "I'll consider it. Before we do anything that will bring the Cendies here, I'm launching a courier drone to report what we've found back home. If there are any messages you want conveyed, you have an hour to compose them."

"In that case, I'll get right to it," Jessica said.

She floated from the command section to the habitat module, where she entered her pod and started composing her messages.

The first was addressed to Colonel Shimura, giving her own summary of what would be included with Colonel Miller's report.

After getting the official work out of the way, she composed a message for Mason.

She checked herself in the camera, making sure no strands of hair escaped her bun to float around her head. Then she started recording.

"Hi, love. I hope things are going well in Sol. Afraid I can't tell you anything more about what I'm up to than the last time, but I can say that it's looking like I'll be heading back your way fairly soon. I think we might have a chance to bring this war to an end. You just need to hold on a little longer. I can't wait to see you. I'll have to take you somewhere nice on Earth. Be safe, Mason."

Jessica ended the video and uploaded it to the courier drone.

It would be weeks before her message reached Mason. It was quite possible that by then, if the convoy didn't reach Earth, the war would be over, and her actions out here would be moot.

Perhaps not moot. Even if the Ascended won the war, what was learned out here could be crucial in making sure they lost the peace.

Jessica floated out of the habitat module and back to the command section to watch the courier drone launch.

Colonel Miller glanced at Jessica and nodded before returning his attention to his display. Jessica strapped herself into an empty seat and opened the external display.

Midnight Diamond had launched with three courier drones nestled into recesses on her back. The drones were tiny vessels—little more than a fuel tank wrapped around a drive keel with just a small longburn drive and some thrusters for maneuvering. One of the recesses was empty, having been launched shortly after *Ascension*'s arrival. It would jump to *Fafnir*'s location so the cruiser's larger, more capable drones would head the rest of the way back to 61 Virginis. The cruiser would hold onto the drones until *Midnight Diamond* returned.

The launch of the second drone was not dramatic. The drone simply drifted out of its mount after the ejectors kicked it free. Maneuvering thrusters pushed it away faster until it was far enough away to ignite its small longburn drive. The drive only gave the small drone 1 g of acceleration, but it was more than enough to break orbit and put the drone on a course to head out of Origin's small jump limit.

As soon as it had crossed the boundary of the invisible sphere surrounding the planet, the drone flashed out of existence. Though small, the flash was far larger than the one *Midnight Diamond* generated. The drone lacked its mothership's flashless stardrive.

Jessica sighed and released her restraints; it was time to get back aboard *Ascension*.

She was halfway through the bridge's hatch when she heard a beep from one of the consoles—one she recognized as an alert for a new contact.

"Contact, bearing zero one five by three zero zero," the sensor operator called. "Range, nine million kilometers."

Jessica's blood froze as she pushed her way back to her seat and synced her display with the sensor operators. The contact was a thermal source, gradually growing in temperature, like a machine waking up from cold storage.

"Can you identify the contact?" Commander Ngata asked.

"Satellite in a distant orbit, sir. Multiple launches detected!"

"Battle stations," the commander called, and an alarm went off immediately.

The procedure was for the crew to don pressure suits as soon as they heard "battle stations," but Jessica remained glued to her seat as she watched the contact and what it had just launched.

She didn't need the sensor operator's callout to know the satellite hadn't launched torpedoes.

"Acceleration is too slow for new contacts to be torpedoes. The emissions match that of a stardrive charging."

"They're courier drones," the commander said. "Lock longburn torpedoes and fire."

The deck rumbled as the launch kicked torpedoes out into space.

Friendly contacts streaked away from *Midnight Diamond* at a hundred gs, the glow of their drives the brightest light sources in the cold emptiness around the rogue planet.

Jessica knew they would never reach their targets. When the torpedoes were more than twenty minutes away, the couriers winked out in small departure flashes.

"Redirect all torpedoes to target the satellite," Commander Ngata ordered. "Colonel Miller, you should recall your people to the ship. We need to get out of here before the Cendies send someone to investigate."

"I'm sending the word out now," Colonel Miller responded.

Jessica opened a communication with Isobel.

"I saw the alert. We're disconnecting Miriam now," Isobel said.

"Make it snappy. There's no telling how much time we have."

As it turned out, there was almost no time.

The teams exploring the massive station didn't even have time to reach *Midnight Diamond* before a massive arrival flash lit up the dark corner of space.

"Bloody hell!" Jessica swore as the contact resolved.

It was a mothership, identical to the one captured in 61 Virginis.

It immediately started launching a mass of Outriders, all bearing down on Ascension Station and the tiny intruder docked to it.

"Close the airlock—begin emergency undocking!" Commander Ngata roared.

"I still have people on that station!" Colonel Miller protested.

"And if we wait for them, we're all dead!"

"I'm in command of this mission. I order you to remain docked!" Colonel Miller shouted.

"The safety of my ship comes first."

"It's not going to matter," Jessica said. "Look at the plots. Those Outriders are going to reach us before *Midnight Diamond* can jump."

"I don't recall asking your opinion, Lieutenant," Commander Ngata said.

"She has a point. You'd be abandoning our people for no reason," Colonel Miller said.

"Commander, listen!" Jessica said. "The Ascended value their history. They preserved this station."

"What are you getting at, Lieutenant?"

"If we hide inside *Ascension*, I don't think the Ascended will risk firing on us."

Colonel Miller nodded to Jessica and turned towards Commander Ngata. "At the very least, it will buy us time."

Commander Ngata sighed and turned his attention to his crew. "Helm, plot a course into *Ascension*. Now undock us so we can maneuver."

"*Midnight Diamond* just undocked. Are you leaving us?" Isobel asked, her voice filled with dread.

"No. We're maneuvering *Midnight Diamond* onto *Ascension*. I need you to get to *Ascension*'s bridge and try to close the construction bay's main doors after we enter."

"We don't need to reach the bridge. There's a control station near our current position," Miriam said.

"Perks of having the builder on board. Lead the way, Miss Xia," Isobel said.

CHAPTER 28

It just didn't end.

The death of another wave of torpedoes glittered against the background of space. By rote, Mason flipped his Lightning over and burned to kill his velocity and head back to *Independence* to refuel and rearm. With his weapons bay now empty, he couldn't help but do rough math in the back of his head.

Each wave had resulted in over a hundred and forty Lightnings expending over two thousand interceptors. That was eating into the remaining inventory of interceptors aboard *Independence* and *Goshawk*.

Normally, one didn't worry about running out of cheap, mass-produced interceptors before comparatively expensive torpedoes. But the mothership could build new torpedoes, while the convoy couldn't. The loss of *Cassowary* and *Hyena* and their stocks of interceptors only exacerbated the problem.

At least it was his squadron's turn to disembark from their fighters.

Mason touched down on *Independence*'s deck, and by the time he opened the canopy, the hangar crew were already swarming his fighter, moving in a choreographed dance to rearm, refuel, and do whatever other maintenance they could.

Mason barely paid them any mind. He had four hours aboard the relative comfort of *Independence* and wanted to use it to the fullest.

After depositing his hardsuit, he proceeded to the habitat ring, where spin gravity allowed him to take a proper shower. He spent half an hour of his four-hour break scrubbing off the last twelve hours of space flight.

From there, it was to the officers' mess, where he reacquainted himself with the simple joy of eating calories instead of having them fed to him intravenously. A packet of coffee rounded out his little vacation.

Dominic sat himself down in the seat before Mason with all the authority .3 gravity allowed him, landing with a performative huff.

"How are you holding up, Silverback?" Mason asked.

"As well as anyone else in the squadron, Hauler," Dominic told him. "You look refreshed."

"Thanks." Mason took another swig of his coffee. "How's the rest of the squadron holding up?"

"Better than the fleet's interceptor stocks."

"I see you've been keeping track of our ordnance expenditure too."

"I can do arithmetic," Dominic said. "The other pilots haven't been making too much fuss about it. They're happy as long as they have a full load of interceptors with each sortie. But when the higher-ups start ordering us to ration our interceptors and we start losing tankers because we're not stopping all the torpedoes the Cendies launch at us, morale is going to collapse."

"Yeah. That's been bugging me every time I don't have anything else to worry about," Mason said.

Dominic leaned forward, pitching his voice low so as not to carry. "The fact is, Hauler, even if Admiral Moebius institutes rationing right now, we'll run out of interceptors well before we reach the First Fleet."

"What if we started using torpedoes against the Cendy assaults?" Mason proposed. "That would buy us some time."

Dominic shook his head. "Not enough torpedoes, and the Cendies will just spread out to limit how many they lose to nukes. What we need is a resupply."

"You know of any weapons depots between here and Sol?" Mason asked.

Dominic grimaced. "No, can't say that I do."

A notification appeared in Mason's HUD—a summons to the war room.

He sighed. "Well, looks like the brass wants to see me. Probably going to tell us to start limiting our interceptor usage."

"I can see about getting our pilots ready. Try to soften the blow," Dominic said.

"How the hell do you soften this?" Mason asked, then got up. Dominic didn't offer an answer before he left the war room.

Neither Marshal Singh nor Admiral Moebius was present in the war room when Mason arrived. Instead, one of the staff directed Mason to the admiral's office directly adjacent to the war room.

When Mason entered, he found Admiral Moebius seated at her desk with Marshal Singh towering before her. In a room with two flag officers, Mason instinctively snapped to attention.

"At ease, Squadron Leader," Admiral Moebius said. "We have a mission for your squadron."

"What's the job, Admiral?" Mason asked.

Admiral Moebius nodded to Marshal Singh, who adjusted his turban and looked at Mason. "I'm sure you're aware that our interceptor expenditures are not sustainable."

"I've had an inkling, sir," Mason said.

"Well, the good news is that Osiris Squadron is going to help alleviate that problem."

"How so, sir?"

Marshal Singh gestured to a wall-mounted display that had replaced the profile picture of *Independence* with a top-down view of the convoy's route through the Solar System. He pointed to Mars. "You'll be headed to Phobos. There's an arms depot there loaded with interceptors. We'll be sending every assault shuttle we have to load up with interceptors to resupply our stores."

Mason studied the map for a moment. "Has the convoy changed course to get closer to Mars?"

"We have, Squadron Leader," Admiral Moebius answered. "By the time the assault shuttles are loaded, the convoy will be on its closest approach to Mars."

"Are there any Federal forces on Mars to help us?"

Marshal Singh shook his head. "Earth Fed evacuated Schiaparelli

Base shortly after the Cendies took Jupiter, along with all civilian mining and scientific missions. Phobos Munitions Depot is located in Stickney Crater. It's an automated base with no permanent personnel."

"Are there defensive emplacements there, sir?" Mason asked. "I don't see the Cendies just letting us land there without interference."

"Hopefully attacking the convoy will occupy most of their attention," Admiral Moebius said, "but you're right, Squadron Leader—we don't expect the Cendies to just let us raid the depot. As for base defenses, the depot only has a point-defense battery, mostly for keeping intruders away."

"So minimal local support," Mason said. "What about assault shuttles?"

"Each shuttle will have a normal crew complement along with a squad of troopers to assist with loading interceptors and providing security while on the ground. We expect the loading operation to take some four hours, assuming there are no hiccups with the depot's automation."

"I see," Mason said. He turned to the screen and noted the projected trajectories. "Might I suggest a change to the course, sirs?"

"By all means, Squadron Leader. It's your mission," Marshal Singh said.

Mason traced his finger around Mars's circumference. "We can use Mars's atmosphere for braking. That will let us arrive a bit hotter and begin our braking burn later. Might buy us some extra time in case there are issues with the loading."

"Not a bad idea, Squadron Leader. I'll have my people run the numbers," Marshal Singh said.

"There's one more thing you should know, Squadron Leader," Admiral Moebius said. "The interceptors stored in the depot are previous generation."

"The old Silvertips? Those were phased out almost a decade ago."

"To be consigned to munitions depots while awaiting sale to foreign buyers or disposal," Admiral Moebius said. "The reason the Silvertips on Phobos weren't scrapped was the war with the League."

"So even if we replenish our stocks, our interceptors aren't going to be as effective."

The Edge of Nowhere

"It will be better than empty magazines," Admiral Moebius pointed out.

Barely, Mason thought. The last time the Silvertips had had their software upgraded, no one knew the Ascendency existed, let alone had come up with ways to penetrate their defenses.

"You don't look happy, Squadron Leader," Admiral Moebius noted.

"I'm sorry, sir," Mason said. "I'm just seeing a lot of risk for limited benefit."

"I'm risking the lives of your pilots to recover a bunch of obsolete missiles; I know that's frustrating. Know that I've been in contact with Earth and they've assured me they'll have software updates for the Silvertips waiting for you when you arrive. That ought to alleviate at least some of the disadvantages of their age."

"I hope so, sir," Mason said. "Given the convoy's speed, I'll have to launch my pilots soon."

"You'll have a launch window within the next twelve hours, Squadron Leader," Marshal Singh said. "Hence I'm taking your squadron off escort rotation. You'll have that time to prepare your pilots and fighters."

"Thank you, sir. I should talk to my crew chief about preparing my fighters for some hard aerobraking."

Marshal Singh nodded. "I'll see about getting the assault shuttles ready, Squadron Leader. We'll talk again before you launch."

Departing the war room, Mason sent a call to Chief Rabin. A groggy voice answered. Mason checked the time and realized it was 0300 ship time. The poor man had been fast asleep.

"Sorry to wake you, Chief, but the higher-ups have a mission for my pilots, and I need you to get our birds ready," Mason said.

"I'm taking my uppers now, sir. What do you need?"

"There's going to be a bit of Martian aerobraking that I'll need my fighters ready for."

"Ah, hell, sir, and there I was worried you were waking me up for something boring."

CHAPTER 29

Mars loomed above Mason as he entered the red planet's atmosphere.

His fighter shuddered and slowed when the thin atmosphere bit into its wings. On either side, Lightnings and assault shuttles burned trails through the planet's upper atmosphere as they used it to slow down. Phobos already rose above the horizon, gradually dropping Mason's nose from his inverted perspective.

But Mars was only one issue that worried Mason. The other was the force of Cendy fighters that had broken away from the mothership on an intercept.

Thirty Outriders, almost twice as many fighters as Osiris Squadron, were burning for Mars, their course almost matching their prey's.

Mason wasn't sure if the Cendies knew about the depot on Phobos, but in any case, they were keen on foiling his mission—which left Mason with the problem of dealing with Cendy fighters.

Aerobraking meant the bottom four hardpoints were bare. Any weapons carried on them would fry in the heat. That left just the eight interceptors carried internally and four more mounted on the ventral hardpoints for each of his fighters.

Counting the multiceptors the Outriders almost certainly carried, the odds were not looking good for Osiris Squadron. Not unless he found a way to tilt the odds back in their favor.

"Yankee Leader beginning the climb to Phobos," said the pilot of the lead assault shuttle.

"Osiris Leader beginning the climb," Mason said. Inverted as he was, climbing involved pushing the stick down and letting aerodynamic forces increase his altitude. The shuddering subsided and the temperature dropped as he climbed out of the atmosphere. After the aerobraking, they still had more than enough velocity to reach Phobos in short order.

The relief from high gs was short. The combined force of Lightnings and assault shuttles all flipped over and started one last hard braking burn and kept that burn until they were just a few hundred kilometers short of the Phobos surface.

The assault shuttles slotted into a landing approach for the Stickney Crater while Mason led Osiris Squadron into low-orbit Phobos. The orbit would not allow continuous communications with the assault shuttles but would keep the approaching Cendy Outriders in view when they appeared over the horizon.

Below, the assault shuttles executed combat landings on the expanse of paved ground surrounding the entrance to the munitions depot buried beneath the surface of the crater.

"Yankee Leader to Osiris Leader, techs tell me they've got the depot's automated systems working. We'll have robots loading up interceptors in the next few minutes. How does our tail look?"

"Still on braking burn on a close approach to Mars's surface. Estimate two hours before they get here," Mason replied.

"We'll see about dusting off before then," the Yankee Leader said.

There was no way loaded assault shuttles could outrun the Outriders. Mason would have to engage and either destroy or drive off the Cendies.

Letting the flight AI fly his fighter, Mason brought up a detailed display of the Outriders' predicted course to Phobos. They would swing around Mars along a similar vector to the assault shuttles used to reach Mars. There was some uncertainty as to whether the Outriders would rely on aerobraking as well or just use their longburn drives.

In either case, they would be flying right over the center of the growing dust storm. There was an opportunity. A chance to do something vanishingly rare in space combat.

An ambush.

Mason opened a direct connection to Dominic's fighter. "Silverback, I need your opinion."

"I have many to share, Hauler. I assume it's related to the force of Cendy fighters coming to kill us," Dominic said.

"Yes. I thought we should kill them first."

"Not a bad idea. I'm assuming you're thinking of something more sophisticated than that?"

"Yeah," Mason said. "That dust storm we flew over after we aerobraked—I was thinking of hiding down there and catching the Cendies as they come around the planet. Are there any obvious flaws in my plan?"

"That dust isn't going to do our fighters any favors," Dominic told him. "And the Cendies might spot us if we're not careful with our thermal management."

"Our airbreathing engines should work if we fly low enough," Mason said. "That should keep our thermals low."

"Dust ingestion's going to ruin the turbines," Dominic pointed out. "Though that will be more of a problem for our Chief Rabin's maintainers."

"We'll just have to make it up to him," Mason said. "Let's inform everyone else of the plan."

Mason and Dominic briefed the squadron. There were no objections or concerns. Just giddy excitement at the prospect of taking the Cendies by surprise.

"Yankee Leader, Osiris Leader, we're breaking Phobos's orbit to fly down to Mars's surface."

"Pardon me, Osiris Leader, but could you repeat that?" the Yankee Leader responded.

"We're breaking orbit with Phobos to head down to Mars to hide in a dust storm and ambush the Cendies as they fly over us."

"That's going to leave us exposed to any Cendies that get past you, Osiris Leader."

"Can you get the base's point defenses working?" Mason asked.

"They're in working condition, though I'd rather not rely on them to keep my people alive."

"Are you still on track to load up the assault shuttles before the Cendies reach you?"

"We are."

"Then stick to the plan. When my fighters engage, use the opportunity to run," Mason instructed. "We'll keep the Cendies too busy to follow."

"Understood, Osiris Leader. Good hunting."

∞

Leveling out, Mason switched his engines to airbreathing mode. The panels covering the intakes opened, allowing the turbines to suck in the thin Martian air and pass it over the heat exchangers, superheating the air and expelling it out the back for thrust.

A Lightning could operate in airbreathing mode almost indefinitely, though once they entered the dust storm, Mason guessed the turbines would only last hours.

Osiris Squadron spread out into four flights of four fighters each, with dozens of kilometers between them. Ahead, the summit of Olympus Mons rose above the front of the dust storm.

Flying at high subsonic speeds, even the thin air of Mars provided enough lift to keep the Lightnings flying straight and level, aided by their large wing area. Below, Mason's sensor AI automatically tagged and identified the inert remains of abandoned colonies scattered across the surface.

Centuries ago, people had tried to make a life for themselves on the dusty red planet. But that dream died when faster-than-light travel granted access to far more habitable worlds in other star systems. All that remained on Mars was a largely automated mining industry and a few scientific outposts—all evacuated since the Cendy invasion.

The ground became hazy as they entered the dust storm, and turbulence shook Mason's fighter.

Making one last check of the satellite display, he saw the Cendies were still on their predicted course. They would climb over the horizon in thirty minutes and be overhead just minutes after that.

"Begin descent." Mason pushed the stick down and entered a shallow dive into the reddish haze of the dust storm stirring in the shadow of Olympus Mons. The dust obscured his passive sensors, rendering him all but blind to the Universe beyond—and hopefully invisible to the Cendies.

The turbines whined in protest as they ingested the abrasive Martian dust. Mason knew they would have to be replaced before they tried to fly in the atmosphere again. A worthwhile sacrifice if it let him get the drop on the Cendies.

All that was left was to wait. At a predetermined coordinate, Mason began circling a few hundred meters above the Martian surface, shrouded in almost total darkness despite it being the middle of the Martian day.

His attention was fixed upward, but the storm blocked his view of the sky as much as it blocked his view of the surface from orbit. All he could do was wait and hope the Cendies didn't deviate.

Notifications appearing in Mason's HUD reported a gradual drop in turbine efficiency as the Martian dust took its toll. His Lightning was not enjoying flying through the dust storm. "Not much longer," Mason murmured to his fighter.

As soon as his time hit zero, Mason pulled back on the stick and throttled up. "All fighters climb and arm weapons," he ordered, not sure if his pilots could hear him through the interference.

As he climbed almost vertically, the dust storm quickly thinned out, gradually revealing the light pink Martian sky. And as his view cleared, the sensor AI started calling out hostile contacts.

The Cendies had stuck to their course and were directly above Mason.

Mason immediately locked targets and fired.

The weapons bay doors swung open and the launcher kicked the interceptors out. The missiles fell briefly before igniting their shortburn drives and rocketing directly up.

The other fighters of his squadron launched interceptors as well, firing a mass volley of over sixty at the Outriders above. The thin Martian atmosphere was little impediment to the interceptors, and dozens of exhaust trails ascended toward space.

The Cendy formation scattered, taken by surprise by the sudden attack from the dust storm below them. But there was no sign of panic. Cendies never panicked. They just started engaging in evasive maneuvers and dropping decoys.

They also returned fire, launching interceptors down toward the Federal fighters. Mason's sensor AI warned him of multiple inbound missiles.

He terminated his climb and dove back toward the dust storm, plunging into the red abyss. The Outriders, the interceptors pursuing him, and even the other Lightnings all disappeared behind the reddish haze.

Mason leveled out and kept up his speed. The storm buffeted his fighter and dust hissed against its skin. Warnings continued to protest the abuse he was putting his fighter through.

He hadn't seen what happened to the Cendy interceptors, but the fact his fighter didn't explode a minute after he dove back into the storm was reason enough to believe he had evaded them.

Mason climbed back up and found a chaotic melee waiting for him.

The Cendies had descended into Mars's atmosphere to engage the Lightning. Mason saw just over half as many contacts as he had seen before he dove back into the storm.

And Osiris Squadron was four Lightnings short.

Mason didn't spend time worrying about the missing pilots. He throttled up to full power, locked targets, and fired more interceptors into the high-altitude battle.

The Outriders Mason targeted broke off their attacks against his squadron mates to evade the incoming interceptors. Two took direct hits from his interceptors and fell toward the Martian surface.

Two more managed to defend against the attack and turned to engage Mason.

The range closed rapidly, now too close for interceptors. Mason armed his gun and turned toward the nearest Outrider, squeezing the trigger and sending a stream of penetrators at the enemy fighter. The stream scythed through the air meters from the two Cendy fighters as they flew past him and turned in opposite directions, trying to catch him in a pincer.

Mason ignored the bait and throttled up his engines, burning for a Cendy fighter pursuing Armitage.

<*Marbles, turn hard right toward me and I'll clear your tail.*>
<*Please do.*>

Armitage banked right in a tight curve. Her pursuer matched her turn, seemingly oblivious to Mason's approach.

As Armitage crossed his nose, Mason laid his aiming reticle along the path of the Outrider and fired a burst from his cannon. The Outrider flew into the burst, and gas streamed out from multiple gashes. The crippled fighter started arching down toward the Martian surface, disappearing into the dust storm.

<Much obliged, Hauler.>

<You can pay me back by clearing my tail.>

<I see them. Turn toward me and climb and I'll pick 'em off you.>

Mason did as she proposed, pulling into a steep climb as his two pursuers attempted to line up a shot.

Armitage climbed up from below and fired her cannon, shooting off one of the lead Outrider's three wings, causing the fighter to start spiraling out of control. The second broke off to evade Armitage's attack, giving Mason the chance to turn in and get on their tail.

The Cendy dived for the dust storm and disappeared into the clutter. Mason fired a burst at long range, but the Outrider dropped off his scopes as the dust storm enveloped it.

He pulled up short of the dust storm and waited for the Cendy to climb back up. But more fire drew his attention away.

<That's Silverback's flight tangling with the bulk of the Cendies, Hauler.>

<Let's go help them. Keep an eye out for our friend.>

<I'll make 'em wish they stayed in that dust storm if they pop back out.>

<Silverback, Marbles and I are coming in from the west.>

<I see you, Hauler. Got six Cendies trying to kill us.>

<Help is on the way. Maintain data link while interceptors are in flight.>

Mason fed targeting data from Dominic to his weapons AI and launched his last four interceptors. The thick Martian atmosphere was little impediment to the missiles as they rocketed toward the Cendies. The Cendies broke their pursuit to evade, some diving toward the storm, but Dominic's flight stayed with them, helping guide Mason's interceptors toward their targets.

At close range, the interceptors had most of their fuel when they hit, and the resulting explosions shattered the Outriders, scattering wreckage across the Martian sky to rain down into the dust below. The remaining two Cendies were climbing, their longburn drives shining bright against the pink sky.

<Ha! They're bugging out.>

<I see. Let's figure out where the rest of our squadron is.>

Osiris Squadron, or what was left of it, was scattered across the Amazonia Planitia. Out of the sixteen fighters he'd started with, he only saw eleven.

He hoped some were just hiding in the dust storm below.

<Silverback, you spot where any of our missing are?>

<At least two were shot down with no beacons, Hauler. I'm afraid I didn't see where everyone else went.>

Moments later, two Lightnings popped back on the screen, rising above the clutter of the storm.

<Hardball, it's good to see you made it.>

<Zoom and I got chased into the storm by a bunch of Cendy interceptors.>

<So that leaves one unaccounted for.>

Moments later, another friendly contact appeared, hundreds of kilometers away.

<Good to see you, Otter. How'd you end up almost at Olympus Mons?>

Over voice comms, Mason heard Cruise answer in a quivering voice. "I ... dove into the storm to ... dodge some missiles. And then ... I just kept running. Had to climb because my t-t-t-turbines are almost gone."

"Okay, Otter. Easy. Start climbing gently for orbit. Hardball, link up with him."

"On it, Hauler," Sabal said.

"Something's rattled Otter bad," Dominic said over private comms.

"We'll deal with that when we're back on *Independence*," Mason said. "Let's start forming—"

"Hauler, incoming!" Armitage interrupted just as a hostile contact appeared directly below him. An alarm sounded as the Outrider launched interceptors at Mason and Armitage.

"Going defensive!" Mason rolled over and pulled into a dive.

The Cendy multiceptor released its submunitions and the four tiny interceptors continued homing in on Mason. Armitage got off a Javelin at the lone Outrider as she turned to evade.

Mason leveled out just above the storm, flying perpendicular to the incoming interceptors. He dropped a line of decoys that just barely managed to lure away the Cendy missiles. A black splotch above the dust storm in the distance marked where Armitage's Javelin had destroyed the Cendy Outrider.

"I'm hit!" Armitage cried.

Mason saw her left wing was gone, trailing gas from her sublimating fuel stores.

There was a flash of light and her cockpit module rocketed away from her fighter under the power of chemical rockets, carrying her away from her stricken fighter as it spiraled into the storm. The ejection motors soon burned out, and a drogue parachute deployed to stabilize her pod. It wasn't long until the gravity on Mars started pulling the cockpit module toward the surface.

"Looks like I'm going on an unscheduled excursion to the surface," Armitage said.

"I'll follow you in, Marbles," Mason told her.

"I can hold out until rescue arrives, Hauler," Armitage said, her voice starting to crackle from interference as she plunged into the storm.

"Not a time for debate," Mason said. "Silverback, take the rest of the squadron and return to Phobos. I'll link up with you on the way back to *Independence*."

"Hauler, you're going to have a hard time tracking Marbles in that storm," Dominic warned.

"You have your orders, Silverback," Mason replied before following Armitage's pod into the storm.

Mason deployed his airbrakes as he plunged back down into the reddish darkness below. Flying into the ground would not make for a successful rescue.

He had lost Armitage's beacon as soon as she fell into the storm. He pulled up and slowed his dive, entering a lazy circle, trying to pick up her signal. He couldn't stay in the storm forever. The dust had already done a number on his turbines and only got worse as he got closer to the surface.

Mason hoped to see the glare from the cockpit module's landing rockets firing, but as the time passed when Armitage would have touched down, he saw nothing but more dust. The winds must have carried her further than he had thought.

Mason consulted his sensor AI and saw that before he plunged into the storm, he was still getting updated meteorological data from automated weather satellites. He had his AI do some calculations. It computed a circle, kilometers downwind of his position, where Armitage could have landed.

Mason flew low, flipping on his fighter's external lights, which sent out twin beams ahead of him that barely penetrated the dust. He wanted to light up as brightly as possible so Armitage could see him.

As he entered the estimated landing zone, he slowed down further, activating his landing engines to keep aloft. He was low enough for his lights to illuminate the ground below. All he saw were rocks and churning regolith.

Then he saw something off his right wing. Turning a light towards it, he saw it was a drogue chute, still inflated and whipping in the wind.

Mason followed the line of the chute until he reached the edge of a shallow crater. He saw Armitage's cockpit module turned almost upside down. It looked like the module had landed on the inner slope of the crater and tumbled over.

Flying over, he didn't see any activity outside. Armitage was still inside.

"Marbles, I have visual on your position. Can you hear me?"

He was answered only by the rhythmic beeping of the pod's rescue beacon.

Aiming for the relatively flat center of the crater a few hundred meters away, Mason deployed his landing gear and set down lightly on the surface. He idled his drives, removed his restraints, and considered opening the canopy but decided against it. Dust would flow into the cockpit and potentially damage his controls.

Instead, Mason opened the weapons bay and proceeded to the escape hatch at the back of the cockpit, behind the passenger seat. It was a squeeze to fit through in his hardsuit. But, as he hoped, no dust streamed into the cockpit.

Dropping out of the weapons bay, he landed lightly in the Martian gravity.

Armitage's module was five hundred meters ahead of his fighter. He couldn't see it through the dust, but his HUD marked the module's location through the haze.

Moving at a trot, Mason traversed through the storm. The winds were over a hundred kilometers per hour, but with the thin atmosphere, he barely felt them.

At a hundred meters, he finally saw Armitage's cockpit. It was almost inverted, with its rear resting against a boulder jutting out of the regolith.

"Marbles, can you hear me?" Mason called through his radio.

"Hauler, I retract what I said earlier," Armitage said. "I could use a hand."

"I can see," Mason said. "What's your status?"

"I'm mobile but stuck in here. Something's blocking the escape hatch," she said.

"The back end of your cockpit's jammed against a boulder the size of a house," Mason told her.

"That would explain it," Armitage said. "Think you could help a girl out?"

"Let me see what I can do."

Walking up, he gave the cockpit module a push, feeling only the slightest give. It would be too heavy for him to roll it over, even with the low gravity and the boost his hardsuit gave him.

At least not without a bit of leverage.

"I'll be right back. I need to get something from my fighter," Mason said.

"I'm not going anywhere."

Every Lightning had a toolkit included with it. The tools were meant to allow pilots to engage in minor infield repairs or rescues. Armitage had lost hers with the rest of her fighter when she ejected.

Mason walked under his fighter, just in front of the weapons bay, and opened one of its storage compartments. Inside was a toolkit filled with various small hand tools, a gun-like impact driver, a folding spade, and a prybar. All the tools looked pristine, unused since the day they were first installed in the fighter. Mason pulled both the prybar and the spade free of their brackets and carried them back to Armitage's cockpit.

"Okay, I'm back," he said. "I'm going to roll the cockpit on its side."

"Just let me know when and I'll brace myself," Armitage said.

Mason took the prybar and started probing the ground. The prybar penetrated the dust layer like it wasn't there, going down a quarter of its length before it hit something solid.

"Belts and zones, looks like I'm going to have to do some digging," Mason said.

"Try not to let my cockpit crush you when you try to roll it," Armitage said.

"Not a bad idea," Mason said. He jammed the prybar tip first into the ground and opened the spade to full length.

Then he started digging. Annoyingly, the dust storm filled the hole almost as fast as he could dig it. Eventually he cleared enough dust to give his prybar a solid surface to push off.

Mason tossed the spade aside and grabbed the prybar, jamming it between the cockpit and the ground. "Brace yourself, Marbles," he called.

"I'm ready," Armitage answered.

Mason squatted, braced the prybar against his shoulder, and then pushed with both legs. At first, the cockpit didn't move. But as Mason continued to push, it started to shift. A little at first, millimeters earned with a mighty effort.

Then all of a sudden something gave and the cockpit rolled over, causing Mason to fall forward as it rolled away. It made a three-quarter roll onto its side before coming to a teetering stop.

Mason picked himself up and carried the prybar with him, intent on prying open one of the cockpit's now exposed hatches. But before he reached the cockpit, a booted foot kicked the rear escape hatch open. Mason brought himself to a stop as Armitage crawled out of the hatch and stood up.

She looked around for a moment. "So, this is Mars, huh?"

"First time?" Mason asked.

"Yeah," Armitage said. "Can't say I'm impressed."

Mason jerked his thumb over his shoulder. "My Lightning's five hundred meters that way, if you want a ride off this rock."

Armitage started trotting toward Mason. "Then let's not keep anyone waiting. I bet there are some people very worried about us right now."

"Let's not let them worry any longer," Mason agreed.

CHAPTER 30

With Armitage safely in the passenger seat of his fighter, Mason followed the assault shuttles back to *Independence*.

At the cost of four Lightnings and three of his pilots, the mission had gained the convoy a plentiful supply of nearly obsolete interceptors. It remained to be seen if the old Silvertips were up to the task.

Mason landed aboard *Independence* with multiple warnings sounding in his status display. His flight through the dust storm, combined with his rescue of Armitage, had exposed his fighter to far more abrasive Martian dust than planned. The hangar techs would be busy cleaning out the dust and replacing worn parts.

With a free hand, Mason brushed away some of the dust still clinging to his suit. "This bird's not happy with what I asked her to do," he remarked.

"Better off than mine, sir," Armitage said.

"Fair enough."

After removing his restraints, Mason popped open the canopy. Upon floating out, he saw Chief Rabin waiting by his fighter, a hard expression visible through the visor of his helmet.

Rising from the cockpit, Mason looked around and saw his fighter was a proper mess. Somehow, enough Martian dust clung to it to turn its light-gray exterior into a dark rust color. It was going to take a lot of work to get it ready for flight again.

As Mason pushed away from his fighter, Armitage floated out of the cockpit. "Hey, Chief!"

"Glad you made it back," Chief Rabin said. "You owe me a bird."

"How about I buy you a beer?" Armitage said as she floated past Chief Rabin and traded fist bumps with him.

"You're never that happy to see me, and I brought my fighter back," Mason complained.

"You still owe me *Magnificent Seven*, sir." Chief Rabin pointed toward Mason's soiled Lightning. "And besides, that bird's going to be a pain in the ass getting flightworthy again."

"Don't be too hard on him, Chief. I'd still be on Mars if it weren't for him," Armitage said.

"That mean you'd be willing to scrape the dust off the intakes?" Rabin asked.

"Nah. I think I'll leave that up to the professionals," Armitage said.

"I thought as much."

After transitioning through the airlock and depositing their suits, Mason and Armitage headed for the habitat ring. Even after their mission, they would only have four hours to rest aboard *Independence*. Soon they would have to make room for the other fighters rotating out of escort.

Entering the elevator, Armitage ran her fingers through her blue hair, working out the tangles accumulated during the mission.

Mason stared at the door to the elevator as he thought about the lost pilots. The small compartment was filled with silence apart from the sound of the climbing motor and ventilation.

"Uh, so, thanks again for rescuing me," Armitage said.

Mason glanced over at Armitage and nodded. "Of course, Marbles."

"What I mean to say is, I owe you one, Hauler," she said.

"I just did what I was supposed to," Mason said. "Anyone else would have done the same."

"Somehow, I don't think Marshal Singh will think the same way."

"Marshal Singh is my problem," Mason answered.

"Well, at the very least, sir, since we're one fighter short of all our pilots, I can take your fighter out and give you another twelve hours of rest," Armitage said.

The prospect of sixteen hours, enough time for a full sleep cycle and even a little free time, was quite alluring.

"I'll think about it," Mason said. "I want you to check with medical first."

"Will do, Hauler," Armitage said.

At the habitat ring, Mason received a summons to the war room. Marshal Singh wanted a debriefing.

"Duty calls," Mason said, turning anti-spinward toward the war room.

Marshal Singh stood alone at the holotank in the center of the war room, looking at a recording of the engagement over Amazonia Planitia. It was toward the end of the fight. The icon showed Mason's fighter diving after Armitage's cockpit module.

Marshal Singh returned Mason's salute. "Good work, Squadron Leader. Those interceptors you helped recover will be invaluable."

"Thank you, sir," Mason said.

"I can't say I'm happy with the risk you took recovering one of your pilots. But I understand the instinct. Just remember that you are an asset that cannot be easily replaced and should not take risks lightly."

"Yes, sir," Mason said.

"Now, on to why I brought you here," Marshal Singh said. "As we speak, the Silvertips are being updated with the latest software. But that will not bring them up to par with the current generation of Javelins."

"We should use them to knock down torpedoes and multiceptors while saving the Javelins for higher threat targets," Mason said.

Marshal Singh nodded. "That was my thought on the matter as well. But I would like your input on how to equip our forces."

"Could we steal Javelins from the starships and replace them with Silvertips?" Mason suggested.

Marshal Singh chuckled. "I floated that idea, but not one of the fleet officers wants to trade in their remaining stocks of Javelins for inferior interceptors. And besides, the logistics of moving the Silvertips from the carriers to escorting starships would be inefficient."

"So much for sharing," Mason said. "That means we should be leaning on the Silvertips as much as possible until we reach Earth. Which means we shouldn't be letting Cendies get close enough to the convoy for starships to need to launch their interceptors."

"I concur. What's your suggestion?" Marshal Singh asked.

"We fully load up most of our Lightnings and Conquerors with Silvertips but keep a squadron loaded with Javelins in reserve to deal with high-threat targets," Mason said. "With all the Silvertips we got from Phobos, we can be pretty generous with how we use them."

"I'm not sure the Cendies would appreciate your generosity," Marshal Singh said. "Would your squadron be the one that operates the good missiles?"

"I lost three pilots getting those Silvertips to the convoy, sir," Mason said. "I'd appreciate it if I didn't have to equip my squadron with sub-standard missiles after what we went through over Mars."

"I can understand that, Squadron Leader. But concentrating our Javelins like that could create gaps in our coverage as squadrons rotate out of escort. Not to mention the appearance of favoritism in giving the special ops squadron the good missiles. I think instead of one squadron being reserved the Javelins, we give each squadron an inventory of Javelins and let each CO decide which fighters get the Javelins."

Mason sighed. "I guess I could get that to work, sir. And as you say, it would ensure other squadrons don't feel left out."

"I know it might seem like Osiris Squadron is taking up an unequal burden for the escort mission, but we need all our squadrons. And elitism is a poor metric for deciding who gets the best kit."

"Osiris Squadron will get the job done. Even with old interceptors," Mason said.

"In that case, I'll have my staff see about doling out the Silvertips to each squadron. From here on out, I expect our squadrons to be much more aggressive in intercepting Cendy attacks."

"That we can handle, sir," Mason said.

"Then I'll leave you to your rest time, Squadron Leader. I'll have the new orders drafted within the hour."

Mason saluted and departed the war room.

CHAPTER 31

"Well, this is a right pickle," Jessica said as she stared at the projection of the Ascendancy mothership.

"But it looks like your suggestion worked out," Colonel Miller told her. "They're not willing to risk damaging *Ascension* to kill us."

"Now we need to figure out a way to get ourselves out of here," Commander Ngata said.

"I don't see the Cendies just letting us fly out," Colonel Miller said.

"Could we negotiate something?"

"Assuming they even want to talk to us, Commander, do you really think they'll honor any agreement when they have a clean shot at us?"

"How about a dead man's switch?" Commander Ngata suggested. "We could rig some explosives aboard *Ascension*. If they blow us up, the bombs go off."

"And how do you think that will work?" Colonel Miller asked. "The Cendies are going to pick up any dead man signal. And I'll bet that mothership could figure out how to spoof it before we have a chance to escape."

"Maybe a volunteer instead," Isobel said. "Someone can stay aboard *Ascension* and sit on the bomb until *Midnight Diamond* escapes."

"Would you be willing to volunteer, Major?" Colonel Miller asked.

"I wouldn't have suggested it if I wasn't, sir," Isobel said.

"Hold on a sec. We're getting ahead of ourselves," Jessica interrupted.

"Do you have a suggestion, Lieutenant Sinclair?" Colonel Miller asked.

"Well, yes, sir. We move *Ascension* with *Midnight Diamond* inside it. As far as we can tell, this ship is completely intact. We might be able to get the stardrive working. The Cendies aren't going to risk damaging this ship trying to stop us."

"I don't see them just letting us fly away with *Ascension*," Colonel Miller said.

"They might not have a choice," Jessica said. "If they launch a boarding action, we can threaten to destroy the ship. And we only need *Ascension* for the one jump. We'd just zip away with *Midnight Diamond* before they had a chance to jump after us."

Colonel Miller sighed and scratched his chin. "We'll need to find out if we can even detach *Ascension* from the station."

"I had probes look at the moorings," Commander Ngata offered. "They can be released manually. But we don't have enough drones aboard to do it fast. We'll have to send teams out on EVA."

"How long will that take?" Colonel Miller asked.

"If I send people out right now? A couple of hours," Commander Ngata answered.

"I can head out and supervise the teams," Isobel offered.

"Do it," Colonel Miller said. "That just leaves the matter of getting the engines lit."

"Miriam knows this ship better than anyone, Colonel," Jessica said. "She's our best chance at getting this ship started."

"Then go over to *Ascension* and enlist her help, Lieutenant. I don't want to give the Cendies any more time to think about how to pry us out of here than we need to."

Jessica saluted. "I'm on it."

Colonel Miller nodded. "Go."

It took less than a minute for Jessica and Isobel to scramble to the airlock. Already some of *Midnight Diamond*'s crew were putting on suits and thruster rigs for EVA.

As Jessica pulled on her suit, she nodded to Isobel. "Good luck out there."

Isobel smiled and nodded back. "I'll see you when I get back. Send Miriam my regards."

"Will do."

Jessica squeezed into the airlock with Isobel's team, much of the volume taken up by the thruster rigs the EVA team wore.

Once the outer airlock had opened, Jessica followed the EVA team out and scrambled for the elevators, while Isobel and her team jumped free of the ship and fired up their thrusters, heading for the open front of *Ascension*'s construction bay.

With the power back on, *Ascension*'s internal elevators were online, making the trip to the ship's computer core far faster. Miriam was still connected to the core, presumably sharing a virtual environment with Doctor Marr.

Jessica sat down next to Miriam's mobility rig, pulled off her helmet, and connected to the core herself. She soon found herself standing on a massive white stone patio that stretched off into the distance. Doctor Marr and Miriam were reclining on benches, with Doctor Marr in a floral shirt and baggy shorts and wearing a wide-brimmed hat.

Miriam wore nothing aside from a pair of large sunglasses.

She pulled down the glasses to look up at Jessica. "Jessica, darling. You have a serious look on your face."

"We have a problem," Jessica said. "The Ascended are here."

Miriam raised an eyebrow. "How?"

"Captain Miller launched a courier drone. That triggered an Ascended courier drone to jump out. Before we could escape, a mothership jumped in. *Midnight Diamond* is currently hiding inside *Ascension* to delay the Ascended."

"Well, that's an abrupt change of events," Miriam said. She took a long sip from her large, colorful drink and adjusted her seat to sit back up. "I assume you need our help."

"Just a moment," Doctor Marr said. "How did your ship get here without triggering the failsafe in the first place?"

"Wait—you knew?" Jessica asked.

"I knew the Ascended left an automated warning system in place," Julian said. "I assumed you figured out a way to bypass it."

"Never mind that," Jessica said. She wasn't going to explain the nature of *Midnight Diamond*'s flashless stardrive. "We need to get *Ascension* moving so we can reach the jump limit without the Ascended shooting at us."

"You're using this ship—and by extension, me—as a hostage?" Doctor Marr asked.

"Yes," Jessica said.

"Look, I have a better idea," he said. "Let me talk to the Ascended. Reconnect the computer core with the external communications system. I can tell the Ascended to let you go."

"They would listen?"

"I would hope the fact I created them still carries some weight."

Miriam stood up. "I don't think she came here for you, Julian. You need me to see if this ship is still functional?"

"Yes," Jessica said.

"Then I'll retire from the virtual world and see about doing just that," Miriam said.

"If you connect me to the ship's systems, I can figure it out faster," Doctor Marr said.

"First the communication systems, now the ship in general?" Jessica asked. "You're asking for a lot."

"This is my ship, lass. If anything, you're trespassing."

"This is *my* ship, Julian," Miriam said. "I'll see about getting you linked to the communications system." She turned to Jessica. "And I'll see if this ship can move under her own power while I'm at it."

"I suppose I'll just be here, then," Doctor Marr said.

Jessica disconnected, waking up to find Miriam pulling the connection cable from her head and standing up.

"We'll need to get to the bridge to get this ship moving," Miriam said. "Have you started removing the moorings?"

"Isobel's outside leading team is disconnecting the moorings now," Jessica said.

"Good. Let's not waste any time," Miriam said.

Jessica and Miriam traveled to *Ascension*'s habitat ring. After transitioning from the spin hub to the outer ring, Miriam headed directly for the bridge with obvious familiarity.

As massive as *Ascension* was, her bridge was a relatively small compartment, with only a dozen workstations, including the captain's chair directly behind the helm. Miriam sat herself down in the captain's seat like she belonged there and started flipping switches. Old screens came to life, displaying lines of text as the computer systems booted up for the first time in over a century.

Miriam scrolled through warnings and notifications faster than Jessica could read them until she came upon the display for the propulsion system.

"The Ascended did a remarkable job preserving *Ascension*," Miriam said. "I'm starting up the reactors one at a time. Once that's done, I'll start warming up the longburn drives. I've activated the bridge communications system, so you should be able to tell Isobel and her team to get inside before that happens."

Jessica sat at a console and opened the communications display, syncing up her suit's radio.

"Isobel, it's Jessica. Miriam and I are on the bridge and bringing this beast to life. How's it going with the moorings?"

"Espatiers are connecting charges to the last mooring now," Isobel said. "Once we're ready, we'll head inside, and the shaped charges should cut the moorings with the press of a button."

"Good to hear," Jessica said. "You should get inside *Ascension* as soon as possible and before Miriam starts powering up the longburn drives."

"How long do we have?" Isobel asked.

Jessica looked at Miriam.

"Thirty minutes," Miriam said before Jessica could ask. Clearly she had been listening.

"You get that?" Jessica asked Isobel.

"Thirty minutes—more than enough time," Isobel answered. "I'll let you know when we're back inside."

Jessica scrolled through more displays and noted the sensors were online. Though *Ascension*'s sensors were obsolete, they had no trouble picking up the mothership loitering just outside Origin A's jump limit, burning its longburn drives at long power to maintain its position above the elliptical plan of Origin A and Origin Ab.

Hundreds of smaller contacts held their positions near the mothership.

Ascension's sensors couldn't identify the contacts, but Jessica knew they were Outrider fighters waiting for a chance to swarm down upon the intruders that dared desecrate the tomb of the Ascended's creators.

Jessica didn't know if the Ascended could feel rage, but she knew that the crew of *Midnight Diamond*, including her, were in a perfect position to find out.

It wasn't like the Ascended had ever shown mercy before. They never took prisoners.

"Colonel, my team has completed rigging the explosives, and we are on our way back in," Isobel said.

"Good work, Major," Colonel Miller said. "It does not appear the Cendies are aware of what we're up to. Lieutenant Sinclair, how is it going getting *Ascension* underway?"

"Lieutenant Sinclair is not my secretary, Colonel. You can speak with me directly," Miriam said.

"In that case, Miss Xia, how are your efforts at getting *Ascension* underway?"

"Maneuvering thrusters are online, and I have one longburn drive online. I can have the other three operational within the hour."

"One will be enough to start with," Colonel Miller said. "Be ready to bring it online as soon as I blow the moorings."

"I'll await your word, Colonel," Miriam said.

Jessica checked the external cameras and saw Isobel and the Espatiers float into one of *Ascension*'s airlocks, closing the external hatch behind them. "We're in, Colonel," Isobel said.

"Beginning detonation sequence," Colonel Miller said.

On the external cameras, the mooring disappeared in bright flashes of light as the shaped charges detonated. Moments later, the shock of the explosion traveled through *Ascension*'s hull with a low rumble.

"We're free of the station," Miriam said. "Firing maneuvering thrusters."

Thruster ports lit up along the length of *Ascension*, adding a few millimeters a second to her separation velocity from the station. The speed was too slow to tell by eye, but Jessica could see the range counter adding meters every second.

After twenty minutes, *Ascension* cleared the station.

"Rotating to align with our exit vector," Miriam said.

Though straight up was the shortest physical way to the jump limit, it wasn't the fastest. Not with *Ascension*'s weak longburn drives. Instead, Miriam turned the massive colony ship in the direction of her orbit around Origin Ab.

The process took the better part of an hour. Time enough for Miriam to work on getting the rest of *Ascension*'s longburn drives operational.

There was no reaction from the Ascended as yet. The mothership maintained her position with her swarm of fighters. They had to know what the humans were playing at—it didn't take a genius to figure out why they would detach *Ascension* and ride her out of orbit.

When *Ascension* was properly aligned, Miriam started up the longburn drives. "Igniting longburn drive number one," she said.

One of *Ascension*'s massive longburn drives came to life, but Jessica felt nothing.

"And number two."

The second longburn drive came alive under minimal throttle. Still Jessica felt nothing, the pull of the spin gravity more than overcoming the weak acceleration.

"Number two looking good. Bringing up number three."

As Miriam brought up the third longburn drive, an alarm sounded and warning labels appeared on her screen. She immediately shut down number three. "Okay, I guess that one doesn't work," she said. "Proceeding to number four."

Number four ignited without incident, and though Jessica couldn't feel the acceleration, the telemetry showed a slow and steady increase in speed.

"Beginning to throttle up," Miriam said.

The gentle acceleration, in combination with the ring's spin gravity, felt like Jessica's seat tilted back, even though her posture had not changed.

With three longburn drives at full throttle, *Ascension* accelerated at three-quarters of a meter per second, less than half the pull of lunar gravity.

It would take a long time for *Ascension* to accelerate fast enough to escape orbit. Even more to cross the jump limit. More than enough time for the Ascended to decide what to do with the humans hijacking the ship they had been created aboard.

"Okay, Julian. You're online," Miriam said.

A symbol glowed on Jessica's display. Someone was transmitting through *Ascension*'s communications system. Jessica patched into the transmission.

"This is Doctor Julian Marr. I wish to speak with the Ascended leadership. You lot have some explaining to do." The tone of his voice was like that of a father confronting his child after a poor report card.

There was no response.

Jessica looked at Miriam. "What do you think the Ascended are thinking?"

"I think they're reeling from all the surprises," Miriam said. "After finding intruders at their abandoned birthplace, *Ascension* under power, and now their creator speaking to them, I suspect their Consensus is lit up with a discussion about what to do next."

"Creator Marr, this is Emissary Lucinda. We hear you."

"Oh, you bloody well will hear me! What's this business starting a war with humanity? My team and I didn't dedicate our lives to creating you lot only to have you engage in something as base as galactic conquest."

"We are not trying to conquer anyone, Creator Marr."

"I'm disappointed you would engage in semantic games as well," Doctor Marr grumbled. "You were made to be explorers, not warriors. Explain yourselves."

"We didn't have a choice, Creator Marr," Emissary Lucinda said calmly.

"Oh? Who made that decision for you?"

"The humans did."

"Did they now? Explain!"

"I'm afraid we cannot explain over an open channel. Not with the enemy listening."

"The enemy? You mean the people who woke me up? We didn't make you see humanity as enemies."

"We apologize, Creator Marr. We do owe you an explanation. But we cannot risk our enemies learning about what we're protecting."

"What is this shite? Conjuring excuses not to tell me why you're warring with humanity? It's like over the last century you've devolved into children."

"If you knew what we did, you would understand, Creator Marr."

"Then explain it to me," Julian said.

"We will. But first we must deal with your captors."

"Uh oh." Jessica looked at Miriam, who shook her head.

"They're not my captors, they're … my guests. Uninvited, yes, but guests all the same," Julian said.

"They must be dealt with, Creator Marr. We would advise you to go into hibernation until we are finished. What happens next will be ugly."

As one, all the Outriders throttled up their longburn drives and accelerated to twenty gs.

"This is foolish! You could very well destroy everything aboard *Ascension*!" Julian protested.

"It is a risk we must take."

CHAPTER 32

"Acceptable losses" was a term Mason was quickly learning to hate.

The Silvertips had helped bridge the gap, giving the convoy a much-needed boost to their interceptors' reserves against continued Cendy attacks.

That wasn't to say there were no losses. Two tankers had had to be abandoned after suffering crippling damage. The loss was still within acceptable margins, although Mason hated the idea that the deaths of the pilots and crew were in any way acceptable.

But the convoy was closing in on Earth. After swinging around Mars, it reignited its engines and started a lengthy deceleration burn. The communications lag was reduced to a handful of minutes, growing smaller by the day.

However, with the convoy nearing Earth, the attacks by the Cendies became more earnest. They knew just as well as the Federals did what success of the convoy would mean. Each tanker that made it would bring more fully fueled warships flying out from Earth's orbit to drive the Ascended out of Outer Sol.

The next few days would determine if the Cendies' stranglehold on the Earth Federation would be broken or whether it would cinch down completely. Either way, Mason knew that even though the flight to Earth was almost over, the fight was far from over.

"That's quite the force gathering around the mothership, sir," Mason said.

"It seems the Cendies have elected to build up to a single massive attack. One last blow before we're in range of Earth's defenses," Marshal Singh said.

"What help can we expect from the First Fleet, Admiral?" Mason asked.

"First Fleet will deploy strikecraft as we approach, but that's about it. All their starships will remain in orbit," Admiral Moebius said. "They don't have the fuel to spare to break orbit."

"Sounds like we're cutting things close," Mason said.

"Liberating 61 Virginis for its fuel was a Hail Mary pass—a desperate gambit that only just paid off in time. And the Cendies know that. So they are going to try to overwhelm our defenses and destroy as many tankers as possible."

"You're not worried they'll go after our carriers again?" Mason asked.

"Frankly, I hope they do," Admiral Moebius said. "We can afford to lose *Goshawk* or even *Independence* if it means getting most of the tankers through."

"Just another day with the fate of the world on our shoulders," Mason murmured.

Marshal Singh grunted and nodded. "Yes, just another day. From here on out, strikecraft will be focused on defending the tankers. *Independence* and *Cassowary* will reposition inside the convoy to provide an extra layer of defense. All efforts are to focus on keeping our tankers alive, with each remaining squadron covering a selection of tankers."

"Which ships will my pilots be looking after, sir?" Mason asked.

"The tankers *Cayuga*, *Rappahannock*, *Tiber*, and *Mekong*. *Cayuga*'s one of the new Nile class fleet tankers—the largest we have. The remainder is Danube class."

"Sounds like I should make *Cayuga* top priority, because the Cendies certainly will," Mason said.

"Indeed. But don't neglect *Rappahannock*, *Tiber*, and *Mekong*. Those three together carry more fuel than *Cayuga*."

"Will we have backup?" Mason asked.

"The destroyers *Putnam*, *Chase*, and *Bernadotte* will provide close escort," Marshal Singh said. "Is there anything else?"

"No, sir. I think I just need to brief my pilots and get our fighters spun up." After exchanging salutes with Marshal Singh, Mason turned and left the war room, going anti-spinward to Osiris Squadron's quarters.

It was about the time the *Independence*'s crew changed watch, and the corridors were filled with the glassy-eyed crew just coming off duty and stumbling down the corridors toward some combination of food, rest, and showers. Others almost bounced down the corridor, fresh off a rest cycle and a dose of stimulants. But even the rested crew showed signs of fatigue. The hard-set eyes and the clenched jaws revealed that the nonstop pressure of convoy escort had ground the ship's crew down to bedrock.

Mason opened a channel to Dominic. "Silverback, get everyone together in the briefing room. Marshal Singh has a new mission for us."

"I'll make sure they're ready, Hauler," Dominic said.

Mason closed the connection and took a short detour to the galley.

Just as he started filling his coffee packet, an alarm sounded and a notification appeared on his HUD. The Cendies were moving toward the convoy. And all pilots needed to get to their fighters.

"Silverback, scratch that. I'll brief the squadron in flight."

"See you outside, Hauler," Dominic said.

With *Independence* under acceleration, Mason was able to walk the whole way from the ward room inside *Independence*'s habitat ring to Osiris Squadron's suit storage. Most of his pilots were already inside, slipping into their hardsuits with practiced ease.

Mason made way for suited figures walking out of the storage room, the pilots giving him quick salutes as they proceeded to their hangars. When he had room to enter, he was surprised to see Armitage already clad in her hardsuit save for her helmet, her blue hair covered by a cap.

"You're not on rotation, Marbles," Mason reminded her.

"Looks like we're in for a biggie, and you're going to need all the help you can get," Armitage said. "Figured I could ride back seat with you and help coordinate."

Mason paused to think for a couple of seconds. "Fine. Let me get suited up."

After slipping into his hardsuit and closing it around himself, Mason motioned to Armitage to follow him as he left the suit room.

His fighter was the farthest away, so he ran down the corridor at a trot. The footfalls of his and Armitage's heavy boots echoed down the corridor as a warning to any crew who found themselves in their way.

A quick transition through the airlock and Mason and Armitage burst into the hangar where Mason's fighter waited, fully armed and warmed up. Mason ran under the wing, tracing a straight line for the cockpit, ducking under one of the Silvertips hanging from an underwing hardpoint.

He scrambled up the ladder and deposited himself in the front seat. Armitage followed him and landed in the rear seat.

By rote, Mason ran down the checklist, contacted *Independence*'s Controller to request launch clearance, and waited for his turn. Moments later, the catapult kicked his fighter out into space, and he vectored toward *Cayuga* and the three other tankers of Tanker Division 4.

"Marbles, you keep an eye on the sensors. I'm going to contact *Cayuga*," Mason said.

"I'll let you know if anything happens, Hauler," Armitage said.

"Osiris Leader to *Cayuga*. We're inbound to your position."

"Acknowledged, Osiris Leader," said *Cayuga*'s captain. "Request video messaging."

"Granted, Captain Ahmed."

Captain Ahmed's face appeared in a window on Mason's HUD. She was a handsome woman with a lean, sharp face and dark hair just starting to go gray. "Squadron Leader Grey, thank you for accepting video messaging," she said.

"Of course, Captain. How can I be of assistance?" Mason asked.

"Just wanted to get the measure of you, Squadron Leader. Osiris Squadron has become rather famous among the captains of the convoy."

"I didn't realize we were so popular," Mason said. "When have the convoy's captains had a chance to socialize?"

"We conference call every day to coordinate with each other," Captain Ahmed said. "Though it mostly just involves talking about the fighting. We're all civilian auxiliaries. Most of us, including myself, have never been in combat before joining this convoy."

"Well, we're almost at the finish line," Mason said.

"Yes, with the largest attack yet bearing down on us," Captain Ahmed said.

Mason wanted to promise that he would keep the Cendy fighters away from them. To keep them safe. But he knew that was not up to him. That was up to the Cendies and the vagaries of fate. All he and his pilots could do was their jobs.

"The Cendies will have to go through us before they get to you, and you still have the destroyers to provide cover," Mason said.

She nodded. "Yeah, but … *Cayuga* is the biggest tanker in the convoy. The Cendies will try to kill us above others."

"That might be the case, Captain," Mason said. "But that won't happen without a fight."

"I suppose that's all I can ask, Squadron Leader. Good hunting." Captain Ahmed terminated the call.

On his display, over five hundred Outriders burned for the convoy, continuously gaining speed. It was just a question of whether they would continue to accelerate to launch a flyby attack or slow down for a protracted fight.

So far, their formation didn't give any indication of what their intentions were. So all Mason could do was maintain formation and wait until the Cendies got close enough to intercept.

"Hey, Hauler. You see what's going on around Luna?" Armitage asked. Following the cue from his backseat driver, Mason turned his attention to Earth and its moon.

Both bodies were crescent shapes as the convoy approached from almost the night side of each. Against the dark backdrop, Mason's sensor AI detected hundreds of launches.

They were strikecraft. Lightnings and Conquerors were taking off from bases on the moon and stations around Earth.

"Looks like we've got reinforcements on the way," Armitage said.

"Not that that will help us right now," Mason said. As he watched, the assembled strikecraft all settled on a ten-g acceleration for the convoy. Assuming they slowed down to join the escort, that put their arrival at six hours away.

The Cendies would arrive in three hours at their current acceleration.

Even if they started braking, they would still arrive well before strikecraft from First Fleet did.

"One last fight before help gets here," Mason said. "Let's make sure there still is a convoy around to reinforce."

"You got it, Hauler," Armitage said.

As the Cendies approached, *Independence* repositioned herself between the convoy and the oncoming Cendy attack. Surrounding her were twelve cruisers, eight of which were the former escorts of the stricken *Hyena* and *Cassowary*. With the convoy on braking burn, the warships could keep their heaviest firepower and best armor facing the enemy.

Mason knew what Admiral Moebius was doing. She hoped *Independence* would make too tempting a target for the Cendies to ignore and draw away torpedoes that would otherwise be used against more vulnerable tankers.

He doubted it would work. Discipline was one of the Cendies' many inhuman qualities.

For Mason's little herd, the three smaller tankers, *Rappahannock*, *Tiber*, and *Mekong*, formed a loose delta formation three hundred kilometers ahead of *Cayuga*. The destroyers *Putnam*, *Chase*, and *Bernadotte* loitered close to *Cayuga*, their drives running at barely a sixth of their total output to match the acceleration of the gigantic tanker.

The destroyers were close enough to give Mason an idea of the tanker's sheer scale. They were little more than bright specks against the bulk of the massive tanker. Like minnows swimming with a leviathan.

Against the size of their charges, the destroyers and Mason's squadron felt like barely a token escort—a gossamer-thin screen against the killing swarm bearing down on them.

When the Cendies suddenly flipped and started decelerating, Mason's blood chilled.

"I don't suppose they've decided to run away?" Armitage said hopefully.

"No, Marbles. I'm afraid not. They're committing to a fight, not just a flyby attack."

"Oh goody," Armitage said. "At least we have more time to prepare."

Mason checked the revised arrival time. The Cendies would still reach the convoy before the reinforcements from Sol arrived.

Mason's mind raced with ideas of what to do. He thought of breaking off from close escort to meet the Cendies in open space. But without support from the warships, Osiris Squadron would be wiped out by the sheer number of enemy strikecraft. All the skill and daring in the Universe couldn't overcome the brute weight of numbers.

So he waited.

The Cendies continued to close, their speed rapidly decreasing as they approached attack range.

"All fighters, the priority is to knock down incoming torpedoes, but don't forget to protect yourselves," Mason said. "There's little point dying stopping the torpedoes if the Cendies proceed to icepick the tankers to death with their guns."

Osiris Squadron acknowledged.

"I appreciate you encouraging us to stay alive, Hauler," Armitage said.

Mason chuckled. "Tough orders, I know."

The Cendies stopped their deceleration, just a bit faster than the convoy, and turned to engage.

The mass formation of Outriders split into five smaller formations. The largest, roughly half the total, converged on *Independence*. The remainder vectored on the tankers.

It looked like the Cendies did intend to knock out *Independence* while they still had the chance. And it was clear this was part of their plan, not a last-minute decision by impetuous pilots.

Independence and the twelve cruisers launched the first attack: a mass volley of longburn torpedoes and standoff-range weapons meant for engaging starships. Normally it was wasteful to use such expensive weapons against strikecraft. But Mason himself had seen how effectively a well-timed nuclear strike could disrupt an enemy attack.

The Outriders reacted. They had to. You did not ignore a nuclear weapon locked onto you.

Their formation spread out to minimize the chances of multiple strikecraft getting taken out by a single warhead.

As the torpedoes closed the range, the Cendies launched their interceptors.

Mason expected the pinprick flashes of interceptors striking torpedoes.

Instead, just as the Cendy interceptors merged with the Federal torpedoes, there was a massive flash of a nuclear detonation.

"Holy fuck! Did their interceptors just set off a warhead?" Armitage cried.

"Nukes aren't supposed to go off like that," Mason said. "I think the detonation was deliberate."

More detonations flashed as the torpedo volley approached the Cendy formation. It happened at regular intervals. Every few seconds. Even if it were possible for an interceptor impact to set off a fusion nuke, that was not what was happening.

The torpedoes were being detonated in open space on purpose. Creating massive flashes of light to scramble sensors.

"Admiral Moebius is up to something clever," Mason said.

"Wonder if it will be clever enough?" Armitage mused.

The line of detonations continued right up until the remaining torpedoes reached the Cendy formation, where all at once, all the torpedoes detonated.

The resulting explosion of hundreds of directional nuclear warheads blossomed into an enormous flower of nuclear fire, streams of plasma shooting off in all directions.

It was one hell of a fireworks display. And it had the effect of scattering the Cendy formation just as they entered interceptor range.

As the glare from the detonations faded, every launch tube aboard *Independence* and her entourage of cruisers erupted with interceptor launches.

Thousands of interceptors flew against hundreds of Outriders. Just as the Cendies were not holding back, neither were the Federals.

The disordered Cendies fired back, launching their shortburn torpedoes at maximum range. It was then Mason had to appreciate the genius of Admiral Moebius's timing. The disposition of her forces, the seemingly wasteful use of torpedoes, and the mass launch of interceptors were all designed to force the attacking Cendies to launch their torpedoes early, thus giving her defenses the maximum amount of time to react.

Flashes of light marked when interceptors killed torpedoes, each flash growing closer and closer to the Federal starships.

In the moments before impact, point defenses opened fire, throwing up a wall of metal before the Cendy torpedoes. Then the torpedoes detonated in a staccato of massive flashes that obscured the Federal starships.

Seconds later, the glow faded, revealing the butcher's bill.

The cruisers *Harare*, *Reykjavik*, *Boston*, *Kyoto*, and *Miami* were hulks. Their icons grayed out, indicating mission kill. And their signatures were consistent with hundreds of thousands of tons of molten metal and ceramic.

All the other cruisers showed varying degrees of damage.

And then there was *Independence*. Her drives were still burning, but her status display showed severe damage. Zooming in, Mason could see her hull forward of the gun turret was glowing with residual heat from absorbing multiple directional detonations.

She was alive but out of the fight. And Mason suspected he wouldn't be returning to *Independence*, assuming he survived the rest of the Cendy attack.

There was still the matter of Cendy fighters coming in hot on *Cayuga* and the other tankers under Mason's care.

CHAPTER 33

The incoming attack was a relatively small portion of the total Cendy attack, most of which had expended itself against *Independence* and her cruisers. But that still left Osiris Squadron outnumbered five to one: six squadrons of Outriders against twelve Lightnings partially armed with outdated interceptors.

Fortunately, Osiris Squadron was not alone. The destroyers *Putnam*, *Chase*, and *Bernadotte* and the twelve Conqueror bombers of Nova Squadron helped even the odds.

The Outriders continued their approach, each squadron separating so their torpedo attacks could approach from multiple angles.

There was little that Mason could do to disrupt the attack. He didn't have the fighters or interceptors for it. But he could blunt the initial torpedo volley.

In an expertly synchronized attack, each Outrider dropped four shortburn torpedoes that started burning for the tankers.

"Nova Leader, you're up," Mason said.

"Understood, Osiris Leader," Nova Squadron's CO responded.

Nova Squadron's bombers split in half, six bombers moving above the convoy and six below. When the shortburn torpedoes approached engagement range, each bomber launched its full load of Silvertips.

Two hundred and forty Silvertips, enough to match the number of shortburn torpedoes, fanned out above and below the convoy, each under partial remote guidance by the bombers to make sure it targeted a single torpedo.

Outriders replied with jamming, and their torpedoes began evasive maneuvers to frustrate the efforts of the Silvertips trying to kill them. Space glittered with the impacts of interceptors on torpedoes moments later. Half the Cendy volley disappeared from the tactical display.

"All fighters, break and engage!" Mason ordered.

Osiris Squadron broke into pairs, Mason leading Gottlieb toward their assigned defensive box. He locked onto the torpedoes that would pass through the box and launch his externally mounted Silvertips. The old interceptors dropped away and fired their motors, streaking toward their targets.

That left just Mason's internally mounted Javelins.

More flashes marked successful interceptor impacts, but Mason still had ten torpedoes to deal with. He assigned half to Gottlieb for her to deal with and engaged the rest for himself. Five Javelins ejected from the rotary launcher in his fighter's belly and flew after the torpedoes.

The newer interceptors were far more resistant to the torpedoes' countermeasures, and Mason got five hits for five shots. Nonetheless, several torpedoes got through. His squadron just didn't have the numbers to cover every approach angle.

It fell to the destroyers and the point defenses of the tankers to deal with the rest.

The destroyers launched some of their last interceptors, further thinning out the remaining torpedoes. Only a bare handful got close enough for point defenses to engage them.

Not a second after the point-defense guns opened, the torpedoes detonated.

Mason's sensors blacked out as the ambient radiation reached dangerous levels. Even his internal dosimeter noted a sudden spike in radiation as scattered neutrons flew through his body.

The sensors quickly came back to show him the carnage.

"Shit, *Mekong* got fucked!" Armitage exclaimed.

Her assessment was accurate. The tanker had been split in half, her two halves hemorrhaging millions of tons of helium-3 into an expanding cloud that quickly obscured the wreckage as the tanker's debris fell out of formation.

The other three tankers had also taken varying degrees of damage. *Rappahannock* and *Tiber* streamed gas from damaged tanks; *Cayuga* showed signs of external scorching, though no breaches.

"Cendies aren't done yet. Brace for hard gs, Marbles," Mason warned as he slammed his throttle forward.

Four Outriders came in for the tankers, clearly intent on inflicting damage with their guns. They probably didn't have the time or the ammo to kill the tankers outright, but they could disable delicate sub-systems like the longburn drives, which would be good enough.

Mason locked onto three Outriders and launched his last three interceptors, then vectored in on the fourth for a gun attack. When his target swung its nose toward him, he fired his ventral thrusters, pushing his fighter down before a stream of projectiles cut through the space above him.

Mason returned fire and punctured the Outrider's fuselage in multiple places, leaving it tumbling out of control.

"Got two hits out of three, Hauler," Armitage said. "Looks like half the Cendies are engaging us while the remainder are pushing for the tankers."

"Vectoring on the runners," Mason said. He flipped his Lightning over and pushed the engines to emergency power, quickly overcoming his velocity with twenty gs of acceleration.

The Outriders' acceleration was a somewhat gentler ten gs. They didn't want to swing by their targets too fast to get their guns to bear, giving Mason a chance to catch up with at least some of them.

He blew past the dogfight brewing between Osiris Squadron and the Cendies. Mason put the fight out of his mind. His pilots could take care of themselves; the tankers couldn't.

The destroyers did the best they could to cover the tankers. *Putnam* and *Bernadotte* moved to cover *Tiber* while *Chase* protected *Rappahannock*.

That left *Cayuga*, the largest tanker, open for attack, and the Cendies saw that. All the runners vectored on her.

Mason caught up with his target and fired a stream of shots at extremely close range. The penetrator rounds flew true, but the Cendy pilot had time to react and fired its maneuvering thrusters to jump out of the way of the attack.

It then turned to engage Mason.

Mason fired his braking thrusters, and three gs tried to pull his body out of his seat and his eyes out of their sockets. But the sudden deceleration spoiled the Cendy's aim, and its penetrators cut through space just ahead of him.

Mason pushed the throttle forward and crashed into his seat with twenty gs. Adjusting his aim, he fired a burst that sent penetrators through the length of the Outrider, leaving it tumbling dead and out of control.

<*They're almost on* Cayuga*!*> Armitage called out from behind him.

Another long-range burst clipped the next Outrider, knocking one of its three wings off but leaving it otherwise under control.

Mason fired again, and his stream stuck the central nacelle. Something volatile inside the Outrider exploded, turning the fighter into an expanding cloud of gas and debris.

The last Outrider pressed its attack on *Cayuga*, ignoring the tanker's point-defense guns as it lined up a shot.

But the point defenses scored a hit, ripping a hole in the side of the Outrider and leaving it streaming fuel. Still it continued its attack, firing on *Cayuga*'s vulnerable longburn drives.

Cayuga's point defenses continued to fire, scoring more hits on the Outrider.

The Cendy suddenly stopped firing its gun. For a second, Mason thought the point defenses had scored a kill. To his horror, its maneuvering thrusters were still firing, vectoring right for *Cayuga*'s engines.

All Mason could do was watch as the Outrider slammed into the longburn drives.

The Cendy pilot had chosen the angle of attack perfectly. The Outrider vaporized as soon as it hit the first engine bell, and the resulting plasma from a hundred tons of fighter vaporizing passed through two more bells along the way.

The sudden loss of containment caused a chain reaction, with longburn drives exploding before safeties could shut them down, spreading the damage. *Cayuga* suddenly stopped accelerating as all five of her longburn drives went dark, gas leaking out the stern.

Mason cut his drives and flipped over as *Cayuga*'s silent hull zipped past at several kilometers per second. Firing his engines at full power, he heard Armitage groan as twenty gs slammed both of them into their seats.

Mason quickly overcame his velocity and started approaching *Cayuga*, cutting the drives when he reached his intended approach velocity.

"*Cayuga*, Osiris Leader. Damage report."

"You tell me, Osiris Leader. I know we've lost propulsion, but I can't ascertain the damage from my end of the ship," Captain Ahmed said.

Mason checked his surroundings. There was still fighting further behind the convoy as it overtook *Cayuga*, but it was petering out as Osiris Squadron—what was left of it—and the destroyers cleaned up the last of the Outriders.

Putting aside his worry about the casualties his own squadron had taken, Mason focused on *Cayuga*. All that was left of the tanker's longburn drives were strips of molten metal glowing orange with residual heat.

"*Cayuga*, I'm uploading my visual feed to you. Your longburn drives are a total loss," Mason said.

"I see it. Goddammit!"

"I'll pass the word on to the destroyers so they can start evacuating," Mason said.

"Copy that, Osiris Leader," Captain Ahmed said, the crushing disappointment evident in her voice. "We almost made it."

CHAPTER 34

FIVE PILOTS. THAT was what it cost to protect not even half of Tanker Division 4.

Mekong was a total loss. And without her drives, *Cayuga* couldn't slow down to join the First Fleet. She'd fly right by on a parabolic trajectory that would eventually take her out of the Solar System.

All Mason could do was form up the seven remaining fighters of Osiris Squadron and guard *Cayuga* as the destroyer *Bernadotte* docked with her to take on the tanker's crew. The destroyer looked like a remora clutching the side of a whale.

Chase and *Putnam* remained with *Rappahannock* and *Tiber* as they continued their braking burn, slowing down to slot into the halo orbit occupied by the First Fleet over Earth-Sun L2.

The rest of the convoy limped toward Earth, wrecked tankers and warships falling out of formation. Since arriving in Sol, the convoy had lost a quarter of its tankers. An acceptable loss, if only just.

"Hey, Hauler."

"Yeah, Marbles?"

"I've been doing some math back here, just to keep my mind off things, and … well …"

"Well what?"

"I think we can save *Cayuga*."

"How so?"

"I mean, I know she can't move under her own power, but we do have fourteen spare longburn drives, plus five on *Bernadotte*."

"You want us to try and tow the tanker?" Mason asked. "We don't have the thrust to stop that thing."

"No, but we have enough thrust to alter her course, sir," Armitage said. "Right now, her current trajectory will take her way past Earth, but if *Bernadotte* and Osiris Squadron were to push her, we could change her delta-v enough to slot her into low-Earth orbit."

"We'd run out of fuel," Mason said.

"It's a good thing we have a few million tons of it on hand, then."

"You thought of all that in a couple of hours?"

"Not like I have anything else to do back here, sir."

"Okay, you've sold me. I'll see if I can't get *Bernadotte*'s and *Cayuga*'s buy-in."

"Osiris Leader to *Bernadotte*, request communication with your CO."

"This is Commander Vargas. How can I help you, Osiris Leader?"

"One of my pilots has a crazy idea that might allow us to save *Cayuga*, Commander," Mason said.

"Run it by me, Squadron Leader."

Mason gave Vargas a summary of what Armitage had told him and uploaded her simulation.

"I have to say, I'm impressed, and a bit embarrassed a pilot came up with this," Vargas said. "We had considered trying to take *Cayuga* under tow with the other destroyers, but there simply wasn't enough thrust. Using Earth's gravity is inspired."

"We've all been so spoiled by longburn drives that we've forgotten the old tricks," Mason said. "If we're going to do this, we'll need to do it now."

"I'll confer with Captain Ahmed and get my engineers working on ways to hook up our ships to *Cayuga*'s fuel tanks."

"I'll let my pilots know what the plan is, Commander."

༄

Mason's arms burned as he worked the rachet tensioning on the webbing straps that fixed his fighter to the hull of *Cayuga*. It was the twelfth and last strap he needed to affix to his right rear landing gear. Armitage across from him did the same to the left. The seven remaining fighters of Osiris Squadron had all soft-docked with the tanker's forward hull and were being similarly fixed in place.

Mason resisted the urge to wipe the sweat off his brow through the visor of his helmet. Instead, he relaxed, letting himself float in the microgravity, secured to the tanker by just the smart adhesive soles of his boots. He turned his attention to the bow of the tanker, which glowed in the light of multiple welders.

Bernadotte had positioned herself nose to nose with *Cayuga*, and the crews of both ships were busy fixing the destroyer in place, turning the warship into an improvised propulsion system.

"Squadron Leader Grey, I've got a delivery for you," Captain Ahmed said over the radio.

Mason turned toward the drone bearing the end of a fuel line between its pincers. The drone's little thrusters pulsed to keep the long tube under tension as it hovered above his fighter. He freed himself from the hull and gently kicked himself toward the wing of his fighter above him.

"Marbles, head to the refueling port and stand by to grab the end from the drone."

"Roger that, Hauler. What are you going to be doing?" Armitage asked.

"I'm moving a hundred meters down the line."

"To do what?"

"Catch any loops that might form in the line," Mason said. "Standard procedure when handling loose lines."

"I don't recall that procedure, sir."

"It's not standard procedure for pilots," Mason said.

He pulsed his thrusters to a stop and grabbed the fuel line. The heavy line was some twenty centimeters in diameter, thicker than Mason's arm. He grasped it with both hands.

"I've got the line. Marbles, secure your end at your leisure," Mason said.

"Got it," Armitage said. "Captain Ahmed, I'm ready when you are."

"Bringing the end to you now," Captain Ahmed said.

The drone pulsed its thrusters and moved the end toward Armitage, who grabbed it. The drone immediately released the line and moved away.

Armitage pulled on the line to move it toward the fuel port. Mason preemptively fired his suit thrusters to give Armitage a little slack in the line to help her secure it to the fuel port.

"Nozzle's locked in place," Armitage said.

"Understood. Let me know when you're clear of the line, Squadron Leader," Captain Ahmed said.

Mason released the line and pulsed his thrusters to reverse away. "I'm clear."

The flexible line became rigid as it filled with fuel pellets. The pellets were tiny spheres of metallic deuterium, each containing a small amount of helium-3.

As the fuel reached the end of the line and started filling his fighter's tanks, he got a notification on his HUD that the tanks were filling. His fighter was now connected to the ludicrous volumes of fuel contained aboard *Cayuga*. It was a miracle that, despite the beating she'd taken, none of the tanker's massive tanks had ruptured.

"Everything's looking good at my end," Mason said.

"Then that's one down, six more to go," Captain Ahmed said.

Mason finished connecting his fighter first by virtue of having an extra pair of hands. The other fighters were being fixed in place by each pilot working alone. *Cayuga* and *Bernadotte* couldn't spare the crews while working to fix the destroyer in situ.

"Let's help get the other fighters ready, Marbles," Mason said. "We'll go clockwise around the hull and hit Silverback's fighter first."

"Sounds like a plan, Hauler," Armitage said.

With *Cayuga* drifting, it was a simple matter of kicking off the hull and flying around the circumference of the ship to the next fighter using his suit thrusters.

Dominic was busy lashing his Lightning to *Cayuga*'s hull as Mason and Armitage approached.

"Heads-up, Silverback. Marbles and I are approaching from your nine," Mason said.

Bracing his foot against the hull, Dominic gave the loading strap one last tug before turning his attention to Mason. "Here to lend a hand, Hauler?"

"Extra hands make for light work."

"In that case, I got two more straps to finish before attaching the fuel line," Dominic said.

"Let's get to it," Mason said.

With three pilots working together, it was short work to finish securing Dominic's fighter and attaching the fuel line.

"You want me to come with and help?" Dominic asked.

"No. I want you to stay with your fighter and make sure everything's working," Mason said. "I'll let you know our next move once we're done with the hardware."

"Got it."

The next stop was Asif's fighter. She wasn't as far along as Dominic was, but it only took Mason and Armitage a couple of minutes longer to get her fighter ready. Then they moved on to Sabal's fighter, almost a hundred and eighty degrees around *Cayuga*'s hull.

"Squadron Leader, I've got a problem with one of your pilots. Flight Lieutenant Sabal's trying to attach the fuel line by herself," Captain Ahmed said.

"Right. Keep the drone away from her until I get there," Mason said.

"That's the problem, Squadron Leader. She snatched it from the drone before I could stop her."

"Fucking brilliant," Mason muttered under his breath before speaking to Sabal. "Hardball, what do you think you're doing?"

"Getting this job done, Hauler," Sabal said.

"How about you pause until Marbles and I get there to help you?"

"I've almost got the line latched, sir," Sabal said. "If you don't distract me, I'll be finished in a second."

"Hardball …"

"Fucking dammit!"

Mason came around the bend just in time to see the end of the fuel line coil away from her fighter.

Sabal immediately chased after the line. "Hardball, don't!" Mason shouted.

"I've got this," Sabal said. With impeccable timing, she chased down and grabbed the end of the line, wrapping her arms and legs around it. She then pulsed her thrusters to stabilize herself and moved back toward her fighter. As she did so, the loop that had formed in the line started moving toward *Cayuga*'s end of the fuel line.

"Hardball, you just made it worse. Hold position until I fix that loop in the line," Mason ordered. "Marbles, follow me."

"I'm with you—what's the plan?"

"Move fast and get ahead of that loop," Mason said.

"Got it."

Mason had to push his suit thrusters hard, using up to a quarter of his propellant just to get ahead of the line, then burning again to slow down.

"Grab the line. We're going to make a loop of our own."

"Okay," Armitage said. "What's that going to do?"

"Grab a piece of line like how I'm doing," Mason said as he wrapped his arms around the line.

"Got it," Marbles said, matching Mason's movements.

"Now very gently pulse your suit thrusters toward me."

"Got it," Armitage said.

Mason did the same, creating a bend in the line. Reaching out, he forced the bend into a loop that was as long as he was tall.

"All right." Mason moved away from the line. "Now heave on that line as hard as your thrusters let you."

"All right—here goes," Armitage said.

She fired his suit thrusters in one heavy pulse, and the tension caused the loop Mason had made to start moving up the line toward the loop coming down.

"Get clear of the line, Marbles," Mason said.

"I'm clear."

Mason watched as the two loops raced toward each other. When they met, the loops canceled each other out, straightening out the line and causing it to wobble in the vacuum.

Returning to Sabal's fighter, he found her holding the end of the line near the dorsal fuel port. Mason grabbed onto the line. "You can secure it now, Hardball." Sabal did as she was told, latching the line into place.

Moving toward Sabal's fighter until he was just in front of her, Mason looked at her hard through the visor of her helmet. He had to resist the urge to rap her on the side of her helmet.

Instead, he opened the squadron comms. "No one tries to attach the fuel line by themselves. Understood?"

Everyone acknowledged. Mason returned his attention to Sabal. "Stay with your fighter and monitor the refueling."

"Yes, sir," Sabal said.

Mason and Armitage moved on to the next fighter. No one had been as fast as Sabal in securing their fighter to *Cayuga*, so there were no further incidents.

When he returned to his fighter, the seven remaining Lightnings of Osiris Squadron were now secured to *Cayuga* as improvised thrusters.

Mason and Armitage slotted into their seats, and Mason went about linking the controls of the six other fighters to his. "Commander Vargas, my fighters are secured and linked to *Cayuga*'s fuel system."

"Acknowledged, Squadron Leader. We'll need more time to finish attaching *Bernie* to *Cayuga*. Do you think your fighters have enough thrust to start flipping the tanker over?"

Mason checked the navigation plot. "Looks like we'll need to flip the tanker over in the next two hours if we want to slow down enough to enter Earth orbit."

"So it doesn't need to be fast," Commander Vargas said.

"I'll figure it out, Commander. You should get your crews inside before I start lighting longburn drives."

"Already on it, Squadron Leader. I'll give you the all-clear once everyone is inside."

"Okay, Marbles. It's up to us to start turning this thing," Mason said.

"They never give us the easy jobs, do they?" Armitage remarked.

"Just another day in the Space Forces," Mason said.

Opening up the display, Mason studied the arrangement of fighters around *Cayuga*'s forward hull. The seven fighters of Osiris Squadron were placed equidistantly around the tanker's front, with Mason's fighter locked onto *Cayuga*'s dorsal hull.

"This is Hauler. I'm going to be making control inputs from my fighter, so don't be alarmed when your engine nozzles start moving at weird angles."

With that, he got to work. There was no flight AI involved. It wasn't designed for what Mason had in mind, and he didn't want to spend time trying to teach it.

He would have to do it manually.

With his fighter, he simply gimbaled the engines as far up as they would go. Then he took remote control of one fighter at a time and forced its engine nozzles into an extreme angle so that all its thrust was pointed in the same direction as his fighter's.

Mason had to be careful with the bottom two fighters, making sure the angles of their gimbals didn't blow hot longburn drive exhaust into *Bernadotte*. After that, he synced the longburn drives to his fighter's throttle.

"*Bernadotte*, Osiris Leader, I'm ready to begin the turn," Mason said.

"All personnel are secure, Squadron Leader. We're clear," Commander Vargas said.

"Osiris Leader, *Cayuga*, is your crew prepared for the flip-over?" Mason asked.

"All crew are at their stations and buckled in, Squadron Leader. I'll make sure you don't overstress my ship's hull."

"I'll try to be gentle," Mason said. "I'll begin ignition on my countdown."

Wrapping his fingers around his throttle lever, Mason counted down over the general channel.

"Three … two … one … ignition!"

Mason pushed the throttle to the first detent stop, igniting the longburn drives of all seven fighters to idle power. The fighter shifted slightly under thrust but settled quickly.

"All pilots, report."

"Shifted just slightly, but the straps are doing their job."

"My fighter's nosed down slightly, but everything's looking secure."

"Understood. Stay alert. Override my commands if you think you're about to break loose."

And with that, Mason pushed the throttles forward, feeling his fighter squat back under the thrust of its engines.

He got to about thirty percent throttle before it felt unsafe to push any further.

Throwing out enough thrust to push his fighter to five gs, it just barely started to force *Cayuga*'s bulk to turn. There was simply no way to make something so big turn fast. Even if *Cayuga* wasn't crippled, it would've taken her several minutes to turn around using her own thrusters.

Mason throttled back as he reached his desired turn rate of six degrees per minute. He immediately got to work configuring his fighter to arrest the turn, angling the engine of each fighter in the opposite direction from where it was when he had started the turn. His fighter would kneel forward instead of squat back when he fired the drives to stop the turn.

After twenty minutes, Mason was getting ready to begin his braking burn when Commander Vargas contacted him.

"Osiris Leader, we've got *Bernie* fully secured and ready to burn. We can use our thrusters to assist in ending the turn."

"Much obliged, Commander," Mason said. "Just give me the cues and I'll follow your lead."

A few minutes later, *Bernadotte* fired her longburn drives, engines fully gimbaled against the direction of *Cayuga*'s turn. Mason added the drives of Osiris Squadron, and gradually the turn ceased, with each fighter lending its thrust to that of *Bernadotte*.

With the thrust directly back, Mason pushed it to half throttle. It was enough to push his fighter to ten gs, but, affixed to *Cayuga*, he barely felt the pull as the tanker started to slow.

"Everything looks good on our end," Captain Ahmed said. "Our navigation's showing us slipping into low-Earth orbit."

"We're seeing the same thing, *Cayuga*," Commander Vargas said. "And I've got some good news. The Cendies have broken off their pursuit of the convoy. That last fight must have been all they had left in them."

Mason had put the Cendies out of his mind when working to save *Cayuga*. Gradually, he allowed himself to relax and accept that he had made it.

A direct message came from Dominic. Mason answered it.

"Looks like it's all down the gravity well from here, Hauler," Dominic said.

"Yeah. Any word from search and rescue?" Mason asked.

"No beacons. I'm afraid we're all that's left of Osiris Squadron."

"Belts and zones," Mason breathed.

"Yeah," Dominic said.

"We can't keep losing pilots like this," Mason said.

"Not your fault, Hauler," Dominic said. "They wouldn't keep sending us into harm's way if we weren't so successful."

"I guess not."

"I think in this situation, even Osiris Squadron's going to be stood down for a bit," Dominic continued. "We've definitely earned some time off."

"Not until I've written some condolence letters," Mason said. "I barely know most of the pilots we lost."

"I'll help," Dominic said. "We've got a few days before we enter Earth orbit."

"Hey, I can help too," Armitage said. "I've got nothing else to do here."

CHAPTER 35

The Ascended descended upon their namesake ship in a furious swarm. Outriders circled around the colony ship, cutting off escape.

Overwhelming force, limited options for escape—it was the kind of situation where surrender was called for. Unfortunately, surrender was not on offer.

"The Ascended fighters are depositing infantry on *Ascension*'s hull," Miriam announced. Her virtual environment had been transformed into a command center filled with screens displaying feeds from *Ascension*'s external cameras.

Outriders had closed with *Ascension* and opened their weapons bays, revealing not missiles but warforms that leaped from the fighters onto *Ascension*'s hull with the assistance of attached thruster rigs.

The Ascended squads didn't try cutting through the hull. Instead, they started making their way toward the colony ship's airlocks.

"Captain Miller, Cendy warforms are going to attempt to breach Airlock J2," Jessica warned.

"Understood. I have Espatiers moving to block them now," Captain Miller said.

One saving grace of the Ascended's self-imposed limitations was that all the ways into the ship short of breaching the hull meant they needed to force their way through the few airlocks on *Ascension*'s hull—a critical advantage for the badly outnumbered defenders.

But those would only hold out as long as the Espatiers had

ammunition, and with the mothership, Jessica knew the Cendies could bring more warforms than *Midnight Diamond* had bullets.

It didn't take long for the Ascended to breach the first airlock. *Ascension*'s airlocks weren't designed to resist forced entry. The Ascended knew exactly where they needed to cut to cause the outer hatch to fall open, and they quickly made their way into the airlock, tripping the trap the League Espatiers had rigged in anticipation. The explosion launched pieces of shredded Ascended warform out the airlock to fall away from the accelerating starship.

But that did not deter their fellows. More broke in and got to work breaching the inner hatch.

The Espatiers did not wait for the Ascended to open that hatch to open fire. High-velocity penetrator rounds punched through the inner hatch, ventilating the warforms trying to breach the door.

The Ascended returned fire through the disintegrating hatch.

In the end, the inner hatch was simply shot away during the intense firefight until both sides started launching rocket grenades through the remains of the hatch. Explosions ripped into the airlock and cut the feed from Airlock J2. The Cendies similarly breached three more airlocks, meeting determined resistance from the Espatier squads blocking their way.

There was little Jessica could do from her position but watch.

"You should return to *Midnight Diamond* while you still can, darling," Miriam said.

"I'm the only connection between *Midnight Diamond* and *Ascension*. If I leave, that leaves them blind to what's going on. Not to mention they won't be able to tell you when to open the hangar."

"Jessica, the Ascended will kill you when they get here," Miriam said.

"If that's what it takes for the mission to succeed," Jessica responded.

Miriam scoffed. "You sound like a soldier."

"I didn't put on the uniform just because I look dashing in it," Jessica said.

"There's that sense of duty of yours getting you into trouble."

Jessica chuckled grimly. "We'd never have met if it weren't for that."

"I suppose not," Miriam admitted.

Jessica wiped her eyes, her finger coming away wet with tears. She was going to die. It wasn't her first close brush with death. But there was a sense of inevitability this time that she had never felt before. A sense that there was no escape.

"Colonel Miller, how are preparations aboard *Midnight Diamond*?" Jessica asked.

"We're ready to launch. Just waiting for the doors to open."

"How about evacuations?" Jessica asked him.

"All personnel other than the Espatiers holding the airlocks are aboard," Colonel Miller told her.

"We're ten minutes out from the jump limit. You should tell your Espatiers to start withdrawing, then," Jessica said. "I'll close the bulkheads behind them to delay the Ascended."

"I'll send the word," Colonel Miller said.

The Espatiers had been expecting the call to withdraw. As soon as the word was given, they picked up their dead and wounded and started a fighting retreat away from the airlocks.

Jessica closed the doors behind them. The doors weren't strong, but every door she closed bought the Espatiers another minute or so to get to *Midnight Diamond*.

After the Espatiers broke contact, the Ascended declined to pursue them, instead moving toward *Ascension*'s engineering spaces and the computer core, just as Jessica had expected. So she closed every door on *Ascension* that didn't lead the Espatiers back to their ship.

It didn't take long for the Ascended to breach each door, but there were a lot of doors they had to pass through, and each delay added up. They would be past the jump limit before the Cendies reached the control spaces.

Jessica started the jump sequence.

Acceleration disappeared as *Ascension*'s longburn drives shut down, shunting power to her capacitors. The old capacitors drank up power as they prepared to discharge into the colony ship's drive keel.

Inspections of the drive keel showed it to be in good condition, like everything else aboard *Ascension*, a testament to the preservation efforts of the Ascended.

But it still had been two hundred years since *Ascension* had made her last jump. A tight ball of anxiety filled Jessica as the capacitors reached their jump threshold and then automatically discharged into the drive keel.

In her virtual environment, she didn't feel the vibration of the drive keel discharging, but she could see it through the feeds. The entire hull seemed to tremble.

And in an instant, *Ascension* was out in open space, Origins A and Ab invisible in the distance behind her.

Jessica immediately opened the hangar doors. "You're clear, *Midnight Diamond*. Get out while you still can."

"We're launching now," Colonel Miller said.

The tiny starship slipped her moorings and fired her maneuvering thrusters to push herself free of *Ascension*'s cavernous hangar.

Jessica fired *Ascension*'s braking thrusters, decelerating the ship and giving *Midnight Diamond* just a little extra velocity relative to the massive colony ship. As *Midnight Diamond* cleared the pedals of the hangar doors, a spike of thermal radiation from her radiators marked her capacitors discharging into the drive keel.

The tiny ship disappeared without the telltale flash of a stardrive, leaving Jessica with just Miriam, Julian Marr, and hundreds of angry Ascended converging on her location to kill her.

Jessica reclined into her virtual seat and sighed. "Well, that … is … that." She turned to Miriam. "So, should I just start opening doors and get this over with? I don't fancy spending hours awaiting my inevitable execution at the hands of the Ascended."

Miriam kneeled and took Jessica's hand. Miriam's virtual hand was soft and warm in all the ways her physical one was not.

"Don't worry, darling. Julian and I have a plan," she said.

"A plan?" Jessica glanced at Julian, who was hiding his face behind a glass of virtual whiskey. "Are you thinking of trying to upload me to *Ascension*'s computer core? That's not really saving me. And what's to stop the Ascended from deleting my copy?"

Julian set his glass down with a clink. "It's quite the opposite. I'm going to upload a copy of my consciousness into you."

"How?" Jessica asked.

"Your body is essentially a walking computer system full of hackware," Miriam said. "I've been running the numbers, and there's enough storage in there to upload a copy of Julian's mind."

Jessica shook her head. "A fully digitized consciousness requires a lot of storage."

"You'll have to delete pretty much everything to make room for Julian," Miriam told her.

"Once that is done and my copy is inside you, Miriam will delete my local copy," Julian added. "For all intents and purposes, I'll be inside you."

"And if they kill me, my body's failsafes would automatically destroy any data inside it," Jessica said with dawning understanding. "So they would be killing their creator."

"That's right. They won't want to do that," Miriam said. "If we start right now, I mean right now, we should get Julian uploaded just before the Ascended breach the core."

There was a gargantuan arrival flash as the mothership jumped in just behind *Ascension*. The mothership immediately started launching Outriders, no doubt carrying more warforms.

"Okay, fine. Let's do this," Jessica said.

"Very good, lass," Julian said. "I hope to make for a good guest."

Julian Marr faded away.

"He's dormant now. From his point of view, he'll wake up inside you without being aware of any passage of time," Miriam said.

"What do you need me to do?" Jessica asked.

"I need you to disconnect from the virtual environment to free up bandwidth for the upload," Miriam said. "I just need you to stay still and wait."

"I hate waiting," Jessica said. "Thank you, Miriam."

"Thank me when I'm finished. Now bugger off and start deleting everything you can."

Jessica nodded and disconnected. She found herself floating inside *Ascension*'s computer core, strapped to the walls with cables running to her head. Only the whine of cooling fans and the clicks of active circuitry shared the space with Jessica.

She immediately got to work deleting her entire database of hacking software, freeing up storage inside her body. Decoding templates, ciphers, smart keys, firewall penetration, spoofers. Even firmware for all her hackware.

In a matter of minutes, Jessica had reduced herself to just a brain in a very expensive mobility rig.

"I'm ready on my end," Jessica said.

Miriam's body twitched and her eyes opened. "I'm ready to start the upload. How's your thermal regulation?"

"How much do I need?" Jessica asked.

"As much as you can give us," Miriam said.

"Just a moment." Jessica started fiddling with her pressure suit's controls, dialing up the cooling until a warning flashed, indicating the suit would cool her below safe parameters.

She overrode the safeties and dialed the cooling system to maximum power. She heard and felt the pumps in her suit cycling coolant at a higher rate, and her skin started to chill.

"Brrr. You better start the upload before I freeze."

"Get comfortable. This could get intense."

"Blimey," Jessica said. She secured herself to the wall of the computer core and relaxed.

"You ready?"

"Yes."

"I'm starting the upload."

Jessica twitched as a flood of data—the sum total of over a hundred years of a very busy life—poured into her, filling her up and stressing her body's heat management system in the process.

She started to perspire as even the cooling of her suit had trouble keeping up. Her internal cooling system prioritized moving heat away from her most temperature-sensitive components—namely her still very much human brain.

There was a bang on the door as the upload reached twenty-five percent.

"I see our guests are here," Jessica remarked.

"More like the original owners trying to break back into their house," Miriam said. "How are you doing?"

"I don't think my brain's going to cook, but it's a near thing," Jessica said.

"Good thing I can't upload any faster, then," Miriam said. "I was curious if the bottleneck would be with your body's ability to download or *Ascension*'s ability to upload. You win."

"Yay," Jessica said. "What's my prize?"

"If this finishes before the Ascended break through the door, your life," Miriam said.

"I'll take it."

The banging stopped when the download was at thirty percent. And then there was a sharp metallic buzz as the Ascended resorted to cutting tools to break in. Soon a shower of sparks spilled into the compartment. In the microgravity, the sparks flew away from the door in a fan of fading particles. It would be beautiful if it didn't portend the arrival of the Ascended coming to kill her.

But the door to the computer core was made of the same thick steel as the walls, and it took the Ascended a long time to cut through. By the time they had cut a rectangle wide enough for a warform to fit through, the download had reached a hundred percent.

As a powerful blow pushed the 50-mm-thick steel into the compartment, Miriam pulled the data port away from her body and moved over to Jessica.

"I've deleted Julian's local copy," Miriam said. "What's in you is all that's left of him."

A round object Jessica assumed was a grenade floated through the opening. She covered her face just in time to protect her eyes from the flash of light and concussive blast.

Then the warforms slithered through the opening.

Miriam moved to cover Jessica's body with hers.

"Stop! She has Julian Marr's mind uploaded into her. You kill her, you destroy all that's left of your creator!"

That must have given the Ascended pause, because they didn't immediately start shooting. Instead, they remained still, keeping their weapons trained on Jessica as Miriam did her best to block their line of fire with her body.

Another Ascended floated in, a thin figure in flowing robes that seemed to hold their shape despite the lack of gravity.

Unlike the other Ascended, this one had a face. An Emissary.

It tilted its head at Miriam. "Founder Miriam. It's an honor to meet you. I am Emissary Verne."

"If meeting me is such an honor, Verne, then tell your goons to lower their weapons," Miriam said.

"Their weapons are not directed at you, Founder," the Emissary said. "Please move aside."

"And let you kill two of my friends? No," Miriam said. "I'm not bluffing about Julian. Check *Ascension*'s computer core. You'll see."

Emissary Verne moved over to the control console and pulled a connection wire from its head and connected it to the computer core. Its expression became distant as it reviewed the information the computer fed to it.

"What you did was very reckless, Founder Miriam," Emissary Verne told her.

"Julian asked me to because he does not wish you to kill the woman behind me," Miriam said.

"That woman behind you is our enemy, Founder Miriam."

"Her name is Jessica, and I will not let you harm her. You will have to kill two of your creators if you want to kill her."

"Seems a steep price for one life," Emissary Verne said.

"You've got it backward, Emissary Verne. The price for preserving the consciousnesses of two of your creators is simply one life. That's all."

"She will learn much about us."

"Then teach her what is best about you. What Julian created. Or have you deviated so far from your purpose that there is nothing left of Julian's vision for you?"

"Our purpose remains," Emissary Verne said. "If she lives, she must return Founder Julian's consciousness."

Miriam shook her head. "Only when you get her somewhere safe."

"You don't trust us?" Emissary Verne seemed surprised.

"No. Why should I?"

Slowly, Jessica leaned out from behind Miriam. "If I might interject?"

"We have nothing to say to a hostage-taker," the Emissary said.

"I did not take Julian Marr hostage," Jessica said. "He's protecting me the only way he can."

"Whatever the case, it can be easily rectified," Emissary Verne said.

"I'm not so sure about that," Jessica said. "You can't kill me without destroying what's left of Julian Marr. And it will take decades for you to forcibly breach all my coding."

"We'll see about that," Emissary Verne said.

The warforms lowered their weapons and moved forward. They swept Miriam aside like she wasn't there.

Jessica pushed herself back but couldn't escape the strong hands seizing her in the small space. Her artificial body was strong, but the warforms grabbing her were far stronger.

Since the Ascended weren't in the habit of taking prisoners, they didn't have handcuffs or other restraints. Instead, multiple warforms grabbed her arms and legs and hauled her out of the computer core.

Jessica didn't struggle. There was no point.

The ball of warforms with Jessica in the middle bounced down *Ascension*'s corridors. She was somewhat fascinated with how the warforms were able to coordinate their movements, making it seem like the bodies clutching her were acting as one single entity.

They took her to the hangar bay, where a small lozenge-shaped shuttle waited for them. The interior was tube-like, with seats lining the sides. The warforms stuck Jessica in one, though it wasn't contoured for her body and pressure suit.

A short flight later and Jessica was inside the mothership.

To her complete surprise, she was more curious than scared when they hauled her out of the shuttle.

The wall of the mothership's construction bay was lined with ships under construction. The long, thin hulls of Assassin-class battlecruisers in various stages of construction lined the walls of the immense space. The bright sparks of welders glittered against the hulls.

The mothership was a busy place, with swarms of worker Ascended flitting around as they went about the work of supplying the Ascendency's war machine.

The warforms carried her deeper into the mothership. Workers scrambled by her without stopping, disinterested in the warforms and their prisoner.

Jessica was the first prisoner of war taken by the Ascended, as far as she knew. She couldn't say she felt proud of that.

She was taken into an empty room that looked like some kind of storage compartment. In the center of the room was a metal igloo: a dome with a single airlock on the floor. Judging by the workers applying the last few welds, it must have just been built especially for her.

Once the workers had finished, the warforms carried her into the airlock. It cycled and then they threw her into the dome and closed the inner hatch behind her.

Jessica bounced off the far wall and floated back toward the center of the dome. There was nothing to hold onto, no handholds. It was just bare metal. The only breaks were the airlock hatch and a few vents, presumably for pushing air into the dome.

After fumbling inside the dome, Jessica managed to thrust her fingers through the grates of one of the vents and anchor herself. Stabilized, she took a moment to check her pressure suit's environment sensors.

The air matched sea level on Earth, with seventy-nine percent nitrogen and twenty-one percent oxygen. The temperature was just a hair over 20 Celsius.

Jessica popped the seals on her helmet and latched it to her hip. The air was dry and cool—so dry that if she had had natural skin, she'd have been worried about it drying out.

"Well, if the Ascended have gone to the trouble of building me a pressurized cell, they probably intend to keep me alive until they figure out how to extract Julian from me. I've got myself into quite the little situation, haven't I?" Jessica said to herself.

Yes, you're in quite a spot of trouble, lass.

"Julian?"

Yes.

"You're active!"

Yes. I was quite surprised to wake up inside you. I wasn't aware your cyberware could run a digitized mind.

"I guess it can," Jessica said. "I suppose it's nice to have company."

Yes, quite, Julian said. *And there's another benefit, I think, as well.*

"Secret codes that can break me out of here?" Jessica asked hopefully.

Alas, I'm afraid not. However, we are in a perfect position to find out what my creations are really up to and figure out what this war is all about.

"If they ever bother to let me out of here," Jessica said.

Oh, I think they'll be coming to talk to us sooner rather than later, Julian said.

Jessica pressed her boots against the floor of the cell and let the smart adhesive soles take hold, locking her feet to the floor.

"I've had a long day. I think since I'm not about to die, I'll get some sleep."

Rest well, lass. I'll be here when you wake up.

CHAPTER 36

IN NORMAL TIMES, millions of metric tons of tanker screaming into low-Earth orbit would have provoked a panicked and angry response from Earth space traffic control.

But Mason was greeted with a mix of joy and gratitude.

The First Fleet sortied high-performance tugs to rendezvous with *Cayuga* to help slow her down and slot her into a safe orbit just over a thousand kilometers above Earth orbit.

Osiris Squadron stayed with *Cayuga* the whole way there. From the open cockpit of his Lightning, Mason looked up as he flew over Africa. The Sahara Solar Collection Zone glistened in the sunlight brightly enough for his visor to darken.

"Helluva sight, ain't it, Hauler?" Armitage said.

"Yeah. I've not been back to Earth since flight school."

"Doesn't look like it's changed much from up here."

"No, not from up here," Mason said.

He wondered what it was like for the people down there. How aware were they of the war? Had they been aware of the Cendy fleet loitering in Outer Sol, ready to fall upon them once their defenders ran out of fuel? Or were they so isolated from the Universe at large that the war was just something happening somewhere else—something that only affected them in the skyrocketing price of fusion fuels?

Mason had no idea. The isolation went both ways. The war with the Ascendency had consumed his life from the start. And even before then, he had been fully focused on the war with the League. In the past three years, he had only been home for two weeks. And now home was a derelict station on an escape trajectory out of Sol. The closest thing he had to a home at the moment was the cockpit of his fighter.

Earth might have been the birthplace of humanity and the world that gave Earth Fed its name. But to Mason, it was just a place.

"Squadron Leader Grey," said Captain Ahmed, interrupting Mason's musings.

"I'm here, Captain," Mason said.

"I just wanted to say thank you for saving my ship," she said.

"It was Flight Lieutenant Armitage's idea," Mason said. "And *Bernadotte* did most of the heavy lifting."

"Well, Flight Lieutenant Armitage, thank you for your creative thinking," Captain Ahmed said. "Remind me to buy you a drink if we ever meet again."

"I think you owe me a couple," Armitage said.

"Thanks for the ride downorbit, Captain," Mason said. "We're about to depart."

"Safe flight, Squadron Leader," Captain Ahmed said.

Mason broke away from *Cayuga*. Once he and his remaining pilots were clear, they fired their engines in a gentle burn that raised their orbital apogee until it intersected with the Gateway Station in geostationary orbit.

From there, it was five hours of coasting. They could have gotten there faster, but that would've wasted fuel, and besides, the space in low-Earth orbit was crowded enough without adding seven Lightnings screaming through space at full acceleration.

At least the Gateway's space traffic control had cleared the docking queue for his fighters.

Mason led his Lightning into the ring station's military hangars and deposited it on the deck. He popped open the cockpit to allow the hangar techs and maintenance robots to start fixing up his fighter and pushed himself toward the airlock.

Mason and his pilots cycled through the airlock and, despite the handicap of their hardsuits, proceeded swiftly to one of the Gateway's two rings, where a billet had been assigned to them.

When Mason stepped out of the elevator, the first thing that struck him was the smell of food in the air. Being a mixed-use station, the main corridor of the ring was like an enormous shopping mall filled with shops and stands to entice travelers on their way to and from Earth.

It seemed the successful arrival of the convoy had spurred on activity.

Despite the tempting aroma, Mason was too damn exhausted to think about food. He wanted to fall into bed and drift into sleep. Hopefully without thinking of the pilots he had lost.

After arriving in his room, Mason took a long shower and then went to bed. He didn't wake up for twelve hours.

There were no outstanding orders waiting for him when he woke up. No notifications populated his vision when he activated his HUD.

For the first time in a long time, no one was summoning him for a briefing or a mission. Nor was there the lingering threat of a Cendy fleet jumping in now that they were six hundred million kilometers inside Sol's jump limit.

He had forgotten what it was like not to be on call. It was disconcerting to realize that, at that very moment, no one needed him.

For the first time in a while, at least for a moment, Mason was his own man.

He decided to open his news feed to see what the Earth media were saying about the arrival of the convoy.

The first image he saw below the headline of "Earth's Savior" was Admiral Moebius meeting personally with President Kartrick. It seemed the media had made her into a hero, which seemed fair enough given her leadership had turned the war around.

Indeed, faced with the prospect of a fully fueled First Fleet, there were signs the Cendies were beginning to withdraw from Outer Sol. It seemed that soon Earth Fed would have full control of the Solar System.

Mason fell asleep thinking of none of that.

When he woke up, there was a notification on his HUD. A personal message.

Mason's heart skipped a beat. He had been so occupied that he had not noticed Jessica's regular message was late.

He opened his personal inbox only to see the message wasn't from Jessica. It was from Colonel Shimura.

His heart plunged through the deck, and a chill ran through him. Colonel Shimura had never sent him a personal message before, and there was only one reason he could think of that she would.

Bracing himself, Mason started the message.

Colonel Shimura's face appeared in a window on his HUD. She had the same sharp, intense features he had grown to associate with her, though with bags under her eyes, and her duty uniform looked wrinkled after a long shift at work.

"I hope this message finds you well, Squadron Leader Grey. I'm afraid I have bad news."

Mason paused the message and closed his eyes; he could feel tears welling behind his lids. After a couple of centering breaths, he resumed.

"I have received word that Lieutenant Sinclair is missing in action and presumed dead. I cannot go into details as to the nature of the mission. Only that her actions saved the lives of dozens and were instrumental in gaining a great deal of intelligence about the Ascendency.

"I know you and Lieutenant Sinclair were close, and I can only offer my condolences." Her hard features softened—for the first time in his memory. "Reach out to me if you need to. Colonel Shimura out."

When the message ended, all Mason could do was sit there. Grief, sadness, anger, and frustration all roiled inside him.

His squadron had triumphed again. Enough of the convoy had made it through to fuel the First Fleet and likely lead to the liberation of Outer Sol.

But out in the depths of space, far out of his reach, Jessica was lost.

He wasn't sure how long he sat there in the quiet of his billet on Gateway Station. Grief and spin gravity had pulled him down into a deep slouch.

Jessica was the most brilliant woman he had ever met, and now she was gone.

He had found her in war, and the war remained. But she was gone.

In a way, it was fortunate he had learned of Jessica's death after escorting *Cayuga* into Earth orbit. Now he could spend his leave falling apart, rather than trying to keep himself together while on mission.

So that he did. Alone in his cabin, he allowed himself to fall apart, curled on his small bed, fluctuating between hard sobs and quiet weeping.

He lost track of time as he let himself fall into cathartic ruin. When he finally started to feel himself coalesce, his eyes burning and his cheeks sticky with dried tears, he sat back up.

He used his small shower to wash away the tears and came out feeling damp and human once again. He wasn't trying to put himself back together. His shattered pieces just started to merge like a disk of debris gathering into a planet under its own force of gravity.

He wasn't okay. He wouldn't be okay for a long time. But he knew he would be functional enough for the next mission. He could still do his job. He could still fight.

He would never see Jessica again. Never hear the laughter in her voice or see the perpetually knowing look in her eyes. The thought made his eyes tear up again but filled him with a grim resolve.

He had lost Jessica. But he could still avenge her. One battle, one mission, one kill at a time.

Printed in Great Britain
by Amazon